THE MRS MACKINNONS

JAYNE DAVIS

Verbena
Books

Development editing: Antonia Maguire

Copyediting & proofreading: Sue Davison

Cover design: SpiffingCovers

PROLOGUE

Seringapatam, India, May 1799

*P*rivate Webb shifted uncomfortably, his hand pressed hard against the gash in his thigh. Sweat trickled down his back, sticking his tattered red coat to his skin. He stood listening to the sounds of fighting drifting further down the narrow street. The wound didn't feel too bad, he thought, cautiously lifting his hand. Blood was oozing slowly, not flowing. He found an almost-clean handkerchief in his pocket and folded it into a pad. He fastened it in place inside his torn trousers with a bit of the string he always carried in his pockets.

The shouting and clashing of steel reminded Webb that the rest of his company were still fighting their way further into the city, so he picked up his musket and limped after them. The lieutenant's voice, high with fear, was trying to keep the company together and stop the usual suspects from sneaking off to look for loot. Webb was about to add his support when he remembered his new demotion back to private. If Lieutenant bloody Dawson thought he knew best, he could damn well manage the company on his own.

He slipped down a quiet alley before he came into sight of the company, grimacing at the unmistakable sight of Fingers Richardson slinking off ahead of him. Last week he would have dragged the thieving bugger back to the rest of the company, but that was when he still had a set of sergeant's stripes on his sleeves. He spat into the dust and filth in the gutter; the true reckoning for yesterday's argument was yet to come. With any luck the lieutenant would get himself killed and maybe he would get away without a flogging. But in the meantime the bloody officers' orders against looting could go hang. Not that they obeyed those orders themselves, oh no. He hesitated only a moment before limping off after Fingers.

Half an hour later, their pockets rather heavier and the best items stuffed uncomfortably down their boots, they came across the entrance to a grimly solid building with high walls and few windows. A prison? Two guards stood by the gates looking the other way, towards the continuing sounds of fighting. Fingers started to creep back the way they had come, but some lingering sense of responsibility made Webb put out a hand to stop him.

"Tipu's enemies are our friends, right?" Webb asked. Fingers nodded reluctantly. "Well, then...?"

Fingers still looked doubtful.

"And maybe they're not just guardin' prisoners, eh?" Webb said. He doubted that the Tipu would keep valuables in the same place as prisoners, but Fingers wasn't the brightest of sparks. He nodded eagerly this time.

They unslung their muskets and checked the bayonets. Shots in the next street masked the small sounds they made, and the guards were taken completely by surprise. Once inside the building, Fingers showed great enthusiasm in dealing with the few soldiers that were still there, searching the bodies carefully for valuables and keys. Webb made him unlock every door they came to, even though Fingers wasn't particularly interested in releasing prisoners. The stench from the cells made even Webb retch, and he hoped that some of the poor bastards locked up here had enough strength to get themselves and their fellows out.

He left Fingers searching the boxes in a storeroom, and descended another flight of stairs. There were only a few guttering lamps, but no guards. Half the cells were empty, or empty of human life, at least. The rotting straw stank, and the rustling noises spoke of rats scuttling through the filth. In other cells there were prisoners chained to the walls, some already dead. Webb almost threw up again. The prospect of death on the battlefield, or even in a stinking field hospital afterwards, was not one he welcomed, but it was a fact of life soldiers were resigned to. Slowly rotting away here in this fetid darkness was a far more hellish fate.

He released as many prisoners as he could, striking their rusting chains from the walls with the butt of his musket. Most were natives, but in the dim light he could just make out one or two paler faces— Europeans, he supposed. But this was only supposition until the last cell, where one dead body and one only-just-living prisoner still had enough uniform on them to be identified as British soldiers.

"Jesus Christ!" he swore, rolling over the one still alive. He struck the ends of the chains off the wall and picked the man up, ignoring the faint groan that interrupted the rasping breathing. He wasn't heavy— although a man that tall should have weighed twice as much. Webb staggered back up the corridor, stumbling and almost dropping his burden as the wound in his thigh shot pain up his leg. He was concentrating too hard on negotiating the steps to hear the footsteps behind him. The first—and last—he knew of something wrong was a fierce pain in his back and the taste of blood in his mouth.

CHAPTER 1

Portsmouth, November 1799

The masts and rigging of the ships along the dock were black against the clouds, the gradual change of the sky from dark to pale grey the only sign that dawn had arrived. A sharp wind blowing off the land brought spatters of rain that soaked into cloaks and overcoats. It also brought land smells—a mix of coal and wood smoke, and a faint whiff of rotting fish and seaweed from the jetties. Thankfully it was just rain in the air, not the sleet that might be expected at this time of year.

"Major?"

Matthew Southam turned from watching the *Amathea's* deckhands start to unload the cargo. "Lieutenant Fanton."

"Looking forward to dry land?"

"It will be good to see England again," Matthew said. Good to see the countryside, perhaps. And it would be good to get off this ship. As for the rest…

"And land that doesn't move? And family?"

Matthew gave an embarrassed smile at this reference to his supposed seasickness. "I haven't seen my family in ten years," he said, responding only to the second question and not indicating whether this was a good or a bad thing.

"I have to thank you once again for helping to keep Captain Beauchamps away from Miss MacLeod," Fanton said. Beauchamps was another returning army officer, although not someone Matthew had come across during his time in India.

"My pleasure," Matthew said. "You had too many duties to keep an eye on him all the time." And at least it meant he was still useful for *something*.

"Mrs Reed-Smythe should have done her duty better," Fanton said. "Or she should have declined to chaperone the girls—then we could have made other arrangements."

Matthew suspected that the recently-widowed Mrs Reed-Smythe had been anxious about her own financial future and had accepted money from Captain Beauchamps to absent herself while he attempted to seduce her young and attractive charge. There was no point in airing his suspicions to the lieutenant, so he just gave a non-committal grunt.

"You're travelling to London?"

Matthew nodded. "Webb has already gone ashore to arrange transport," he said. "Four seats," he added, guessing what the lieutenant's next question would be. "I will escort Miss MacLeod and her sister to London and see they reach their relatives safely." He shivered as an icy gust found its way under his coat. "I'll be glad to get some warmer clothing too."

"Too long in India thins the blood," the lieutenant stated, and held his hand out. "I wish you a good journey, sir," he said. They shook hands, and Matthew returned to gazing at the land as the lieutenant hurried off to supervise the unloading of baggage and cargo.

These last few days, waiting until the wind changed so they could enter port, had seemed interminable—a final climax to the horrendous journey. At times the ship had seemed like just another prison, albeit with more people, air and food. But a prison just the same. He pulled the flask from his pocket and took a big mouthful of brandy, the spirit warming his mouth and throat. The flask was nearly empty, and he hoped Webb would remember to buy some more while he was arranging a carriage and driver. Assuming, that is, that Webb didn't just pocket the money and disappear. He still wasn't sure why the man seemed to have appointed himself as his orderly, but he had been useful during the voyage and, as long as he returned, was likely to be so in future.

Another passenger stood further along the rail, a gentleman dressed in clothing far more suitable for the weather than Matthew's. The man looked his way, then abruptly turned and moved further off. Matthew recognised him as one of the passengers who had embarked in Gibraltar. The one who had shown him a copy of the London Gazette after dinner one evening, and asked if the reports of the siege at Seringapatam were accurate. Matthew recalled with shame his rude response that the man should mind his own damn business, before he escaped the dining room to spend the rest of the evening on deck, as usual. He'd tried to apologise, but he'd clearly caused offence and the man avoided Matthew for the remainder of the voyage.

There were more footsteps behind him, lighter ones this time. Miss MacLeod and her younger sister. Matthew could see why Captain Beauchamps had been intent on seduction—the elder Miss MacLeod had quantities of curling brown hair with intriguing blue-green eyes and a winning smile. If he had been interested in such things he might have been tempted himself—although taking advantage of a pair of orphans as Beauchamps had attempted was not something he would ever have actually done.

"We've come to say goodbye, Major Southam," Miss MacLeod said. "And to thank you for your help."

In truth, they had done more for him than he had for them—although whether he was grateful for this he had yet to decide. Standing by the rail, watching the Indian Ocean roll past, then the Atlantic, had been strangely mesmerising. Each wave subtly different from the next, their shapes and the pattern of blown spume changing with the wind, the colour varying from deep blue to green to gunmetal grey with the changing skies. He had more than once felt the urge just to lean over until he joined the waves. The thought of dying didn't worry him. The urge was particularly strong when he hadn't slept for days. A few times it had only been the thought of what would happen to Miss MacLeod and her sister without his protection that had kept him on the deck side of the rail.

He realised that Miss MacLeod was waiting patiently for him to reply.

"My apologies, Miss MacLeod. Wool gathering again, I'm afraid." He glanced down at the younger girl, clutching her sister's hand. "It is too soon to say farewells. I will ensure that you reach your relatives in London safely." The girl's shoulders relaxed, and Matthew realised she had been worried about the rest of the journey. "I could not abandon you on the docks," he said.

"We are giving you so much trouble." She looked apologetic.

"Nothing of the sort!" Matthew said. "You helped immensely to relieve the boredom. Particularly as I could spend so little time below decks."

"You will be glad to be on dry land again, sir?" Matthew suspected she did not quite believe in his seasickness, but did not challenge his story. "Do you know how much the stagecoach costs?"

"Webb is arranging to hire a carriage," Matthew said. "No, don't protest! You'll need to conserve your funds. Allow me to take the pair of you to London."

"I should not allow you to pay for us," she said, a small frown creasing her brow. "But I thank you."

"Miss MacLeod, I do not know my plans, but if you are in need of assistance in the future, apply to the East India Company offices. They are likely to know where I may be found."

"I suspect Mrs Reed-Smythe would not approve of my asking assistance from you, sir."

"I think you need not worry about her," Matthew said. "She is not the best example of proper behaviour." That produced a small smile.

"You are ready to go?" he asked, spying Webb's skinny frame in his scarlet uniform approaching the gangplank.

"Yes, our trunks are there." She pointed to two small trunks placed close to his own. He had several much larger trunks—having no intention of returning to India, he had brought all his possessions with him. He frowned—the pile included a smallish trunk with his name stencilled on that he did not recognise. He rubbed his eyes, and took another mouthful of brandy, deciding not to worry about it. Likely his mind was playing tricks again.

"Success?" he asked, as Webb arrived on deck, wheezing noisily after climbing the gangplank. Webb did not have enough breath to speak, nodding instead.

"Carriage, horses and driver arranged, sir, ready within the hour," he confirmed as soon as his breathing returned to a more normal rate.

"Good man," Matthew said. It would be cold riding on the box, but better that than cooped up inside. "Can you make sure my trunks are sent to the right place? And make sure the MacLeods' trunks go too."

"Sir!" Webb saluted, and hurried off to organise the luggage. Matthew muttered a curse as he realised he hadn't got his flask refilled, but there would be time for that before they left. He retreated a few steps into the lee of the main mast—the biting wind was still finding its way into his ill-fitting coat, making him shiver. The two girls' clothing, although worn and now travel-stained, was of good quality and they'd had the sense to wrap up warmly. They stayed at the rail watching the comings and goings on the dock. Thus it was that Captain Beauchamps did not notice Matthew leaning on the mast as he approached them.

"Excuse me, Miss MacLeod," the captain said politely, lifting his hat as he came to stand in front of her. Miss MacLeod turned to face him, looking wary but not frightened.

"I don't think we have anything to say to each other, Captain," she said, managing a very good frosty tone for one of her few years. Matthew was about to intervene, but she seemed to be managing well on her own so far.

"I wish to apologise for my earlier behaviour, Miss MacLeod, and to make amends if possible," the captain said, bowing slightly. "I understand from Mrs Reed-Smythe that your destination is London. That is a long way for an unaccompanied young woman to travel. If you permit, I will escort you and ensure you arrive safely."

"Thank you, but that will not be necessary. Arrangements have already been made."

A fleeting expression of annoyance crossed Beauchamps' face, quickly controlled. "May I enquire as to what those arrangements are? Just to be sure you will be safe," he added, trying for a reassuring tone.

"Major Southam has arranged a carriage."

"Alone with Major Southam?" There was censure in his voice.

"What had *you* in mind, sir?"

"Mrs Reed-Smythe has agreed to act as your chaperone, so there would be no impropriety, Miss MacLeod. Please allow me to make amends—"

"If Mrs Reed-Smythe does as well at chaperoning me as she did during the voyage, I hardly think her presence in the coach will be of any use. As I said, arrangements have already been made." She turned her back on the captain to end the conversation. Beauchamps stared at her back for a moment then turned away himself, swearing under his breath. He finally noticed the major watching him.

"Think you're so clever?" he hissed through clenched teeth. "What business is it of yours?"

"Common decency?" Matthew suggested.

Beauchamps consigned Southam to the devil and stalked off. Matthew shrugged, dismissing the man from his thoughts. He wished he could dismiss thoughts altogether—he could not, but the brandy helped a little.

CHAPTER 2

"*M*r Brock and his family settled down to a nice dinner of worms, snails and slugs.*"

Charlotte MacKinnon put down her quill and pushed the stopper into the bottle of ink. She spread the last few pages out across the table and read through them carefully. Then, checking that the ink on the last page was completely dry, she shuffled them together into a neat pile. Just the covering letter to write before parcelling it up to send to Mr Berry in London. She stretched her back and arms, cramped from sitting too long, and grimaced at the usual ink stains on her fingers.

She removed her spectacles and glanced at the clock on the parlour mantelpiece. Davie would be back from his lessons at the squire's house soon. Squire Thompson allowed Davie to share in the lessons with the tutor he hired for his son, in return for Charlotte's help with other matters. She frowned, remembering that Bertie Thompson would be going off to school next year. She would have to make other arrangements for Davie's education. He was ten years old, but she couldn't afford to hire a tutor, nor to send him away to school.

Charlotte rubbed a hand over her eyes. Her stories helped, but didn't make enough money on their own. Perhaps she should consider accepting Sir Vincent if he offered for her again? It must be nearly six months since he had last proposed, so he would probably try again fairly soon. Putting that unwanted thought out of her mind, she tried to plan her next story. Was it was time for the fox family to have another adventure?

A gust of wind spattered raindrops against the window. It had rained all week, but not heavily enough to make the paths through the Birchanger woods impassable. The sloping ground prevented flooding, but too much mud made the steep sections slippery, which meant that Davie would have to walk the extra mile along the road instead.

Flooding... hmm. She reached for one of the pencils she used for everything except her final copy.

Half an hour and several sheets of scribbled paper later, she became aware of voices coming from the kitchen. Not Davie, and not Sally—she would have gone home by now. It must be Mary talking to someone else. She'd been so deep in her flow of ideas she hadn't heard anyone being let in. Charlotte put the papers into a drawer. At least half of the things she'd jotted down wouldn't be of any use, but she had the beginnings of the next *Woodland Tale*.

In the kitchen, Davie sat at one end of the long table, eating biscuits. He looked remarkably clean; Mary must have made him wash when he arrived. Mary sat at the other end of the table with Emma Wilton from the bakery, her petite figure contrasting with Emma's rather plump one—too much sampling of her own baking, Charlotte suspected. They both sat drinking tea, and Mary had set a third place with a cup and plate.

"Wondered when you'd appear!" Mary said. "I popped in a while ago, but you was writing. Didn't want to distract you."

"Quite right, thank you." Charlotte sat down, and Davie handed her a folded note. It was from Letty, the squire's wife, asking if she could go over to Northridge Hall a day earlier next week. She put it into her pocket and poured herself a cup of tea. She was about to ask what brought Emma here, when she noticed the red eyes and quiet sniffs.

"Emma's come about the accounts," Mary explained.

"It's not time, is it? It's not been six months..." Charlotte stopped as Mary shook her head.

"Losing money," she said. "Wondered if you could tell why."

Charlotte sighed.

"I'm sorry, Mrs MacKinnon," Emma said tearfully. "I wouldn't ask, but I don't know who else to turn to. It took my Billy years to build up the business, but now he's gone and I'm not..." Emma stuck her face back into her handkerchief, shoulders shaking.

"Of course I'll take a look," Charlotte said, managing to sound cheerful. "Did you bring them with you?" Emma sniffed, and reached into a large bag on the floor beside her chair.

"Why don't you stay for supper, Emma?" Mary said, with a quick glance to get Charlotte's agreement. "You'll have to help get it ready, mind, if Mrs Captain's going to be checking your accounts."

Emma nodded and Charlotte smiled. Mary, practical as usual, had not only given her time to look over the accounts, but ensured that Emma wouldn't be hovering behind her as she did so.

"I can make you my apple pie," Emma offered hesitantly. "If you've got apples..."

"Come along, then. Sally's left the vegetables chopped, you can help put the stew on then make your pie."

Charlotte sat and drank her tea as the two women moved Davie away from the table and started preparing the meal. Davie grabbed the last biscuit, and disappeared before Charlotte could ask him if the squire's tutor had set him any work. She fetched her spectacles and some paper from the other room and opened the accounts book.

By the time dinner was ready she had an inkling of the problem. Since the death of her husband, Emma had religiously kept records of money taken and money spent, but Charlotte suspected she didn't really understand why such records were necessary. She jotted down some questions.

Their meal was ready by the time she finished her list, and Mary kept Emma talking village gossip while Davie concentrated on eating as much as he could. Charlotte allowed her mind to wander to the adventures of Mr Fox again.

When the apple pie had been eaten and the dishes washed, Davie settled at one end of the table with his mathematics while the three women gathered at the other. Emma looked rather apprehensive.

"D'yer know what I be doing wrong?" she asked.

"I'm not sure yet," Charlotte said. "But I've got some questions for you." She looked at the list she had written. "The price you pay for flour seems to have risen."

Emma nodded. "Mr Weekes, he says the price of wheat has gone up."

"It seems expensive, Emma. I'll check what Weekes charges the squire's cook for their flour." She looked at the list again. "You're selling more white bread?"

"Folks like it."

"But did you put the price of the loaves up when Mr Weekes started to charge you more?"

Emma frowned. "I did try, but folks complained."

Charlotte sighed inwardly. "And the new fancy cakes, how did you decide how much to charge for them?"

"Dunno, Mrs MacKinnon. Just seemed about the right price to me."

"How much flour does it take to make a batch?"

Emma's brow creased. "I don't rightly know—half a sack for a big batch, maybe. I always check I've got enough before I start," she added earnestly.

Charlotte rubbed a hand across her eyes, not knowing where to begin. She'd checked Billy Wilton's accounts for him annually for several years, and he'd had a good head for business. Emma was an excellent baker, especially of cakes and pies, and had helped her husband run the bakery for fifteen years. But if she still hadn't grasped the business side of things, Charlotte wondered how she could make her understand what was needed.

"Make some more tea, shall I?" Mary asked, seeing Charlotte's

THE MRS MACKINNONS

expression. Charlotte, about to answer, was interrupted by a loud knock on the front door. Mary went to see who it was, so Charlotte got up to fill the kettle.

"Mrs MacKinnon?" It was a man's voice, not one she recognised.

"I'm one of the Mrs MacKinnons." Mary's voice was quieter. "Did you want Mrs Captain or Mrs Sergeant?"

"Bring him through, Mary," she called.

The man following Mary back into the kitchen wore practical clothing, somewhat travel-stained.

"Who's the letter from?" Mary asked him.

"Lady Henbury, ma'am, in London."

"That'll be for Mrs Captain," she said, taking the proffered letter and handing it to Charlotte.

"I'm to wait for a reply," the man said.

Mary waved the man to a seat and asked if he needed anything.

"No, thank you, ma'am. I got money to stay at the inn tonight." He paused for a moment. "Mrs Captain and Mrs Sergeant?"

"It helps when there's two of us with the same surname," Mary explained with a laugh. "She married Captain MacKinnon and I married Sergeant MacKinnon. Not related," she added.

Charlotte's amusement disappeared as she took in the contents of the letter. She must have made some sound, for Mary asked if she was all right.

She took a deep breath, clutching the letter in shaking hands. "I will be." She took another deep breath, then read the letter again carefully. After a moment's thought she spoke to the messenger. "Can you be here at ten tomorrow?" she said.

"Yes, ma'am." The man stood, gave a small bow in their general direction, and headed for the door. Emma looked around uncertainly, and stood up to leave as well.

"I'm sorry, Emma," Charlotte said. "I won't be able to do anything for a few days. Mary can explain."

"I'll be round tomorrow," Mary promised Emma. "We'll sort something out, don't you fret!" Looking somewhat reassured, Emma

15

followed the messenger to the front door. Mary shut and bolted it behind them.

"Mama, who's Lady Henbury?" Davie asked.

"My Aunt Elizabeth," Charlotte said. "My mother's sister." She looked at the letter once more, as if she didn't really believe what it said.

"She writes to tell me my mother is very ill, and not expected to live."

Davie's eyes widened, but he said nothing. Mary unearthed an ancient bottle of brandy from a cupboard, poured a small glassful and thrust it into Charlotte's hand. Charlotte took a sip and coughed, then firmly put the glass down.

"I'm all right, Mary. It's a shock, that's all."

"You're to go to London?"

"Yes. Benning, the messenger, he's to take me to Bath tomorrow and put me on the mail coach. I'll be in London the next day."

"Your father's not written?"

Charlotte shook her head—she wouldn't have expected any communication from that quarter.

"Where will you stay? With your aunt?" Mary concentrated on the practicalities.

"It is she who invites me, but I'll see if Ann Hamilton can put me up."

"You'll not need to take much then. Is Davie to go?" She glanced at the boy, who was following the conversation with interest.

Charlotte shook her head. "Davie… Mama only saw him when he was very small, he doesn't remember her. I don't want my father to get any ideas…"

Mary nodded in understanding. "Well, you just go and pick out what clothes you need to take and get a good night's sleep. I can look after everything while you're gone." She glanced at Davie. "*And* I'll make sure he don't miss his lessons! You'll miss your day with the squire—I'll send a message with Davie."

"Emma…?"

"I reckon I've got enough idea what she's bin doin' wrong from what you said. I'll go along and see what I can sort out. Davie can come too—good practice for him to see why he should be studyin' his numbers!" She gave a small smile at the fleeting look of dismay on Davie's face, before he remembered that the bakery was also a splendid source of cakes, pies and other delightful offerings.

"You finish your sums, Davie," Charlotte said sternly. "Then I'll read you my latest story and you can tell me if it's any good before I take it with me tomorrow." Davie reluctantly pulled his book towards him again, and Charlotte went upstairs to pack. She hesitated over the mourning gowns she hadn't worn for nine years, but eventually packed one, hoping she wouldn't need it.

"Charlotte!"

Charlotte sighed with relief as Ann opened her front door.

"Ann, I'm sorry to spring myself on you like this—"

"Don't be silly." Ann took in Charlotte's expression, and her own face changed from welcoming to anxious. "Something is wrong? But come in, do. Let me have that."

Ann took the bandbox from Charlotte's hand and led the way into the parlour. A chubby toddler played with a doll on the floor, looking up with interest at this new arrival.

"You look in need of tea before you tell me why you're here."

"Yes, please." Charlotte sank into a chair with relief. She'd slept very little on the overnight mail.

"...make it myself, Betty is in the middle of washing."

Charlotte opened her eyes to see Ann's amused smile, before her friend left to make tea. Not wanting to doze off now, she looked around the room, little changed since her last visit here back in the spring. The table next to her chair held a packet of letters tied with ribbon, and beyond it stood a basket full of mending. If Ann was reading old letters, then Lieutenant Hamilton must be at sea again.

The little girl held her doll out to Charlotte, who took it. She absently straightened the dress it wore, wondering how things might be different if she'd had a girl instead of Davie. She wouldn't be so worried about paying school fees, for one thing. *Silly—I wouldn't change him for the world!*

"Now, tell me why you're here," Ann said, handing over a cup of tea and placing a plate of bread and butter on the table. "Your mama?"

"Yes. How did you know?"

"She wasn't well when you visited in the spring. And you—" She broke off, biting her lip.

"I?" Charlotte prompted.

"You are sad. I didn't think your father being ill would cause too much sorrow."

Charlotte frowned. "No. He married Mama for money, despised her for being the granddaughter of a merchant, and seemed to go out of his way to make her life a misery." Not to mention trying to force *her* into an insupportable marriage.

"Charlotte," Ann said gently, reaching out a hand to pat her knee. "I wasn't criticising you."

Charlotte drew a deep breath and rubbed her forehead. "I know, I'm sorry. I'm just… well, she was a good mother, as far as he let her be."

Maria Metcalf hadn't held the aristocratic view that children should be inspected and conversed with for half an hour a day, and left to their nurse or nanny for the rest of the time.

"I can still picture her sitting on a blanket in our back garden, reading to us, or playing battledore and shuttlecock." Charlotte's voice ended on a wobble, and she felt tears prick the backs of her eyelids.

"And you're being a good mother to Davie," Ann said, patting her knee again. "I'll get Betty to make up the spare bed when she's finished the laundry. Have some more bread and butter before you go to see your aunt." Ann picked up the packet of letters with a fond smile.

"You have some good news?" Charlotte asked. "Does Thomas have some leave?"

"Even better," Ann said, a beaming smile crossing her face. "He writes that he is to be transferred to the *Lothian* after his leave."

"Promotion? That is good news."

"And the *Lothian* is part of the Channel Fleet—he may be able to get short amounts of shore leave quite often. I am looking into moving to Plymouth."

"Now *that* is even better news!" Charlotte wondered what it would be like to desire someone's presence so much, then gave a mental shrug. She was doing well enough as she was, with no man to make her dance to his tune.

The residence of Viscount Henbury was an imposing mansion on Grosvenor Square, with a small portico and Greek columns flanking the windows on the upper floors. Charlotte gave her name to the liveried footman who answered the door, and he showed her straight into her aunt's parlour.

Lady Henbury was in her mid-fifties, her hair grey but still thick and curly. Her husband had died only six months earlier, so she was still in mourning clothes. Charlotte had not seen her since Lord Henbury's death, and, in spite of the sad occasion, she thought her aunt was looking very well. The blacks even suited her colouring.

"Charlotte! Come in, my dear." Lady Henbury stood, and Charlotte could see the news in her expression. "I'm so sorry, my dear. Your mother died yesterday morning."

Just as Charlotte was travelling to Bath to catch the mail; she had been too late even before she set out. She sank into a nearby chair and put her face in her hands, trying hard to swallow against the lump in her throat. The worry of the journey changed to an aching sense of loss.

"I've ordered some tea," Lady Henbury said after a few minutes. "Have they taken your luggage to your room?"

Charlotte looked up and shook her head. "I'm staying with Ann, Aunt Elizabeth. I wasn't sure if cousin Cecil would be in residence."

Like her mother, her mother's sister had been married for her money. In Aunt Elizabeth's case, to the much older Viscount Henbury. He had been glad enough to spend her dowry, but his enthusiasm for the match had not extended to welcoming any relatives of his wife, only a generation removed from trade. Her son, the current viscount, had inherited many of his father's prejudices.

Lady Henbury shook her head. "He's at the Yorkshire estate at the moment," she said. "But of course, you are tired," she added. "The funeral is tomorrow afternoon. Your father and brother, and your sisters' husbands, will be in attendance from the family. Refreshments will be served at the house afterwards. I have arranged to pay my last respects tomorrow morning, with Lady Meerbrook. You can come with me then."

She handed Charlotte a cup of tea and a plate of small cakes. Charlotte ate and drank a little, and leaned back to rest her head on the back of the chair—still exhausted, but also relieved she didn't have to cope with hostile relatives until the next day. Her aunt sat in sympathetic silence.

"Does my father know I am coming?" she asked eventually.

Lady Henbury shook her head. "I doubt it—unless you had a letter from him?"

"No. But if he did not write to me straight away, a letter could be awaiting me at home."

Lady Henbury gave an unladylike shrug. "I did not tell him I had written to you. I informed him I would be paying my respects tomorrow."

"How…" Charlotte asked, not sure how to phrase the question. "I mean, what happened? It was sudden?"

"Not so sudden, really, now I look back," Lady Henbury said. "She was not well when you visited in the spring, if you remember?"

"I thought that was just a temporary indisposition."

"We thought so at the time, but she never really got her full health back. Then she caught the influenza, and she was still so weak." Lady Henbury shook her head sadly. "I think she just gave up."

Reaching over, she patted Charlotte's shoulder. "Now you are not to start feeling guilty, Charlotte," she said. "She enjoyed seeing you every year—and she would have loved to see Davie but she understood very well why you did not want to bring him. You visited as often as you could, and if Augusta and Beatrice—" She pressed her lips firmly together and shook her head.

Charlotte's sisters had been married to titled men, with the assistance of what was left of their mother's dowry. These husbands, like the late Viscount Henbury and his heir, did not wish to be reminded that trade was not too many generations earlier in their wives' backgrounds. And neither Augusta nor Beatrice cared to defy their husbands' instructions that they should stay away from their mother.

"Will he even let me into the house?" Charlotte asked, remembering his cold fury when she told him, all those years ago, that she was leaving.

Her aunt smiled, although with little humour. "That's why I invited Lady Meerbrook. She is a friend of mine more than she was a friend of Maria's, but she is influential in society. I doubt your father will cause a scene in front of her."

"Aunt Elizabeth!" Charlotte exclaimed, both surprised and impressed at her aunt's small rebellion.

Lady Henbury smiled with genuine pleasure. "You have no notion, Charlotte, what a relief it is to be free of Henbury," she said. "My son, although he has some of his father's ways, can be managed!"

She patted Charlotte's shoulder again. "I wish I'd had your courage when I was your age, my dear, to avoid my own father's plans for me. But enough of that! You should go back to Ann and rest. I'll get Simmons to call a hackney for you, and pay in advance, so don't be gulled into paying again. I shall call for you at eleven tomorrow morning. Give Simmons Ann's direction."

Charlotte did as she was bid, glad to have someone else to make decisions for her.

CHAPTER 3

*M*atthew did not rush the journey from Portsmouth, ordering the driver to stop at an inn when the grey day darkened into early dusk. The inn was not luxurious but it was clean, with enough rooms for them all, and a private parlour. The brandy was decent, too—much better than the stuff he'd drunk on the ship. A bottle ensured he slept for most of the night, and some concoction supplied by the landlord settled his stomach sufficiently in the morning so he did not disgrace himself while the girls ate breakfast. He even managed to shave without slitting his throat.

Once back on the box next to the driver, the cold air and a little hair of the dog helped his stomach and his pounding head—it made his insides feel warmer too.

They reached London just after midday. Matthew paid the driver at the White Hart while Webb supervised the unloading of the luggage and then went to find a hackney.

"It might be best if you say Mrs Reed-Smythe accompanied you as far as here," Matthew said to Miss MacLeod. "I'll send Webb in the hackney with you as an official escort. He'll make sure your aunt is at home before he leaves you."

"Thank you again, Major," Miss MacLeod said, obviously nervous at the prospect of meeting an aunt she had never seen. Matthew wished he could be of more help, but he was having enough difficulty managing himself. In any case, turning up with a strange officer would do nothing for her reputation, even though she was accompanied by her younger sister, whereas Webb would have little difficulty representing himself as an official escort from the 74th. He handed the girls into the hackney, told Webb to straighten his coat and stock, then sat down on one of his trunks to await the sergeant's return.

He knew he must have made a strange sight, sitting in the bustling inn yard in the drizzle instead of enjoying an ale in the taproom while he waited, but he ignored the curious glances. He debated whether to find some better, and warmer, clothing, but decided that calling at Gleason and Gleason should be his first order of business. His unexpected inheritance of a title and more property from a distant cousin was the reason Lieutenant-General Stuart had shipped him out so hurriedly, after all. He supposed he should find his proofs of identity, but opening his trunks in the rain would only get everything wet. It was easier just to sit and wait. And drink.

Matthew was in a warm, mellow haze when Webb eventually returned, reporting that the MacLeod sisters had been handed into the keeping of their aunt. Webb arranged for the larger trunks to be stored until they were collected, then directed the hackney to Holborn.

The journey took some time through the streets packed with carriages and delivery carts. Matthew put his flask away, trying to dispel some of the brandy fumes in his brain with deep breaths of the acrid air.

The offices of Gleason and Gleason were not difficult to find. However, according to the clerks, Mr Gleason the elder had passed away some time ago. Mr Gleason the younger was in court today and so unavailable, but the senior clerk was most helpful when Webb produced Matthew's papers. Two other clerks were instructed to write notes cancelling all Mr Gleason's appointments for the following morning so he could attend to his new lordship.

"Where now, sir?" Webb asked when they once more stood in the drizzle.

"Mayhew, Mayhew, Dunstable and Broadstairs," Matthew recited. "The Southam family solicitors—in the next street, as I recall."

"Nice short name," Webb commented as he traipsed behind Matthew, breathing hard to keep up. Matthew sent him inside to find which of the partners was present.

"Wouldn't speak to me," he told Matthew, two minutes later. "Right rude little bugger, thinks 'e's the dog's bo—"

Webb cut short his complaint when Matthew caught his eye.

"I get your drift, Webb, but if you wish to remain in my employ you will attempt to express yourself more politely. Understood?"

"Yessir!" Webb drew himself to attention.

"Don't overdo it, man," Matthew muttered, and Webb grinned. Matthew sucked in a deep breath before shoving the door open hard enough for it to bang on the wall. He strode into the room.

"Sir, what is the meaning of this?" a clerk protested, jumping to his feet.

"I need to see one of the partners as soon as possible." Matthew put all his officer's authority into his voice. "As you refused to deal with my man, I am forced to discuss an appointment with you myself." He seated himself in an armchair some distance from the clerk's desk, compelling him to come out from behind it and stand in the middle of the room to continue the conversation.

"I'm afraid both Mr Mayhews are away on business today," the clerk said, apologetic now. "Mr Dunstable is not well."

"When will the Mayhews return and Mr Dunstable recover?" Matthew asked. There should be a fourth partner, but there seemed little point in enquiring about him.

"If I could ask your business, sir?" the clerk said hesitantly. "If your business is urgent I'm sure one of the partners could see you in a few days."

"You have been dealing with the affairs of my family, the

Southams, for decades. If you wish that arrangement to continue, you will make an appointment for me at noon tomorrow with the appropriate partner."

"You're not Mr Southam," the clerk said with certainty. "He was here only last month—"

"I am Major Matthew Southam." he stated, "I—" Matthew fell silent, for the clerk's eyes had widened and his mouth hung open.

"But... but you're dead..." the clerk managed to stammer.

"Really? I hadn't noticed."

Webb snorted a laugh, hastily suppressed.

"What made you think I was dead?"

"Mr Sou—" The clerk must have decided that silence was a better idea. "I think Mr Mayhew should explain, sir."

"Very well. Noon tomorrow. In the meantime, I wish you to advance me some funds."

"I... I lack the authority to do that, sir. Even if I did, I would need some proof of your identity."

Matthew gave the clerk his officer's stare. He suspected that Webb's best sergeant's glare was also aimed at the clerk, for he swallowed hard. However, the request for proof of identity was not unreasonable. Matthew got to his feet, keen to bring the interview to a close before the walls started to move in on him.

"Noon tomorrow," he repeated. "I shall want funds advancing, and a full accounting for business since I have been away. It has been at least two years since I have received an annual report." He didn't wait for a response, but strode out of the building, Webb on his heels.

Matthew took a deep breath of the drizzly, smoke-laden air. How in heaven's name was he going to manage *two* interviews with solicitors the following day?

"'Ome now, sir?" Webb asked, when Matthew made no move. The hackney still waited, the driver's expression of relief showing he'd been anxious about being paid for his time.

"I wouldn't call it home, precisely," Matthew muttered. The dingy, cramped hackney looked even less inviting than it had earlier. "I'll walk," he said. "It's only a couple of miles."

Webb made a faint sound of protest, hurriedly suppressed.

"You take the hackney with the luggage," Matthew went on. Webb's lungs wouldn't cope well with walking in this stinking air. "Brook Street, number 49. If you arrive before me, wait outside."

"Sir." Webb smiled in relief, gave the driver the direction, and then climbed inside.

Matthew set off at a brisk pace that warmed him up nicely, but left him feeling breathless and slightly dizzy by the time he reached Brook Street. As he suspected, he made better time on foot than the hackney had managed through the crowded streets. He leaned on a handy stretch of wall at the end of the street until he spotted the hackney approaching. Quickly checking that the knocker was still on the door, he motioned to the driver to unload the items of luggage they had brought with them and paid him off, including a generous tip for the time he had waited.

Webb mounted the steps and banged the knocker. A young footman opened the door, looking enquiringly at them.

"Major Southam," Webb announced, jerking his thumb over his shoulder. The footman looked blank.

"This *is* the Southam residence?" Webb asked.

The footman nodded. "Perhaps I can take in your card, sir?" he asked.

"I don't have any cards," Matthew snapped. "This is, however, *my* house."

The footman gaped as Webb rolled his eyes and pushed past him. "Here, you can't—" the footman protested, in vain, as Matthew strode into the hall.

Matthew looked around curiously. When he had last seen the place it had been newly decorated by his stepmother in garish colours, with modern furniture in place of the pieces passed down from his grandparents. The hall still looked over-bright, but in a different set of colours from those he remembered. How many times had it been redecorated in his absence? Each time at great expense, no doubt. He put the thought of dealing with the family's finances firmly from his mind.

"Sir?"

An older man, in his late thirties, came through the baize door leading to the servants' quarters, and the footman gave up his protest. "Mr Baldwin, these men... er, gentlemen..."

"Baldwin?" Matthew said, regarding the man before him. "Weren't you a footman at Farleton Manor?"

The man looked surprised, then pleased, before assuming a neutral but polite expression. "Welcome back, Mr Matthew, sir." He gestured. "If you would step into the parlour I will arrange for some refreshment. I'm afraid the family are not at home at the moment." He murmured an instruction to the footman, who scurried off, then led the way into the front parlour.

Red and white striped paper covered the parlour walls, contrasting with heavy curtains of gold cloth with a woven pattern of flowers. Matthew took in the furniture of gilded wood, upholstered to match the walls, and wondered again how much money was being spent on this house. A fire glowed in the hearth and the room was reasonably warm.

"Mrs Southam is likely to be back shortly, sir, as she has a dinner engagement this evening. Would you care for some tea while you wait, sir, or something stronger?"

"Tea," Webb said firmly, before Matthew could answer. Matthew shrugged, aware of Webb's disapproval but remembering that his flask was still fairly full and he had an emergency bottle. And surely his half-brother, Charles, would have his own supplies somewhere in the house?

"Will you be staying, sir?" Baldwin asked.

"A day or two, possibly longer."

"I'll have Mrs Malplass make up a room for you, sir. I'm sure we can find a place for your man..."

"Webb."

"For Webb in the servants' corridor." He bowed himself out.

Matthew wandered around the room, looking at the pictures and ornaments. There was nothing here he recognised, other than the portrait of a sharp-featured woman hanging above the fireplace.

"Your mother, sir?" Webb asked.

"Stepmother," Matthew said abruptly. "The Honourable Mrs Serena Southam. The 'honourable' is from her father."

"Married down, eh?"

"*She* certainly thinks so." Matthew frowned. Webb was being altogether too familiar, but he couldn't even find the energy for a reprimand. Webb, and possibly Baldwin, made a grand total of exactly two friendly faces in this damp and gloomy country. Although still only mid-afternoon, the solid clouds outside made the room dim. He poked a taper into the fire and lit all the candles.

"Shall I get the rest of the luggage sent round, sir?" Webb asked.

"Very well. But send that young footman. You don't need to go out again unless you want to."

"Thank you, sir."

Matthew wondered how long it would be before Webb was flattering the cook, and possibly one or more of the housemaids. Webb's appearance was not prepossessing, with a thin frame, sandy hair and a scar beside one eye. But he could charm the women when he chose to, and make friends of the men. Matthew wasn't sure how he managed it, but it did have its uses.

Refreshments arrived. The warmth of the tea was welcome, but the plate was soon empty as each sandwich was little more than a mouthful. Matthew stood when he had finished, catching a glimpse of himself in the over-large mirror between the two windows.

He moved towards the mirror, examining his reflection with a frown. He hadn't done too bad a job with the razor this morning, but no-one would call it a good or a close shave. He grimaced at the reflection of his gaunt face and short hair, still growing out after having his head shaved in the hospital. He ran his hand through it—it was still thick enough, at least, with no grey that he could see. He supposed he would have to wear his wig if he couldn't avoid strictly formal occasions, but thankfully the current fashion for shorter hair would mean he wouldn't stand out.

The sound of the front door opening, and voices, roused Matthew from his abstraction. A moment later, two fashionably-dressed women entered the parlour.

"Well, I do think you could have let us know you were coming back!" were the first words out of his stepmother's mouth.

Matthew gave the merest nod of his head. "So pleased to see you, too, Serena," he said.

She still looked fairly youthful, in spite of being in her mid-forties, her skin unwrinkled apart from a few lines of discontent around her mouth. Definitely not laughter lines.

The younger woman must be Julia—as sharp-featured and discontented as her mother. She was not an improvement on his memories of his ten-year old half-sister. She looked him up and down critically.

"Julia," Matthew acknowledged, with a brief nod. "I did write, Serena, but perhaps the letter went astray." He doubted it—she had not looked or sounded particularly surprised to see him, just annoyed.

"Well, I suppose it won't be *too* inconvenient to have you around for a few days," Serena said. "You'll be seeing about your new title? If only your father—"

"What? If only he'd had the decency to hang on to life for another few years, then you'd be Lady Tillson?"

The clock on the mantelpiece chimed the hour. Mrs Southam glanced at it, lips pursed. "I haven't time for this now. Julia, go and get changed. Ring for Presson to attend me—we mustn't be late to the Gotheringtons' dinner."

Matthew raised an eyebrow, but made no comment. Unless things had radically changed since he'd last been in England, she had at least two hours before the earliest dinner party would be starting. But if it took so long for her to get ready, that was fine by him. He really didn't feel like having the inevitable confrontations now.

"I will see you tomorrow, then," he said. He gave the briefest of nods and brushed past them to get to the door. It was time he had a bath himself, after a couple of days on the road, but it would not be fair on the servants to ask them to prepare a third bath now.

He found his way through the kitchen and out into the small

garden behind the house. The drizzle had now turned to more enthusiastic rain, but there was a small covered area with a couple of benches near the door. He sat, leaning his head against the wall.

"All right, sir?" Webb's voice made him jump.

"Any of those cigars left, Webb?"

"Think so, sir."

"Get me one, will you? I'll have a bath once the women have finished."

"Yessir. Would you like to be shaved as well, sir?"

"I'm not letting you near me with a razor, Webb! What d'you take me for?"

"Hah! Not me, sir. Your brother's... your 'alf-brother's valet says Mr Charles won't be back tonight, nor yet in the mornin', so he can do for you if you want."

"A proper shave in the morning, then. And get a couple of the footmen to go up into the attics. I left some clothes here when I was posted to India. If my dear stepmother hasn't thrown them out, they're probably packed in trunks somewhere."

"Very good, sir."

CHAPTER 4

*L*ady Henbury collected Charlotte at eleven, as promised, arriving with Lady Meerbrook. Although not related to the deceased, Lady Meerbrook wore a lavender gown as a sign of respect. Introductions were made and Lady Meerbrook was both polite and friendly. She refrained from remarking on Charlotte's blacks, nearly ten years out of fashion with their lower waist and fuller skirts.

As both Charlotte and her aunt had expected, gaining admission to the Metcalf house in Wimpole Street was not straightforward. The butler, recognising Lady Henbury, asked to know the names of the other two ladies before showing them into the drawing room where Maria Metcalf's body rested.

"This way, if you please, Lady Henbury, Lady Meerbrook," he said, gesturing to a doorway near the end of the hallway. "This person..." He gazed at Charlotte. "This person may await you outside. I have instructions that she is not to be admitted."

"Very well," Lady Henbury said, tilting her head back to look down her nose at him before turning away. "Come, Sarah, Charlotte. We will *all* wait on the steps until such time as Metcalf changes his mind."

"But other callers will see us there!" Lady Meerbrook said, on cue.

"So they will. And you, Sarah, can explain to them why two peer-esses are sitting on the steps of a gentleman's house. I'm sure the story of Metcalf's unnatural behaviour towards his daughter will spread—"

The butler cleared his throat. "Er, if you ladies would take a seat here in the hall, I will enquire..."

They entered and took their seats, as requested. After only a few minutes, Charlotte stood up again and moved around, looking at the pictures hanging on the walls, and peering into the front parlour. None of it seemed to have changed much in the past ten years. Everything was clean, but it all looked tired and slightly shabby. Charlotte shivered—seeing the parlour again brought back that last argument, with her father shouting that she was now dead to him.

Finally, the butler returned. "Please come this way, my ladies." He bowed. "This person may accompany you," he added stiffly, his gaze avoiding Charlotte. "Please do not take long. Lady Santon and Lady Fairford are expected shortly."

Charlotte flushed at the insinuation. Her sisters seemingly did not want to speak to her either. Or perhaps their father still considered her to be a corrupting influence, even ten years on when both her sisters were married with children of their own.

Lady Meerbrook took a quizzing glass out of her reticule and surveyed the butler through it. The man shifted uncomfortably and cleared his throat.

"My apologies, my lady. I am only relaying Mr Metcalf's orders."

"Very well," Lady Meerbrook said. "You have done as you were bid. Now *we* will pay our last respects without being hurried. If *Mister* Metcalf objects he can come and tell us so himself, and I will be clear that you passed on his... er... *instructions*."

Charlotte almost smiled as Lady Meerbrook sniffed. The butler would be in no doubt of her opinion of a mere 'mister' giving such impolite orders to a viscountess.

The back parlour was draped in black bombazine, gloomy with the curtains closed. A low table in the centre of the room supported the coffin, and one of the maids kept watch in a corner. Charlotte thought her mother looked peaceful, resting there with her eyes closed. She did not look happy, but neither did she look unhappy or in pain. Tears started to run down her cheeks as she gazed on her mother's face for the last time. She made no attempt to stop them.

Lady Henbury put a comforting arm around her shoulders, and she was dimly aware that Lady Meerbrook had gone to stand in the doorway. Some time later she heard a heated discussion conducted in whispers, rousing her. She sniffed, blew her nose and mopped her eyes, then braced herself.

"Thank you, Aunt," she whispered, and looked towards the doorway where her sisters stood. Augusta had the same rich brown hair as all the Metcalfs, but hers was now showing streaks of grey, and her forehead was marred by lines of discontent. Beatrice, a few years younger than Charlotte, appeared well, although she was becoming rather plump. Both looked as if they had just bitten into a lemon.

"Come, Charlotte," Lady Henbury said firmly. "We will let your sisters pay their last respects." She nodded to her other two nieces briefly as she passed them. "We will see you later, after the funeral."

Charlotte felt as surprised as her sisters looked, for she had not expected to be invited to the small reception that afternoon.

Nor had she been invited, as it turned out when she asked Lady Henbury about it. "But your mother's last will and testament will be read then," her aunt explained.

"Surely my father would not have allowed her to leave me anything?"

"Oh, he didn't. But there are some things he does not know." She gave her niece what could only be described as a smirk, then put her hand on Charlotte's arm. "Forgive me for being amused at such a time, my dear. But your mother planned this, as her last small act of defiance. I hope you do not find it too upsetting, but it is something she thought about often during the past months when she was ailing. However undutiful some people might consider it, she took considerable comfort in the idea that she would be thwarting him from beyond the grave."

Charlotte wondered what her mother could have done. As far as she knew, her mother had had no money of her own. A substantial dowry had become her husband's property on marriage. The will would only specify who got various personal possessions such as jewellery, although Charlotte thought her father would claim it all belonged to him. He would not want her to inherit anything.

"... looking much better than your sisters," Lady Henbury said.

Charlotte looked up to see her aunt regarding her quizzically. "I'm sorry, Aunt Elizabeth—"

"No matter, my dear. I was only saying how well you look."

"Having to walk everywhere works wonders," Charlotte said. She put a hand to her cheek. "I probably look too... tanned."

Her aunt smiled. "You look healthy, my dear."

"I never really thanked you, Aunt, for helping Mama to receive my letters, and to send her own."

When she had run away to get married, her father had tried to ban all communication between Charlotte and the rest of her family. Her mother, with Aunt Elizabeth's help, had ignored this instruction, and when Charlotte moved to Edgecombe had even managed to send her some of her pin money. Although not large sums, these gifts had helped to make life in Edgecombe comfortable for all of them.

Charlotte tried not to think about that for now, but sat for a little while, reminiscing with her aunt. Then, still tired, she took a short nap in a spare bedroom before it was time to return to Wimpole Street.

Charlotte, Lady Henbury and Lady Meerbrook arrived back at Wimpole Street ahead of the family members who had attended the funeral. Lady Henbury had also brought along a rotund man in a powdered wig and black suit. He took a seat in the hall, carefully placing his leather satchel on his knees.

This time the butler showed them straight into the parlour and sent for fresh tea. Augusta and Beatrice were already there, awaiting their husbands' return from the funeral. Charlotte said good afternoon to them and, under Lady Meerbrook's sharp eye, they gave stiff but polite replies. They didn't have long to wait.

The butler must have warned Mr Metcalf that his errant daughter was once more in the house, for he did not look surprised or even angered to see her when he entered the parlour. Charlotte, though, had to hide her shock at her father's appearance. He must be around sixty now, the deep wrinkles around his eyes and mouth making him look his age. He was much more portly than she remembered, with an unhealthy flush to his complexion.

Metcalf inspected Charlotte carefully, casting an occasional glance from her to Beatrice. Charlotte smoothed her gown self-consciously.

"Charlotte," he said coolly.

"Father," she said, responding in kind.

"You look well," he said, an odd note in his voice.

Lady Henbury stood just behind Charlotte's father, watching the meeting. Charlotte saw her brows draw together in a frown.

"How is David?" her father went on. "Your son is still healthy, I hope? Thriving?" He paused a moment, his head tilting slightly to one side and his eyes running down her dress again. "You have not brought him with you? He must be of an age to start school soon."

"I left him at home," she said. *I don't want you to get your claws into him, or infect him with your view of life.* Such things were better not said aloud.

Her father looked thoughtful, but was distracted by condolences from other guests and moved away. It was half an hour before he approached her again—half an hour of partial silence, interrupted by stilted conversations with her sisters.

"Well, Charlotte," he started, with suspicious friendliness. "Perhaps it is time to let bygones be bygones and for you to return to London."

Charlotte waited. There would be more to this offer than was immediately apparent.

"A pity you did not make that offer while Maria was still alive," Lady Henbury said tartly. "She would have loved to have had Charlotte back."

Her father's lips thinned. "If you please, madam, I would like a private conversation with my daughter!" Lady Henbury regarded him for a moment, looking down her nose, then moved off a couple of paces. As far as Charlotte knew, Lady Henbury's hearing had not deteriorated with age; she suspected her aunt could still hear them quite clearly, for which she was grateful.

"I don't suppose what MacKinnon left you goes very far," her father said, with a meaningful glance at her skirts, which were unfashionably full and showed signs of fading along the folds.

"Far enough," Charlotte said. Her mother had known that she earned money from writing and various other things, but her father had probably never bothered to enquire.

"And David? How is his education progressing? He must be, what, ten now?"

"Very well. He has a tutor—"

"But surely, you would wish him to go to school? A man cannot develop properly under only female influence."

"It is a little late to put him down for Eton or Harrow," Charlotte said, a sinking feeling in her stomach. What was he planning?

"There are other schools," her father replied. "Mixing with other boys of his class will be useful for his future, and will help to develop a love of sports and other manly activities."

If other boys of his class were similar to the squire's lumpish son, Charlotte thought Davie might be better off without their company. Nevertheless, few boys grew up with only a mother's influence. If Davie were too different from his peers he might face problems later.

"Your point, sir?" Charlotte asked impatiently.

"Return home and live here, and David will be sent to a good school. It is my duty to ensure my grandson is educated properly."

"That is all? If I return to London, you will pay for Davie's education?"

She didn't believe it, and she was right.

"Why, yes! You can take your place in society again—you are young yet, and looking very well." He couldn't stop another glance at her waistline, and Charlotte realised what he was after.

Although ten years too old to be a debutante, she had borne a healthy son and so would be attractive to a man in need of an heir. Her father wanted to marry her off to advance his own social status, and probably also his finances.

She was about to point out that she no longer needed his help or permission to marry, nor had any desire to remarry, but suddenly thought better of it. She couldn't afford to give Davie the things other boys of his class took for granted—and possibly giving him her love wasn't enough to make up for that.

She could see Lady Henbury shaking her head; even without that, she was not going to make an answer now. She might have no choice but to marry again if she were to do right by Davie, but it need not be a man of her father's choosing. Far better *not* to be one of his choosing! He could no longer coerce her, after all—he had lost his legal power over her when she married.

"I will think on it, sir," was all she said.

Metcalf, having expected an outright denial, raised his eyebrows a little and moved off to talk to other guests. Charlotte didn't want to agree to his proposition, but she had to think about Davie's future.

An hour later, many of the guests had departed, and Metcalf announced that his wife's will would be read. Charlotte looked around—her sisters and their husbands were still present. Lady Henbury and Lady Meerbrook had been joined by two other men she did not recognise.

Metcalf rang the bell and the butler ushered in a man who looked to be a solicitor, complete with a rolled paper tied with ribbon. The rotund man who had arrived with Lady Henbury slipped into the room behind him.

Metcalf gestured for everyone to be seated, glancing in puzzlement at the three strange gentlemen. "If you will excuse us, Lady Meerbrook, sirs? This is a family matter."

The rotund man coughed. "Lord Meerbrook and Lord Etherington are witnesses to the will, Mr Metcalf." The two lords nodded briefly. "I am Josiah Renwick, the late Mrs Metcalf's solicitor."

"Nonsense!" Metcalf said. "Smeaton, here, represents our family. Tell them, Smeaton."

Metcalf's man of business unrolled his paper and cleared his throat. "This is the last will and testament of Maria Sophia Metcalf, dated 10th August 1799, prepared by myself and witnessed by—"

Renwick coughed again. "Excuse me," he said, opening his satchel and taking out a paper. "I have here the last will and testament of Maria Sophia Metcalf, dated 20th August 1799, and witnessed by these two gentlemen."

"What? Give me that!" Metcalf strode across the room and pulled the paper from Renwick's grasp. "A forgery!"

"Metcalf, are you really calling Lord Etherington and myself liars?" Lord Meerbrook's voice was calm, with an undertone of vague surprise, but no-one was fooled into taking his mild tone at face value. Lady Meerbrook and Lady Henbury exchanged a small smile.

Metcalf paled. Charlotte could almost see the implications dawning on him—the second son of a baron calling two peers of the realm liars—he could be called out, and would certainly no longer be welcome at his clubs.

"Papa!" Augusta hissed.

"Let us hear them out, Metcalf," said Lord Santon calmly, and Metcalf reluctantly sat down.

Renwick cleared his throat and began to read. The will was simple —as a married woman, Mrs Metcalf had owned nothing in her own right so there were only personal items to be disposed of, mostly jewellery. The items of jewellery were divided fairly equally between Maria's three daughters and her sister.

Metcalf nodded as the reading concluded, his expression once again calm. "Very good," he said. "Augusta, Beatrice, Lady Henbury, I will have the items sent round tomorrow."

He turned to Charlotte. "I assume you will be travelling back to..." he paused, unsure where his daughter lived. He cleared his throat and continued. "It would not be safe for you to travel with such expensive pieces. I will keep them for you until you move back to London."

Charlotte opened her mouth to protest, but a painful pinch on her arm stopped her. She glanced round in surprise to see Lady Henbury shaking her head. *What's going on?* But she trusted her aunt more than her father, so she kept quiet.

"If that is all...?" Metcalf asked, his hand reaching for the bell to call the butler.

Renwick cleared his throat. "Not quite, sir. There is the matter of the trust."

"Trust? What trust?" Metcalf's voice was loud, but he took a deep breath and closed his mouth, pinching his lips together firmly.

"The trust that Mr Sloane, your late wife's father—"

"I know who Sloane is, damn it!" Metcalf snarled. Lord Meerbrook cleared his throat; Metcalf took another deep breath.

"I believe you were informed when the trust was set up, sir," Renwick said. "The letter would have been addressed to Mr Smeaton."

A fulminating glance at Smeaton from Metcalf promised retribution later, but he said nothing more.

"As I was saying, there is the matter of the trust set up by the late Mr Sloane. At present this contains around fifteen thousand pounds, invested in the funds, to be disbursed by the trustees as directed by Mrs Metcalf, or according to her written instructions."

"My wife's money should be mine to dispose of," Metcalf started, but Renwick shook his head.

"The money never belonged to Mrs Metcalf, sir, and is not yours to dispose of as her husband. Her instructions are that the sum is divided equally between her three daughters, for their sole use."

Charlotte closed her eyes for a moment, hardly believing it. That would be plenty to buy some decent schooling for Davie, and hopefully there would be some left over to invest for the future. It could keep her out of her father's clutches.

The thought had clearly occurred to her father as well.

"I will contest that," he announced. "Who are the trustees?"

"Lord Meerbrook and Lord Etherington, with myself as the legal representative," Renwick said. "The late Mrs Metcalf's wishes also state that if there is a legal challenge that aims to prevent Mrs MacKinnon getting her share of the money—" Metcalf's expression

39

darkened. "—she will accept that Mrs MacKinnon should not be paid."

Charlotte could see her father's shoulders relax as he smiled.

Renwick cleared his throat again, and continued. "However, Mrs Metcalf did not think it right that her daughters should be treated differently and in that case the whole sum is to go to Lady Henbury."

"What?"

Metcalf positively roared this time, and there were also protests from Augusta and Beatrice. Nor did their husbands look pleased. Lady Henbury, on the other hand, looked like a cat who'd been at the cream.

"I think our presence is no longer required, Meerbrook," Lady Meerbrook said to her husband, who obediently rose and gave her his arm. Etherington offered an arm to Lady Henbury, and Charlotte followed them from the room. The last she heard was Renwick suggesting that Metcalf think carefully before he took any action, and perhaps Smeaton should come to see him the following day.

Lords Meerbrook and Etherington excused themselves at the front door, with Lady Henbury's thanks, and the ladies rode back to her house together.

"Thank you so much, Sarah, for helping, and getting your husband to help too," Lady Henbury said as they entered the house.

"Our pleasure, Beth," Lady Meerbrook said. "Meerbrook doesn't care much for your brother-in-law."

"I can't think why," Lady Henbury muttered, and both Charlotte and Lady Meerbrook laughed.

Lady Henbury led the way into her parlour, and rang for her maid to fetch something from her bedroom. The maid returned with a leather case, which Lady Henbury handed to Charlotte.

"Your jewels from your mother," she said.

Charlotte opened the case with trembling fingers. Inside lay the simple pearl necklace, the locket with a miniature portrait of her mother, and the diamond tiara that had been left to her in her mother's will. She looked up at her aunt, her vision blurred by gathering tears.

"Your mother brought them to me on the day she came to make her new will," Lady Henbury explained. This, then, was why her aunt had stopped Charlotte from protesting against her father's plans to keep hold of them.

The gazes of the two older women met, and they smiled. Charlotte, while appreciating their pleasure at allowing her mother one final protest against her overbearing husband, felt mostly sadness at the unhappy life her mother had lived. Lady Henbury's married life had not been much better, by all accounts.

She picked up the diamond tiara, tilting it so the gems twinkled in the light from the window. This alone might be enough to ensure Davie's schooling, even if her father did contest the trust and tied up the money in chancery while lawyers' fees consumed most of it. It was a course of action that would ultimately benefit no-one except the lawyers, but she wouldn't put it past him to do so out of spite. Particularly after he discovered that Charlotte had the jewellery in her possession after all. She was certain that her sisters and their husbands would try to dissuade him, in the interests of keeping their own shares of the money.

"What are you going to do with the jewellery, Charlotte?" Lady Henbury asked. Charlotte put the tiara down and picked up the pearl necklace, running it through her fingers slowly.

"I remember Mama wearing this," she said. "I'd like to keep it, and the locket. But the tiara—can I sell it?" She looked at it doubtfully. "I hate to admit it, but my father may have been correct about the danger of me carrying it back to Edgecombe."

"I'll ask Meerbrook to sell it for you, if you wish," Lady Meerbrook said. "Let me know what your banking arrangements are, and he'll deal with it."

"I don't know how to thank you, my lady," Charlotte said.

"Just keep writing those stories, my dear," Lady Meerbrook said with a smile. "My grandchildren love them! If you could do more about Mr and Mrs Hedgehog..."

Charlotte blushed, both surprised and pleased. "Another fox story is in progress, my lady, but I will see what the hedgehog family can get up to next!"

"Why does your father dis—" Lady Meerbrook stopped, pressing her lips together. "I'm sorry."

"Why does he dislike me so much?" Charlotte asked. "Don't worry, my lady, you have not offended me by asking." She glanced at Lady Henbury, who waved a hand. "I ran away instead of marrying the man he chose for me."

Lady Meerbrook's eyebrows rose.

"Whiston," Lady Henbury stated.

Lady Meerbrook's eyebrows rose even further, if that were possible. "Viscount Whiston? Good God in heaven—he must be sixty if he's a day, and still a lecher." She looked at Charlotte. "How long ago was this?"

"Twelve years ago, when I was seventeen."

"And Mr MacKinnon, if you don't mind me asking?"

"A captain in the East India Company army, home on leave, my lady."

"You fell in love?"

"No, we were just friends, but he agreed to help me. We married and went to India." She glanced at Lady Meerbrook, wondering if she was really interested.

"Do go on, my dear." She smiled. "To be frank, it's a pleasure to hear how one of our sex managed to thwart the… er… *superior* sex!"

"He died of cholera a couple of years later, and I had Davie a month or so after I got back."

"I'm sorry."

"It is a long time ago, my lady, and I have my son. *And* my freedom. My father wanted to marry me off again. The widow of one of Angus' sergeants travelled back with me on the same ship. I approached her, and we bought a house together."

"Well, you thwarted him twice! Well done indeed, my dear."

"I'm afraid today will not have endeared you to him, Charlotte," Lady Henbury said.

"No, I'm afraid not." Charlotte rubbed her forehead. Her father was planning something, she was sure, but she tried to put that out of her mind.

"Do you have any friends there, Charlotte?" Lady Henbury asked. "Is there much local society?"

"I visit the squire's wife regularly," Charlotte said.

"Yes, they would naturally wish to associate with you," Lady Henbury said, nodding.

Charlotte suppressed a smile—her status in the local area was far lower than Lady Henbury assumed. Charlotte's weekly visits to Northridge Hall had started only a couple of years ago, when the squire remarried. Letty had been a younger daughter kept at home to look after an ailing mother; she had accepted the squire's offer with relief, having thought her chances of matrimony were long gone. Unfortunately, she had no idea how to manage a large house and its servants, much less her nine-year-old stepson.

Arthur Thompson hadn't known what to say when his new wife was regularly reduced to tears over the management of his household, but he did have enough sympathy to find someone who did. Charlotte had been invited to call, and Letty had welcomed her with relief, the two soon becoming friends.

"Davie shares his son's tutor," Charlotte went on, "and there are dinner parties now and then." Her aunt was not likely to regard Mary MacKinnon as suitable company, even though the two shared the house as equals. She decided not to mention Sir Vincent and his mother, not wanting to deal with the speculation about her marital prospects that would inevitably follow.

After another request for more hedgehog stories, Lady Meerbrook took her leave, and Lady Henbury rang for tea. They discussed what might happen with the trust, and came to the conclusion that Charlotte would eventually get some of the money, at least, but it might take some time.

Charlotte finally parted tearfully from her aunt, and went back to tell Ann what had happened, and to rest before catching the overnight mail for Bath.

CHAPTER 5

*M*atthew awoke the next morning to a firm knock on the door, followed by the sound of the door opening. He squinted out of gritty eyes; the man entering was middle aged, running a little to fat and baldness, with neat, plain clothes. He held a jug of water and a box.

"Good morning, sir. I am Gregson, Mr Charles' valet. Your man, Webb, said you had an appointment this morning and would require a shave?" The valet looked around the room, taking in the untidy piles of clothing and the empty, and dusty, trunks with a neutral expression. He put the jug and shaving kit down on a table then went over to the window, tutting quietly as he closed it against the cold air and pulled the curtains partway across.

"Coffee first," Matthew said. His head wasn't too fuzzy this morning, thankfully. He picked up his watch from the table beside the bed. "I've a couple of hours before I need to set off."

"Very good, sir."

"Ring for it, will you? And could you look through that lot?" He waved his hand at the garments over the back of the chair. "Sort out a set and see if it can be made presentable."

Gregson rang the bell, then started to pick through the clothes.

Although obviously not new, the garments had not suffered months of salt-laden air and damp cabins like the clothes he had brought back from India. A hacking cough from the dressing room next door reminded Matthew that Webb had turned down the offered place in the attics, preferring a hard cot in the dressing room to a shared room with one of the footmen.

Half an hour later, Webb had disappeared below stairs for his breakfast and Matthew was feeling almost human. He wore a set of his old clothes, tailored for the stripling he'd been when he set out for India, waistcoat and coat lying ready on his bed. At the moment they fitted him better than his newer garments. He settled himself in a chair while Gregson sorted out his shaving gear.

Webb installed himself at the table in the servants' dining room. Though not yet time for the servants' breakfast, he asked nicely and the cook made him some tea, porridge, and toast. Genlowe, the young footman who had not wanted to let them in the day before, arrived, rubbing sleep out of his eyes. He sat down, grinning cheekily at the little kitchen maid who brought him a drink.

"You stayin' long?" he asked Webb.

"Dunno," Webb grunted, continuing to eat.

"Just come from India, you said last night? How was it?"

"'Ot."

"Bit of warm weather'd be good right now," Genlowe went on, not seeming bothered by Webb's curt responses. "Still, at least the mistress keeps us in coal. It's not so bad here, not like the last place I was at." He took a bit of toast from the plate in front of Webb.

Webb pointedly moved the plate out of his reach.

"Where you off to today, then? Mr Gregson'll turn him out a bit smarter than when you arrived. Good with clothes he is."

"'E's a valet," Webb muttered.

"Does a lovely shave, too," Genlowe went on. "Did it for me once— lovely and relaxing, it was."

"He's probably ready for the hot water now," Baldwin said from behind Genlowe, making him jump.

Genlowe reluctantly got up and checked if there was hot water in the kettle. He poured a jug-full.

"Save some of that toast for me," he said with a grin as he headed for the back stairs.

"What's 'e doin' with that?" Webb asked.

"Hot towels," Baldwin said. "Like the lad said, lovely and relaxing. Not something we have time for, though."

"'Ot towels?"

"Yes, he dips them in hot water, wrings them out then puts them on your face. Warm and damp. Might do your breathing good, you know. You sound awfully wheezy…"

But Webb had gone.

He was too late. He'd managed one flight of stairs at a brisk pace, up to the ground floor, but had to stop halfway up the next flight and lean on the wall until he got his breath back. Genlowe had passed him on the stairs on his way back down to the kitchen, giving him a puzzled look, but Webb didn't have the breath to explain. Once in the corridor leading to the major's room he heard the crash of over-turning furniture, but he had to stop again when he reached the door-way. He couldn't see either man at first, but then there was a movement and the valet's feet came into view beyond an overturned chair.

"Shit!" He hurried over. The major had the valet on the floor with his hands around his neck.

"Major!" He tried to pull him off the valet, but the major ignored him. Webb tried to pry the hands away, but was nearly head-butted for his pains.

"Oh, bugger it," Webb muttered. He might not be able to run any more, or even walk fast, but he could still throw a decent punch. He made a fist and swung it.

The major went limp, the force of the blow rolling him away from his victim. Gregson lay on the floor for a minute, gasping for breath, then Webb helped him to sit in the now-righted chair.

"He… he attacked me!" the valet said indignantly, then seemed to recall that his attacker was still in the room. He tried to stand up, but Webb put a firm hand on his shoulder.

"You're safe now, lad," he said, in spite of the fact the man was old enough to be his father. "What did you do?"

"It wasn't my fault!" the valet snapped.

Webb shook his head. "Never said it were." He looked at the major, now beginning to stir.

"Let me go before he wakes up!" Gregson said in renewed panic.

"'E won't attack you again," Webb said. "Wet towels, was it?" He thought for a moment, then added in a confiding tone, "The major don't like folks to know, but 'e nearly drowned when 'e were a nipper. Don't like water over 'is 'ead. Baths are fine, but not swimmin'. I reckon them wet towels took 'im back."

Gregson looked a little doubtful, and rubbed his neck. Webb could see red finger marks where the man's neckcloth had loosened.

"I don't reckon that'll show," Webb said. "Not dignified, is it, to be rollin' around on the floor—"

"He attacked me!" Gregson protested again.

"Asked 'im about the towels first, did you?"

Gregson frowned. "Everyone else liked it," he muttered weakly.

Webb shook his head. "Well, you'll not do that again." He glanced down the valet's clothing. "You'll likely need a new neckcloth. Is that a bit o' damage to your shirt? Will a couple of guineas cover it, d'you think? And you've done a real good job on the major's clothes." He looked around, spying the brandy flask on the floor beside the bed.

"'Ere, take this with you. A little nip now and then'll stop your throat feelin' too sore."

The valet took the flask—an expensive silver one. Webb could see him calculating its value.

"Feelin' a bit better?" Webb asked. The valet nodded. "Good man. Tell 'em in the kitchen we'll get our breakfast out. Maybe we'll be back for dinner."

The valet stood up, rubbed his neck gingerly, and adjusted his clothing. Checking his appearance in the glass, he gave a quick nod and an uncertain glance at the major still lying on the floor, and then left. The door shut with a click behind him, and there was silence for a moment.

"What did I do?" the major asked, sitting up and rubbing his jaw. "And did you *have* to give him my best flask?"

"You nearly throttled the bugger," Webb said laconically, and picked up the towels scattered on the floor. "'Ow long was you awake?"

"Long enough to learn that I nearly drowned when I was a child." The major rubbed his jaw again. "Why are you still here, Webb? Haven't you got family to go home to?"

"You want me to leave, sir?"

"No, just wondering."

"Seems a decent billet to me, sir. Ain't got no family, and I ain't fit for labourin' neither." Webb kept a wary eye on the major as he finished tidying up, but he just rubbed his face again and shrugged.

"Very well. Get my coat, would you? We'd best make ourselves scarce, before Gregson spreads his little story."

"Oh, I don't think 'e will, sir. 'E won't want me to ask for your silver flask back."

The major just shook his head and shrugged into the coat. "Breakfast," he said, and the two men headed for the nearest inn.

Mr Gleason the younger was not young—far from it. His wisps of white hair showed his age, as did the purple veins visible through the papery skin on his temples and the backs of his hands. Nor did he look to be in the best of health. However, he was polite and welcoming, read through the documents presented to him with care, and finally gave his verdict.

"All seems to be in order, Major Southam. Rather, Lord Tillson, I should say." He ran one hand across his bald pate. "You have no idea how glad I am to be able to say that. It has taken four years to trace the heir to the title and the entailed part of the estate. We had to go back four generations from the previous baron to find a surviving heir of the male line."

"That's it then?" Matthew asked, surprised at how little had been required. Somehow he had imagined that the formalities of inheriting a title would be more involved.

"Well, no. There are various applications to be made, documents to be signed, et cetera. But any challenges to the inheritance would have been made long ago, so they should all be straightforward."

"And the estate consists of…?"

"Birchanger Hall is an old house near the village of Edgecombe, on the western side of the Cotswolds. There is a respectable acreage of farmland with it, and some woodland, but that is the only land covered by the entail."

"Who is running it at the moment?"

Mr Gleason seemed to wilt a little at this question. "There was a steward, but I understand he left. I have not been able to appoint a replacement. I'm afraid Cyril Southey, the last baron, was somewhat of a skinflint and allowed the estate to run down."

"Southey?"

"Southey, Southam. It seems someone in one line or the other changed the spelling at some point. That did not help to expedite tracing the heir," Gleason said with downturned mouth.

"There is no mistake?"

Gleason shook his head. "You sounded rather hopeful, my lord?"

"It is beginning to sound like a poisoned chalice," Matthew said. "An estate run into the ground, with but a single farm to support it…" He had never even heard of the barony until the letter informing him of his inheritance had reached India. Farleton, the estate in Somerset he'd inherited on his father's death, was easily sufficient for his needs. Birchanger sounded as if it would be more trouble than it was worth.

"I'm sure you will be able to bring it around, my lord. You will wish to see the place as soon as possible, I suppose?" He indicated a box standing by the door. "The papers in there may be of interest;

they pertain to the running of the estate. I am afraid I have other appointments. I will let you know when there are more documents to be signed, but there is no impediment to your taking possession as soon as you wish."

Interpreting this as dismissal, Matthew picked up the box, shook the man's hand and left. He supposed he'd have to at least go and see the place. Or, better, just get the family solicitors to sort it all out.

Once outside he took a deep breath, then wished he hadn't. The acrid tang of coal smoke stung the back of his throat. It was far worse today—perhaps yesterday's drizzle had actually been a blessing, washing smoke out of the air.

He sent Webb to deliver the box to Brook Street and to buy a replacement flask, telling him to be outside Mayhews' in an hour. Matthew wandered down the road to Lincoln's Inn Fields to wait in the green space there. It was too cold to sit still, so he walked around the grassy patch a couple of times, noting a few other men also taking the air, but not passing close enough to exchange greetings. In one corner of the park a pie-seller called for trade. Matthew had only managed more coffee when he and Webb ventured out for breakfast, and now he felt the need for a bit of brandy. The pies smelled good. Perhaps eating something would help take his mind off his lack of a flask?

Unfortunately, they smelled far better than they tasted. Matthew managed a couple of mouthfuls, then nearly gagged at the amount of gristle and grease inside. He'd eaten far worse at times on campaign, but he really wasn't hungry enough to eat such a thing now. He tossed the remains of the pie into a bush. As he did, a blur of mud-coloured hair dashed past, and a skinny dog ate what he had thrown away. Then, looking around hopefully for more, the filthy creature came and sat at his feet.

"Out of the way," Matthew muttered, putting out a foot to push the dog gently off the path. The animal cringed sideways, then edged forwards a little, its stomach to the ground and the tip of its tail stirring slightly. Matthew couldn't tell its colour beneath the mud, but its dirty, matted coat couldn't hide its prominent ribs. He shrugged, sorry for the animal, but he couldn't feed all the strays in London. He walked on—another lap of the grass and he would head for Mayhews', early or not.

"Yer wan' another pie fer the mutt?" the pie man asked, hopefully, as Matthew passed him again. Matthew looked up in surprise, and the man jerked his head. Matthew turned around to see the dog sitting a couple of feet away. "Follered yer right round, 'e did," the man said.

Matthew moved off a couple of paces and the dog followed, sitting down when he stopped.

"Lie down," Matthew said experimentally, pointing downwards. The dog obeyed. "Stay." He walked a bit further away. The dog twitched with the desire to follow this potential source of food, but managed to restrain itself.

"Come," Matthew said quietly, and snapped his fingers. The animal bounded over, but instead of jumping up at him as he'd half expected, it sat again.

"Reckon 'e use ter be someone's pet," the pie man said. "Poor bugger—'e'll not know 'ow ter fight. Bet the other strays don't let 'im get near no food."

"Two pies," Matthew said, digging in his pocket. He gave the pie man his best officer's glare. "Preferably ones with meat in them!"

The pie man opened his mouth to protest, then thought better of it. "They're all the same, sir," he said regretfully. "But I kin give yer two fer the price o' one?"

Matthew handed over the coins, took the greasy packet, and walked over to a nearby bench. The dog followed him, a little more of its tail waving this time. He broke off a piece of pie and dropped it on the ground in front of the dog, feeding it a little at a time until the first pie was gone. He didn't think it would do the animal good to gorge itself, and he started to reach for a handkerchief before realising that the grease on his hands would get everywhere if he touched his coat.

"May I be of assistance?" an amused voice asked. Matthew looked up to see a man of about his own age, fair-haired and dressed in gentleman's clothing. "A handkerchief, perhaps?"

"Thank you—but I have one—if you wouldn't mind reaching into my coat?" Matthew stood, indicating the relevant pocket, then gratefully wiped his hands. He gingerly used the now-soiled handkerchief to pick up the greasy paper holding the remaining pie.

"Phineas Kellet," the man said, holding out a hand.

"Matthew Southam." He eyed his own hand. "Perhaps you'd better take the handshake as done?" he suggested. Although no longer dripping with grease and bits of pastry, his hand could not be said to be clean.

Kellet nodded and smiled. "Pleasure to meet you, sir. I think you have a new friend there, as well." He glanced at the dog, then pulled a watch from his waistcoat pocket. "Sorry to dash off, but I've an appointment."

Matthew watched him walk off, then looked back at the mutt at his feet. "Time for me to go too." He set off for Mayhews', not surprised to hear the click of claws once he reached the stone paving in the street. "I suppose I'm stuck with you for a bit," he muttered.

Webb was waiting for him outside the Mayhews' office, having a coughing fit. When he had regained his breath, Matthew gave him the greasy packet with the pie in it.

"Don't give the animal the whole thing in one go."

Webb grunted, holding out a small flask.

Matthew took a mouthful from the flask and almost spat it out—what on earth had Webb found to fill the damned thing? Furniture polish? He'd have to manage without for a bit longer.

His second interview that day with the legal profession was both longer and less satisfactory than the first. It appeared that Mr Gerrard Mayhew was the partner in charge of the Southam concerns, but unfortunately only Mr Anthony Mayhew was available. Mr Anthony was very apologetic, and could only suppose there had been some misunderstanding leading to their firm's belief that Major Southam had passed away. He advanced Matthew a hundred guineas in return for a signed receipt, but informed him that all the accounts were with Mr Gerrard, who was currently out of town.

"Visiting Farleton, is he?" Matthew asked. He could think of no other reason why the books for the Farleton estate should not be here in the main offices.

"Indeed," Mayhew said, a faint look of relief crossing his features. "I will notify you as soon as my brother returns, so you may inspect them."

"And the accounts for the town house? And my stepmother's allowance?" Matthew raised an eyebrow.

"They are stored in the basement, Major. We have a regular time of the month for dealing with them. It would take time to retrieve them today—perhaps if you could call back in an hour?" He stood up, apparently ready to usher Matthew to the door.

Matthew did not move. "When I called yesterday I told your clerk I wanted a full accounting, together with the last two annual reports I should have been sent."

"I'm terribly sorry, Major, I was not informed," Mayhew said smoothly. *Too smoothly?* "I shall speak to the clerk about his ineffi-ciency. An hour?"

Matthew nodded, keen to get out of the over-warm air in the office. Shown out by the clerk, he waited until the door closed behind him before cursing. Unless he was indeed losing his mind, he had just been treated to the longest list of lies he'd heard since sitting in on a regimental sick parade.

"Hello again, Major Southam! What a co-incidence!" Phineas Kellet stood at the bottom of the short flight of steps to the street. Webb stood behind him, wiping his greasy fingers on a grubby hand-kerchief.

Matthew nodded a greeting.

"Not a satisfactory meeting?" Kellet asked.

Matthew ran his hand through his hair. "You could say that. You don't know..." He cut himself off, glancing at the door with the Mayhews' business plate on it. This conversation would be better conducted elsewhere.

He descended the few steps down to the street and set off along the pavement, inclining his head in tacit invitation for Kellet to accompany him. "Can you recommend a good solicitor? One who can take on my affairs at short notice?" Birchanger business as well as taking over from the Mayhews.

"As it happens, my younger brother is in the business," Kellet said, falling into step beside Matthew as they walked down the street, Webb wheezing along behind them with the dog at his heels. "He's not as well known as many—still trying to make a name for himself. I don't think I'm being over-partial..." He finished with a shrug.

"I'd take it most kindly, sir, if you could furnish me with his direction."

Kellet nodded, and the two men paused while Kellet took a card from his case and wrote a name and address on the back. Then he touched the end of his cane to his hat and bade Matthew farewell again.

"Seems like a nice gent, sir."

Matthew started, having forgotten Webb's presence for the moment. Not to mention the dog.

"You don't think I'd be too trusting to turn my business over to his brother? I don't know the man."

"Seems 'onest enough to me, sir," Webb said, not quite meeting his eyes. "What you goin' to do with this mutt, sir?"

"Nothing, Sergeant."

"Can't just leave the poor bugger on the streets again, sir!"

Matthew made the mistake of looking down into the pleading brown eyes, noting the barely moving tail.

"Mind you," Webb added, with no trace of guile in his face, "maybe it's better not. Your stepma would 'ate to have it around the 'ouse."

Matthew grinned. "So she would, Sergeant. But you will be responsible for getting him clean!"

"I reckon it's an 'er, sir—or else it's 'ad a very nasty accident to its—"

"Yes, thank, you Sergeant."

"Very good, sir."

"Get a hackney, would you? I'm just going to call back at Gleasons'. Meet me there."

Half an hour later Matthew had determined that the younger Kellet, although relatively inexperienced, had a good reputation and was generally considered to be going far.

The hackney delivered the major, Webb, and the dog to the address Phineas Kellet had provided. Webb was relegated once again to waiting outside with the dog.

Mr Joshua Kellet, unfortunately, was in court this afternoon, and likely to be busy for the next few days. However, on Webb sticking his head in the door to find out how much longer Matthew was going to be, "Cos the mutt's whinin' somethin' 'orrible, sir", the clerk thought he could manage an hour or so later the following morning.

Matthew decided against returning to Mayhews' for the family accounts. Kellet could deal with them, and any remaining business with Gleason.

CHAPTER 6

Baldwin informed Matthew that the family were dining at home that evening. Gregson had selected another two sets of clothing from the garments Webb had unearthed, then had them cleaned and pressed. As a result, Matthew looked almost presentable when he entered the dining room, although his clothing still hung loosely off his frame.

This room had been decorated with turquoise walls which, to Matthew's eyes, clashed horribly with the orange curtains. The mirror over the mantelpiece had an ornate gilt frame, matching the frames on the family portraits around the walls. He stood looking at one showing his father, a lump coming to his throat as he studied the familiar features.

He turned as the door opened behind him. Serena and Julia entered, both clad in ornate ball gowns trimmed with yards of lace, and a quantity of jewellery bordering on the vulgar—at least in Matthew's opinion. Charles followed them into the room.

Mr Charles Southam had not changed as much over the years as Julia had. He still bore a certain resemblance to his sister, with similar dark blond hair and grey eyes, but without her sharp features. His bland, neutral expression contrasted with the discontented appearance of his sister. He, too, was dressed expensively, in a velvet coat and embroidered silk waistcoat, with a number of jewelled fobs hanging at his waist. The style was not to Matthew's taste, but he was ten years out of date on his knowledge of men's fashions, and had cared little even then.

Just how much have they been spending since Father died?

Although it was only a family meal, the table was laid as if for a formal dinner. Charles took the seat at the head of the table and Serena sat at the foot, leaving Matthew to face Julia across the middle. He sat back in his chair, toying with his glass while two footmen placed dishes of food along the table. It felt odd, seeing Charles in the place his father had occupied, beneath the painting of the house and grounds at Farleton hanging on the wall behind. As the current head of the family, that place should be Matthew's, but no doubt Charles had got used to sitting there in the years since their father died.

"Good journey home, brother?" Charles asked, once all the food had been served. Matthew guessed from his demeanour that his valet had not related this morning's unfortunate incident.

"As any sea voyage," Matthew replied. "Tedious, damp and uncomfortable."

"What have you been doing today, Matthew?" his stepmother asked, eyeing his attire. "I hope you found time to visit a tailor?"

"No, I went to see the solicitor about claiming the title." Best not to mention the other visits.

"That took all day?" Serena looked at his waistcoat, then peered at his short hair. "You're not looking at all the thing, Matthew. I hope you won't intrude on my guests until you have improved your appearance."

Matthew narrowed his eyes. "Are you seriously telling me what I can and cannot do in *my* house?"

She stiffened, the corners of her mouth turning down. "It is our home, Matthew. You have no right to—"

"I think that, legally, he does, Mama," said Charles. "So, brother, are you going to your new seat, then? Take a look around, and so on?"

"I suppose so—I haven't really decided yet. Perhaps I'll see how things are going on at Farleton first. It's not so far away from Birchanger, after all."

"I'm sure all will be in order," said Charles, his face emotionless. Matthew was reminded of Mayhew's expression when excusing the non-appearance of the account books. *Something to think about later.*

"We'll see, won't we? Have you been overseeing things?"

Charles waved his fork. "Oh, I leave that to the men of business— not the done thing to take too close an interest. Besides, it's your place, brother."

Matthew detected a touch of resentment in Charles' tone, faint but discernible.

"Perhaps, now you're back, you could see your way to increasing my allowance, brother?" Charles went on. "Tailors' bills get more extortionate every year, you know."

Julia sniggered. "He obviously doesn't know!" she said, glancing pointedly at Matthew's clothing with a shrewish expression remarkably similar to her mother's.

"I'll have to see how things are before I make any decisions like that," Matthew said, hoping to end the discussion. He was not about to commit himself to anything at the moment.

He addressed himself to his food, all fancy sauces with little substance, and not even hot. The richness and mingled flavours made his stomach queasy, so he settled for another glass of claret instead. The meal was over-elaborate for a small family gathering, with numerous dishes to choose from, and he noticed many returned to the kitchen untouched. The wine, though, was of excellent vintage.

"You should have given us some warning of your arrival," Serena said again.

Matthew couldn't be bothered to reply, but she didn't wait for him to speak.

"But why I should have expected any consideration when you spoiled your own father's last years by refusing to write to him, I don't know. How could you have been so unfeeling? It was bad enough you running away to the opposite side of the Earth without cutting off all contact like that!"

Matthew frowned. He had a packet of his father's letters in one of his trunks upstairs, and the contents of the letters were clearly replies to his own.

"I did—"

He stopped as Baldwin stepped into the path of a footman carrying a loaded tray. The loud crash as the crockery hit the floor drew everyone's attention.

"So sorry, ma'am. An unfortunate accident," the butler explained in a calm voice. "It will be cleared up immediately." He waved the footman away, and began to pick up pieces of broken china.

The Southams returned their attention to their dinner, except for Matthew. He regarded the butler thoughtfully; the upset had been no accident. Baldwin caught his eye and gave a small shake of his head.

Matthew took another mouthful of wine. Baldwin had deliberately interrupted Serena's diatribe about his correspondence with his father; he'd have to talk to the man after dinner to find out why.

"What happened to your arm?" Julia asked as he reached to put his glass down. His shirt cuff, too loose now, had ridden up to show the scars around his wrist. He pulled his sleeve down.

"Just a minor accident," he said.

"Oh, dear. It must have been painful." Her words were sympathetic, but her eyes held avid curiosity, not sympathy. "What happened? Was it in a battle?"

"No," he said abruptly. "Just an accident."

"You seem accident-prone, Matthew," his stepmother said. "When Gleason wrote about this barony, the firm was told you were missing." She met his gaze, one neatly drawn eyebrow raised.

"Communications can be difficult in a country as large as India," he said. The statement was accurate, even though it didn't answer her question. "I expect they just meant they hadn't heard from me for a while."

"But they can't have lost touch with a whole regiment, brother, surely?"

Matthew took a deep breath before replying. Being called 'brother' by Charles was beginning to grate on him. "I wasn't always with the rest of the regiment."

"You were at Seringapatam, though, were you not? At the siege? What was that like?"

Matthew's fist clenched beneath the table.

"Do tell, Matthew," Julia said. "We've only had the newspaper reports. It will give me something—"

"I hardly think this is a proper subject for the dinner table," Matthew said, forcing his jaw to relax enough to speak. *Or for any other time. If they knew...*

"Oh, come, Matthew, we—"

"Where's Richard at the moment?" Matthew asked, his voice over-loud and cutting across his sister's wheedling tone. Matthew's younger half-brother was in the army, so it wasn't surprising that he wasn't at home. Matthew drained his glass and signalled the footman for more wine.

"Oh, still on the continent," Charles replied, eyebrows rising slightly. "He was mixed up in that Bergen affair. Bit of a wound, I think."

"Bergen?"

"September—bit of a disaster in the Netherlands. You haven't heard?"

"It's a little difficult getting the newspapers delivered at sea," Matthew pointed out, working hard to keep his voice level. Charles' lack of interest in Richard's health suggested there was as little love lost between the brothers now as there had been before he'd left for India.

He changed the subject again. "Where do you go this evening?"

"Oh, Boodles, then perhaps some other clubs." Charles waved a hand in a languid gesture.

Matthew wondered for a moment if he was to be invited along, but then his half-sister spoke, as if the question had been addressed to her.

"The Stanhopes' ball," Julia said. "We are invited everywhere, you know."

"My dear, you must make sure you get your two dances with Lord Westham," her mother said. "There are so few entertainments this late in the year, you must make the most of them."

"A suitor?" Matthew asked, not really interested, but happy to steer the conversation away from his past.

"One of many," Julia said, with a smug air.

"Your first season is going well?"

She flushed. "This is not my first season, Matthew."

"Your second?"

She shook her head, lips pursed.

"Never mind, perhaps now you are related to a baron you may have more success?" Taunting her was petty, he knew, but this wasn't the sweet ten-year-old sister he remembered leaving behind when he set off for India.

"I've had several offers," she said, an angry colour rising to her cheeks.

"You don't want to hold out for a title too long, Julia," Charles said. "You're getting to be a bit long in the tooth, you know."

"Thank you, Charles," Julia said. "That is very helpful advice. But if Father had arranged a bigger dowry I wouldn't have this problem. And if you hadn't gambled—"

"That's enough," Serena cut in.

Charles said something else, but Matthew stopped listening. He finished his claret, staring at the portrait beyond his stepmother's head. *Tailors' bills might not be the real reason Charles wants more money, then?* No doubt it was only a matter of time before Serena and Julia asked him for a bigger allowance.

When the ladies withdrew, Matthew turned down Charles' offer of port, saying he had things to see to. He headed out through the kitchen to the mews behind the house; the company of Webb and the dog was a more enticing prospect than any further contact with his family this evening.

He looked over a smart curricle, painted glossy black with its wheels picked out in red and gold. The stalls held a fine pair of matched greys and a bay gelding—Charles', he supposed; the gelding looked too big for a comfortable lady's mount.

He found Webb sitting in an empty stall on an upturned bucket, trying to comb out the dog's matted hair. Webb's clothes were liberally streaked with mud, and a large wet patch on the floor suggested that the mutt hadn't taken kindly to being bathed. Matthew suppressed a grin.

"Going well, Sergeant?"

Webb muttered something foul in reply, flinging the comb down. As Matthew held out a portion of a sausage, the dog jumped out of Webb's hold and came to sit at his feet, tail thumping on the floor.

"I've fed 'er as much as you," Webb grumbled. "She ain't so pleased to see me!" He picked up the comb and handed it to Matthew. "Mebbe you can comb 'er?"

Matthew ran his fingers over the dog's body gently, feeling her wince as he touched what must be some tender spots. "Better just to cut most of it off, eh?" he suggested, running his hand reflectively over his own head.

"Likely you're right," Webb said. "It's time for servants' dinner now. I'll find some scissors after."

Matthew waved him away. "Go to dinner, I'll sort her out."

It took some time, and involved much wriggling on the part of the dog, but in the end Matthew managed to clip away most of the matted hair, revealing a black and tan spaniel. A very odd-looking spaniel after his amateur barbering, but the short hair also allowed him to inspect her for wounds. There were a few cuts and sores. He washed these carefully then settled her on a bed of fresh straw in the back of the stall. He considered tying her up, but thought she wouldn't desert a source of food. If she did, well, there would be one less responsibility.

Matthew was contemplating the state of his breeches and coat, now covered in dog hair, when he heard someone approaching.

"My lord?"

"Baldwin?"

"Webb said you were out here, my lord." Baldwin hesitated.

Matthew peered at him in the dim light. Now he was here, the man seemed uncertain what to say next, his gaze sliding from Matthew's face to a point somewhere above his head.

"Letters?" Matthew prompted. "The letters that never were?"

"Er, yes, my lord."

"Please stick to 'sir', Baldwin. Why does Mrs Southam think I stopped writing?"

"I... er..." Baldwin ran a finger inside his neckcloth.

"Baldwin," Matthew said patiently, "anyone who helped to ensure that my father continued to receive my letters is to be praised, not censured."

"I... yes, sir." Baldwin took a deep breath. "Your father became ill a couple of years after you left, sir, as you know." Matthew nodded encouragingly, and Baldwin continued with a rush. "Mrs Southam took charge of correspondence while he was ill. I was butler at Farleton by then, and Mr Southam used to talk to me sometimes. He said he hadn't had a letter from you for some time, and wondered if there was a problem with the post. I think he meant between England and India, sir, or perhaps within India. I set a couple of the staff to watching, and Mrs Southam was taking your letters before he got them."

Matthew frowned, running one hand through his hair. His step-mother had never liked him, always favouring her own children. Stealing his letters to spite *him* wasn't surprising, but it was sad to realise that she'd had no compunction in hurting his father as well.

"She was trying to turn him against you, sir. Wanted him to leave everything he could to her children." The butler allowed himself a small smile. "I have to say the old staff, the ones who knew you, were pleased when they found out he had done no such thing!" He cleared his throat.

"But the letters I received from him were replies to mine," Matthew said, puzzled. "He commented on things I'd said..."

"Yes, indeed, sir. I ensured one of the footmen took his letters directly to the post after that, so she never knew he was writing to you. And arranged for anything from India to be given to us and not delivered with the normal post."

"So, she truly believes I'd stopped writing to him, and he to me?"

"Yes, sir. And she made a great fuss about you not coming back when he was dying, and missing the funeral."

"Good God—he'd been in the ground for months before the letter telling me he was ill even arrived!" Matthew had obtained leave to return to England when he heard of his father's illness, even though the length of the voyage meant he almost certainly would not arrive in time. But another letter had arrived only days before his departure with news of his father's death. There hadn't seemed much point in going back then; he would have arrived months after the funeral. And he'd had things to do in India.

"Yes, sir."

"Never let facts get in the way of a complaint, eh? In that case, I owe you thanks for managing this business, Baldwin. Is there anything I can do?" He suspected an offer of money would not go down well.

"Perhaps a more congenial post when you have settled somewhere, sir?" Baldwin suggested.

Matthew laughed, and clapped him on the shoulder. "Done! Now, perhaps you can get a few bottles of my brother's finest sent up to my room?"

"Certainly, sir." Baldwin bowed and glanced uncertainly at the dog. "Er, the rest of the family have left the house for the evening, sir, should you wish to use the parlour."

An hour later Matthew was soaking in a hot tub with a large glass of rather good port, the rest of the bottle standing within reach. He fancied a cigar, but decided it wasn't fair on Webb's lungs to fill the air with smoke. Webb, looking much put-upon, had taken Matthew's coat and breeches away to try to remove the dog hairs, and he could hear him stamping back up the servants' stairs. But he was not alone.

"I left her in the stables," Matthew said, as the dog followed Webb into the room.

"Whinin' again, sir."

"Well, we wouldn't hear her from here!"

"Stable lad could, sir. Was threatenin' to kick 'er when I went to take a look. Gerroff!" The last was addressed to the dog, who was taking too great an interest in the newly brushed clothing over Webb's arm.

Matthew sighed, then snapped his fingers. "Here, girl. Sit!" The dog came and sat beside the tub. Webb grunted and put the clothing away.

"Want anythin' else, sir?"

"Hand me that towel, would you?" He stood and towelled himself off. It wasn't late, but he decided to stay and read in the room rather than venture downstairs. He really didn't feel like facing his relatives when they returned. "I won't need you again."

"Thought I might try the nearest ale-houses, sir."

Matthew nodded. "Enjoy yourself, Sergeant. But don't get too foxed, we've a busy day tomorrow." He carefully ignored Webb's mutter about one of them needing to be relatively sober in the morning.

Putting on his nightshirt and a robe, he drew a chair nearer to the fire. He had a book, but couldn't concentrate. He finished the port instead, staring into the flames.

Private Benson came to him that night, for the first time in weeks. Sometimes he cursed Matthew for leaving him, and the army for taking him to India, but tonight he sobbed and whimpered. He apologised to Matthew, tearfully, over and over, then cried for his mother. He begged for water, but Matthew hadn't any to give him. He'd breathed it all himself. Matthew shouted his own anger to the walls, then there came a banging on the door and the clank of a bucket being put down. He could reach the water, but he couldn't reach to give some to Benson. He swore again, loudly, then someone slapped his face. Had they come to take him away again? He lashed out with one hand, but it wouldn't move. Rage was better than cringing in fear, so he tried again—

"Wake up, sir!"

This time someone was shaking his shoulder. He became aware that it was Webb, not Benson, but he could still hear banging. He sat up abruptly.

"Hellfire!"

"Yessir. You properly awake now, sir?"

Matthew swore again, and swallowed bile, determined not to be sick in the bed.

"'Ere, 'ave a swig o' this." Webb handed him his new flask. It still had the morning's foul-tasting drink in it, but at the moment he didn't care. He gulped down a large mouthful, coughed as the spirit burned his throat, then sat with his knees drawn up and his head in his hands, concentrating on breathing steadily until his heart-rate returned to something like normal and his hands almost stopped shaking. The banging came again, then a voice through the door.

"I say, are you all right, brother?"

"Want me to get rid of 'im, sir?"

Matthew nodded.

Webb went over to the door. "Nothin' wrong, sir," he said to Charles as he opened the door. "Bit of a nightmare, that's all."

"Nightmare? Sounded like someone being murdered. I'll just see—"

"No sir," Webb said firmly, unmoving as Charles took a step forwards.

"Stand aside, man!" Charles said, trying to peer around him.

"I'm quite all right, thank you, Charles," Matthew called from the bed.

"You didn't sound well, Matthew. Let me make sure." He tried to move forwards again as he spoke, but Webb blocked the doorway.

"Excuse me, sir," Webb said firmly, placing a hand against Charles' chest and pushing until he could close the door in his face. He turned the key in the lock. "Nosey bugger," he muttered.

"Thank you, Webb."

"No trouble, sir." He yawned widely.

"Go back to bed, Webb. I'll be all right now."

And he would be, as long as he didn't fall asleep again. And as long as the walls didn't start to close in.

Webb muttered and went back into the dressing room, shutting the door behind him. Matthew got up to open the window, then dragged the chair over to it. He reached for his robe, but the night air was too chilly for that, so he got into his clothes and tucked the robe over his lap.

A soft whimpering in the room reminded him of the dog, and he snapped his fingers. She slunk out from her hiding place under the bed and came to sit at his feet. He scratched the back of her head, and she soon settled down and went to sleep.

Matthew's watch said it was the early hours of the morning—it was going to be a very long time until daybreak. He looked with envy at the sleeping dog, then tried to think through tomorrow's plan. He was too fuzzy-headed to decide on anything more than sending Webb to buy tickets for the mail coach. The pair of them could leave for Birchanger the following afternoon.

CHAPTER 7

*C*harlotte arrived in Edgecombe a little after midday. She had planned to take the stage, which was slower but much cheaper than the mail. But her aunt had already bought a ticket on the mail coach for her, and insisted on buying her some books as a gift. One of the books she wanted wasn't in stock, so the bookseller agreed to send them on when they were all available. Charlotte bought a present for Davie, too, settling on a magnifying glass. She wasn't going to rely on money from the sale of the tiara or her mother's trust fund until it was actually in her bank account.

Once in Bath, she had been lucky to find the local carrier nearly ready to depart. The thought that she was nearly home helped her endure the jolting ride through the small towns and villages between Bath and Edgecombe. She left her small bandbox at the inn, too tired to carry it the extra mile up the narrow lane to her house in Upper Edgecombe.

She paused as the cottage came into sight, the recent confrontation with her father making her thankful for the independent life she had achieved here. The cottage stood at the end of a row of similar houses, the warm creamy colour of the stone walls and mullions welcoming in the pale sunshine. The roses trained around the front door—Mary's doing—still had a few late blooms showing red. She averted her eyes from the slipping stone slates on the roof; they were a problem for another day.

Sally was alone in the kitchen, busy ironing some of Davie's shirts, and eagerly stopped work to put the kettle on the range for tea. She must have sensed that Charlotte was tired, as she refrained from her usual chatter, simply stating that Davie was playing in the garden and Mrs Sergeant was sitting in her room. She placed the pot on the scarred wooden table when it was ready, and set out a plate with bread, ham, and some small cakes. Charlotte decided to let Davie continue to play for a while, so she hung up her pelisse and bonnet in the scullery and changed her muddy shoes for indoor ones. She sat close to the range, leaning back in her chair and enjoying the warmth coming from the range while she ate and drank.

Finally she began to feel a bit more relaxed, the anxieties and grief of the last few days fading now she was back in familiar surroundings. It occurred to her that it was a little odd for Mary to be sitting alone in her room.

"Is Mrs Sergeant unwell?" she asked, concerned.

"Don't think so, ma'am. Reckon she's watching them sailors."

"Sailors?"

Sally continued with her ironing as if her cryptic comment were self-explanatory. Charlotte topped up the teapot and set it on a tray with milk and two cups. Time to find out how things had gone in her absence.

As Sally had said, Mary was tackling a pile of mending while watching two men working in the garden. She looked round, smiling when she saw Charlotte.

"I didn't hear you come in!" She tied off the thread and put all the mending back into the basket on the floor near her chair, clearing the small table for the tray. Charlotte fetched another chair from her own room.

"Are you all right, my dear?" Mary asked.

"I will be. I'm mostly tired." She looked out of the window, rubbing her forehead. "Digging out a new vegetable plot?"

"Yes. I've a mind to grow a bit more next year, and that grassy bit was only growing weeds."

Charlotte nodded. Mary ran the house with practical economy, and took most of the domestic decisions. After their first year, when they had shared the household work between them, it had become clear that things would run more efficiently if Charlotte concentrated on earning money with her writing, and assisting some of the local tradesmen with their book-keeping. Mary had happily settled into the role of housekeeper cum gardener, although Charlotte and Davie did help with digging and harvesting now and then.

"Who are they?" Charlotte asked.

"Discharged sailors, they said. Looking for work—well, mebbe looking for free handouts, one of 'em, but I reckoned they could work for their supper and some coin."

Charlotte poured the tea. The two men were digging up the grass, working from opposite sides of the patch. She couldn't make out much detail through the window, but the man on the left seemed to be moving awkwardly, thrusting the spade in but then bending much lower than the other to lift the soil. He'd only dug over half the area the other man had.

"Why are you watching them? Are they so untrustworthy they cannot be left in the garden?"

"I was wondering..." Mary paused.

"Go on."

"While you was away... Emma Wilton..." Mary took a deep breath then started again. "Emma, she's got no idea about business at all. Billy must have done everything but the mixing and baking."

Charlotte nodded, trusting that this explanation would eventually involve the two men in the garden.

"I reckon Emma needs a partner with a bit of sense. It were a right good business before Billy died, and it ain't gone so far downhill that it couldn't be sorted out again. I thought if we had some help here, maybe I could..." Mary paused yet again.

"There's no reason you can't spend time there," Charlotte said, wondering what was making her friend hesitate. "You know you don't have to ask me."

"Nearly all my time, I'm meaning," Mary said. "I've still got a little bit saved, so I could put that into the bakery, all legal, like. But you'd need someone here to do for you. Sally's fine for indoors, though maybe it's time she were moving on. But she don't have time for growing the fruit and veg. I were thinking where to get some help, when these two turned up."

Charlotte sipped her tea while she worked through the implications. She could help with the housework, and perhaps it was time Davie learned to peel potatoes. She smiled to herself as she imagined his likely protest.

A man to work the garden would need to be paid—but if Mary would be earning money in the bakery perhaps they could manage to pay his wages between them. With her mother's death, the occasional gifts of money she used to receive would stop, although she had gained the tiara and possibly more. She would have a little less than she was expecting to invest for Davie's schooling, but she'd manage that somehow.

She looked up to see Mary frowning slightly. "Sorry, Mary, I was just thinking things through. It sounds an excellent opportunity for you." She smiled, raising an eyebrow. "Tell me, what time does Emma get up to put the day's bread on?"

Mary grimaced. "Aye, that's the down side to it. But it's a good challenge."

Charlotte looked more closely at the men in the garden. "The slower one—he's lost a hand? Shame for him, but he'll have a smart ticket from the navy." That would allow him to claim an annual pension from the Chatham Chest.

"Didn't say—but I reckon he'll need to get home first," Mary said.

"I thought the navy gave them the stage fare home?"

"I reckon they drank it."

"And you want to employ one of them?" Charlotte tried not to sound too incredulous, but Mary just nodded.

"I've been watching. He'd likely make a good worker—and there'll not be much lost if it don't turn out right. Once the bakery's running proper it'd bring in enough to pay his wage and make up for me not being here. Can I take him on, then?"

"You know you don't need my permission to do things."

"Thank you." Mary smiled and they finished their tea, then Mary opened the window, calling to the men to finish up and come in for their pay.

Charlotte decided that Mary could manage perfectly well on her own, so she went to change her dress and have a wash. She descended the stairs as the two men came in through the scullery door. Davie followed behind. Spotting her, he gave a brilliant smile but did not come to greet her; instead he remained lurking just inside the door.

Her curiosity aroused by her son's behaviour, Charlotte stayed in the kitchen doorway, watching. The man who'd lost a hand was brown of hair and beard, with an odd, baggy look as if he'd lost weight and wasn't quite filling his skin. Filled out, he would be burly. His face was damp, as was the hair around it; he must have had a quick wash in the scullery before coming into the kitchen.

The other man was slimmer; blond, with blue eyes. He looked around as Charlotte appeared in the doorway, his eyes running down her body then back up to her face. He turned his attention back to Mary, but not before Charlotte saw a quirk of his lips that looked more like a leer than a smile.

"Supper'll be ready in a couple of minutes," Mary said, pointing at two places set on the kitchen table.

"I thought you was payin' us in coin!" the blond one protested.

"Very well, Mr... Mr Smith," Mary said. She handed over some money.

Smith looked at it, then back at her, his brows drawing together in anger. "This ain't what you said!"

Charlotte wondered for a moment if Mary's judgement was not as good as she had thought, but put the doubt from her mind. She'd never met anyone as sensible as Mary.

"That's exactly what I said," Mary stated calmly. "That's your pay."

"But I look after both of us."

"Well then, Mr…" She hesitated, looking at the other man.

"Deacon, ma'am," the other man said quietly.

"Mr Deacon can give you his pay later, if that's the way he wants it." She cleared one plate, knife and fork away. "Now, I might need someone to work for a few days—"

"I'm sorry to have complained, mum," Smith said. His tone was conciliatory, but his chin still thrust forward aggressively.

"No matter. It don't seem fair to just take on one of you, but I can't afford two men permanent-like."

"Oh, Johnny won't stand in my way, will you Johnny?"

John Deacon just shook his head. Mary looked pleased, as if her plan, whatever it might be, was working. Charlotte looked more closely at Deacon; he looked… defeated?

"Very well. I'll think on it. Come back in the morning. You can both have a bit more work, and I'll decide then. Mr Deacon, do you want your supper?" Deacon looked up, but before he could speak Smith interrupted.

"Come on, Johnny, you need the coin to get home, remember?"

"Thank you for the offer, ma'am," Deacon said as he stood up. Mary handed him his own pay and escorted them out of the back of the house, where they picked up a small bag each. She stood watching them until they had set off down the hill towards Edgecombe.

"Do you want your supper now, Mrs MacKinnon?" Sally asked. Charlotte looked at Mary.

"Not yet, thank you, Sally," Mary said. "If you've left it ready you can be off home now." Sally washed a couple of dishes in the scullery and set them to dry, then collected her cloak and said her goodnights.

"Now then, Davie," Mary said, beckoning him further into the kitchen. He came over, giving Charlotte a quick hug before sitting down at the table and looking hopefully at the tin where the biscuits were kept.

"Report first," Mary said.

"The one-handed one—"

"Deacon."

"Yes. Deacon—he only dug about half the amount the other one did."

"Spying, Davie?" Charlotte asked.

"Not exactly, Mama, Mary asked me to keep an eye on them."

"A good way of telling who was worth employing," Mary said. "If either of them are! So, Davie, which of them should we be having here to work?"

Charlotte had initially assumed Mary was thinking of taking on Smith, the able-bodied man, but now she was beginning to think the opposite. She made more tea while Mary and Davie talked.

"How *well* did they do the digging? Did you see?"

"The one... Deacon—he was digging deeper, and there weren't as much—"

"Wasn't," Charlotte corrected automatically as she spooned tea into the pot.

"—wasn't as much grass left in the part he was working on when he'd done it."

Mary nodded. "Anything else?"

"Deacon wiped off his spade before he put it away, the other one didn't."

"Anything else?" Mary prompted again. "Did they go into the house at all while they were supposed to be working?"

"Well, they used the outhouse, and I wasn't watching them all of the time." Davie frowned, trying to remember something. "The other one, he spent longer in the outhouse each time, and once he went round to where they left their bags."

Mary went over to the larder and peered through the door.

"Ham missing," she said succinctly when she came back. She took her cloak and bonnet from the hook behind the scullery door and put them on. Charlotte suppressed a grin—crossing Mary wasn't a wise move.

"You have your supper," Mary said. "I'll be havin' mine when I get back." The door clicked closed behind her.

"What happened in London, Mama?" Davie asked, reaching for a biscuit.

Charlotte moved the tin out of his reach. "No, it's time for supper," she said. "Then you can see what I've brought you from London." That cheered him up, and he helped her to set out the meal.

It was not late, but dusk came early in December, making it difficult to see the muddy track down to Edgecombe. Although Mary had set off behind the two men, she was familiar with the way and walked quickly. She hadn't quite caught up with them by the time she reached the village, but she suspected that Smith would be heading for the Hare and Hounds.

She pushed open the door to the taproom quietly and peered in, breathing in the scents of ale and Mrs Minching's stew. Smith was sitting at a table with a pint of ale and leering at Toby Minching's serving girl, his blond hair showing up in the dim light. Deacon sat next to him with a smaller mug, looking longingly at one of the other customers eating a plate of food.

"Can I help you, Mrs MacKinnon?" It was Toby himself, waiting behind her to enter the taproom, plates of food in his hands.

"Sorry, Toby," Mary said, stepping out of the way. "I need to speak to those two," she pointed. "One of them stole a ham."

"I'll sort them out for you as soon as—"

"No, no, that's all right," she said, putting a hand on his arm. "I don't want a fuss, but if you could just back me up?"

"Right you are, missus," Toby said. Mary walked over to stand in front of Smith, arms crossed, as Toby put the plates of food in front of two customers at the far side of the room.

Smith looked up in surprise, then noticed her stern expression. Mary's suspicions were confirmed when he looked pleased rather than puzzled or apprehensive.

"What can I do for you, ma'am?" he asked, giving a reasonably good impression of being respectful.

"I'll have the ham back that one of you took," she said. Smith almost suppressed a smirk, then assumed an expression of bland innocence. Very like one of Davie's expressions, Mary thought, when he was trying to pretend his latest mischief was nothing to do with him.

"Ham, missus? I don't know nothing about a ham." He nudged Deacon, who seemed to have been in a world of his own. "Johnny boy, you didn't steal a ham from those nice ladies, did you?"

"No, ma'am," Deacon said, looking at Smith with a worried frown.

"Our bags is there, ma'am," said Smith, indicating the two bags beneath the table. He pulled one out. "This one's mine," he said, standing up and emptying it in front of her. There were only a couple of dirty-looking shirts and a coat.

"Is that bag yours?" Mary asked Deacon, pointing at the other one. By now there was a small audience watching closely.

"Yes, ma'am," he said. He looked at Smith, then at Mary, then down at the bag again. Moving slowly, he took a shirt out, followed by the missing ham.

"Johnny, how could you?" Smith said, sounding horrified. "After the nice lady gave us work as well!"

"I didn't take it, ma'am," Deacon said, glancing sideways at Smith. The slump of his shoulders indicated he didn't think he would be believed.

"I'll send for the constable, shall I?" Toby asked.

"Yes, please do," Mary said. "But I ain't got the time to hang around here all evening waiting for him. Send him on up to the cottage, will you?" She turned and looked down at Deacon. "I've got Mrs Captain's box to fetch as well. He may as well be of some use. He can carry it up, and Mrs Captain can talk to the constable about what's to be done."

Toby opened his mouth to protest against this plan, then caught Mary's eye. "I'll get the bandbox," he said, leaving the room.

"You can't be trusting him, ma'am, after he stole from you!" Smith protested.

"Well if I come to any harm he can be arrested for assaulting me as well as for theft," Mary pointed out. "It's not like no-one knows who walked up the hill with me!" She held his eyes until he looked away, then picked up Deacon's bag with the ham in it.

"Come along," she said. Deacon stood up and followed without a word. Toby was waiting in the door with the bandbox. Deacon didn't seem to know how to manage with one hand, so Toby helped him to hoist the bandbox onto his shoulder. Once it was up he steadied it easily enough and followed Mary along the lane in silence. She didn't say anything until he had followed her through the gate of the cottage.

"You didn't notice the weight of the ham in your bag?" she asked.

He gaped at her, taken aback.

"Well?" she said impatiently. "I didn't think it was you what took it. Am I wrong?"

"No, ma'am," he said, his gaze dropping. "It wasn't me. I wouldn't—"

"But you didn't notice?"

"I don't always notice things, these days," he admitted, with a grimace.

"You can put the box down," Mary said. She helped him to steady it as he lowered it to the floor just inside the front door. "Did you have something heavy in your bag he could have taken out?"

"Books," he muttered. Mary heard the regret in his voice.

"Well, at least it's not raining. We can bring a lantern out later and have a look for them. Come on in now."

There was no-one in the kitchen, but there was still plenty of stew left and a large potato in its jacket keeping warm next to the range.

"I'm back!" Mary called. An answering murmur came from the front parlour. Mary turned up the lamp and put the kettle on to boil. She laid two places at the table, then dished out the stew, cut the potato in half and brought out some bread.

"Sit and eat," she said, and Deacon did so. He struggled a bit with the potato, until Mary leaned over to cut it into smaller pieces for him. He muttered his thanks, flushing slightly, and seemed embarrassed at needing such basic help. He ate quickly and without speaking, managing not to shovel his food in too fast. Mary poured two mugs of tea and put one in front of him.

"Sugar?" she asked.

"No, thank you ma'am."

"You said you were in the navy," she said.

Deacon sat up straighter. "Yes, ma'am. Carpenter on the *Wessex*."

"An important position, then!" Mary was surprised. "What happened to you?"

"Splinter when a ball came through the side of the ship. Didn't make a big wound, but it got infected."

"Where are you headed?"

Deacon shrugged. "Home, I suppose. Lancashire." He didn't seem particularly enthusiastic at the prospect, so Mary didn't try to get more out of him at the moment.

"Smart ticket?"

"Purser bought it off me."

"Did you get money for the stage fare home?"

"Yes." He stopped and rubbed his face, while Mary waited for some explanation.

"My hand hurts," he said, looking at Mary warily. "The one I haven't got."

"I've heard of that," she said with a brisk nod. "Go on."

"The surgeon said he could give me some poppy syrup for it, but that it wasn't a good idea in the long run. But having a drink helps."

"You drank your fare?"

"And the money the purser gave me. Drank more than I meant to," he admitted. "Jud Smith said he was going my way. Helped me with..." He broke off, frowning. "I don't suppose he *did* help, really."

He looked directly at Mary. She could see only self-reproach in his expression. "I've been bloody stupid, excusing my language, ma'am. But that's how I come to be needing work." He looked down at the hand that wasn't there. "I can't manage carpentering, leastways, not on a moving ship. But I'm finding ways to manage. And I'll work hard—"

They were interrupted by a knock on the door. Mary went to see who it was, and came back with Bennett, the constable, his hat in one hand. Charlotte came out of the parlour and followed him into the kitchen. Bennett eyed Deacon suspiciously, until Mary explained what had happened.

"Ah, that be the way of it. Toby Minching said as how he thought it wasn't as plain as it seems. You'll be wanting this Smith fellow arresting then?"

Mary looked at Charlotte, who gave an unladylike shrug. An arrest would mean one of them having to go to the magistrate to explain.

"No," Mary decided. "Just make sure Smith is sent on his way tomorrow."

Bennett nodded, looking pleased to avoid further trouble, and took his leave.

"Mr Deacon will be working here," Mary said to Charlotte. "I thought he could sleep in Davie's room tonight, till we sort out something better? Can Davie share with you?" Davie's room was the only one with a lock on the door. "And can I send Davie to ask Emma if she can lend some clothes?"

Charlotte, her head obviously still full of the story that had been interrupted, agreed to both requests and went back to the parlour.

Mary sent Davie on his errand. She showed Deacon the little laundry room outside, then sent him to pump water while she lit a fire under the cauldron. Deacon went back and forth to the scullery pump until the cauldron was half full. By the time he made his last trip Mary had dragged in a tin bath. She told him to fill it when the water was hot, and went back into the house, returning with a large towel, a long handled brush and a bar of soap. When Deacon had finished transferring the hot water into the bath, he touched his cap. He headed for the doorway where Mary stood, but she didn't move.

"Get in," she said, pointing at the bath. "Preferably without your boots."

He gaped. "Me, ma'am?"

"You don't think you'll be sleeping in my clean house in your state, do you?" she asked sternly. "How long since you even had a proper wash?"

He flushed.

"Never mind," she said, more gently. "Looks like you've been sleeping rough as well?"

He nodded, and bent down to untie his boots. He struggled to undo the laces with one hand, but Mary let him get on with it, hanging the towel on a hook in the wall. He took off his coat, then hesitated.

"I'll leave you to it, if you can manage," she said.

"I'll manage," he muttered.

"When you're done, leave the water in and put your clothes in. A good soak won't do them any harm, and you can rinse them out in the morning."

Twenty minutes later, wondering if he had fallen asleep in the hot water, Mary knocked on the door.

"You decent?" she called, but didn't wait for an answer. Still sitting in the tub, he hurriedly moved his hand to cover himself. But she didn't look in his direction, only hanging a set of men's clothing on the hook where the towel was.

"I've buried three husbands, Mr Deacon—I've seen it all before!" she said, but she didn't embarrass him by looking. "These are from a friend, until your own can be cleaned." Emma had been happy to lend a set of her late husband's clothes.

Deacon came into the kitchen ten minutes later, damp hair sticking in all directions. Was it her imagination, or was he standing a little straighter than before? He definitely looked more civilised. She offered him some tea then sent him to bed and locked him in.

CHAPTER 8

*M*atthew felt stiff, tired and drunk, his rear end tender from sitting on the hard seat of the wagon as Webb drove it slowly over the rutted roads.

The overnight mail had delivered them to the centre of Bath in the middle of the morning, and they bought breakfast at the coaching inn. After a night sitting beside the driver, all Matthew wanted was more brandy, so Webb had ended up eating most of Matthew's breakfast as well as his own.

They had spent several hours shopping, Matthew managing to find a simple wagon and a gelding to pull it, along with a mare for riding. Neither animal would win any prizes for looks, performance or good temper, but they would have to do for now.

While Matthew tracked down horses, Webb bought supplies. From the unpromising discussion with 'young' Mr Gleason, Matthew wasn't expecting much in the way of comfort or service at Birchanger, so Webb bought coffee, bread, cheese, ale, butter and jam, and a ham. These things would see them through until tomorrow, at least. Matthew had surveyed the purchases, then sent Webb off again for brandy and port, and some candles, just in case, and oats for the horses.

The rain had set in again as they left Bath, gradually soaking through their outer garments and running down their necks. Now, with their destination nearly in sight, they had come up behind a carrier's wagon. Much more heavily laden than their own vehicle, it was struggling on the short, steep sections of the road that swung along the sloping edge of the Cotswolds. Their single horse couldn't get up enough speed to pass, particularly with the mare fastened on behind, and Webb wasn't the best of drivers. Matthew was too tired and too cold to want to take the reins, particularly with the brandy's disorientating influence making it hard to focus.

It was the middle of the afternoon by the time they arrived in Edgecombe. The place was little more than a village, Matthew realised, looking around. The houses lining the sloping main street were built from the local limestone, topped by steep, stone-tiled roofs, and drifts of smoke from their chimneys mingled with the misty air.

The carrier pulled to a halt in front of a grocery shop, and Webb managed to squeeze their own vehicle past before a small crowd of people rushed over to collect parcels. The next building along was an inn—the sign proclaimed it the Hare and Hounds.

Matthew got down to stretch his legs, discovering too late that his legs didn't want to co-operate. He hung onto the side of the wagon for a moment before his knees gave way, sending him sprawling in the muddy street. The sudden jolt stirred his stomach, and he swallowed hard, trying to stem the rush of nausea.

There was a muted sound above him, rather like one of Serena's tuts of disapproval. He lifted his head, opening his eyes to see a muddy pair of stout boots below a muddy hem. Tilting his head back a little further, he saw more skirt, black above the mud caking its hem, with faded streaks along the gathers indicating its age. He hadn't time for more than a glance, as his stomach gave warning that it was about to embarrass him. Scrambling awkwardly to his feet, he managed to reach a couple of small bushes planted against the front wall of the inn before casting up his accounts.

The contents of his stomach expelled, he dragged out a handker-chief to wipe his face, leaning against the wall to take a few slow, deep breaths. His emptied stomach felt a little better, and the circulation was returning to his legs, so he straightened, managing to stay upright.

Webb was talking to a woman in faded black, the muddy skirt he had noticed before topped by a somewhat battered black bonnet. From here, she looked like an old witch. He rested against the inn wall for a moment, taking a very small sip from his flask to wash the acrid taste of vomit from his mouth. The woman waved a hand, pointing up the road. Giving directions?

Webb said something to her and she shook her head emphatically before stalking off up the street, her face hidden by the bonnet but her gait radiating disapproval.

"The new Lord Tillson's made a right good first impression with the locals," Webb commented as Matthew returned to the wagon and climbed up. Webb flicked the whip to get the horse moving again.

"Stow it, Webb," said Matthew, without rancour.

"Yessir. A couple of miles more, sir," he added, turning the horse off the main street, along a narrow lane heading north and gently upwards around the end of a wooded ridge. The lane hugged the edge of the woodland, which sloped steeply up to their right, then started to descend.

Webb drew the wagon to a halt as the next dip came into sight, the fields in the valley bottom surrounded by more wooded slopes.

"Problem?"

"Nossir. The woman... lady... said the turnin' was just after we could see the next valley. On the right." He flicked the reins and the wagon lurched into motion again, making Matthew grab for the rail. Webb pulled to a halt just beyond a bend in the lane, next to a couple of stone gateposts. A rusting gate hung open crookedly from one hinge. The grass and weeds growing through it indicated that no-one had touched it for a considerable time, much less attempted to close it. Beyond, a rutted track wound up through the woods.

"Promising..." Matthew muttered, taking another pull at his flask.

Although it was less than a mile up the track to the Hall, it proved slow going. A fallen tree beside the wheel ruts had been dragged clear of the road some time ago, but there were also numerous dead branches scattered across the drive. They had to keep stopping to clear them out of the way, occasionally stumbling over unseen obstacles in the gathering dusk.

When they eventually came out of the trees near the top of the hill, Birchanger Hall was visible ahead, a pale shape against darker woodland rising steeply behind it. The drizzle had resumed, making it difficult to discern any details other than the two short wings either side of the main door and the mullioned windows half-covered with ivy.

The wheels crunched across gravel as the drive took a sweeping curve through a weed-covered lawn. The turning area in front of the house was also well covered by weeds growing through the stones. Not a light could be seen through any of the windows.

Webb brought the wagon to a halt in front of the door. Matthew climbed down and tried the knocker; it was stiff, but he managed a couple of loud raps. There were no signs of life, so he banged again, then tried the door. Although the handle turned, the door would not move.

"Try round the back," he said, climbing up next to Webb. He looked up towards the windows as they rounded the building, turning between the north side of the Hall and a long wall. There were a few cracked panes; if all else failed, they could probably climb in through a window.

Luckily, it did not come to that. The gravel led around to the back of the Hall and into a yard surrounded by low stone buildings, all with the local stone-clad roofs. A pump stood in one corner, almost hidden by weeds around its base. Next to it, a wide, open entrance indicated a coach house, and Webb pulled up in front of that. A quick look inside revealed stalls, some still with straw strewn across the floor; although it gave the appearance of having been there for some time, the straw had not yet gone mouldy.

Webb set about unharnessing the wagon horse. He got the two horses settled with some measures of the oats they had brought with them and a bucket of water from the pump, while Matthew wandered around the yard. He opened various doors, finding rusty tools, a few logs in an otherwise empty store, and finally a way into the back of the house through a scullery and the kitchen. There were no shutters on these back windows, but the grime and the fading daylight made it almost impossible to see once indoors. He went back to the wagon and retrieved the packet containing the candles, but it took him a few minutes and several curses to find the tinderbox.

The kitchen appeared cavernous in the gloom, with draughts from cracked windows making the candle flames flicker and sending shadows dancing across the walls. Webb joined him, lighting his own candle and peering into cupboards and under the large central table. This was the only piece of moveable furniture left. Matthew thought it was probably only still there because it was too big to fit through the doors without dismantling.

"Nowt 'ere, sir. Looks like the place 'as been cleaned out."

Webb was correct. Dusty shelves and cupboards held a few cracked plates and cups, and some rusting pans, but not much else. Certainly not the crockery and cooking implements to be expected in a house of this size. Matthew supposed he would have to try to find out from Gleason, or Kellet, if he was supposed to have inherited the contents of the house or just this dilapidated shell. But those details could wait; it was too much for him to cope with now.

They made their way through the kitchen and along a narrow service corridor before coming out into the main part of the house through a door opening into one corner of a cavernous space, the ceiling beyond the reach of the light from the candles. Matthew worked out that they must be facing the front of the building. The wall to their right held a large fireplace, beyond which a door opened into an empty room. Ahead, the main entrance door was flanked by two large diamond-paned windows; Matthew thought they would provide a good view across the front lawn in daylight. When they had been cleaned.

Turning, he saw another fireplace opposite the first, the large entrance hall taking up what must be a third of the width of the building. A staircase faced the front door, going up a little way before branching left and right to reach the first floor. Exploration of the upper floors could wait.

Matthew crossed to the entrance door, which opened into a small vestibule. The large, oak-studded front door was bolted from the inside. The bolts were stiff with rust but he managed to pull them, opening the door to let in a welcome gust of air. Although cold and damp, it was a relief from the musty air inside the main hall.

"Reckon there's any beds, sir?"

"I doubt it, Webb, but do go and look."

Webb wheezed his way up the staircase, treading warily as various boards squeaked and groaned. Matthew crossed the hall to investigate the two doors flanking the far fireplace. One led to a library with empty bookshelves, the other to a room anonymous without its furniture. These rooms had shutters closed over the windows.

Back in the hall he inspected the fireplaces. It was impossible to tell whether they would work or if years of disuse had encouraged birds' nests in the chimneys. Perhaps that should wait for the morning. Although it was still only late afternoon, Matthew felt bone-weary and incapable of planning anything. Thank goodness they had brought some supplies with them.

"No luck?" he asked, as Webb reappeared.

Webb shrugged. "A few broken chairs, an' a bed without a mattress, but nowt else. Smells damp, an' all."

"The stables are beginning to seem attractive."

Webb just grunted at this, but the two men made their way back through the kitchen and out into the yard. The stables had offices to one side, with a loft above where the grooms and stable-hands must have slept. He didn't fancy the loft himself—too small, dark, and airless—but Webb went up to take a look. He came back down with an armful of blankets, several of which had escaped the worst depredations of moths, mice, and damp, and would do for now. The building appeared to be watertight. The offices boasted a small fireplace, a cupboard containing a single saucepan, a battered table, and a couple of chairs, one leaning drunkenly due to a broken leg. Things not worth taking.

With the efficiency of an old campaigner, Webb soon had a small fire going with a pan of water put to heat, coughing in the initial smoke. Matthew found enough dry straw to keep the chill of the stone-flagged floor off them, then both busied themselves eating and drinking the supplies they had brought with them.

Bits of ham and bread went to the dog as they ate, and were snapped up quickly. He'd have to give her a name soon.

Fed and happily tipsy, Webb brought out a small knife and passed the rest of the evening finishing off the ale and whittling bits of wood retrieved from the log store. It was quiet, with only the crackling of the fire, the sounds of Webb's knife, and some rustling noises coming from the horses shifting on their straw.

The dog sat up and looked towards the stalls with interest. Perhaps not all the rustlings were due to the animals they'd brought with them.

"Rats?" Matthew asked.

"Reckon so," Webb replied, giving the mutt a little push with his toe. "Go on, girl, get 'em!"

She looked round at him, but did not move.

"Go on," Webb said encouragingly. When the dog still did not move, he cursed and got to his feet, picking up the lantern.

"Come, then!" The dog obediently followed him over to the stalls and sat down, looking up at his face with interest, her shorn tail waving slightly. The rustling had stopped, but Webb tried a couple more times to get her to investigate what might be living in the straw.

"Useless bitch," he muttered as he finally stamped back into the office.

Matthew wasn't sure why that comment inspired him, but once he had thought of the name he couldn't resist. "I think I'll call her Serena," he said.

Webb shrugged, and then Matthew could almost see the cogs turning in his brain.

"Weren't your step-ma...?" he started, then one of his big grins spread across his face and he laughed. "Ain't that a bit unfair on the mutt, sir?" he asked eventually, wiping his eyes with a grubby handkerchief.

"Reena for short, then?" Matthew said.

Webb nodded and went back to his whittling, with only the occasional chortle showing he was still enjoying the joke.

Matthew made further inroads into the brandy, wondering whether he should retreat to London and just let Birchanger Hall carry on rotting. If he managed to drink himself to death, Charles was welcome to inherit this pile of liability.

He took another mouthful of spirit, remembering Charles' ingratiating behaviour in London, and the way he'd treated their younger brother in the years before Matthew had left for India.

It might just be worth the effort of staying alive to thwart him.

Maybe.

CHAPTER 9

*C*harlotte watched drops of rain running down the window and contemplated staying indoors—but the carrier should be bringing the books she'd ordered to the inn today. Hopefully the rain would stop at some point during the morning.

Mary must have let Deacon out of Davie's room before leaving for the bakery, as Charlotte could see him in the garden, digging up more of Mary's planned new vegetable patch. Davie had slept in her room, but she hoped Deacon was trustworthy enough not to need to be locked in again. Davie didn't seem to need enough sleep for a growing lad, and she'd got no rest from the moment he'd woken up that morning.

She sent Davie to see if Deacon had been given any breakfast. He returned dripping wet and shivering.

"He says he had some, Mama, but he looked hungry to me."

"Fetch him, then," Charlotte said. There was enough porridge for three, even with Davie's appetite. Deacon carefully wiped his boots before coming into the house, hung his damp coat behind the door, and washed in the scullery. For once, Davie went to wash his hands without having to be told.

Deacon hesitated as he entered the kitchen, looking around, and it dawned on Charlotte that he didn't know who she was. She made a gesture for him to sit at the kitchen table. He waited until she had taken her own seat.

"I'm Mrs MacKinnon," she started. Deacon shook his head, and Charlotte smiled. "Yes, we're both called MacKinnon. Mary's husband —late husband—was my husband's sergeant."

"Yes, ma'am." Deacon still looked confused.

"She and I own the house jointly," Charlotte explained. "Do eat."

He ate neatly, without bolting his food as Davie would have done if hungry. Charlotte waited until Deacon had eaten most of his porridge, then asked him how he came to be here. She realised as she did so that she must be asking the same things that Mary had asked the night before. She would compare notes with Mary later, and if he'd told them both the same thing, it would be a good sign that his story was true. Or it would show he was an accomplished liar, she acknowledged, suppressing a smile.

He didn't seem to be a particularly talkative man, but he wasn't taciturn either, answering her questions fully and politely.

Sally arrived to wash the dishes and start the cleaning, while Charlotte made sure Davie was wrapped up warmly before he set off for the squire's. Settling herself in the parlour, she managed a couple of hours with Mr Fox and had a quick bite to eat before it was time to meet the carrier. The rain had not stopped, and she sympathised with Deacon, still digging in the wet, as she donned her oldest cloak and bonnet. She found her old gardening boots and put them on. She was only going to the village, so there was no point in getting her better shoes muddy and wet.

She reached the village just as the carrier's cart approached from the opposite direction and pulled to a halt in front of the grocer's shop. A small wagon with two men on the driving seat pulled around the cart and stopped in front of the inn.

The carrier spotted her amongst the crowd of waiting people and held out her parcel. Taking it with a smile of thanks, she backed away again, finding a less crowded spot outside the inn. The rain had eased, so she risked undoing the string then taking out her spectacles so she could check that the correct titles had been sent. She peered cautiously inside the wrapping paper so the books themselves did not get wet. There was also a letter for her, but she put that in her pocket.

She was brought back to her surroundings by a scuffling noise in front of her, and looked over her spectacles as a man descended from the wagon and stood, clutching the side of it. She jumped backwards with a gasp as he suddenly sprawled onto the road in front of her.

She wondered if he was hurt or ill, but he scrambled to his feet, mud adorning his hands and knees, and much of the front of his coat. He staggered away, and she heard the sounds of retching behind her.

She shrugged and walked around the wagon to regain the road.

"Excuse me, ma'am?" The voice came from the wagon, and she looked up. The man holding the reins wore a faded soldier's uniform. He was thin, with sandy hair and a scar around one eye. A dog curled up at his feet, its fur ragged but clean.

"Yes?"

"Is this Edgecombe, ma'am?"

Charlotte nodded.

"Can you tell me the way to Birchanger 'All?"

Charlotte looked at him with more interest. "It's empty—there's no-one there."

"Yes, ma'am. We expected that. Lord Tillson—the new Lord Tillson—'as come to see about it."

Charlotte looked from him to the inn, where the stranger had been sick. He was standing again now and she could see him properly. His clothing did seem to be good quality, but it was ill-fitting and now plastered in mud. He had very short, brown hair, and his skin had an odd appearance, as if he were pale beneath skin that was normally tanned. A large bruise marred one side of a thin, almost gaunt, face. As she watched, he took a flask from his pocket and put it to his mouth.

Charlotte sighed, turning away. Birchanger Hall had been empty so long, people in the village had almost given up hope that someone would come and spend money in the local shops. But now someone *had* finally come, he appeared to be the kind of drunkard that was castaway even in the middle of the day.

"Drunk as a lord, indeed!" Charlotte muttered under her breath, then realised that the man on the wagon was waiting for an answer.

"I'm sorry?" she said.

"Do I carry on up this road, ma'am?" the driver said patiently.

"No." She turned and pointed. "Go as far as that house with the red door and turn up the lane just beyond it." She gave him further directions that he listened to carefully.

"Thank you, ma'am," he said when she had finished. "Can we take you up? It's nasty weather to be out."

"Thank you, no." Charlotte said, glancing back at the new Lord Tillson, still standing by the inn wall. She set off up the lane, passing the turning before the wagon caught up with her. The rain returned, and she made sure her parcel was safely tucked under her coat.

She arrived back at the cottage tired, hungry, and thirsty. Sally was busy chopping potatoes, so Charlotte put the kettle on to boil. Looking out of the back window, she couldn't see Deacon anywhere. Sally said she hadn't seen him for a while. The patch of grass he'd been digging over wasn't finished.

Men! Charlotte supposed she should check on him before she took off her outdoor clothes, so she let herself out of the scullery door. She looked into the laundry room on her way past. A set of wet clothing hung above the empty bath. They wouldn't dry out here, and she made a mental note to bring them into the kitchen on her way back. The outhouse was empty too. Beyond that was the small wooden shed where Mary kept the garden tools. The door to this stood open.

Mary kept a clean and tidy house, but for some reason this did not extend to her gardening tools. A small pile of tools outside the door was getting wet in the rain, and a scraping sound came from inside. She stepped forward.

The scraping sound stopped. Charlotte realised she must be

blocking whatever light the grey sky provided. Deacon sat on an upturned bucket, a pair of shears awkwardly clamped between his knees and a sharpening stone in his hand. A spade and hoe leaned on the wall beside him, both of them clean, shiny, and showing the marks from sharpening. Beside the bucket, a small pile of other tools waited to be cleaned. He was out of the rain, but the air felt raw and damp—it could not be pleasant sitting there without exercise to warm him, especially as the coat he was wearing looked threadbare and worn.

"'Afternoon, ma'am," he said, touching a finger to his forehead. "Mrs MacKinnon set me to digging, but the soil's really too wet—standing on it will compress the lumps and make it harder for the frost to break them up later."

That sounded like sensible reasoning to Charlotte. "You know about growing?"

"Used to help in our garden, ma'am, before I went to sea."

"Well, it looks as if you've found yourself something useful to do," she said. "Have you had anything to eat?"

He looked up. "No, ma'am, not since porridge this morning."

"Come on in, then."

He seemed much more alert than he had that morning, looking about the kitchen with interest while he ate a simple meal of cold pie and bread. She tried to look at the place as a stranger might, noticing the wobbly leg on one of the chairs, the loose shelf in the pantry and the squeak every time the scullery door was opened. Not to mention grubby whitewash on the walls. She'd had the place painted when she and Mary had bought it nine years ago, but had done little since. All little things that were annoying, but not quite annoying enough to do anything about.

"You were a carpenter, Deacon?"

"Yes, ma'am."

"So you can fix squeaky doors and stuck drawers?"

He nodded.

Charlotte smiled. "Perhaps not quite so much of a challenge as fixing ships? You can write?" she asked.

"Yes ma'am. Those are my books," he pointed to a pile of three small books next to a stack of plates on a shelf. "Smith took them out of my bag when he put the ham in, and hid them outside. Your lad found them last night."

"Very well. I'll get you some paper and a pencil. Come around the house with me and make a list of repairs, then you can let me know if you need any materials or tools. It might depend on how much it will cost, but you can at least get some of the things fixed. You can ask Sally if she knows of anything else that needs fixing, as well."

She recalled Davie's early morning exuberance, and considered for a moment. Deacon had shown no sign of being anything other than respectful and polite. "There is a small room next to Davie's room," she said, making up her mind. "We use it to store trunks and so on. If you can move enough things out of the way, you can sleep in there."

He smiled—a real smile that reached his eyes. "Thank you, ma'am."

"You haven't seen how small it is yet," Charlotte said, surprised at the effect her offer had on him.

After a quick tour of the house, she left him to his lists and retired to her parlour. She still had her letter to read.

It was good news and bad news. The letter was from her publisher. Mr Berry wanted more of the *Woodland Tales* she wrote under the name Cicely Hawkesbury. He was thinking of publishing a collection of them as an illustrated book, instead of as magazine articles. The *Cotswold Diary* articles she wrote about country life were still popular with the readers, so he wanted her to continue writing one of those each month, and he was interested in the other ideas for articles she'd sent him.

All that was good, although she would have to work hard to get so much writing done. It was the reference to illustrations that dismayed her. Mr Berry wanted to know if she could provide the drawings or if he should commission an artist, with payment to be taken from her earnings.

Damn. The enquiry about the drawings was a sensible one. Like all young ladies of her class, she'd had lessons in drawing and watercolours, although why this was thought to make them more marriage-able Charlotte had never worked out. The only problem was that Charlotte was not very good at drawing.

She sighed. She would have to try. But first she would try to finish the next Mr Fox story.

CHAPTER 10

*M*atthew woke the next morning to the smell of coffee brewing. He'd fallen asleep readily enough, his bed in the straw more comfortable than many places he'd slept on campaign. However, the rustling of the straw as he turned over in his sleep had somehow turned into the noise of rats in his cell, the unseen walls around him starting to press in on him, trapping him…

Untangling himself from the blankets, he had shifted a pile of straw into one of the stalls, hoping that the cold air coming in would make the place seem less closed-in. He lay there for some time, hearing the soft breathing of the sleeping horses and making out the dim shape of the entrance arch against thin clouds lit from above by the moon. He'd put the list of problems out of his mind, and had tried to think of this place as his new home, with no memories of Serena or Charles, no failures…

Eventually he'd fallen asleep again.

"Coffee, sir," Webb said, handing him a steaming mug. "Thought I'd take the mare, sir, and go an' get summat for breakfast in Edgecombe."

"There's nothing left?" Matthew rubbed sticky eyes.

"Nossir. There was some ham left, but the dog…"

Oh, well. He could hardly blame the mutt. Matthew dragged himself up and over to his coat. His purse felt remarkably light. They must have spent more than he'd thought yesterday—but then when he'd got the money out of Mayhew, he hadn't been thinking that he would be buying a wagon and horses. He hadn't really been thinking much at all.

He handed a few coins to Webb. "You'll have to ask for credit for a few days. Shouldn't be a problem—most tradesmen just submit monthly accounts."

Webb looked doubtfully at the coins in his hand. "If you say so, sir."

Matthew had a quick wash in the icy water from the pump, then made sure the horse had enough to eat and drink. He brewed more coffee, added a good dash of brandy, and took the cup out to the front of the house with the dog sniffing around at his heels.

The weather was still gloomy, sucking the colour from the grass and trees around him. At least the rain had stopped; the air beneath the layer of cloud was clear. There wasn't enough sun to judge directions, but his pocket compass told him that the front of the house faced south-west. Beyond the overgrown lawns the land sloped downwards, covered in woodland. A few gaps in the trees allowed more distant views; a river that must be the Severn, and the rising, tree-covered ground of the Forest of Dean beyond.

He turned to survey the house, limiting himself to walking around the outside for now. The diamond-leaded windows had a few broken panes; not many, considering the place seemed to have been abandoned for some time. Most of the windows he could see appeared to have closed shutters behind them; he was hopeful not too much rain would have got in. Beneath the ivy, the walls were built from the local pale limestone. The building was laid out in a shallow E-shape common for houses from Elizabeth's time, with another floor above the one Webb had explored in search of beds.

To the east, the woods rose behind the house—perhaps the birches that gave the place its name? The wall they had driven past on their way to the stables last night was around twelve feet high, with the side facing the Hall covered in ivy, and brambles and nettles pushing up through the gravel at its base. The wall turned a corner, then another some distance away where the gardens gave way to fields. A walled garden? Perhaps a kitchen garden, Matthew thought. An overgrown path led to an arched doorway. Matthew tried the handle; it turned, and the door moved a little when he pushed it with his shoulder, but then it jammed on something. He set his cup down and put all his effort into pushing the door, but he only achieved a few inches of movement. His feet slipped on the wet leaves on the path; putting out a hand to stop himself falling, he earned himself a long, jagged line of blood across his hand from the brambles beside the path.

Swearing at length, he kicked at the door, gaining nothing more than a bruised foot. He took a deep breath, then another, leaning with one hand on the wall and attempting to control his frustration.

It's a stuck door, an inanimate object. It's not deliberately thwarting you, it's just stuck!

He picked up the cup, resisting the urge to throw it at something. Perhaps more drink would help? Before he headed back to the stables, he tried to peer through the small gap between the door and the wall. All he saw for his trouble was a tangle of vegetation.

Back in the stables he was tempted by the brandy bottle, but the memory of sprawling in the mud the day before stayed his hand. Instead he made fresh coffee, using up the last of the supply.

He took advantage of the daylight to have another look around the stables and offices, but found nothing else of use. Making better use of his time until Webb returned, he drafted a letter to Kellet, describing the state of the house. Kellet might need to consult Gleason about the reasons for the lack of contents, but Matthew suspected that he was more likely to get an answer via Kellet than by writing to Gleason directly. He had almost completed a neat copy when he heard the crunching of wheels on gravel.

He went outside to see Webb sitting next to the driver on a wagon loaded with the trunks he had left in London to be sent on, their riding horse tied behind. The carrier helped to stack the trunks in the stable and Matthew gave him one of his few remaining coins as a tip. Webb chatted to the carrier in a friendly fashion, but he grimaced once the man was heading back down the drive.

"Problem?"

"You could say that, sir," Webb muttered, dumping a loaf of bread, a lump of cheese and a couple of bottles of ale on the table. "No bugger'd give me any credit. Said you already owed them money."

"*I* owe them money?"

"They said Lord Tillson, sir. I tried to explain, but they said they couldn't afford to give any more credit till summat 'ad been paid. All of 'em."

Matthew swore, and emptied his pockets onto the table. They had enough for another day's worth of food, but not for more brandy. Kellet should be making arrangements for banking in Bath, but he was unlikely to have done it yet.

"Any idea how to catch rabbits, Webb? It will be a few days before I can draw money in Bath."

"Nossir. City boy, sir." Webb felt around in his own pockets and dropped a few more coins on the table. "Reckon we can last another day or two?"

"We'll take a look in the trunks. Must be something I can pawn to tide us over." Matthew unfastened the strap on one of the large trunks and opened the lid. He tried to remember what had gone into them, for he hadn't seen the inside of most of them since putting his gear into store before his last mission in India. This trunk only contained uniforms—he couldn't imagine getting much of a loan with the security of a major's dress uniform, but it might have to do. The other trunks held mostly books and papers. Not much use for feeding them, but they might to help pass the time. He mentally added lanterns and oil to the shopping list of things he couldn't yet afford to buy.

Webb cleared his throat. Matthew dropped the uniform back in the trunk and turned around. Webb held out a necklace made of delicate gold links, studded with red stones. Matthew merely raised an eyebrow as he took the necklace over to the door to look at in better light.

"Gold and rubies?"

"Dunno, sir, but they look like they could be."

"Where the—" Matthew belatedly remembered his own instructions to Webb not to use bad language. "How did you come by this, Webb?"

"Found it, sir."

Matthew suppressed a smile. Webb, whether consciously or not, had reverted to the age-old soldier's strategy of answering an officer's question with the minimum possible information.

"Sergeant?"

"In India, sir," Webb added reluctantly. "Bit late to give it back now, sir."

"So we won't have the runners after us?"

"Nossir."

"Pawning this should tide us over. You can get it back when my money comes through."

"You can 'ave it, sir. You might get better for it at a proper jeweller's than in a pawn shop."

"Not to look a gift horse in the mouth, Webb, but why give this to me?"

"I got more…"

Matthew shook his head. "I don't think I want to know, Sergeant."

Webb shrugged. "I'd never 'ave got it back 'ere without you, sir. And I'm like to be arrested if I try sellin' it in a shop."

Matthew recalled the small additional trunk he'd noticed when they disembarked at Portsmouth. Was that how Webb had got the jewellery back to England?

"You stuck with me across half the world so you could keep your loot?"

"Nossir. That were just a bonus, sir." Webb's face had a carefully expressionless look that meant he was hiding something. Matthew thought about enquiring further, but someone who'd been a sergeant as long as Webb was likely to be a master prevaricator. He gave up and reached for his flask.

"Very well. Back to Bath, then."

Webb stood motionless.

"Sergeant?"

"With all due respect, sir, you should 'ave a shave and put a better coat on."

"Turning into a valet, Webb?"

"Less likely to be asked where it come from if you look respectable, sir."

"Oh, very well. Get the wagon harnessed, can you? We can eat breakfast on the way."

The trip to Bath could be counted a success, Matthew thought as the wagon jolted back up the muddy road towards Birchanger. He also thought that Webb had missed his calling in life. The three jewellers he had visited had all offered similar amounts for the necklace, and he had accepted the last offer. But he couldn't help overhearing Webb's gossip—there was no other word for it—with the clerks in each shop. The words 'inheritance' and 'distant relative' appeared to be explaining the origin of the necklace, and other snippets he overheard implied that Matthew was expecting a good deal more to come, at which point he would be wanting to *buy* jewellery for his sisters and fiancée, not sell it.

They found a carrier to deliver the purchases they couldn't take themselves that afternoon, then spent hours buying food, brandy, port, ale, wine, coffee, kitchen implements, blankets, tools, lanterns, oil... the list seemed endless. But at last it was over and they were on their way... home? It felt as much like home as the London house did, which was to say, not very much. At least here, he didn't have to suffer the presence of his stepmother and her offspring. Hell, having to think about buying food was preferable to inane small talk with people he didn't like, about things he cared nothing about.

When they got back to Birchanger, Matthew decided to use the last few hours of daylight to attempt to open the door in the wall again. He found the billhook they'd bought, and he managed to push it through the gap between the wall and the door, hacking away some of the brambles blocking the doorway. He succeeded in freeing the door enough to slip through it, cursing as the thorns caught on his coat and trousers.

Once inside, he could see that the wall enclosed an overgrown kitchen garden. The remnants of paths criss-crossing the area could still be made out, and overgrown trees with rotting fruit at their bases had once been trained tidily against the walls. A row of roughly rectangular humps down one edge of the garden might be a row of cold frames.

Matthew swallowed a sudden lump in his throat, seeing instead the sun-filled kitchen gardens of his childhood at Farleton. He remembered one long-ago summer when he had followed Harris, the head gardener, watching the weeding and planting. Looking back, Matthew was impressed at the patience Harris had shown as he'd pestered the man with endless questions. Harris must have been relieved when Matthew's enthusiasms had turned to guns, forts, and soldiering. He had been old then, Matthew recalled with sadness—he must be long in his grave by now.

Voices behind him roused him from his nostalgia, and he squeezed back through the door to help Webb unload their purchases from the carrier's wagon.

Webb cooked dinner, proudly serving up a large bowl of overcooked vegetables almost too mushy to eat with a fork, with lumps of chicken boiled to tastelessness. The sergeant didn't seem to be too fussy about his food, tucking in with a will. Matthew ate a few mouthfuls before surreptitiously feeding his portion to the dog, who was still hungry enough to eat anything. Instead he forced down a bit of bread and cheese, then uncorked a new bottle.

. . .

Later, Matthew gathered more straw to make a better bed for himself in the stall. He lay wrapped in his blankets, thinking about the walled garden and drifting on an alcoholic haze. Then he was looking at other walls, sweltering under a blazing sun, with bodies flying in all directions...

He sat up, heart racing and gasping for breath. The chill air and moonlight in the yard reminded him that this was not India, but the old shame washed over him. Gradually his heart rate returned to normal, and he rubbed his eyes.

Not wanting to risk another similar experience, he got dressed, found the billhook and an old pair of gloves, and made his way back into the kitchen garden by lantern light. If he was too afraid to sleep, he could at least try doing something useful.

The moon shone fitfully through gaps in the clouds, allowing him to see well enough to hack away the brambles and ivy choking the doorway. The task proved frustrating and painful, the thorns on the bramble vines catching in his clothing and stabbing him through his gloves. Ignoring the discomfort, he kept on hacking and pulling, piling the cut stems into a large heap near the door. *If only physical labour could atone for the past.*

Several hours later, the sharp ringing of the billhook hitting metal brought him to a halt. He must have hit some kind of support structure. He straightened his back, lifting the lantern to look around properly. For all the time he had spent, he'd only managed to clear a small patch of ground. The sight was discouraging, but it wasn't sensible to carry on hacking in the dark. He'd take a better look at what he'd done in daylight.

Back in the stable block his muscles let him know how physically unfit he'd become, but the aches and twinges in his arms, back, and legs felt good. Even the sting of the scratches and stabs from the bramble thorns didn't bother him. He'd *earned* the aches and pains.

Moving quietly, he made up the fire and brewed some coffee, and then lay wrapped in his blanket in the draught from the door, thinking about the kitchen garden. At the moment, sorting out the house and other buildings seemed a huge task—digging out the kitchen garden was much simpler, much more achievable, and it wouldn't require hiring teams of workers or making a lot of decisions.

His contemplations lasted until the sky began to lighten, then he dozed off. His language when Webb tried to wake him must have convinced the sergeant to let him sleep on, and when he awoke again a few hours later, he felt almost refreshed. Even the sound of rain pattering on the cobbled yard sounded comforting, wrapped up and warm as he was.

The feeling didn't last beyond lunchtime. Webb suggested looking over the house properly to make a list of what needed doing. It was almost enjoyable at first, opening the shutters in the various rooms to find good proportions and lovely oak panelling. Unfortunately, upon closer inspection, many signs of damp around windows and in the ceilings of the rooms on the second floor hinted at extensive, and expensive, repair work. Webb suggested a trip up into the attics to inspect the roof from the inside, but Matthew vetoed it. He wasn't going to subject himself to such a small space, and Webb's breathing was already laboured from coughing on the dust they'd raised. Besides, the damp ceilings told their own story.

The weather improved steadily during the morning, leaving the sky clear with only a filmy sheet of high cloud making the sunshine rather watery. Matthew found his spyglass and went to sit in one of the upstairs windows, inspecting what he could see of his land from a high vantage point. He was observing the edge of the woodland where the track up from the road emerged from the trees when he noticed a person striding up the drive. A woman, in a black coat and black bonnet.

He frowned. She looked familiar. He handed the spyglass to Webb.

"It's the woman from Edgecombe what gave me directions," Webb said. "The one what saw you…"

That's what he'd thought. "I'll be in the kitchen garden, making a bonfire," he announced. "I am not at home to visitors."

"But you *are* at home, sir?"

Matthew sighed. "What I mean, Webb, is if she is coming to call here, you are to say I am not at home."

"If you say so, sir." Webb shook his head as Matthew made his escape out of the back of the house, where the woman coming up the drive would not see him.

CHAPTER 11

*S*unday dawned damp, cool, and gloomy. Charlotte and Mary took Davie to church, accompanied by Deacon. Charlotte was not surprised to see the pew belonging to Birchanger Hall still empty. Deacon turned out to have a pleasant bass singing voice, and for once Davie did not fall asleep or fidget too much during the sermon.

After the service, many of Charlotte's acquaintances in the village came up to her to pass on condolences; news of her mother's death had spread around the village. The vicar was particularly effusive.

"You are holding up so well, dear Mrs MacKinnon. It is not easy to lose the support and advice of a loving parent, and you without a member of the stronger sex to help you through this difficult time." He smoothed his thick hair back as he spoke.

"I lost my mother, not my father, Mr Bretherton," Charlotte said, trying to stem the flow.

"Indeed. No doubt you and your father found great consolation in supporting each other through your loss."

Charlotte sighed. The vicar was so sympathetic at her separation from her natural source of male guidance that he freely offered his own advice whenever possible, oblivious to the fact that it was not only unwanted, but usually ignored. He continued speaking, but Charlotte stopped listening. Eventually Mary took pity on her and asked the vicar about the arrangements for Christmas decorations in the church.

Charlotte's relief was short-lived.

"I must have a word with you, Mrs MacKinnon." The rather high voice belonged to Mr Halliton, the local apothecary, jowls quivering with irritation as he spoke. "Mrs Jenson tells me you advised her when her son was ill last week."

"I was not in Edgecombe last week, Mr Halliton. Excuse me." Charlotte turned away, but that did not stop the man.

"You or that other one—it makes no difference! You are not qualified to give medical advice!"

"Mr Halliton, people are entitled to ask anyone they wish for advice."

"It is not proper for a woman to set herself up as…"

Charlotte, walking away, did not hear the rest. She had no idea what Mary might have advised Mrs Jenson about, but it would have been sensible advice, based on experience, and would *not* have included recommending one of the more expensive concoctions sold by Mr Halliton.

Halliton's voice continued behind her, and she felt his hand grab her arm, but suddenly Deacon was there. He didn't say anything, but plucked Halliton's hand from Charlotte's elbow and then offered her his own arm to escort her from the churchyard. She smiled in thanks as they headed back to the cottage. Deacon was turning out to be an exceedingly useful addition to the household.

The next morning, Charlotte was still worrying about Mr Berry's request for drawings to accompany her tales. Rather than tossing and turning in bed, she decided to get up. She could, at the least, get more writing done if she was at her desk. She'd heard Davie get up, then call out that it had stopped raining and he was going into the garden before breakfast.

She sighed. She still could not see the attraction of damming the small stream at the far end of the garden, or building model mill-races with clay and bits of wood. Particularly on a freezing morning like this one.

She had heard Mary get up and leave several hours before. Mary must really want to be part of this bakery business to get up so early.

No-one was around when she went downstairs, although the range had been stoked up and the kitchen was warm. There was no sign of Deacon, and the door to his little room had been open when she passed it. She frowned. Surely he couldn't be digging the garden this early? It was barely light but she could see that there was no-one working on the vegetable patch.

It was Sally's morning off, so Charlotte put the kettle on and prepared porridge. After touring the house with her on Saturday, Deacon had taken a lantern into the attic to inspect it, and then had spent the rest of the afternoon looking around the outside. He had made a list—a long list—and presented it to Charlotte and Mary after the evening meal.

Mary had gone through it in detail with him, checking what the various tools and materials were for, and which ones were most urgently needed. Then she had given him what looked like a lot of money from her housekeeping fund. Charlotte guessed from his shocked expression that it was enough for his stage fare back to Lancashire with plenty to spare. He had been about to protest about the amount when Mary raised an eyebrow and asked, "You ain't planning on running off with it, are you?"

Deacon had just shaken his head and placed the money safely into his coat pocket. Now, Charlotte wondered if perhaps Mary's confidence had been misplaced.

She called Davie in for breakfast, then made him wash and change into clean clothes before he walked over to the squire's place for his lessons.

She was seeing him off, reminding him to try not to get too

muddy, when she saw Deacon trudging up the hill with a heavy bag in his hand, using his other arm to balance a ladder on his shoulder.

Ashamed of her suspicions, she returned to the kitchen and put the rest of the porridge on to warm again, then made more tea. Deacon came in, leaving a pile of coins on the corner of the table before going to wash in the scullery.

"It didn't seem right, Mrs MacKinnon walking out in the dark on her own," he explained while he was eating. "And there's a bit of heavy work to be done, shifting flour and the like for the bread." He glanced at the bag. "I borrowed some tools instead of buying them. I had to order some things, but Mrs MacKinnon came with me for them and they'll send an account when the things arrive. I hope that is all satisfactory, ma'am?"

"Perfectly," Charlotte said, and his face lightened.

Deacon washed his cup and plate then put his coat back on, saying it was time to re-fix the loose tiles he'd noted before it started to rain again.

Charlotte went into the parlour to concentrate on Mr Fox, reaching the stage where she'd finished the story and would need to leave it for a couple of days before reading it again with a fresh mind. She stretched her arms and fingers out, and went into the kitchen to make more tea. Deacon was there, working on the pantry shelf, and they discussed how the repairs were going while she waited for the kettle to boil.

Back in the parlour, the next task was January's *Cotswold Diary*. She'd kept a detailed journal for the first couple of years after she'd moved here with Mary; this was now proving very useful for writing articles about the countryside a month or more ahead of time. There wasn't a lot to say about January, really; not much was happening for those who worked on the land, nor would there be many wild flowers in bloom. December's article, written five weeks ago now, had been easy to fill with descriptions of Christmas preparations. She looked through her old journals, jotting down a few ideas. Now all she needed to do was to find someone who knew about hedge laying. That might have to wait until her next visit to the squire in a couple of days' time, so she turned to thinking about other possible animal stories.

Mary arrived home in the middle of the afternoon. Charlotte saw her approaching through the parlour window, and decided this was as good a time as any to take a rest from her work, even before she saw the three men accompanying her.

She recognised Samuels from the grocery shop in Edgecombe, Jenson the blacksmith, and was that the butcher? She heard them wiping their feet, then being taken through to the kitchen. She was about to go and find out what the men wanted when Mary knocked on the door.

"Quite a delegation?" Charlotte said.

"I'll let them tell you," Mary said. "It's you they wants to talk to. A letter come for you as well." She put the letter on the table.

In the kitchen, the three men stood close together, turning their hats in their hands and shuffling their feet uncomfortably. Charlotte knew them all, for they each paid her a small sum every quarter to check their accounts for them.

Mary sat down at the table, so Charlotte joined her. There weren't enough chairs for all the men to sit, but Charlotte suspected that they would be more comfortable standing in any case. After a little muttered conversation between them, Samuels took a small step forwards.

"We was wondering if you could speak to Lord Tillson for us, ma'am," he said.

That was unexpected. "I don't know the man, Mr Samuels."

"No, ma'am. But..." He dropped his gaze, his fingers tightening on his hat.

"Perhaps if you start by telling me what it is you wish me to speak to him about?"

Samuels cleared his throat. "Yesterday morning, ma'am, his man came to buy food and such. He wanted to have it on credit, with an invoice."

"That is usual for someone wishing to supply a house the size of Birchanger, is it?"

"Yes, ma'am. But he still owes from when he was here before."

"But he only arrived a couple of days ago. I saw him—he arrived after the carrier." Drunk, she added mentally.

"Yes, ma'am. But this new one was here in the spring as well."

Charlotte looked at Mary, puzzled.

"I don't remember, neither," Mary said. "Perhaps it were when you was in London?"

"April, it was, ma'am." Samuels said. "Ordered a lot of stuff, an' got a horse re-shod." He nodded to the blacksmith. "Sent our bills up to the house, we did, with the goods, but never got no reply. Jenson went to enquire a couple of weeks later, but the place was empty then."

"It's the same man?"

"Dunno about that, ma'am. It wasn't Lord Tillson what done the ordering, it was his man."

"The same one as yesterday?"

"No, ma'am. Never seen this one before."

That didn't prove anything. A lord would have more than one servant.

"You could send new accounts, now he's back."

"We could try, ma'am. But his man said Lord Tillson didn't owe nothin'."

"You could try explaining to him. After all, he'll need to buy supplies from you."

"That's just it, ma'am," Jenson put in. "Yesterday afternoon, we seen that wagon of theirs coming through the village again. It was piled with stuff. They must 'ave bought all their food an' such somewhere else."

"Birchanger used to help us all make ends meet," Samuels added.

"Even with the old lord arguing about every bill?" Charlotte had not had direct dealings with the man himself, but she'd certainly heard complaints about him. Many, lengthy complaints.

"He allus used to pay up in the end, at least for ordinary goods, ma'am."

Charlotte sighed. "Why don't you go and explain to his lordship?" Not only was it none of her business, but she had no desire to confront a potentially drunk aristocrat.

The men shuffled their feet and looked at each other. Finally, Samuels spoke. "He might take against us, ma'am, then we'd never get the custom. If it come from someone like—"

"Someone who has no personal stake in the matter," Charlotte finished for him, acknowledging the sense in this.

The three of them nodded gratefully.

Charlotte sighed again. "He may not even see me, you realise?" she warned them, but they still looked more cheerful than when they arrived.

"Thank you, ma'am," they said, as they filed out.

Charlotte waited until they had gone. "Thank you *so* much for bringing them, Mary!"

Mary grinned. "It weren't my idea, honest! That's what you get for knowing everything and giving advice. There's more than one reason they call you Mrs Captain, you know!"

She got up. "Now you go and get more writing done. I'll brew some tea and get started on the dinner."

Charlotte picked up the letter waiting on the parlour table, breaking the wafer. It was from her aunt, and started with general enquiries about her health.

I have decided to buy the tiara myself. You may not know, but it belonged to our mother, your grandmother, so it has two-fold sentimental value for me. I suspect this is why it was left to you, rather than the more valuable items left to your sisters.

I had it valued. I'm afraid it isn't worth nearly as much as you hoped, but that does mean that I have enough pin money saved to give you a fair price for it. Meerbrook thinks there is less likelihood of your father trying to reclaim it, or the money, from me.

A smile of relief spread across her face. The money from that meant they could afford to pay Deacon a proper wage, even if it took some time for the bakery to show a profit.

Charlotte put off her errand until after lunch the next day. The sky was clearing after a wet morning, so she decided to take along a few pieces of paper to try to sketch some trees. She'd have to draw lots of woodland scenes, and there was no point in attempting to draw the animals if she couldn't even manage trees. She debated walking around by the road—the way she had directed Lord Tillson's man a few days ago—but decided to take the shorter path through the woods.

That had not been a good decision, she thought, after she crossed the stream. The path here went up a steep slope, and she very nearly slithered down it again as her boots slipped in the mud. After another, more cautious attempt, she managed the slope with no more than the usual coating of mud around the hem of her gown

When she came this way, she normally crossed the drive up to Birchanger, continuing north through the woods to Northridge Hall, the squire's place. Today, she turned along the drive towards Birchanger Hall.

Charlotte had seen the building from this edge of the woods, but had never been right up to the house itself. The weak afternoon sun brought out the warm buttery colour of the limestone, and made the leaded windows twinkle. If one could ignore the signs of neglect, it was a beautiful building, surrounded by this meadow which had once been a lawn.

The front door gave the impression of being a wooden section of wall, rather than something that opened. The knocker was very stiff, and although it did make a noise she wasn't convinced that the sound would carry as far as the kitchen, if that's where the servants were. She looked around for a bell pull, but couldn't see one.

After waiting for someone to respond to her knock, she decided to try at the back of the house. There were tracks in the gravel leading around the north side of the house, so she went that way. At the corner, the gravel continued around the house to a stable yard, passing a wall with a wooden door, probably a kitchen garden. She stopped at the corner when she saw the soldier who had been driving the wagon.

"May I see Lord Tillson?" Charlotte asked.

"He said he is not at home, ma'am," the man said politely.

Charlotte met his eyes and he shuffled his feet. "Do you mean he is not here, or that he doesn't want to see me?"

The man opened his mouth to reply, but then a voice called from beyond the door to the kitchen garden.

"Have you got rid of the old witch yet, Webb?" It was the voice of an educated man, not a servant. It could only be the new Lord Tillson.

Charlotte felt her face flushing. She pressed her lips together hard, her temper flaring for the first time in several years. A few deep breaths brought better control, and she looked Webb in the eye again.

"I came to clear up a misunderstanding," she said, keeping her voice steady with an effort, then turned on her heel and stalked off down the drive, fuming.

How dare he? He doesn't even know what I wanted to see him about. Drunken wastrel! Fine! If he wants to pay carrier's charges for all his supplies from Bath, let him!

CHAPTER 12

$\mathcal{M}$atthew hacked at brambles morosely. Webb had come into the garden after getting rid of their unwanted visitor, his disapproving expression making clear that the woman had heard Matthew's words. Yet another good impression made.

Perhaps they'll leave me alone, then!

The weather continued to improve as he worked, sunshine warming his shoulders and the back of his neck. His mood gradually lightened as he made a little progress, chopping brambles and feeding the bonfire. Towards the end of the afternoon he stopped and surveyed the kitchen garden with a certain satisfaction, stretching his back and arms to relieve the pains and stiffness caused by the unaccustomed exercise.

He could now see the layout of the garden more clearly—the remains of support structures showed where beans and peas had once grown, and the row of humps he had spotted on his first visit were indeed what was left of cold frames. Matthew kicked a couple—the wood felt reasonably sound. With new glass in the lids they would help to get the garden started in the spring. There was still a huge expanse of overgrown ground to clear, and then the beds would need to be dug over, with manure added and persistent weeds removed.

The kitchen garden he remembered at Farleton had had a succession house against the south-facing wall that produced peaches, grapes and early vegetables, even an occasional pineapple. Warmth provided by the sun had been supplemented in winter by stoves that also served to warm the head gardener's office and the stables. Here, the north wall of the garden backed onto the end of the stable block. Perhaps something could be built along the inside of the north wall and a boiler installed in the stable office, or a new building beyond that.

Pulling his notebook from his pocket, he began to sketch ideas.

He stopped sketching when it was too dark to see—not late at this time of year—and suppressed the faint thread of guilt about planning unnecessary improvements before he had even begun to think about fixing all the things wrong with the main house.

Webb emerged from the stables to ask if he wanted his dinner yet.

"Nice bit of beef I've got stewing, sir," he said.

"Not just yet," Matthew said, his stomach roiling as he recalled the overcooked mush of the previous evening. "You have yours, leave mine by the fire to keep warm."

If he dished it up when Webb wasn't there, he could feed it to Reena and make do with bread and cheese again. He wasn't hungry anyway.

Hacking at the brambles had been hard work, but he felt the need for a walk to stretch his legs and loosen the muscles in his back. It might even tire him enough to get a couple of hours of uninterrupted sleep.

He got no response when he whistled for the dog. She didn't seem too enthusiastic about the cold at the moment; perhaps, when she had put on more weight and her coat had regrown, she might be company on a walk.

There was still some light in the sky, with an almost-full moon rising behind the house. Matthew checked that his flask was still in his pocket, then picked up a lantern and his tinder box. Setting off down the drive, he turned just before reaching the trees, which allowed him to keep to the top of the woodland clothing the slope that descended to the west. The stretch of grass between here and the Hall had once been a lawn, but now the grass was long, with dead remains of thistles standing out here and there in the gloom. Further on, the edge of the woodland swept away to the west, and he turned downhill to follow it.

He hadn't gone more than a few paces before he found himself falling. Twisting as he fell, he managed to land on his back. He lay still for a moment, winded. When his breath came more easily he found he couldn't move; something was holding fast to his arms and legs.

Panic seized him, his pulse hammering in his ears as he yanked against his bonds, trying to push away memories of being shackled in the dark. It took several minutes of useless, energy-sapping struggle before he regained sufficient control to realise that the only sounds were his own ragged breathing and the wind in the trees. Taking deep breaths, he forced himself to be still and work out what had happened. He finally recognised the springy branches beneath him, and the cause of the pain in his hands.

Damned brambles again!

Moving carefully and using his elbows rather than his bare hands to help him, Matthew rolled over, tearing his coat and breeches free. He managed to regain his footing, not without further damage to his hands and clothing, and took stock. A hard line of shadow was just visible at chest height. He'd walked over the edge of a ha-ha, and was now standing in the ditch beyond it.

Although the moon was bright, the nearby trees cast deep shadows. He peered around for the lantern, eventually finding it at the expense of more damage from the plants. Luckily it was still intact, and the oil had not spilled. He lit it, holding it high to survey his surroundings.

The brambles around him were fairly well trampled, so he shouldn't have too much difficulty climbing the low wall of the ha-ha and retracing his steps. In the other direction, the brambles gave way to a narrow path, parallel to the ha-ha, with tangles of gorse and the distinctive shapes of yet more bramble bushes beyond. He carefully made his way to the path, treading on the brambles and flattening them with his boots so he didn't get caught up again. He turned towards the main drive.

The path soon meandered back into the trees and down the hillside, crossing a small stream, then forking. The right-hand path headed back up a muddy slope, with only tree roots across the path providing enough grip to climb the bank. That looked as if it would take him back to the drive, but he didn't feel like going back just yet, nor did he feel like tackling the muddy incline. He took the other path, moving slowly downhill in the dim light from the lantern and gradually losing his sense of direction as the path wound through the trees. Pausing to reconsider the advisability of retracing his steps, he heard the crack of a rotten branch breaking.

He was not the only one wandering in the woods, then. He closed the shutter on the lantern and remained still, listening. The other person was coming towards him, making no effort to move quietly. There was no light in the shade of the trees, so the intruder must be familiar with the path.

Matthew waited until the sounds were close, then unshuttered the lantern. The man he faced was short, thin, unshaven and dressed in layers of ragged clothing, a shapeless hat sitting askew atop his head. Three dead rabbits dangling from one hand explained his presence, but not his lack of stealth.

Instead of trying to run or make excuses as Matthew expected, the man just stood there. If it wasn't for the sudden defeated slump of his shoulders, Matthew would have thought he was unafraid and had every right to be trapping rabbits in the wood.

"Your name?" He made it more of a polite enquiry than an accusatory question.

"George Jackson," the man said.

"Whose land is this?" Matthew was fairly certain the woodland belonged to the Birchanger estate, but it was well to be sure. If this was not his land, the poacher was none of his business, and besides, the man looked as if he needed the food.

"Lord Tillson's land," Jackson muttered.

"And your position here is…?"

The man started blankly at him.

"Where do you live? What do you do?" Matthew asked again.

"Cottage." The man jerked his head sideways. South, Matthew thought, but it didn't really matter at the moment. "Used to work on the estate, but there ain't been no work for more'n a year now."

That made sense. As there had been no steward for a couple of years, no directions would have been given to the labourers, nor would there have been seed to plant.

Without warning, the enormity of the problems he needed to address overcame him: the farm, his tenant labourers, no doubt their cottages as well, the house, whatever the Mayhews and his half-brother had been doing with his income from the Farleton estate while he was in India…

He rubbed a hand across his face, the throb starting in his temples making him reach for his flask. It was too much. Far too much.

"Report to the stables at Birchanger tomorrow at noon," he said, turning on his heel to retrace his steps without waiting for the man to acknowledge the command. With any luck, the poacher would run off and he wouldn't have to decide what to do about him.

The list of problems marched relentlessly through his mind as he walked back to the Hall. He knew nothing about farming, and little about buildings such as the Hall. Yet he held the livelihoods of many people in his incapable hands.

Webb was absent when Matthew reached the stables; Matthew guessed he was poking around somewhere inside the Hall. The promised dinner was keeping warm in a covered pot by the fire. Matthew prodded at it with a fork, then summoned the dog, enthusiastic now food was on offer. Brandy would do for himself.

The day's physical work had tired him, and although it was still fairly early, he fell asleep almost as soon as he lay down.

"…knew a bloody sight more about plantin' and keepin' cows than Lord Everall…"

Havers? Havers is dead.

"...Bristol. No money to give us decent 'ouses..."

Benson's voice faded away, together with the shrill of cicadas and the crackling of the small fire. Matthew stared upwards in the dark, the cold, damp British air chilling his face. The only real sounds were his own unsteady breathing, and the horses shuffling in their stalls. He shivered, and reached for his flask.

A memory, not a hallucination.

They had camped in a hollow, where the light from a small fire would not be seen. Havers, from the Kent countryside, had complained about landowners who cared more for their hunters and carriages, or their wives' ornamental gardens and fine clothes, than for ensuring the land was worked properly. Benson, from the Bristol slums, had talked about money spent on fancy houses and gardens, clearing more people into the slums. Their voices had held venom.

He took a pull from his flask. Had they included *him* in the ranks of the uncaring rich? The list of things he had to do marched through his head again, and he drank a little more. Eventually he slept again, fitfully.

To Matthew's disappointment, the list of problems seemed no shorter in daylight. Webb unceremoniously dumped a plate of food in front of him, and he sat for some time with a cup of coffee, staring at the box of papers Gleason had given him and feeding bits of blackened bacon to the dog. The persistent drizzle outside made looking through the papers the only sensible option at the moment.

Matthew forced down a couple of pieces of bread and butter. He refilled his coffee cup, laced it liberally with brandy, then resolutely opened the box. There were several sets of ledgers, the most recent from three years ago and the oldest from the 1770s. No doubt there were more somewhere, but they would be ancient history. He supposed that a study of the accounts would explain the decline in the estate's revenues, but might also reveal what the place should be capable of. Examining them would take days of being stuck indoors poring over lists of numbers; he could not face that at the moment. It was bad enough having to be indoors at night. He stacked the ledgers on a dusty shelf, nicely hidden in one corner where they wouldn't catch his eye.

Beneath the ledgers were bundles of letters. Opening a few, he skimmed the contents with caution, hoping they weren't too personal. However, the first packet appeared to be a set of angry exchanges between the previous Lord Tillson and the owner of a brewery in Bath, complaining of the poor quality of barrels of ale supplied and demanding a refund of the cost. Flicking through the rest, Matthew thought the previous baron must have been the world's most unlucky purchaser—from poor quality wood for panelling, seeds that failed to grow and cheese not fit to eat after only a month, to builders who could not rebuild walls straight.

Matthew put the bundles on top of the ledgers in their hidden corner. Some time, if he was really, really bored, he might go through them and find out how many battles the old curmudgeon had won. But this might explain why the shopkeepers in Edgecombe weren't falling over themselves to oblige the new baron with credit.

The last bundle in the box contained plans. There were plans of the house, some of which were so old they were almost falling to pieces. Others looked like plans of the gardens, and of the fields and woodland making up the estate. He put those to one side and started to pack the others back into the box.

"Sir?"

Matthew looked up as Webb came into the room. Webb nodded towards the doorway, and Matthew sighed when he saw Jackson, the poacher, standing there. The man had three dead rabbits in one hand. Matthew took a minute to wonder if they were the same three rabbits he had caught last night, or if the man had had the sense to wait until Matthew had gone and then trap more for his dinner. But looking at the hopeless expression on the man's face, he doubted it. If he followed the law, he should be sending the man to the local magistrate for trial, and then jail or transportation. Not only was that too complicated, it didn't seem fair either.

"Put the rabbits down, man," he said.

Surprised, Jackson did as he was bid.

"Webb, get some more coffee on, will you?"

Matthew looked the poacher over. His clothing, although worn and patched, looked fairly clean, and he had made an effort to brush his hair and shave.

"I'm Lord Tillson," Matthew said. "Sit down." He indicated a chair across the table.

"Why did you come here today?"

"You told me to, my lord."

"Poaching's a hanging offence. Why didn't you run?"

"I got nowhere to run to," the man said, twisting his cap in his hands. He raised his head and looked Matthew in the eye. "I was only trying to feed my family. There ain't bin no work on the estate. I... I hoped you might be lenient, my lord."

Lenient, yes. He couldn't send the man off to be locked up, or worse, and neither did it seem right just to send the man away without saying anything. So he had to do *something*, which meant making a decision. He should have retreated to the kitchen garden, where the only decisions to be made were whether a plant was to be dug up or left.

"Too many rabbits ain't no good for crops, right, sir?" Webb asked.

Matthew realised that he must have been staring at the poacher without saying anything for some time. He digested Webb's question. "That's right, Webb. So?"

"Reckon anyone trappin' the little bug... the rabbits is doin' you a favour, like."

He could see what Webb was getting at, but thinking about, and then discussing, the details of employing Jackson to trap rabbits on the estate was beyond him at the moment; one more thing added to a rotting building, neglected fields, greedy relatives. And his own failings...

He got to his feet abruptly. "Good idea, Webb. Just sort things out, will you?" Picking up his flask, he abandoned Webb to the details and headed outside.

122

Retreating to the kitchen garden, Matthew determinedly kept his mind on digging bramble roots and thinking about what might be planted in their place. He managed a couple of hours in the cold drizzle before the chill reached his bones and he could no longer ignore his aching back. Reena had accompanied him out, sniffing around the garden for a while before returning to the warmer spot near the fire indoors.

In the stable office he laced a cup of coffee and investigated the pot of stew Webb had left by the fire. It seemed to be the usual mush, making the decision to stick with a couple of mouthfuls of ham an easy one.

Once he warmed up, he found the sheaf of plans he had put aside when Jackson arrived. Maybe it was time to see what the rest of the estate was like. He looked over the map of the fields and woods again, getting the rough outline fixed in his mind. Although the drizzle had finally stopped, the air was too damp to take the map itself outside, but a walk around would help him match the map with the land. It would be dusk in around an hour, so he collected the lantern then set off to the woodland above the house to the east.

He started with the fields on the flat land at the top of the slopes, beyond the birch hangar wood behind the house, doing his best to keep his mind on the land rather than on his past failures. These upper fields were all fallow, with thistles and dock amongst the grass, and brambles escaping from the hedgerows to encroach on the fields. There were great soggy areas in some of the fields, with mud that stuck to the soles of his boots. He mentally added drainage to the list of renovation work he was trying not to think about.

Leaving the fields, he walked north. That direction should take him down into the valley cutting eastwards into the high ground of the Cotswold scarp. The steep slope was clothed in woodland, dense in many places. It took him some time to pick his way down through the trees, consulting his compass occasionally so he didn't wander round in circles. At the foot of the woodland was more pasture. He walked west, thinking to pick up the road from Edgecombe then follow it south until he came to the end of the drive leading into his estate. But before he reached the road he came across a well-trodden path across the fields, leading back into the woodland.

His eyes had adapted to the gathering gloom as he walked across the pasture, but the trees blocked any remaining light from the sky, so he paused to light the lantern before carrying on. The path was narrow, and slippery with mud in places, but it was clear of brambles and did seem to be heading in roughly the right direction. He noticed fainter paths leading off here and there, but decided he'd had enough damp and cold for one evening and so stuck to the more obvious route.

The lack of vegetation on the path meant he was moving quietly enough to hear the rustle of other things disturbing bushes and dead leaves, and the occasional snap of dead branches. He frowned. Jackson again? But if Webb had employed the man to trap rabbits there was no need for him to be out in the dark. Matthew was wondering how many other unemployed labourers-turned-poachers were roaming the estate when he heard voices, and stopped to listen.

As on the previous evening, the others were making little attempt to keep quiet, but there the resemblance ended. Two boys came into sight; they were rather muddy, but beneath the mud their clothing looked respectable, and neither had the gaunt look caused by a lack of adequate food. They had their own lanterns, but were oblivious to Matthew standing on the path until they were almost on top of him. Then they stopped with an audible gasp.

"Who are you?" the older of them asked. He was rather plump, with hair that looked fair in the dim light from the lanterns. The question had been put in a confident, almost aggressive, tone.

"I could ask the same of you," Matthew said mildly. The second lad, a little shorter, thinner and darker, nudged his friend.

"You are trespassing!" the larger boy said. The smaller lad nudged him again, hissing something under his breath. The larger one nudged back.

"This land belongs to Birchanger, does it not?" Matthew enquired.

"I... er... yes, I think so."

"And you do not belong to Birchanger."

The lad, no longer so sure of himself, shook his head reluctantly.

"So, you are the trespasser."

"You don't belong here..." the lad said, his voice tailing off uncertainly.

"If you please, sir," the younger of the two spoke up. "I'm Davie MacKinnon, and I live in Edgecombe. I've been over to visit Bertie and I'm on my way home. Lots of people from the village use this track through the woods—it cuts more than a mile off the way by road."

"Pleased to meet you, Davie," Matthew said. "I'm Major..." he hesitated. He'd hardly begun to think of himself as Lord Tillson so the old rank had come naturally. But then why complicate things now? "Just call me the major," he said. "Such a polite lad is welcome to use the path."

Davie nudged his companion again.

"I'm Albert Thompson," the larger one said, grudgingly. "My father's the squire at Northridge Hall."

"So your way lies there?" Matthew asked, pointing back the way he had come.

The lad hesitated, then agreed.

"See you next time," Davie said as Bertie reluctantly set off home. Matthew wondered what they had been planning on doing, then decided he didn't really want to know.

"So, Davie," he said, once they could no longer see Bertie's lantern. "Does this path cross the drive up to Birchanger? I'm still getting to know my way around, and it can be a bit difficult in the dark."

Davie nodded. "Shall I go first, sir? I know where the slippy bits are."

"Thank you." Matthew followed the lad, acknowledging the occasional warning to mind the muddy bit, or to watch out for a low-hanging branch. The lad was bright enough to warn Matthew of obstacles well above his own head, but low enough to catch Matthew's much greater height. He set a brisk pace, and it wasn't long before they reached the overgrown drive.

Davie stopped on the drive, shining his lantern up the hill. "The

Hall is up there, sir," he said. "The path to Edgecombe goes on there."
He shone the lantern across the drive.

"What does your father do?" Matthew asked, wondering whether
he should have a word about the lad's nocturnal wanderings.

"Oh, I haven't got a father," Davie replied with a disarming
candour. "Goodnight, sir."

"Go carefully, Davie," Matthew said as the boy disappeared into
the darkness.

CHAPTER 13

orthridge Hall was a square mansion, solid and unassuming. Rather like the squire himself, Charlotte thought, as she walked up the frosty drive with Davie. The squire was a man of simple tastes, happy as long as his home was warm and dry, food and wine were plentiful, and he could ride to hounds every week.

Davie took himself off as soon as he had wiped his feet and the butler had taken his coat. Charlotte was shown into the south parlour where Letty was lying down resting, as the child she was expecting in a couple of months was making its presence felt. She was the same age as Charlotte, but there the resemblance ended. Letty was slight, apart from her swelling belly, with wispy hair and pale blue eyes.

This was Charlotte's first visit since her mother's death, so Letty said her condolences while Charlotte poured the tea.

Charlotte had never shared with Letty the details of her disputes with her father, so she confined the description of her trip to the jewellery she had inherited, showing Letty the locket she wore beneath her gown.

"How are you feeling?" Letty asked, handing the locket back.

"I forget much of the time," Charlotte admitted. "I only saw Mama once a year, and only had the occasional letter from her. Things are going on here mostly as they were. I just remember now and then..." She rubbed the locket between her fingers, then dropped it back down into the neck of her gown, sudden tears pricking her eyes.

"One of the maids said there is a new Lord Tillson," Letty said.

Relieved at the change of subject, Charlotte took a deep breath and blinked hard.

"Have you seen him?" Letty went on. "How old is he, do you know? Is he married?"

"If he is, I'm sure his wife will call on you," Charlotte said. "Hasn't Lord Tillson called on Mr Thompson?"

Letty shook her head. "Arthur is talking about riding over to pay his respects." She smiled mischievously. "I'm sure he'll actually do it in a week or two! But tell me, have you seen this new lord?"

"Only for a moment, when he arrived."

"What is he like?"

"Tall and thin," Charlotte said. "And drunk."

"All men drink, Charlotte," Letty said. "Arthur likes his port."

Arthur certainly did, Charlotte thought, but refrained from saying so. "Arthur doesn't cast up his accounts in public in the middle of the day," she said tartly.

She wouldn't normally repeat things to the detriment of another, but she still harboured a bit of a grudge about the rude way she had been dismissed at Birchanger a couple of days before. Besides, at least ten other people must have seen him, so she was not saying anything that was not being talked about by others.

"Is he as handsome as Sir Vincent?" Letty asked, with a sly smile.

"Give up, Letty," Charlotte said with a laugh. "I will not be marrying Sir Vincent, no matter how many times he asks me." *Just because marriage suits you, doesn't mean it would suit me.*

A little voice of doubt whispered in her mind. Her vague concern about Davie's education had been brought into sharp focus by her father's proposition—her return to London for Davie's schooling. If the money from her mother's trust *was* blocked by her father, she would struggle to afford fees, extra clothing, and bed and board. Not

to mention university. Marrying again could solve some of her problems, albeit at the expense of her independence. It wasn't a choice she
relished. Sir Vincent had been persistent; perhaps she should think
more carefully before rejecting him again.

She smoothed a hand absently over the black cloth of her gown.
The tiara money would solve her immediate worries. For now, she
could claim that she could not make a decision until she was out of
mourning.

"… and so what do you think, Charlotte?"

Charlotte looked up, startled to realise she hadn't heard a word of
what Letty was saying.

"Sorry, Letty."

Letty smiled and shook her head. "I was just saying that Arthur's
mama was called Sophia, but one of my aunts is called Sophia too and
I don't like her…"

Charlotte tried hard to pay attention, but although this was better
than Letty expressing her worries about how Bertie would take to the
new addition to the family, she had discussed the same thing, at
length, on Charlotte's last two visits.

"You could use Sophia as a middle name," Charlotte suggested
when Letty finished, as she had last time. "You should rest, Letty."

Letty rubbed her back, and awkwardly put her feet up again. "I'm
so glad Arthur likes discussing the papers with you, Charlotte," she
said. "It saves me having to take an interest. It's too difficult to think
about anything at the moment."

"Ah, Mrs MacKinnon." The squire stood as she entered his study—
although the newspapers were the only things she had ever seen him
studying. "What do you think of this new proposed constitution in
France? There's an article in here." He handed over a copy of *The
Gentleman's Magazine*.

"I'm afraid I haven't seen many details on it as yet, sir," Charlotte
said, taking the paper and sitting in her usual chair. "If I take
this away—"

"Yes, yes—good idea! Next week, then. Now, it seems Pitt said..."

~

Matthew awoke to a hard frost. The damp air had cleared during the night, and the sun made a pale disc above a thin veil of cloud. The grass was rimed in ice, but he suspected that the muddy paths through the woods would not yet have frozen solid. Webb wasn't around, so he got himself a mostly liquid breakfast. He found the map showing the field boundaries of the estate and put a piece of bread into his pocket, checking he had his notebook and a full flask before setting off.

The cold air was invigorating. If he concentrated on noting down the state of each field, rather than thinking about what needed to be done, he found he was almost enjoying himself. He covered the fields to the north of the Hall, roughly checking the map against the bare hedges forming the boundaries, and ending up at the top of the woodland through which he had descended the previous evening. Following the edge of the woodland east took him up the scarp, and he made a loop to end up crossing his earlier route. Most of the land lay fallow, like the fields he had seen the previous day, a few scrawny cows and goats grazing some of them. The whole conveyed an air of neglect he tried hard to put out of his mind. Glancing from the map to the lines of hedgerows in front of him, he realised that not all of the boundaries matched those on the map.

He was puzzling this out when he heard a noise behind him. The kind of shuffling and throat-clearing noise made by someone who doesn't want to interrupt, but is getting a little weary of waiting to be noticed. He turned, and saw the younger of the two lads from the previous evening. What was the boy's name? Ah, yes. Davie.

"Can I help you?" Matthew asked.

"I was interested in the map, sir," Davie said.

Matthew raised an eyebrow.

"Honest, sir! I... I sometimes walk through the fields instead of the woods when I go over to the squire's. I was wondering if you were going to start farming properly again. It seems an awful waste."

Bloody hell, now I'm being nagged by a fatherless brat from the village!

Something of his thought must have shown on his face, for Davie backed off a few paces, drawing his brows together slightly.

Matthew made an effort to smooth his expression. "At the moment I'm just seeing what is here," he said, managing a neutral tone. "I was given this map, but it doesn't seem quite right." He held it out slightly, and Davie approached and took one edge. "You know about maps?"

"I have had some geography lessons," Davie said. "But that's mostly foreign countries."

He stared at the map, looking puzzled. Matthew was so used to maps that he didn't need to have it aligned with the countryside, but most people didn't have that skill. He took hold of Davie's edge and turned it.

"Try it this way round," he said, fully expecting the lad to get bored quickly. But instead Davie traced the field boundaries with his finger, frowning in concentration and looking between the map and the landscape.

"Well?" Matthew asked eventually, interested to see what Davie made of it. "Worked it out?"

"Sorry, sir." Davie handed back his edge of the map. "I'm taking up too much of your time."

"I've got plenty of time. Did you spot where the map is wrong?"

"There's an extra field here," Davie said, putting a finger on a part marked as woodland. "And the hedges up there don't meet like that," he added, indicating another part of the map. "Why do you need a map?"

Matthew thought that 'because I like maps' probably wasn't the kind of answer the lad wanted. "It helps to know how much land there is, so you can work out how many cows can graze, or how much seed you need to plant. You can work out the area of each field from the map."

Davie nodded. "But only if the map shows things properly," he said. "Do you have to get a new map done? Who does that?"

"I can do it," Matthew said. He should have a chain and surveying compass somewhere in his trunks. It would be a nice little job, with no decisions to be made other than where to take the measurements for each field.

"How do you do it?"

Matthew looked at him—the lad really *did* seem to be interested. "If you come along tomorrow, I can show you," he said. "It will be much easier, and more accurate, with two." He could get Webb to help, he supposed, once Davie lost interest.

"Really?"

"If you won't get bored. And if you aren't supposed to be somewhere else," he added, belatedly thinking that Davie might have either work to be done or lessons to attend.

"What time?"

"Ten o'clock?"

Davie gave him a huge grin, and skipped off down the field towards the woods. Matthew rolled up the map and set off back to the house, wondering if he would regret the offer. What if Davie chattered the whole time? It was too late now; he would not go back on his word.

As he entered the yard behind the Hall, Matthew was met with the sound of more childish voices. A couple of grubby children, smaller than Davie, struggled to carry a heavy bucket from the pump towards the kitchen. They dropped the bucket in surprise when they saw him, abandoning it in the middle of the yard and dashing into the house.

Matthew rubbed his eyes and headed for the stable office, shouting for Webb.

"What the hell's going on?" he asked, when the sergeant appeared.

"Gettin' the kitchen cleaned, sir," Webb said cheerfully. "It ain't near as bad as it looked."

"Whose brats are those?"

"Jackson's."

"The poacher?"

"Gamekeeper, sir. You said to sort things out."

"I meant to get the man killing rabbits, Webb." He recognised the bland expression on Webb's face. "As you very well knew!"

"Yessir. But the place does need cleanin', and they need to earn a bit o' money. Starvin', they was."

"How many brats are there?"

"Four, sir. And their cottage needs fixin'. Leaks like a bleedin' sieve when it rains." He eyed Matthew warily. "Thought they could move into the stables in a day or so."

"*We're* in the stables, Webb," Matthew pointed out.

"When they've done dustin' in the 'ouse you can move in there. Bigger rooms," he added encouragingly. "And we reckons we can see daylight up one of the chimneys in the big 'all, so we can get some fires goin'."

"So we're going to be over-run with Jackson, his wife and four children?"

Webb said nothing.

"Oh, very well," Matthew conceded. "As long as Mrs Jackson can cook!" He looked at the map in his hand as another thought occurred. "Just how many tenants are you planning on housing here?"

"Just the Jacksons, sir. Couple of the others went and found some work on the squire's estate, some of 'em went to Gloucester, some to Bristol. Temp'ry, like." He paused. "Mebbe some of the womenfolk can be paid to 'elp with the cleanin'?"

"Good idea."

"Nice bit of rabbit stew for dinner, sir," Webb added.

Matthew groaned, and went to put a bucket of water near the fire to take the chill off it before he had a wash.

Late in the afternoon Charlotte looked up as footsteps scrunched on the gravel path. A shabbily dressed woman with a couple of small children passed the parlour window on the way to knock at the back door. Charlotte heard Mary letting them in. No-one came knocking on the parlour door, but as her concentration was already broken, she decided to take a break and get a cup of tea. If her curiosity was satisfied at the same time, well, so be it.

The woman stopped talking when she entered the room. Charlotte vaguely remembered her as one of the tenants on the Birchanger estate. The woman had asked about sick children a couple of times, not being able to pay the apothecary's fee.

"Mrs Jackson's come for advice," Mary said, unnecessarily. A slight turn of her head told Charlotte that her opinion would be helpful, so she pulled out a chair and sat down.

"He said we could only stay if I could do the cooking," Mrs Jackson said.

"Who said?" Charlotte asked, rather bewildered at being thrust into the middle of the story.

"His lordship. Lord Tillson."

"The cooking?" Charlotte asked. "At the Hall? Didn't he bring a cook with him?"

Mrs Jackson shook her head. "There don't seem to be more'n the two of 'em," she said. "Mr Webb, he's bin cooking, but now he says I've to do it if we want to stay. Otherwise he'll turn us out!" She started sobbing, rubbing her eyes with one corner of the shabby shawl draped over her shoulders.

"Turn you out?" Charlotte was shocked. "But he can't just—"

"We're a long way behind on the rent," Mrs Jackson sniffed. "My George hasn't had no work for near on a year."

"You can stay if you do the cooking?" Charlotte asked, not understanding the problem.

"I can't cook for a lord!" Mrs Jackson wailed. "I can cook stew, and porridge, and fry an egg—but that's not what a lord should be eatin'!"

"Don't worry, we'll sort something out," Mary said comfortingly, putting an arm around the woman. The two children were sitting on the floor by the range, silent and wide-eyed. Charlotte decided tea and biscuits were in order, and put the kettle on while Mary tried to soothe Mrs Jackson.

Davie appeared as soon as the biscuit tin was taken down. Deacon came in after him, as if the two of them had been doing something together. Charlotte was curious, but now was not the time to enquire. Deacon took a good look at the scene in the kitchen then retreated, saying something to Davie, who paused only long enough to grab a couple of biscuits before following him.

By the time the tea was brewing, Mrs Jackson had calmed down a little. "It ain't just knowin' what to do," she said, still sounding a little tearful. "But there's nothin' there!"

Mary and Charlotte glanced at each other, puzzled. "What do you mean, nothing there?" Mary asked. "No food?"

"There's a bit of food," she said. "But there's only one cooking pot and one knife. Mr Webb said I should make a list of things and he'd take me into Bath to buy them. But I don't know what to get for a lord's kitchen!"

Not to mention not being able to write, Charlotte suspected.

"Now, don't worry," Mary said, patting the woman's shoulder. "First thing is to sort out dinner for tonight. In a minute you're going to tell me what food's there, then I'll explain what to do with it."

Mrs Jackson sniffed and nodded.

"Then I'll come up to the Hall tomorrow," Mary went on. "I'll help you make a list for Mr Webb. And tonight, me and Mrs Captain will have a chat about what to do."

Charlotte poured the tea out, gave everyone a couple of biscuits, then resolutely took her own cup back to her parlour to carry on working. Mary had the situation well in hand.

"Gave her some onions and lard," Mary said over dinner. "There's enough else there for one meal, by the sounds of it. Explained what to do. She's got a reasonable head on her shoulders—but no experience. I'll go up there when I've finished in the bakery tomorrow. Make that list she was talking about—"

"And have a good look around?" Charlotte asked with a laugh.

"I might!" Mary said. "I was thinking I could take Sally along. Time she knew more'n just managing in a small place like this."

Charlotte nodded. "Good idea."

She finished her dinner in peace, as Davie talked animatedly to Deacon rather than chattering to her. Or rather, Davie asked questions and Deacon tried to answer them in between bites of his dinner. They were talking about Deacon's life at sea, and Charlotte realised that this might be the first time Davie had met anyone whose life was different from the people in the village and the surrounding countryside.

There *were* things she could not do for her son. Mary deciding to employ Deacon had been a very good decision indeed.

CHAPTER 14

*T*he following evening Charlotte made sure that Davie sat next to Deacon again at dinner, wanting to ask Mary about her visit to Birchanger without Davie asking questions.

"What's Birchanger Hall like inside?" she asked in a low voice, once everyone had a full plate and Davie was safely concentrating on his food.

"Empty and filthy."

"Empty?"

Mary nodded. "Nell Jackson was right about there being only one pot. Someone's stripped the place."

"Where's Lord Tillson staying, then? Is he living up there?"

"Seems to be. I didn't see him, only that man Webb. Sergeant Webb, or ex-Sergeant, mebbe." Mary's eyes narrowed as she said his name. Charlotte was about to ask what was wrong, but Mary glanced at the other end of the table and back, shaking her head slightly before Charlotte could speak.

Charlotte glanced that way herself. Davie was now safely involved in a low-voiced conversation that seemed to be about some project he had in the stream.

"Far as I know," Mary went on, "there's only his lordship and this

Webb there. And the Jacksons. He's got the Jacksons trying to clean up the place. Nell can manage cooking for them, Webb said they don't need nothin' fancy. But once he gets hisself sorted out with proper staff she won't be able to manage. Nor yet if he starts entertaining other folks."

"So what did you do?" Charlotte asked.

"Wrote a long shopping list," Mary said. "Pity I can't go tomorrow —it'd be fun spending someone else's money!"

"Go where?"

"Bath." Mary frowned. "I did say they could get a lot of stuff in Edgecombe, but Webb said if he had to go to Bath anyway he may as well get it all there."

"Did you explain about the money owed?"

"I tried, but I dunno if he was listening." Mary hesitated. "You might have to try speaking to his lordship again."

Charlotte grimaced. "What about Sally, how did she get on?"

"Good. Seemed to get the idea of what's wanted for cooking for more than just us. I did wonder…" She broke off and shook her head. "I'll talk to you later."

Looking down the table, she made what she knew would be a welcome interruption. "Who wants some bread and butter pudding?"

After dinner Deacon took one of his books off the shelf to read, and Davie asked Charlotte if she had any large sheets of paper.

"No, but you could paste some smaller pieces together. What do you need it for?"

"Mathematics," Davie said.

It seemed odd to Charlotte, but she went for some paper and Mary found a pot of paste. They left him working on the kitchen table while Mary followed Charlotte into the parlour.

"All right, what didn't you tell me?" Charlotte asked as they sat down.

"I was thinking of mebbe Sally getting a job there, now she's ready. She's learnt all she can here. You was too?"

Charlotte nodded. "But you don't think so now?"

"No. Mrs Jackson can manage fine, only cooking for the two of them and her own family. And there's that Webb as well." Disapproval was obvious in her tone.

Charlotte waited.

"Most impertinent!" Mary said.

"Admired you, did he?" Charlotte couldn't help smiling. Mary was only a couple of years older than she was, and still remarkably pretty, with her gently curling blonde hair and trim figure.

"Admiring I can allow," Mary said tartly. "Feeling the goods is something else!" Then she smiled in satisfaction. "I reckon he'll have a right good shiner in a day or two."

Charlotte laughed. "I'll wager that surprised him."

"Oh, yes!"

"Have you ever thought of marrying again?" Charlotte asked, suddenly curious. It was not a topic they discussed often.

"I was used to thinking burying three was enough," Mary admitted. "Not to mention the babes. But I might be changing my mind." She looked wistful. "Mebbe children wouldn't be so sickly in this climate."

She just shook her head when Charlotte demanded to know who she had her eye on, and said she had mending to do. Charlotte debated with herself whether to try to get some more work done, opting instead to sit in the warmth of the kitchen with the others and read. It would soon be time to send Davie to bed, in any case.

Davie had his piece of paper spread out on the kitchen table, and was carefully marking angles and making measurements with a ruler. Occasionally he stopped to scratch his head.

"Mr Hayes set you this work?" Charlotte asked. Mr Hayes was the tutor the squire employed.

"Um…" Davie finished a line he was drawing before he replied properly. "Not exactly."

"*How* not exactly?" Charlotte pulled up a chair. "Davie, that question can be answered with a 'yes' or a 'no'!"

"No, then." Davie put down his pencil reluctantly. "When I came back from Northridge this… today… I helped the major do some measuring in the fields. I wanted to see if I could do a proper map."

"Who is the major?"

"Met him in the woods a couple of days ago when I was walking home. I think he works on the estate."

"Birchanger?"

"Yes."

Charlotte frowned. Perhaps the major was an estate steward? That seemed likely if he was surveying the fields. She glanced at Mary with a raised eyebrow, but Mary shrugged and shook her head.

"What's he like?"

"Old," Davie said. "He doesn't talk to me like I'm an idiot, though," he added with approval.

"Who talks to you like you're an idiot?" Charlotte asked, surprised. "I don't, do I?"

"Only sometimes," Davie muttered. "When I'm in trouble."

"Ah. I think that may be allowed," Charlotte said seriously, ignoring Mary stifling her laughter in the corner. "Who else?"

"Sir Vincent. Last time he came he patted me on the head and told me to run along and play."

"Hmm."

Sir Vincent hadn't called for several months, although she'd seen him at the squire's once or twice. That reminded her—she must write to his mother to say she could not attend the Christmas festivities this year—not when she was less than a month into mourning.

Matthew's breakfast was bacon and eggs again, but this morning Mrs Jackson had cooked it. Although he still wasn't hungry, it didn't take much effort to finish the plate of food put before him, wiping up the remains of the egg yolks with a piece of fresh bread covered in thick butter. Last night's stew, too, while far from the best he had ever tasted, had at least been recognisable as cooked rabbit and vegetables, rather than the formless mush Webb usually produced.

It was Tilly, the oldest Jackson child, rather than her mother, who came to collect his dishes. He put her at about the same age as Davie, perhaps ten or so. She was skinny, her lank hair neatly tied back and her clothing ragged, but clean. Well, not completely clean, but the marks on it didn't have the ground-in look of never-washed clothes; likely they were the result of yesterday's work.

"Where's your mother?" he asked. When she did not answer, he said more gently, "Come, girl. I don't bite, you know."

"Sorry, me lord. She gone off with Mr Webb."

"Where to?" Come to think of it, he hadn't seen Webb since yesterday morning.

"They've gone to Bath on the wagon, sir."

He waited, and she went on, getting over her initial shyness as she talked.

"It be a powerful long way! Mrs Sergeant come up yesterday, an' Ma's got a long list of things to buy. Leastways, Mrs Sergeant wrote it out, and Mr Webb, he said he could read it."

"What kind of things?" He wondered who Mrs Sergeant was, but Tilly was already answering his question.

"Pots and pans, she said she had to get. And knives. And food." The girl's eyes went big at the thought of buying a wagon-load of food.

Matthew felt shame wash over him. He'd been moping about the estate for days, bemoaning his fate, while this family, and no doubt others, didn't even have enough to eat. He managed to keep his thoughts from appearing on his face, and realised that the girl was still talking.

"... not proper clean, but ma said they'd do for now. Mr Webb said maybe you'd like the front room cos it's got lots of windows. He said it ain't a proper bedroom, but the downstairs is better for now."

"What are you going to do today?" he asked, when she paused for breath.

"I bin tellin' you, sir," she said sharply, and then put her hand over her mouth in dismay, cringing back slightly.

"I do apologise for not paying attention," he said seriously, and she relaxed again. How had the dour Jackson, and his equally untalkative wife, managed to produce a child like this? "Perhaps you could show me what you and your mother have managed to do in the house so far?"

He followed her into the main building, Reena at his heels, then waited while she deposited his cup and plates in the scullery. Without its film of dust and grime, and with clean windows letting in the weak winter light, the place looked much better. The walls still needed new limewash, and the wooden shelves opposite the range needed a good sandpapering and a new coat of paint, but it was usable. The kitchen was in a similar state—parts of it could do with a good scrub, but it was no longer looking like an abandoned dungeon rather than a place to prepare food.

He moved his thoughts firmly away from that analogy.

"We just done the kitchen yesterday," Tilly said, leading him through the corridor and the hall, into the dining room. This room still had its dust in place, as Reena found out when she sniffed into the corners and sneezed.

"Mr Webb said to leave this one," she excused herself, and opened the door into the main hall. "We ain't had time to do the windows in 'ere, but Mr Webb 'ad a fire yesterday. A right big one," she said, her face lighting. "We swept it, like, but I reckon it needs another go."

Matthew reckoned it needed another go, too, but at least his feet weren't stirring up clouds of dust. Across the hall, Tilly went into the twin of what would become the dining room. The shutters were already open, but the light highlighted the cobwebs and dust, and the grimy outlines on the painted walls above the wainscoting where pictures had once hung.

"Mr Webb said as this'll be your room to start with. He said we are to sweep out today, and try cleanin' the windows." She looked up at him, and he realised she was waiting for his approval.

"Very good." Who was he to gainsay Webb? "Have you got every-thing you need?"

She shook her head. "We could do with more brushes and cloths and such, but Ma'll get some today."

"Do you know if Mr Webb tried the fireplace in here?" The room felt cold, with the strong smell of damp that permeated the whole house. The sun, if it ever came out from behind the thick clouds, would not be shining through these windows until later. Matthew could almost feel the cold seeping into his bones from the walls, despite his warm clothing.

"He said he was goin' to get someone to sort out all the chimneys, sir. He said best not to light any more fires." She didn't complain, but there was a droop to her shoulders.

"Have we plenty of wood, do you know?"

"Dad brought in some dead trees yesterday, and Mr Webb chopped some of it up. Dad's gone off for a bit more now."

Another wave of shame. He'd spent yesterday taking bearings and measuring distances, a familiar routine needing just enough concentration to stop other thoughts intruding, but requiring no decisions more complicated than which edge of the field to measure first. While he'd been occupied with that, Webb and the Jackson family had been doing things that were immediately useful. At least he could manage to light a fire.

"Right then. You and your brother and sister bring some wood in, and we'll get another big fire going in the hall." Tilly looked a little more cheerful. "If you leave this door open, this room might warm up a bit. But if you wash the floor in the hall first you'll be a bit warmer. How does that sound?"

"That's a good plan, thank you sir. My lord, I mean." She blushed.

"Excellent."

Matthew paused in the stable doorway, wondering what he should do next. Following Tilly's tour of the ground floor, he'd warmed himself up by chopping the rest of the wood Jackson had brought in the day before, stacking most of it next to the fire now roaring in one of the hall fireplaces. He could dig the garden again, he supposed, although that was one of the least urgent jobs.

He glanced at the grey clouds, deciding to see what he could do with all the measurements he'd taken yesterday. He wished Webb had told him he was off to Bath again; he would have added drawing paper to his list. In the meantime he could use the measurements to check and amend the existing plan for now. He went back into the stable office, threw some more wood on the fire, and unrolled the plans.

Three hours later Tilly arrived with a plate of bread, ham, and cheese. Matthew was surprised how the time had flown. He'd managed to work indoors for half of the morning, without once feeling trapped, concentrating on transforming measured angles and distances into accurate shapes on paper. Now he'd been interrupted, however, he realised his head felt stuffy—probably a result of the close air and a few too many alcoholic additions to the coffee he'd been drinking. Thanking Tilly, he waited until she'd gone before giving Reena half of the food.

He put water on the small fire to boil, then made fresh coffee. Checking that the ink on the maps was dry, he rolled them back up. He contemplated examining the estate ledgers, but although this morning had gone well, it was enough indoor work for one day. Besides, trying to puzzle out crabbed handwriting and work out costs and profits was not the same thing as the familiar routine of map making. He was going to need an estate steward, but finding a trust-worthy one would not be easy.

He'd have some coffee, then perhaps dig some more bramble roots in the kitchen garden, whatever the weather was doing.

A horseman approached the house as he was opening the door into the kitchen garden. The temptation to hide in the garden, as he had done when the woman from the village had come, was strong, but there was no Webb this time to deny him. He sighed, put down the spade, and walked around to the front of the house.

He recognised the cheerful face of Joshua Kellet as the rider approached.

"Mr Kellet," Matthew said, hoping he didn't sound too grumpy. "What brings you so far?"

"Various bits of business, my lord." Kellet dismounted, looking up at the house with interest. "It's always good to actually see a place," he added. "Makes it all seem real, not just an idea on paper."

"And does the reality match your expectations?" Matthew asked.

"Oh, no," Kellet said with a smile. "I've found that whatever you think a place, or even a person, might be like before you set eyes on them, the reality is always different." He looked Matthew in the eye. "Sometimes better, sometimes worse."

Kellet looked up at the house again. "I have to admit to my paper version being little more than debts and problems."

Matthew gave a grunt of agreement.

"But I never expected it to be such a beautiful building."

Matthew raised his eyebrows in surprise, turning to follow Kellet's gaze.

"Oh, I can see it needs repairs," Kellet said. "But underneath the ivy it looks to be a splendid example of Elizabethan architecture."

"You are an expert on architecture?" Matthew suppressed his irritation with the man's unrelenting cheerfulness, annoyed with himself for feeling that way.

"No, no. But in my business there are often buildings to be bought and sold, or argued over in court. I take an interest."

Shaking off his annoyance, Matthew finally remembered his manners. "It was good of you to come. I hope you had a good journey?" He led the way to the stables.

"Yes, thank you," Kellet said. "I took the mail, and managed to hire this fellow in Bath. Nice to get a good ride, really. I don't see much of the countryside now I'm based in London."

"I must apologise for the state of the place," Matthew said, showing him where to put the horse and then ushering him into the stable office. "I'm afraid this room is the most civilised part at the moment. Have you had lunch? I think there might be—"

"Oh, don't worry about all that," Kellet said, waving a hand and looking around with interest. Matthew mentally winced, looking at the place with new eyes. He'd been here a week now, and the only furniture was still the battered table and the mismatched chairs.

How much effort would it have taken to send to Bath for more furniture?

"Just as well you didn't buy any new furniture, really," Kellet added, and Matthew wondered if the man was a mind-reader.

"Oh?"

"I know where most of it is, but I haven't seen it yet." Kellet glanced around doubtfully, his cheerful expression slipping slightly. "Do you wish to talk here? There's quite a lot to get through." He indicated the fat satchel he carried. "I've taken a room for the night at the Hare and Hounds in Edgecombe, we could talk in the private parlour there?"

Matthew rubbed his unshaven chin. "You go back. If you've come straight here from the mail you must need a bit of a rest. I'll follow you down in half an hour."

"May I look around the house instead? It would be helpful for me to see the state it was left in. I'm happy to show myself around."

Matthew, pleased to get out of viewing the damp stains and cracked window panes again, agreed. He had washed, shaved, and changed and was just saddling the mare when Kellet reappeared.

"It'll be a nice place once it's clean and repaired," Kellet said. "Not very big, mind, but I don't suppose you need a big place at the moment. And there's always Farleton Manor."

Once they were in the inn's private parlour with tankards of ale in front of them, Kellet started by giving Matthew details of the banking arrangements he'd made for him in Bath. Then he took more papers out of his satchel and appeared unsure how to proceed.

"The furniture?" Matthew prompted.

"Ah, yes. Well, in a way that's linked to the disrepair of the house. I've all the details here if you want to see them."

Matthew shook his head.

"Well, to summarise then: Cyril Southey, the last baron, never married. He left all his unentailed property to his sister's family. His sister died many years ago, as did her daughter. Her son is still alive, the late baron's nephew, and there are a total of four great-nieces and nephews. The unentailed property was an estate in Wiltshire which has now been sold, and the proceeds divided between the five people I've mentioned."

"You've found all this out very quickly," Matthew said, impressed.

Kellet looked slightly embarrassed. "Not really, my lord. Mr Gleason found another box of papers and sent them over to me. It seems that a Mr Daniel Fulbeck, who I think is the son of the niece, was in communication with Mr Gleason about six months after the old baron died. He explained that he was going to take the contents of the house for safekeeping, to stop them being stolen or ruined by damp. He also explained what had happened to the rest of the property inherited by his branch of the family."

"Why would he bother doing that?"

"I'm not sure. I intend to call on him on my way home to enquire. But it occurred to me that, in law, the owner of an entailed estate is required to maintain it properly for his descendants. You might be able to take the other beneficiaries to court to obtain some of the money and land they inherited in order to bring Birchanger back to the state it should have been in."

"How does... Fulbeck?"

Kellet nodded.

"How does his explanation that the rest of the land has been sold prevent me doing that?"

"It doesn't prevent it, my lord. But it is a strong hint that the money has been spent or dispersed, so any court case could well cost you more than you would gain from it."

Matthew sighed. "I suppose at least I don't need to refurnish the whole place."

"I was going to ask you what you wanted me to do about that," Kellet said. "I don't imagine you want all the furniture until you've had some repairs done? Unfortunately there was no inventory made when the old lord died, so I cannot say at the moment what furniture and other goods are with Fulbeck."

"Nor how much of it there was originally," Matthew said cynically.

He thought for a moment. "I'd like to have whatever there is in the way of kitchen equipment, if he took that as well, and enough furniture for a bedroom for me, perhaps with a desk, if there is one. And any smaller beds for servants and so on—at least seven, if they've got them."

Kellet noted the requests in a little book, then put it with some of the papers on the table and stowed them back in his satchel.

"What else?" Matthew asked.

"Farleton Manor," Kellet said. "The Mayhews were not happy about handing over the responsibility for that. I had to show your written orders to a magistrate to get them to hand over all the paperwork." He paused, a frown crossing his face. "I also had an irate interview with your brother. Your *half*-brother, Charles," he amended.

"What did he want?"

"It was unclear," Kellet said. "I assured him the allowances your father had arranged for him and your stepmother would continue for now, but that did not pacify him."

"And have you any suppositions?"

Kellet hesitated.

"Spit it out, man," Matthew said. "You must realise there is little love lost between us. I'd rather you just spoke your mind."

"Very well. The Mayhews took several more days to produce the estate accounts after the magistrate ordered them returned." He noticed Matthew's frown. "This *is* relevant, my lord."

"Sorry. Please continue."

"I need to go through them in more detail, but it appears that a larger amount than I would have expected has been spent on maintenance and improvements at Farleton. At the town house as well."

"The town house had certainly been redecorated since I last saw it, but I don't know how long ago."

Kellet nodded. "You or I should visit Farleton to check the detailed ledgers at the estate. Also check that the repairs and so on that are listed in the accounts were actually carried out."

"You are accusing the Mayhews of fraud?"

Kellet shook his head. "You asked for a supposition, my lord. This is pure speculation at the moment, and I have not mentioned it to anyone else, but the accounts for the last few years also looked remarkably... uniform."

"Uniform?"

Kellet put several sets of papers in front of Matthew and spread them out on the table, pointing out specifics. "The ink all looks exactly the same. The handwriting, too."

Matthew glanced through them briefly. "The same person—the steward, possibly—would have done the accounts for Mayhew each time," he said. "That isn't suspicious, surely?"

"Most people's handwriting varies a little from time to time."

Matthew frowned, remembering Charles' mention of needing a larger allowance. "Are you saying one of the Mayhews colluded with my stepfamily to take more than they were entitled to, and have forged new accounts to hide the fact?"

"I'm not saying they have done so, my lord. I'm putting the idea forward as one possible explanation for why the Mayhews took so long to produce the accounts. It would probably also involve the steward at Farleton, if such a thing has been going on."

Matthew rubbed a hand across his face. One more thing to deal with, and not a pleasant thing, if Kellet were correct. His relations with his stepfamily were already strained.

"My lord?"

Matthew started as Kellet spoke, and realised he had been silent for some time. "I suppose I need to go to Farleton then?" he asked, his lack of enthusiasm obvious in his voice.

"I don't think it is particularly urgent, my lord," said Kellet. "If I am correct, they have already had time to forge any ledgers and so on. There is little to gain by rushing." He hesitated. "I could go, but I have other commitments. Besides, even with a letter from you, I fear I may not have the authority to find out what you would need to know if the steward or other members of the staff decide not to co-operate." He put the remaining papers back into his satchel. About to speak, he hesitated again.

Matthew raised his eyebrows. "What else?"

"I was just going to suggest, my lord, that if you are to be living at Birchanger some of the time, it might be better to concentrate on keeping the building from deteriorating any further before turning your attention to Farleton. I will write to the steward to say no more repairs are to be carried out without authorisation from you—"

"From *you*," Matthew stated.

Kellet nodded. "If you wish, my lord. The same for the town house? No further redecoration or refurnishing?"

"Yes, please."

"The expenditure on food and so on at the townhouse also seems to be rather high, and your family are all routinely outspending their allowances. Including Lieutenant Southam, it appears, although he has somewhat less scope to do so while he is overseas."

Kellet noted Matthew's expression. "I think that can wait for a month or two," he added. "The current levels of expenditure could continue for another year or so without causing any great difficulties."

"Thank you Mr Kellet. You have done exceedingly well in a very short time."

"My pleasure, my lord."

"There is one more matter. The tradesmen in Edgecombe refused to extend credit when my man attempted to buy supplies, claiming I already owed them money."

Kellet's eyebrows lifted. "Interesting," he said. "There was nothing in the paperwork Gleason gave me to indicate any spending in the year prior to your arrival."

"If you could make some enquiries before you leave in the morning?"

"By all means, my lord."

"My thanks." Matthew waved a hand. "For everything. Now, can I stand you a meal?"

Kellet agreed, with a small smile; Matthew smiled ruefully in return. "I'm standing you dinner anyway, aren't I?" he said.

"Expenses, my lord. Yes, I'm afraid so."

"Well, make the most of it!"

The dinner was good, as was the wine, and although the two men had little in common they passed an agreeable couple of hours with Matthew reminiscing about the Farleton estate and Kellet sharing anecdotes from his own childhood in Kent. But at the end of the meal Matthew was glad to get out of the cosy parlour and back into the open air for the ride home.

CHAPTER 15

*S*words stabbed through Matthew's head. Some soon-to-be-court-martialled idiot was shouting at him, holding a lantern in his face. Even with his eyes screwed shut, the light burnt.

"Coffee, sir?" Webb bellowed again.

Matthew swore. He gingerly opened one eye to see that the blinding light was a thin shaft of pale sunlight shining through the stable door. The smell of the fresh coffee wafted towards him, and his insides nearly rebelled.

"Water," he managed to mutter, and thankfully Webb took the coffee away. He came back and handed Matthew a mug of water, ordering him to drink it.

Matthew lay in misery for a while, but must have drifted off to sleep again. When he next opened his eyes, thick clouds covered the patch of sky he could see. Now it felt as if his skull was only being gently squeezed. The taste in his mouth…

He fumbled around until he found his flask, and took a quick mouthful. A bit more water, another mouthful of brandy, and he felt as if he might be able to remain upright if he stood up.

Perhaps he wouldn't try just yet.

He sat up cautiously and his head swam. Why did he feel so bad?

Most mornings he just had a thick head and a dry mouth when he awoke—if he'd managed to sleep at all.

Yesterday's discussion and dinner with Joshua Kellet returned in bits and pieces. The dinner hadn't been the problem—he had been no more inebriated than usual afterwards. It had been when he got back, he recalled dimly. He'd started thinking about his family again, and that train of thought had led him to the subject of women in general, and to more brandy.

Serena. He had some memories of his mother—of her laughing, playing, and singing songs with him. Then there was no mother or new baby brother, only a father who kept himself to himself and drank too much. Not that he could blame him for that, he thought, eyeing his own flask. When Serena appeared, his father became happier again, as far as a seven-year-old boy could tell. Serena, however, wasn't a replacement mother; far from it.

After his father's remarriage, the closest thing he'd had to a mother was Mrs Scovell, the nanny. Mrs Scovell was firm and fair, but the limited affection she felt for her charge could not replace what he remembered of his mother. And when Charles was born, Mrs Scovell had been required to share her attentions.

He rubbed his face, looking around. Webb had left a cup of coffee within reach. It was cold, but drinking it seemed a better option than getting up and making fresh, or having to shout loudly enough to summon Webb back.

Other women in his past had wandered through his mind. A few short liaisons, ending by mutual agreement. Pleasant memories, most of them. He sipped his coffee, lips twisting as he recalled one that wasn't.

Annette Lisburn, wife of one of his best friends. She had been bored with the life in India, with the social events and charitable works that other officers' wives used to fill their time. Matthew wasn't the first she'd propositioned, but he thought he may have been the first man who had rejected her. Politely at first, but she'd taken that as a challenge. She was trying again when Freddie had come across them. He had believed her when she cried and told how

Matthew was trying to seduce her. So that was the end of that friend-ship. And this memory had led him to finish off the brandy in his flask.

He drank the rest of the coffee. The usual can of washing water stood by the fire. He rose, slowly and carefully; his head would not appreciate any sudden movements. Splashing water over his face helped to relieve his aching eyes, but also reminded him of those women in the hospital: officers' wives, doing their charitable duty by visiting the sick. The ones who made small talk for five minutes, or bathed a face or two, but could not look directly at the patients with head wounds. Had they really believed they were helping? They had tutted in sympathy over the bandages around his infected wrists, avid curiosity in their eyes. *So* sympathetic, on the surface, but so, so curious about all the details.

His recollection of those women must have been what prompted his opening of a new bottle, he thought. He'd eventually passed out thinking of Serena and her attempts to poison his relationship with his father. He shook his head at the memory, then wished he hadn't. He looked down at himself; he'd slept in his clothes, and felt sticky. He dipped his hands in the can of water and splashed his face and neck again, then went over to his trunk. A clean shirt, at least, might help. Then he'd venture into the kitchen for coffee, and maybe something to eat.

Webb entered the stables as he was pulling his last clean shirt over his head.

"Feelin' better, sir?"

Matthew grunted, noticing that Webb had a black eye. "What happened to you?" he asked, taking the proffered cup of coffee. Webb hesitated, and Matthew added, "Don't say someone hit you—I can see that!"

"I… er… well, my attentions to a young lady weren't welcome, sir." He looked embarrassed.

"Ha—already has a husband?"

"Nossir."

"Her sweetheart objected?"

154

"No, sir. Er… *she* 'it me."

"Big lass, eh?" Matthew couldn't help smiling.

"Not really, sir." Webb held his hand horizontal, level with his nose. "One of the Mrs MacKinnons, sir."

Matthew laughed, in spite of the effect it had on his aching head. "Misses MacKinnons?" he asked, when he regained his breath. "Who are they?" MacKinnons? That was the name young Davie had given him. So, Davie's mother was a Miss MacKinnons? He had said he had no father.

"Live in the village, sir. One of 'em came up to write a list of things to get for the kitchen."

"Ah—I've some news on that." Matthew finished his coffee while he told Webb about the furniture. The coffee, and the laugh at Webb's expense, had made him feel a little better, and he recalled part of his discussion with Kellet the previous evening.

"I asked Kellet to enquire in the village about the money we supposedly owe," he told Webb.

"Er, I reckon the Mrs MacKinnons might know summat about that, sir."

He hesitated. Matthew was surprised to see his face start to turn red.

"I… er… I could ask there, sir?"

"Good idea."

Webb seemed about to say something else, but he just turned on his heel and headed back to the kitchen.

Matthew finished dressing and considered his options. His stomach had settled, more or less, and his headache had subsided to a dull ache. A little gentle physical activity might help? He could chop some more wood for the fires, perhaps. He grimaced as he held his right hand in front of his face, observing the tremor. This might not be the best of times to start wielding an axe. Muck out the stables? A cursory glance at the stalls showed that Webb or someone else had already taken care of that, and besides, the smell…

He settled on a bit of bramble-clearing. His clothing was already a mess, so he didn't bother to change. The physical work kept him warm, but did nothing to stop his thoughts returning to his loving family.

Charles. It hadn't seemed long until Charles, Mama's little darling who could do no wrong, was old enough to want things. Usually things that belonged to his older brother. And what Charles wanted, Charles got. Strangely, Serena hadn't been as doting on her other offspring.

And Richard... how had he fared after Matthew left for India? Charles had been twelve then, and Richard only nine. Charles used to hit his siblings when he didn't get his way, until Matthew stepped in and gave him a thrashing Charles hadn't forgotten for years. The beating Matthew had received from his father as punishment had been painful, but he didn't regret his action at all—not at the time, and not now. But there'd been ten years of dear Serena's influence since then, so he wasn't hopeful that Richard would be any better than the other two.

He had enough bramble shoots cut now to make another bonfire. He needed kindling and his tinder box from the stables, but Webb came through the garden door before he reached it.

"Someone to see you, sir," he said.

Matthew, his head and stomach still feeling delicate, and his thoughts still on his family, told him to get rid of the visitor in language suited more to the stables than to a drawing room. A moment later he realised he had heard Webb talking to someone else.

Going over to the doorway, he saw Webb standing by the corner of the house, watching a horseman ride away down the drive.

"Who was it?" he called.

Webb came over. "Card, sir."

He handed over a piece of pasteboard, inscribed with the name Arthur Thompson. That rang a bell.

"Local squire, I think, sir."

"He heard?"

"'Fraid so, sir."

Matthew swore. The father of the other lad he'd met in the woods. Yet another good first impression made with the local people.

"Said you wasn't feelin' well, sir," Webb added, carefully not meeting Matthew's eyes.

Matthew swore again, and morosely went back to uprooting brambles.

~

Charlotte tried to ignore the knock on the front door, hoping someone else would answer it and say that she was not at home to visitors. The knocking came again, louder this time. She sighed. Mary was still at the bakery, although she should be back soon. Deacon? She shook her head. Probably digging the garden or doing something on the roof, as the day was dry. But Davie...?

Whoever it was knocked a third time. Charlotte put her pencil down, reaching the parlour door just as Davie appeared from the kitchen.

"Sorry, Mama," he said. "I was concentrating..."

"Never mind. Put the kettle on in case we want to give them tea." Charlotte opened the door.

Webb stood at attention just beyond the step, holding his hat under his arm. His uniform, although very faded and shabby, looked as if it had been recently cleaned, and his hair was neatly combed. But, as Mary had predicted, he did have a rather splendid black eye. Charlotte pressed her lips together; it would not be polite to laugh at him.

"Sergeant Webb," she said, blocking the doorway and resisting the temptation to cross her arms—that would look too much like Mary on the warpath.

"Ma'am," he said. "I called to see the other Mrs MacKinnon, but, if possible, I would like to ask you something as well."

Charlotte regarded him for a moment. It hadn't been his fault Lord Tillson had been so rude when she called, but it *had* been his choice to bother Mary. "What do you want with Mrs MacKinnon?" she asked sternly.

He hesitated.

"To apologise, perhaps?" she asked.

He looked embarrassed. "Er, yes, ma'am."

"Very well then, you'd better come in."

She led the way back into her parlour, not wanting Davie to over-hear her discussing Webb's habits with women. She sat at her desk, turning the chair so she faced him.

"At ease, Sergeant," she said, after a moment.

He looked surprised at the military term, but relaxed a little.

"Mrs MacKinnon is not at home, but she will be back shortly. What did you want?"

"Everything all right, ma'am?" Deacon knocked on the parlour door, opening it without waiting for permission to enter.

He looked Webb up and down with no change in expression, and Webb stared back. Charlotte's lips twitched—they looked like two dogs measuring each other up before deciding whether to fight, although that was probably rather unfair on Deacon.

"Yes, thank you, Deacon. Sergeant Webb has one or two things to discuss with me."

"I'll be in the kitchen, ma'am, so call if you need anything."

Charlotte nodded. Deacon returned to the kitchen, pulling the door to behind him but not quite closing it. She heard his footsteps along the corridor to the kitchen. He was not trying to eavesdrop, just making sure she could be heard if she called.

"Mrs MacKinnon is a respectable widow, Sergeant Webb," Charlotte stated.

"Yes, ma'am. I know that now. I want to apologise to 'er, ma'am. I'd never 'ave done it if I thought—"

"If you thought she was respectable? Tell me, Sergeant, do you do the same to Mrs Jackson?"

Webb opened his mouth, then closed it again, shaking his head instead of replying.

"Because she has a husband?"

He nodded.

"Sally… you recall Sally? She was with Mrs MacKinnon when she visited Birchanger."

Webb nodded again.

"She's a maid of all work," Charlotte went on. "Not someone who runs a business and owns a house, like Mrs MacKinnon."

Webb looked surprised at this, but still said nothing.

"Does Sally count as respectable?"

Webb stared at her for a moment, then drew himself up to attention again, staring rigidly ahead. "Ma'am, I should not be doin' that to any woman, unless she allows it."

"Very good, Sergeant." She gestured to a chair. "You may take a seat." Webb sat down gingerly on the edge of the chair, placing his hat on the floor. "What did you wish to speak to me about?"

"I come to apologise to you, ma'am, for Lord Tillson."

"He sent you?"

"Er, not exactly, ma'am."

Charlotte waited patiently.

Webb looked at her, appeared to recognise authority, and gave in. "'E don't know I'm 'ere, ma'am. I thought if I knew what you was wantin' to see 'im about, I might be able to 'elp."

"Unpaid bills, Sergeant Webb."

He frowned. "Are you sayin' Lord Tillson owes you money too, ma'am?"

"No. But he owes money to several tradesmen in the village. They asked me if I could discuss it with Lord Tillson."

"They said they was owed money when I tried to buy food. But that's not possible, ma'am. We only got 'ere last week."

"The goods they require payment for were apparently supplied..." She'd forgotten the details, but she'd made some notes before she'd gone up to Birchanger. "Last April," she said, finding the jottings in her notebook.

"No, ma'am. It weren't this Lord Tillson. 'E were in India in April. We only got to Portsmouth a few weeks ago."

"Well it can't have been the last Lord Tillson," Charlotte pointed out. "Unless his ghost was spending money!"

Webb looked thoughtful.

"You know something, Sergeant?"

"No, ma'am. But I've got an idea. But I'd best ask the... Lord

Tillson about it."

"I hope you can sort it out, Sergeant. The local tradesmen were rather hoping they could supply Birchanger again. It can't be convenient for you to have to go further for supplies."

"Yes, ma'am. Do you have a note of what they say they's owed?"

Charlotte handed him the batch of invoices she'd been given. Webb looked through them briefly then, glancing at Charlotte for permission, folded them and tucked them into a pocket.

"Thank you, ma'am."

"You may wait for Mrs MacKinnon in the kitchen, if you wish."

"Thank you, ma'am."

Rather than going back to her futile attempts to draw a recognisable fox, Charlotte sat in thought. Either Webb was lying, or someone had been posing as Lord Tillson before the current one returned to England.

Then she wondered why a man like Webb would come to apologise for touching a woman? For many men of his class it would be normal behaviour. He'd smartened himself up as well; surely asking her about the bills didn't warrant such an effort? Perhaps Mary had made a conquest? She smiled, then found a clean sheet of paper and mended her pen.

> *My dear Ann*
>
> *I write to thank you again for accommodating me at such short notice when I came to London. But now I have another request, if you can spare the time.*
>
> *Do you recall taking a look at the deserted Hall above the village when you came for a visit in '97? Well, the new Lord Tillson has finally arrived, four years after the last one died. I have not yet seen him to speak to.*

Charlotte looked at that last phrase. It *was* true, in a way—she hadn't spoken to him. She debated describing her first encounter with him, but decided against it, not wanting to suggest any bias.

His man says Lord Tillson arrived in England from India only a few weeks ago, about the same time I was in London. He has not called on the squire, as far as I am aware, and no-one seems to know anything about him. I wondered if the London papers had said anything? Four years between lords seems rather a long time.

I also suspect that the man with him, Sergeant Webb, has an interest in Mary. If you can find out anything about him as well, I'd be grateful. I don't know what regiment he was with, or even if he is still serving, but he implied that he, too, has only just returned from India.

That was the main thing Charlotte wanted to say, but since Ann was going to have to pay for the letter she may as well fill the paper. She described Mary's venture into the bakery business and, as an afterthought, promised to repay Ann anything she needed to spend while making her enquiries. Mary could post the letter when she finished in the bakery tomorrow.

She went into the kitchen to give Mary the letter, and found that Webb had gone. There was no sign of Davie or Deacon. She pulled up a chair and sat next to Mary at the table. Mary handed her a small box full of candied orange slices. They smelled wonderful. She took a piece, then handed the box back.

"Peace offering?" she asked, when she had finished savouring it.

Mary nodded. "He came to ask if I'd step out with him."

Charlotte raised a brow, ready for a gossip. "Will you?"

Mary shrugged. "If I need to."

Charlotte was about to ask what she meant, but Mary went on talking.

"I said I'd be up to the Hall again in a day or two to see how Nell Jackson's getting on, and maybe to see if they want to take on Sally. Else Mrs Fakenham, over towards the Tetbury road, said she'd be wanting a trained maid."

"Sally would prefer to stay nearer home, I suppose?"

"Yes. As long as that Webb can keep his hands to hisself. I'll have a think about it."

Charlotte nodded. "Have you found anyone to replace Sally here?"

"I reckon Mrs Tyler's lass, Jane, is old enough now. Had a talk with her the other day. She already knows general housekeeping, so it'll just be a matter of cooking."

Charlotte smiled, grateful for Mary's efficiency. "That sounds like an excellent plan."

CHAPTER 16

*I*t rained continuously overnight, and by morning the soil in the kitchen garden had turned to sticky clay. It stuck to Matthew's boots, clung heavily to the spade, and persuaded him to give up after only a few minutes.

Retreating to the stables for more coffee, he wondered what to do with himself. Checking the locations of the remaining field boundaries wasn't an option, as he wouldn't be able to see the far edges of the fields clearly during the heaviest showers, and the rain would turn his notepaper to mush. But he had to be outdoors doing something, so he decided to explore the woods around the house.

He put his empty cup down and snapped his fingers for Reena. She raised her head from her place by the fire, but did not move. Matthew frowned—a proper dog would *want* to go for a walk in the woods, rain or no. She was looking much better now, with more meat on her bones and the signs of his clumsy barbering beginning to grow out.

He went over to the kitchen and asked Mrs Jackson for bread and ham for his lunch. As he hoped, Reena showed more interest in following him once she could smell what he had in his pocket.

Matthew started uphill to the east, circling around to the north once he was in the birch woods, and heading for the place where the

Birchanger estate abutted Squire Thompson's land. There were a couple of fairly well-trodden paths through the woodland but he ignored those, following fainter tracks that were most likely made by deer rather than humans. With most of the vegetation dormant for winter, it wasn't too difficult to pick his way between the trees. His boots kicked up dead autumn leaves, now soggy and beginning to rot.

Once Reena realised that whining wasn't going to get her back to the fire right away, she started to enjoy herself. She sniffed around, occasionally dashing off to paw at the soil or run after movements in the undergrowth. But the local wildlife was cannier than the dog, and all she managed to collect was a coating of mud and a lot of burs stuck to her fur. Perhaps he could get one of the Jackson brats to give her a bath when they got back.

A crashing noise interrupted his musings, then a strange scream that turned into something between a yelp and a whine.

Reena!

Matthew ran in the direction of the noise, slipping on the mud and tripping over fallen branches. Reena was stuck between a pair of huge iron jaws with vicious spiked teeth, her paws flailing. Hell—someone had set a mantrap!

Please, no!

Matthew cursed. Reena's small weight must have been just enough to set it off. But she was still moving and crying, so it hadn't killed her. He took a deep breath, gradually bringing his fear and anger under control.

His hands shook, but he managed to suppress other, distracting memories. He crouched down next to the whimpering animal, trying to soothe her with his voice to stop her wriggling. Her panicked movements were likely to be making her injuries worse. Her snaps subsided as he soothed and calmed her.

Inspecting the trap more closely, he could see that it wasn't particularly rusty. It couldn't have been in place for more than a year or so. The mechanism, too, was obviously working, but when he ran his hands along the line of the toothed jaws he realised that they had stopped before they had closed fully. It wasn't Reena's body that had stopped them. He carefully felt along her flanks, and his hand came away red with blood. But if all the spikes were the same length, the ones sticking into her would have made only small surface cuts. He gave a small sigh of relief.

The base of the trap had been disguised by leaves and small branches, some of which had been forced upwards as the trap closed. But there was also a thicker section of branch in there—something that had possibly fallen in a storm. The branch had stopped the jaws closing completely, and was why Reena was still alive.

He had to get her out, but he couldn't risk allowing the trap to spring any further closed. It would be an easy job with two people, but when he stood up and moved away to go for help, she let out such a pathetic whine that he couldn't leave her.

He'd have to open the trap himself. He found a piece of strong branch and jammed it between the jaws, ensuring that it wouldn't spring shut any further. Talking soothingly to the dog, he carefully cleared away the vegetation concealing the mechanism to allow him to examine it.

The two jaws were pushed together by metal loops on the ends of long springs, one on each side. He'd need to push the ends of both the springs down at the same time before the jaws would open. Matthew crouched down again, stroking Reena's head gently while he thought. Standing on the end of the spring nearest the jaws should compress it fairly easily, but to do that to both at once would involve a balancing act. One slip and the jaws would snap closed again; he didn't want to put all his trust in the branch he'd added.

He rubbed a hand over his face, regretting the brandy he'd had this morning. One spring he could have managed...

Matthew stood up and removed his belt. Careful to disturb the trap as little as possible, he pushed the end of one spring down with his foot, threaded his belt around it and fastened it. He cautiously lifted his foot, relieved to see that the spring did not move.

Reena yelped as he pushed the second spring down and the jaws slackened. He bent down, keeping one foot firmly on the spring, and lifted her out of the way. Moving the dog dislodged the branches between the jaws, and they snapped fully closed as he took a step back.

Shaking with relief, he gently put Reena on the ground and took a long pull at his flask. He poured a little into his hand to see if Reena wanted some. It might help dull the pain a little for her.

Matthew gathered some more fallen branches and threw them on top of the trap—they would help him to find it again later. He picked up the dog and made his way carefully—very carefully—to the nearest trodden path. If he was stepping on bare earth he couldn't spring another trap.

Reena whimpered quietly when he jolted her by stumbling on rough ground, but was otherwise fairly calm, and he hoped she wasn't hurt too badly.

He reached the house and took the dog straight to the stables, shouting for Webb and Jackson as he went. He settled her on some clean straw then stepped outside and shouted again. The only person who came was Mrs Jackson.

"They be cleanin' windows inside the other side of the house, sir," she said, still wiping her hands on her apron. She caught sight of the dog. "She's hurt?"

"Mantrap in the woods," Matthew said curtly. "I want to know why your husband didn't warn me about them." He could see the answer from her expression before she managed to speak, for her face went white.

"Mantraps?"

"Jackson didn't know they were there?"

She shook her head, wordlessly, backing out of the stable. "I'll get 'em, sir," she said faintly, and disappeared back into the main building.

Matthew went back to Reena and moved her closer to the door for more light. He ran his fingers gently through her coat, lifting the hair so he could see her skin. Jackson arrived just as he was completing his examination, Webb panting along some yards behind.

"I never knew, sir…" Jackson started.

"She hurt bad, sir?" Webb asked at the same time. Matthew stood up, spotting Tilly and the other Jackson children lurking outside the door.

"I don't think so. Some cuts, and probably bruises as well. Tilly!" The girl crept around the door. "Tilly, can you stay with her for a little while?"

Matthew left Tilly stroking the dog's head, taking the two men into the steward's office.

"Mantraps, sir?" Webb asked.

"Yes. Jackson, you really had no idea there are traps in the woods?" The man just shook his head. "You have probably been very lucky."

"I ain't been poaching long, sir. And there wasn't no staff 'ere so I didn't 'ave to go off the paths far."

Matthew nodded. "The one I... Reena... found wasn't on a well-trodden path. Although I'm surprised it hadn't caught a deer. The odd thing was, it didn't look as if it had been there long. Jackson—what was my predecessor like? The last Lord Tillson," he added, when Jackson just looked blank.

"Don't rightly know, sir. Steward ran the farm. There wasn't much poaching then. We 'ad enough work to feed us, mostly. An' the old lord didn't go shooting so he wasn't all that bothered. I don't reckon he'd have set traps—an' it's four year ago now."

"There ain't no notices," Webb put in.

"Notices?"

"If someone 'urts 'isself in them they can get money if they didn't know there was traps there," Webb explained.

"Thought you were a city lad, Webb?"

"We 'ad a few ex-poachers in the company, sir."

"Notices—good idea. We'll get notices sorted out right away." Matthew frowned. Anything written on paper would just disintegrate. "Webb, can you get hold of some paint?"

"You're leavin' them there, sir?" Webb looked disappointed.

"Any reason I shouldn't?" Matthew raised his eyebrows.

"Nossir," Webb said woodenly.

"Apart from common decency," Matthew said, wryly. He wondered, not for the first time, what Webb really thought of him, with his nightmares and his drinking. But now was not the time for that kind of speculation. "I have no intention of leaving them, but it will take us some time to be sure we've found them all. People from the village use some of the tracks through the woods. Best to warn them while we try to find where they are."

Webb's face lightened. "Paint, yessir. All right if I take Daisy?" They had finally given the mare a name.

Matthew nodded. "Jackson, you and I will walk the main paths through the woods. We'll need to check a little way either side of them. That will do for a start, I think. Get yourself a stout stick, and something to keep the rain off."

They arrived back at the house, soaked and chilled to the bone, just as dusk was making the gloomy day even darker. They had not found any traps on the main paths, and searching further would have to wait for another day.

No-one was in the stable office, so Matthew wandered through the kitchen into the main building. To his surprise he found Webb busy poking through a large pile of furniture in the central hall. Mrs Jackson followed him.

"There was a young man come with it, my lord," she said. "Wanted to see you. Said he'd come back this evening, if you didn't go down to the village. Said he was stayin' at the inn tonight."

Matthew groaned. "His name?" But Mrs Jackson just looked blank.

"Best go down, sir," Webb said. "There won't be too many strangers at the inn. You'll find him easy enough. Bath'll be ready in five minutes, sir."

"Very well," Matthew said. It was easier to do what Webb said than to think for himself. "Sort this lot out, can you?" He waved a hand at the furniture and Webb nodded. Matthew felt uneasy; the last time he'd told Webb to sort something out, the sergeant had moved the whole Jackson family into the Hall.

~

As Webb had predicted, there was only one stranger staying at the inn. The innkeeper showed Matthew straight to the private parlour, recognising him after the evening spent there with Kellet a few days before.

The man waiting for Matthew looked to be in his late twenties, with neat black hair, a slightly tanned face, and a friendly smile. His clothing was of good quality, but the cut indicated a provincial tailor.

"Lord Tillson?" he asked, standing as Matthew entered the room. Matthew took a moment to register the title, then nodded.

"Daniel Fulbeck, my lord." He held out his hand, and Matthew shook it. "The late Lord Tillson was my great-uncle."

"Mr Fulbeck," Matthew acknowledged. The innkeeper still lingered in the doorway, so Matthew ordered a bottle of port.

"It was a trifle disconcerting to arrive to find the place completely empty," Matthew started, once they had sat down.

"I did let Uncle Cyril's solicitors know I'd taken some of the furniture—"

"*Some* of the furniture?"

"Why, yes!" Fulbeck looked surprised. "I only took the good pieces, and all the mattresses and upholstered things. You mean there was *nothing* there when you arrived?"

"A few bits and pieces in the stables, and the large kitchen table," Matthew said.

Fulbeck frowned. "I give you my word, my lord, I did not empty the place. But the building wasn't well maintained even before my great-uncle died, and I thought the furniture would rot. I've stored it in a barn, but a dry one!"

"Why would you go to the bother?" Matthew asked, remembering what Kellet had said about the state of the entailed property.

"Guilt," Fulbeck admitted cheerfully. "I know Uncle Cyril hadn't been keeping the place up properly, and he left everything he could to me and my cousins. Selling his other estate gave Edith, my sister, enough of a dowry so she could marry her sweetheart. The rest of it

169

will keep my Uncle George in comfort now he can't work. Some will help Cyril—my cousin Cyril, that is—pay his way through Oxford. And Sophie won't have to go governessing."

"And yourself?" Matthew asked.

"Oh, my farm was doing well enough, but it did allow me to improve the livestock and bring some more fields into cultivation."

Matthew mentally added up rough estimates of all these costs.

"It wasn't a large estate?" he asked, but barely listened to Fulbeck's continued explanation. If the man was telling the truth, the old lord's money had been needed by his late sister's family far more than Matthew himself needed it. And Fulbeck had not prevaricated about his actions. If only his own family were as honest! The idea of suing for some recompense for the state of the property had not been particularly appealing when Kellet mentioned it, and he finally let go of the idea without regret.

"My lord?"

He roused himself, realising he had missed a question. "Sorry, Fulbeck. Wool gathering…"

"I've a list here of what I've brought you this time, and what is left." He hesitated. "I could use the barn…"

Matthew glanced at the lists, folded them, and put them in a pocket. Webb could deal with it.

"I'll let you know as soon as we can take the rest," he said. "I *will* try to ensure it is a matter of weeks, not years! But it would also help if you could recall roughly what you left behind at Birchanger when you removed what you did?"

Fulbeck nodded. "I don't suppose there's much chance of getting the rest of the furniture back," he said.

Matthew was beginning to have an idea what might have happened to it, but said nothing. He asked instead about the mantraps.

"Uncle Cyril would never have done that!" Fulbeck said, shocked, and Matthew believed him.

"The steward?"

Fulbeck shook his head. "Too lazy," he said firmly.

"Very well. Thank you for looking after the furnishings," Matthew said, standing up. "If you could write a list of what you left behind, you can just leave it here—I'll have it collected." He bade the man goodnight and went to find Daisy, not looking forward to getting wet yet again.

~

Two mornings later, Matthew sat at his desk in what was currently his bedroom, but would one day be a front parlour. He had a proper bed with a mattress, sheets, blankets, and bed hangings. He could see through the windows, from which years of dust and grime had been removed. One of the small diamond panes was missing, but he didn't mind that. It let some air in, and the curtains could be partly drawn to stop the draught from it if the room got too cold. The chimney sweep arranged by Webb had arrived the day after the furniture, so he also had a roaring fire in the grate.

He also had yet another servant. Sally Tivers was only about eighteen, but she seemed to know more about cooking and generally managing a household than Mrs Jackson did. The older woman had gratefully relinquished her role as cook and taken on the task of cleaning. Webb had come to him the day before, asking how much Sally should be paid. Matthew had no idea.

"What was she paid in her last post?"

"The Mrs MacKinnons paid her five pounds a year, but she lived out."

Matthew frowned. It didn't seem much for someone who could cook. Not much at all.

"She said she should be gettin' more here, sir, even when she can live in and she'll be gettin' her bed and board."

"Fifteen shillings a month?" Matthew suggested. "I'll find out how much it should be. I suppose we should be paying the Jacksons too?"

Webb had agreed, which was why Matthew was sitting at his desk with the old estate books spread out in front of him. He squinted at the crabbed handwriting, trying to work out how much had been paid in wages for different members of staff. No doubt he'd soon have to employ a proper cook and housekeeper, not to mention grooms, gardeners...

He rubbed his eyes and looked out of the window. It was too early in the day for the sun to be shining into the room, but the morning's clouds were clearing and it looked like a lovely day. He tried to ignore the sunshine, but after only a few more minutes he gave up and reached for his coat. He could at least have a stroll around the lawn— well, the meadow—before going back to the ledgers.

Matthew was half way around a circuit of the lawn when he noticed movement ahead. Someone was walking along the path below the ha-ha, but disappeared down into the woods before he could see who it was. Curious, as he hadn't noticed many people using the path, he walked along the edge of the lawn until he could see the place where the path came out onto the drive. He had to wait a few minutes, for the woodland path twisted and turned, but eventually the person —people—came into view.

A woman in a black cloak and bonnet, and a boy. Davie? The woman must be Davie's mother—one of the Misses MacKinnons Webb had mentioned. Her shape and clothing looked familiar, then he realised that this Miss MacKinnons was the woman he had avoided seeing the week before. As he watched, the pair of them stopped. Davie wiped the knees of his breeches, but his mother pushed his hands away. Matthew could almost hear his old nurse: 'Let it dry, Master Matthew, then it will just brush off!'

The woman searched in a bag and brought out a handkerchief, wiping the boy's hands. Davie turned and marched on to the path beyond the drive—literally marched, with arms swinging, his mother following suit. Matthew's throat closed up; seeing them together brought back memories of his own mother encouraging him to march along with her, in the days when she spent time with him—a time when someone had cared what happened to him, someone other than a few servants who depended on him for a living...

He gave himself a mental shake—what was he thinking? A grown man shouldn't *need* people to look after him. That's what came of pottering around like this without a purpose.

Walking on, he reached the drive and turned down the path Davie and his mother had emerged from. He stopped at the top of the steep section, inspecting the marks in the slope where they must have slipped. He frowned; it would almost be better for the villagers to have no path at all through the woods than have something as hazardous as that.

Back in his room, Matthew shouted for Webb.

"Sir?" Webb must have been in the kitchen, as he arrived quickly, not even out of breath.

"Get a few men with axes to chop down some trees. Small ones, the kind of size you could use for fencing."

"Yessir. Where d'you want them, sir?"

"Leave the poles on the path near the stream, where the slope is."

Webb frowned.

"Jackson will know, I'm sure," Matthew added.

"Yessir." Webb left and Matthew sat down. That was one decision made today. He hesitated, staring at the account books spread over his desk. Back to the ledgers? Or perhaps he should call on the squire to apologise. He could not ignore his neighbours for ever.

Running a hand over his jaw, he grimaced. A bit of smartening up was in order before making social calls.

CHAPTER 17

"*I* will see if Mr Thompson is available, my lord." The butler ushered Matthew inside Northridge Hall, bowed, and walked ponderously across the black and white flagged entrance hall. Matthew looked around as he waited, taking in the slightly worn carpet and grimacing at the still-life paintings of dead game. Fragments of talk drifted from his left as the butler opened a door.

"...appears that Bonaparte has more power than the other two consuls."

A woman—Mrs Thompson, no doubt. She had an attractive voice, lower-pitched than Serena's. More intelligent than Serena, too, from the sound of the conversation. He rubbed the back of his neck; he knew virtually nothing about the political situation at the moment.

"He vetoed Sieyès' idea of—Yes, Tenby, what is it?"

"Lord Tillson to see you, sir."

"Oh, very well. Send him in." A pause. "I hope we can discuss this further some other time?"

"By all..."

"Mr Thompson will see you now, my lord," the butler announced. Behind the butler, Matthew saw a woman leave the squire's study. A woman in black, looking vaguely familiar. She headed further into the house, not looking in his direction, and he only had time to take in rich brown hair fastened back in a bun, and a glimpse of creamy skin.

Miss MacKinnons?

Charlotte pushed open the door to Letty's parlour, catching her friend lowering herself carefully into a chair, awkward in her advanced pregnancy.

"Spying, Letty?" Charlotte asked, smiling.

Letty blushed, but nodded. "He's very thin. I wonder how old he is? It was difficult to tell."

"Arthur will tell you later, I'm sure."

Letty shook her head. "He won't even ask the right questions. He'll find out how many hunters he has, and hounds, and if he prefers port or brandy."

Charlotte laughed as Letty picked up her embroidery. It had a pretty floral design and reminded Charlotte of one of her current problems.

"Letty, are you good at drawing?"

"Hopeless!" Letty said cheerfully. "Why?"

"My stories might sell better with illustrations," Charlotte explained. "I've tried drawing them myself, but I can't even draw something that looks like a real tree."

"We must both have had very deficient educations!" Letty said. "Speaking of which, I forgot to thank you for taking on Bertie while Mr Hayes is away. You must be keeping him busy; he always seems quite tired when he comes back."

Charlotte frowned. "Taking on Bertie? Letty, what do you mean? I didn't know Mr Hayes was away. Davie has been coming here for his lessons as usual."

"He's been gone for just over a week. His father was taken ill again, so he had to go—" Letty finally seemed to register what Charlotte had said. "Davie's been coming here? I thought Bertie was with you all day." She sat up straight, suddenly worried too. "Bertie stayed with you overnight a few days ago."

Charlotte shook her head. "Davie stayed here with Bertie."

The two women stared at each other, eyes widening in alarm.

"Davie walked over with me this morning," Charlotte said. "If they aren't with Mr Hayes, they should be playing in your nursery or in the grounds."

"Ring the bell, Charlotte, please," Letty said. When the butler came, she asked him where the boys were, and he went off to enquire. Charlotte paced the room while they waited; Letty picked nervously at her embroidery.

"I'm afraid they are not in the house, madam," the butler said when he returned.

"You have looked everywhere?" Letty asked.

"We have looked in the rooms, madam, but not inside cupboards or under beds," the butler said. "Do you wish me to do so?"

"No, thank you," Charlotte said, when Letty was about to agree. The butler bowed himself out.

"Why not look properly?" Letty asked.

"Davie usually returns muddy, and you said Bertie does too. They are more likely to be outside than hiding inside the house. What's the fun in hiding if no-one is looking for you?"

"Oh, yes, I see," Letty said. "I'd better tell Arthur."

Charlotte helped her up, and followed her across the hall. Letty knocked on the study door, opening it and going in without waiting for an acknowledgement. The squire and his guest stood up when they entered.

Matthew continued to sip his port, ignored by the two women who had just come in.

"Arthur, do you know where Bertie is?" The heavily pregnant woman interrupting the squire must be his wife, her pale colouring making a striking contrast with the squire's rather ruddy face.

"—we have a guest. Come, let me introduce—"

"Bertie's missing, Arthur. And Davie."

Matthew turned his attention to the other woman. She was taller, with glossy brown hair pulled into a tidy bun behind her head. Her features were currently contorted into a frown. The fleeting glimpse of a creamy complexion he'd gathered earlier was confirmed; her skin had a warm, healthy glow rather than the fashionable white. A very attractive glow.

"...his lessons with Charlotte this week." Mrs Thompson wrung her hands.

How had he come to think of Miss MacKinnons as an old witch? He had only seen her up close when he had sprawled on the ground at her feet. All he really remembered from that embarrassing moment was a sturdy pair of muddy boots beneath a muddy black hem. She was still in black, but she must have either changed or cleaned her clothing after the slip he'd seen this morning.

"... turn up later, when he wants his dinner." The squire moved over to pat his wife's shoulder. "After all, Letty, if he's been doing it all week he hasn't come to any harm yet! They are probably just playing in the woods. Damned cold time of year to be doing it, but boys will be boys, eh?"

Their words finally registered with him.

"Excuse me," he said, breaking in on Mrs Thompson's continuing lamentations. "Did you say, sir, your son is wandering around in the woods?"

"It's a likely place," the squire said.

"Whose woods?" Matthew asked, a sinking feeling in his stomach. Reena getting injured was bad enough, but if one of the lads got caught...

"There's a lot more woodland on Birchanger than there is on my land," the squire said. "You've no objection, have you? They won't do any harm. I remember playing in those woods when I was their age." There was a slightly dreamy look to his eyes.

Matthew interrupted before the squire could get carried away with reminiscences. "It's not that," he said. "There are mantraps in the woods. That was one of the things—"

"Mantraps?" Davie's mother was sharp-voiced now, and white-faced. "You've set *mantraps* in your woods? That's... that's inhuman! And Davie is wandering around out there?" The last bit of her speech ended on a wobble, as she turned and almost ran out of the room.

"What—" said the squire, bewildered.

"She's gone to look for Davie, of course!" Mrs Thompson interrupted, waving a hand impatiently. "Arthur, Bertie is out there too. Hadn't you better get some men?"

"Yes, yes. Of course!" He moved over to her and patted her shoulder before turning to his guest. "Tillson, you've no objection to me sending some of my people to search?"

"By all means—tell them to report to Birchanger Hall first, though, will you?" Matthew said. "And to go along the road and up the drive to get there. We don't want the *searchers* getting caught."

While he was talking, Mrs Thompson had waddled over to the window, peering out into the drizzle. "Charlotte's not going by road," she said, worried.

"Now then, Letty, my dear, don't worry about Charlotte. She usually walks over through the woods, remember? She'll be fine—she's just worried."

"If she sticks to the path. What if she goes off looking for Davie?" She rounded on Matthew. "How many are there? Where are they?"

"I didn't set them, Mrs Thompson, so I don't know. I only found out about them myself a couple of days ago." He was puzzled. He thought Webb had painted signs about the mantraps the day before, so why didn't Miss MacKinnons know about them? But that conundrum could wait—it was more important to find the boys.

He turned to the squire. "Thompson, can you send a man to follow her—make sure she doesn't wander off the main path, and bring her up to the Hall? I'll ride back to organise a search, and I'll send word when I have any news."

. . .

Matthew pushed the mare as hard as he could along the road, then up the drive, seeing no-one on the way. Birchanger Hall, too, seemed deserted, but after a couple of shouts Tilly came out into the yard.

"Where is everyone?"

"Ma and Sally went to Edgecombe, sir. The rest is cutting trees, like you said."

"Where are they working, do you know?"

"Dunno exactly. But Mr Webb said they should start near where the poles was wanted."

"Right—I'll go and find them. You stay here, and if any men come from the squire's, tell them I said they were to stay here until I get back. We need to look for the squire's son and Davie before they find themselves in a trap." He looked at her doubtfully. "Have you got that?"

"A'course!" she said indignantly, standing taller. "I ain't stupid!"

Matthew managed not to smile as he nodded at her, then mounted Daisy again and trotted back down the drive. He left the mare tied to a tree where the woods started, setting off on foot to follow the sound of axes hitting wood, until he came to the place where the men were working. Webb had found several men to help with the task; they must all have been working diligently, for there was a large pile of slim trunks, stripped of their branches, ready to be used. Webb was standing to one side, leaning on an axe and breathing heavily.

Matthew called out as he approached. "Webb, there's two lads wandering the woodland somewhere, and they don't know about the mantraps. We need to find them."

The sounds of chopping stopped.

"Webb—did you paint signs yesterday? Miss MacKinnons walked this way this morning, and she didn't seem to know anything about the traps."

"I tried, sir," Webb said apologetically, "but the board was too wet. I was goin' to—"

"Very well. But for now we've got to make sure those boys don't get caught in one of them." Matthew looked around. "Any of you know the main paths through these woods?" There were nods all round. He was trying to think how to cover the most ground without risking any of the men when Jackson spoke up.

"There's the hut, my lord."

"Hut?"

Jackson gestured vaguely to the east. "Stone hut in the woods above the Hall, my lord. It's mebbe worth lookin' there first." He glanced at the sky, as if any of them needed to be reminded of the chilling drizzle.

"Very well. Jackson, you come with me to show me the way. Webb, you organise the rest of these men to search this strip to the west of the house. Stick to the main paths and shout for them. If you do need to go off the paths, poke ahead of you with a stout stick every step."

There were a few murmurs of assent, and one of the men picked up his axe to make suitable sticks, trimming thin branches from the pile waiting to be burnt.

"Webb," Matthew went on, "when you've sent them off, come up to the Hall. Squire Thompson was going to send some men over." Webb nodded, and Matthew set off with Jackson.

It took them half an hour to come in sight of the hut—on foot, as there was only one horse. It was rather tumbledown, but still had four walls and most of its roof, although the door was partially rotted and hanging crookedly from one hinge. The smell of wood smoke hung in the air.

When they entered the hut they found that it was empty, but a small fire under the gap in the roof was still smoking. Matthew wondered if vagrants were using the place; they would run if they thought they were about to be discovered. He examined one of the candle ends stuck to a fallen stone, then sniffed it. It smelled like good beeswax. Conkers had been piled in one corner, several of them with string through their middles. That settled it.

"Hidin'?" Jackson said.

Matthew nodded. He called their names, as loudly as he could, but there was no response.

"Might be too far away to hear?"

"Perhaps," Matthew said. "Perhaps not."

He felt in his pocket for his notebook and pencil, wrote a couple of sentences, then tore out the page and propped it up behind one of the candle stubs. Anyone coming into the hut could not fail to see it. The two men walked back down to the Hall, making as much noise as they could without being too obvious about it. He'd give the boys five minutes to be sure that he and Jackson had really gone, then maybe another five to decide whether or not to come down and face the consequences. Perhaps he'd better give them a bit more time still, since they may not walk as fast as he and Jackson. He remembered his own dragging footsteps as a child when being summoned to face reprimands or punishment for some misdemeanour.

There seemed to be no-one at Birchanger Hall when Charlotte arrived, accompanied by the man the squire had sent after her. She went round the side, as she had last time, gradually getting her breath back after almost running most of the way. An open door led into the kitchen, where she found Tilly Jackson watching a large kettle on the ancient range.

"Where's Lord Tillson?" Charlotte demanded, the knot of fear in her stomach and her racing heart almost choking her. From what the squire's man had said, she'd expected him to have reached Birchanger before her. She'd stuck to the path, as he insisted, but now she needed to know that someone was searching.

"He went out," Tilly said. "He said as how anyone who come to help should stop here till he gets back."

"I can't just wait here!" Charlotte protested. "Davie might be—"

"Mrs Captain!" Tilly said firmly. "His lordship's sortin' it out. Please sit down, mum. If you runs off you might step in one, then what would happen?"

Charlotte saw the sense in this, and collapsed into a chair, unfastening her coat and setting her bonnet on the table.

Tilly brought a mug of coffee over to her, and she sipped it absently, her eyes on the door. She drank half of it, then set the mug down on the table and got to her feet. She had to do *something*...

She reached the door, ignoring Tilly's protests, just as Webb arrived.

"You're 'ere safe, then, ma'am?" he said, taking Charlotte's elbow and guiding her back to the table. Charlotte tried to pull her arm away, but Webb had a surprisingly firm grip.

"No need to worry, now," Webb went on. "There's a bunch of men comin' to 'elp search. We'll find 'em, don't you worry." He sniffed. "'Ave some... 'ave some *more* coffee while you're waitin'."

"If they got any sense, mum," Tilly added, "they'll be hidin' in a shelter somewhere in this rain, not wand'rin' about."

"So waitin' till the others get 'ere won't make no difference, ma'am," Webb added, with an approving wink at Tilly. Charlotte sat down, gripping her mug of coffee but not drinking it.

It wasn't long before there came the sound of feet on cobbles, and male voices. Webb went out. Charlotte could hear him telling the squire's men to wait in the stables.

When Webb came back in he was followed by Lord Tillson, who nodded to Charlotte as he removed his wet coat. He didn't stop to speak, but walked on through the kitchen with a gesture for Tilly to follow him.

Charlotte watched him depart in disbelief, springing to her feet to follow. Had the man *no* concern for the safety of the boys? Webb put a hand on her shoulder.

"Just wait, ma'am," he said, and she reluctantly sat down again.

Matthew found his telescope and gave it to Tilly, quickly showing her how to focus it. "You know the old hut in the woods, and the path to it?"

"Yes, sir."

"I want you to go upstairs, and use this to keep an eye on the path. Come and tell me as soon as you see anyone on it."

"Yes, sir," Tilly said eagerly, setting off for the main staircase at a run.

Matthew found a map of the estate and went back into the kitchen.

"Why aren't you out looking?" Davie's mother was on her feet, glaring at him. "It's appalling, using mantraps, but to allow two boys to wander around putting themselves in danger..."

Matthew tried to speak but she wasn't listening, so he pulled his flask from his pocket and took a drink.

"How could you be so irresponsible?"

She's beginning to sound like Serena.

"...of all the despicable things to do..."

Although she's got a much nicer voice.

"...I cannot believe you don't realise just how..."

Her eyes were a riveting shade of grey, flashing now with emotion, and high spots of rose stood out against her cheeks. He took another sip.

He realised she had wound down and was waiting for an answer. "It's always best to have a plan, Miss MacKinnons," he said. "Webb, where did you send the men?"

Webb repeated the instructions he had given, and Matthew moved a finger across the map, tracing the locations Webb was describing. "How many have come from Northridge?"

"Six, sir. Three of 'em says they knows their way around a bit."

"Why aren't you sending them out to search?" Davie's mother demanded again. "Does it mean *nothing* to you that two boys may be out there, fatally injured, as we speak?"

Matthew looked at his watch—he'd been back for ten minutes. When he looked up again, Miss MacKinnons was half way to the door.

"Just wait, ma'am," he called, managing to put enough authority in his voice to make her stop. She turned to face him, her mouth opening, just as Tilly burst into the room.

"Seen 'em, my lord!" she said. "You was right!"

"What? Where?" Miss MacKinnons' voice was sharp, but hopeful.

"Show her," Matthew said, and Tilly led the way out of the kitchen. Matthew and Webb followed.

"I think they've been in a hut in the woods," he explained, but Davie's mother didn't wait to hear his explanation. She picked up her skirts and set off up the field at a run as she spied the two boys walking towards her.

She stopped a few feet in front of them, crouching down in front of Davie, then standing up and putting her hands over her face. Instead of the scold he expected, she just turned and stalked off on a route that would take her around the Hall and back to the main path through the woods. Heading for her home, he thought. The speed she was walking, and the stiff way she carried herself, made it clear she was still angry, but her hand went to her face now and then. Matthew wondered if she was also crying.

He suppressed a sudden urge to go after her and try to comfort her. That would go down well, he thought, recalling her scold. He shrugged and finished his coffee.

The two boys came towards him, Bertie Thompson looking belligerent, but Davie on the verge of tears.

"I'm sorry for trespassing, sir," said Bertie stiffly and unconvincingly.

"I'll talk to your father about it tomorrow," said Matthew. Good, that got the lad looking a little more worried. "Webb, get the squire's men to escort this miscreant home, and thank them all for turning out." He waited until Bertie and Webb had moved off, then turned to Davie.

"We weren't in any danger, sir," Davie said.

"Mantraps are no danger?"

"Not if you know where they are, sir."

Matthew stared at him for a moment. "You *knew* there were mantraps in the woods? And you didn't tell me about them?"

Davie hung his head.

"Did you know that my dog was nearly killed by one?"

"I thought you would have known, sir," Davie said. "I'm sorry sir, if I'd known you didn't know…"

"I think you'd better get home now, before your mother starts to worry again. You frightened her, you know."

Davie nodded wordlessly, and took off down the drive at a run.

CHAPTER 18

*D*avie caught up with Charlotte as she reached the drive and automatically turned down the path through the woods. Charlotte said nothing more to him, and he apparently had enough sense to follow on behind in silence.

She was still furious with Davie for lying to her, her anger blown out of all proportion by the fear she had felt for his safety. That anger was easier to deal with than her simmering fury with the drunken Lord Tillson, who not only had mantraps on his land, but had treated the search for the boys with such a lack of urgency. The sight of trimmed and sharpened stakes near the steep section just fuelled her wrath—the path many of the villagers used was about to be fenced off.

Davie followed her into the kitchen when they reached home.

"Wet clothes off. Now."

Davie stripped to his underclothes obediently, leaving his wet and muddy garments in a pile on the floor. Mary poked her head around the door to see what was happening, but retreated when she saw the expression on Charlotte's face.

"Bed," Charlotte ordered.

"But it's only three o'clock..."

"Now." Charlotte took a deep breath after repeating the order, her anger beginning to fall away now they were both home and safe.

"I'm sorry, Mama, I never—"

"More lies?" Charlotte's voice faltered, as relief finally overcame anger and she came close to tears.

"How long—"

Charlotte cut him off. "You can come down when I tell you."

Charlotte watched him make his way to the foot of the stairs and turn up them, then sank into a chair and buried her face in her hands. She couldn't believe Davie had been lying to her for more than a week. This, on top of all the other emotions she had recently experienced, made her feel weak and trembly.

She felt a hand on her shoulder.

"Brandy or tea?" Mary asked.

Charlotte took a deep breath and sat up. "Tea, please."

Realising she was as wet as Davie had been, she took off her pelisse and went upstairs to change her dress. She paused outside her son's door as she returned, but there were no sounds from inside. Her hand was on the latch, about to open it, when Mary cleared her throat. Charlotte looked down to Mary, standing at the bottom of the stairs. Mary shook her head.

In the kitchen, Mary put tea and a couple of fresh scones in front of Charlotte, and sat down. "It ain't a punishment if you give in that quick," she said. "What's he done?"

Charlotte explained, weary now.

"He didn't frighten you on purpose," Mary observed.

Charlotte had to admit this was true. A large part of her anger was due to the fright she'd had, and Davie could not have anticipated that.

"And boys are bound to wander off the path to explore," Mary went on. "He uses the path through the woods most days."

"But he wasn't anywhere near the path to Northridge. And I think the pair of them have stayed in the woods overnight once or twice. In the middle of winter."

"He hasn't come to any harm by it," Mary said encouragingly. "You don't want to be mollycoddling him, do you?"

"But he lied to me."

"Now *that's* something to be punished for," Mary agreed. "Is he going to get dinner?"

Charlotte hesitated. But Davie probably hadn't eaten anything since breakfast, and he'd come home cold and wet. "I'll take him something in a while," she said eventually.

"Maybe we should have them sprouts tonight?" Mary said with a grin—Davie hated sprouts. That almost coaxed a laugh from Charlotte.

When Charlotte awoke the next morning, Mary and Deacon had already left for the bakery. She knocked on Davie's door as she went downstairs, telling him to come down to breakfast. He looked rather red-eyed, but ate his breakfast in silence, then sat waiting to be told what to do.

"Dishes," Charlotte said. He cleared the plates and cups away then washed and dried them with none of the usual protests. Charlotte sat watching him, wondering what to say. Facts first, she decided, when he came back to stand in front of her, head down.

"How long has Mr Hayes been away?"

He screwed up his face in thought. "All of last week, and up to now."

"And where were you when—" But she was interrupted by a knock on the front door. "Stay there."

It was Sergeant Webb.

"What do you want?" Charlotte asked ungraciously.

Webb took his hat off. "Lord Tillson's compliments, ma'am. Your lad said something yesterday about knowing where the mantraps were. Lord Tillson wondered if you would allow your lad to come and show us where they are."

Charlotte just stared at him for a moment, concentrating first on why Lord Tillson would need Davie's help.

"Why can't he just get whoever set them to take them up again?"

"We didn't know they was there, ma'am, until two days ago. They've been there long enough for stuff to grow over them. Months, at least."

Charlotte thought he was telling the truth. Did this also mean that his explanation for the money owed in the village was true?

"You'd better come in," she said at last, and led the way into the kitchen. "Davie, do you know where the mantraps are?"

"Yes, Mama. So I wasn't in any danger," he added hopefully.

"I didn't know that, did I? How did *you* know?"

"I…" Davie gulped. "I saw them being set."

"When was this?"

"I didn't lie to you, Mama! It was back in the spring, when you were away in London. Not last week."

"Could you lead us to the places, lad?" Webb asked.

"I think so, sir," Davie said.

"Very well. We have not finished this discussion, David Angus MacKinnon," Charlotte said. "Sergeant, he can accompany you if you will escort him back here as soon as you are finished with him."

"Yes, ma'am. And thank you."

Davie put his outdoor boots on, and his coat. Charlotte went into the parlour to watch them go. Webb was on horseback, and pulled Davie up to sit in front of him before kicking the horse into motion.

She massaged her temples, worried. It seemed that Davie had effectively been lying to her for some time. She should really be writing, but this problem would weigh on her mind if she did not think what to do about it.

She went into the scullery to put her coat and boots on, then made her way down to the bottom of the garden, to the stream where Davie seemed to spend so much of his time. She'd seen the dam he'd made last month; now there was also a strange contraption made of wood, propped up on stilts.

"Model mill-race, Mrs MacKinnon."

Deacon's voice behind her made her jump. He stood, looking down at Davie's project. "Still needs a bit of work," he added.

Charlotte wrapped her arms tightly around herself against the cold air. She couldn't see the attraction of wandering the woods at night, or messing around—building—in a muddy stream, but she realised that, to Davie, such activities were far preferable to Latin and mathematics lessons.

She took a deep breath. "Deacon, could you give me some advice, please? Let us go indoors."

⁓

Davie slid down from the horse in front of Birchanger Hall. The major was waiting for them, a rolled map in one hand. Davie's heart sank as he saw the frown on his face.

"Well, Davie," the major said, his voice less friendly than on previous occasions. "*Do* you know where the mantraps are?"

Davie nodded.

"Can you show me where on the map?"

"Not exactly, sir," Davie said in a subdued voice. He looked carefully at the map. "The ones I saw were around here somewhere." He pointed to a section of the east woods. "And a couple down near the road, I think."

"Right. We'll start with the ones near the road. Lead on." The major headed for the drive, striding out so fast that Davie had to trot to keep up. Jackson soon caught them up, carrying some stout sticks and a few poles with bits of white cloth tied to the tops.

"*How* do you know where they are?" the major asked, slowing down a little.

"I… we saw them being put down, sir."

"We?"

"Me and Bertie, sir."

"Did you see *who* put them down?"

"Yes, sir, but I don't know who they are." He glanced up at the major. "I haven't seen them again, sir."

"When was this?"

"In the spring."

"When you were supposed to be having lessons?"

Davie flushed. "Yes, sir." The major said nothing. Eventually the silence grew too much for Davie. "I didn't tell any lies, sir!"

"I didn't say you did, lad."

"My mother thinks I did."

"Upset, was she?" Davie just nodded. "Because she thought you might have got hurt?" Again, he could only nod.

The major strode along, the silence stretching out until Davie had to speak.

"She was upset because she thought I'd lied to her, as well."

"Do you lie to her often?"

"I did when I was little," Davie admitted. "But this time I didn't say anything that wasn't true!"

"You don't need to convince me, lad."

They had reached the edge of the woods. Davie led them off to the north, walking briskly along the main path for a while, then hesitating where the path crossed a small stream.

"No, don't walk where you can't see what you're putting your feet on," the major said hurriedly, as Davie stepped into the accumulated leaf mould. "Just in case you can't remember accurately. Tell me where to go, then you walk exactly where I do."

The major took a stick from Jackson, then followed Davie's directions, carefully prodding ahead of him as he led the group along a faint trail. They came to another vague trail crossing it. Davie hesitated, then shrugged.

"It's somewhere near here, sir. There was more of a path last time, I think."

"You stand there and don't move," the major said. "Jackson, give him the flags to hold."

Davie took the sticks, holding them in one arm so he could rub his hands and breathe on them, trying to warm them up. He watched anxiously as the two men cautiously walked in increasing circles around him, prodding carefully ahead of themselves.

Eventually Jackson gave a grunt of satisfaction. "Found it, sir." He banged the end of his stick hard in the centre of the ironwork. The thing snapped shut, breaking the stick. Davie gave an audible gulp.

"Never seen one in action, eh?" the major asked, his voice kinder than it had been.

"No, sir." He swallowed hard. "How did your dog... I mean, why wasn't it killed?"

"Some branches had fallen on the trap and stopped it closing completely. Now, where's the next one?"

Jackson stuck one of the flags in the ground next to the sprung trap, and the two men followed Davie as he set off back towards the main path, then northwards again. Davie led them to the approximate position, and the men prodded around carefully. This time the major set the thing off.

"The rest are east of the Hall?" the major asked when Jackson had planted the second flag.

Davie nodded. "Yes, sir, but it's just as quick to go on round the edges of the fields."

"Lead on, then."

It was further to walk this time, and Davie had time to think.

"Sir?"

"Yes?"

"I didn't tell Mama anything that wasn't true."

"I never said you did. You don't have to justify yourself to me."

But he did. It didn't feel right, the major not thinking well of him. "Bertie told his mama... his stepmama, that my mother was giving us both lessons. But he said women can't teach useful things to boys so we played in the woods instead. *He* told lies."

The major sighed. Davie flushed, wishing he hadn't spoken. Everyone was cross with him at the moment.

"Do you know what the term 'accessory' means, Davie?" the major said after a moment.

"No, sir."

"It is someone who has not carried out a crime, but may have helped to plan it. They knew about it and did not try to prevent it. They can be punished, as well as the person who actually committed the crime."

Davie tried to puzzle this out. The silence was broken only by the sounds of rain beginning to patter on the bare branches and the ground.

"Do you know what a 'lie by omission' is?" the major asked, eventually. "'Omission' means not doing something."

Davie frowned. "You mean I knew Mama thought I was having lessons with Mr Hayes, and I did an omission lie by letting her think that, even though it was not true?"

"Exactly."

The major did not seem inclined to talk any more. Davie led them to the places he thought the mantraps were concealed, but didn't say anything else in case he made the major angry again. They found five more, but failed to find anything in a couple of places Davie thought they should be.

"But I might not have remembered properly," he admitted.

"Never mind, we've done well so far," the major said. "I need to find out how many there were, if I can."

"Sir?"

The major looked down at him.

"Why don't you know?" Davie asked

"I only got here a couple of weeks ago—I didn't set them."

"Yes, but Lord Tillson must have paid for them—doesn't he know? And what about the man in charge here before you came?"

The major rubbed his face, then shook his head, but did not answer the question. "Come," he said, "we'll get a hot drink at the Hall before Webb takes you home."

Webb let Davie down off the horse, then set off back down the lane. Deacon was in the front garden, cutting back some overgrown rose bushes near the front door, but not managing too well with just one hand.

"You're back, then," he said, unsmiling.

Davie nodded. He could see there was a lamp on in the parlour where his mother worked, but she did not come to the window or the door, and Deacon made no move to get out of the way.

"You're to help me dig the rest of that patch in the garden," Deacon said, putting his pruning knife into a pocket.

"I'm hungry." Davie said. He was also wet and cold.

"You've missed dinner," Deacon said, with an uncharacteristic lack of sympathy. "Come on, now."

He led the way around the house and into the back garden, handing Davie a heavy spade. "Not much more to dig over, so you get on with that now. I'm going to look out some wood to make new edges for the vegetable beds."

Davie looked up miserably at the grey sky, drizzle still falling, then at the large rectangle of sticky clay soil. With a sigh, he started to dig as Deacon disappeared into the dry outhouse where the tools were stored. He thought he saw Deacon waving at someone, but when he looked round no-one else was in the garden.

An hour later Davie was even more tired. His legs were caked with mud almost up to his knees, his hands and arms were sore from wielding the heavy spade, and the drizzle had now soaked through all his clothing, right to the skin.

"All done?" asked Deacon, coming up behind him. "Hmm. You haven't dug it very deep, but I suppose it will do." He went back into the shed and sat on a bucket. His legs blocked the way, forcing Davie to stand outside with the rain still falling on him. "Now, I measured the beds so we'll need to cut up the planks. Can you measure things?"

"Of course I can!"

"Well, I dunno about that. A lad who doesn't like his mathematics isn't going to be much use for planning and making things."

"I helped Mary and Mrs Wilton at the bakery!" Davie protested.

"Helped them move the flour around, did you?"

"No, I helped Mrs Wilton work out how much flour and other things she puts in her cakes!"

"Really?" said Deacon, his tone sceptical. "Dunno how you managed to do that."

Davie began to explain in detail, then gradually stopped talking as Deacon started to smile.

"Get another bucket and come and sit in here." Deacon moved his legs out of the way.

"Enjoyed the digging, did you?" he went on when Davie had settled himself in the dry. Davie shook his head. "Folks with no education end up doing jobs like that," Deacon went on. "All day, every day, in the cold and the wet."

"Am I having a lesson now?" Davie asked, wrapping his arms around himself to try to get warmer.

"Smart lad! What do you think you are supposed to be learning?"

"To do my lessons?"

"That all?" Davie didn't reply.

"Did you see the sense in knowing how to measure angles when you were first taught it?"

Davie shook his head.

"But you needed to know that to draw maps?"

Davie nodded.

"I went to the village school for a bit before I learned carpentry," Deacon continued. "I always wanted a bit of adventure, and being a ship's carpenter was good for that. I practised reading and numbers, which helped me get promoted, and I ended up in charge of all the carpenters on the ship. Now I read well enough to enjoy it. I always thought I'd be busy enough at sea, but I never planned on *this* happening." He held up his left arm with the hand that wasn't there. "I was very lucky to be taken on here. Now I've time for reading, and your mother lends me books. But I never thought I'd need to read more than just plans and bills."

"Learning anything is useful?" Davie began to shiver, but didn't complain, not wanting to end this conversation and be sent back out to dig in the wet.

"Not necessarily—but anything you learn *might* turn out to be useful." Deacon ran his eyes over Davie. "Get yourself into the kitchen, lad—I think Mrs Sergeant will let you have a hot bath."

~

An hour later, there was a hesitant knock on the parlour door.

"Come in," Charlotte called. Davie appeared, neatly dressed but with his hair still wet from his bath. She put her pencil down and turned her chair to face him.

"Well?"

"I'm sorry, Mama."

"Sorry you are in trouble?" Most people were sorry when they were caught.

"No. Well, yes, but..." He took a deep breath and started again. "I'm sorry I missed my lessons. Mr Deacon said you never know when things you learn might be useful." He frowned. "I dunno about Latin..."

Although Charlotte shared his opinion about the Latin, letting him know she agreed with him was probably not a good idea at the moment. "Anything else?"

"I'm sorry I lied to you. I never *said* anything untrue, but I let you think I was still going to my lessons. So I did an omission lie."

"Lies by omission?" Charlotte asked, surprised.

Davie nodded.

"You certainly did learn something from Deacon this afternoon!"

"That was the major, Mama. He talked to me when we were looking for the traps."

Charlotte was impressed. "I'll have to meet this major, to thank him, then."

"But you've met him, Mama," Davie said, frowning again. "You were with him yesterday when we came out of the woods."

"That was Sergeant Webb and Lord Tillson."

They stared at each other, then Charlotte spoke again. "So it was Lord Tillson who let you help him with the mapping?" She was having difficulty reconciling the drunken wastrel who wouldn't go out immediately to look for her son, with what Davie had told her about 'the major'.

"Must be," Davie said.

"He wouldn't go looking for you yesterday, when we all thought you might be in danger." She sounded doubtful, even to herself.

"He knew where we were, I think." A loud growl from Davie's stomach interrupted the conversation. Charlotte felt a twinge of guilt: she'd conspired with Deacon to make sure Davie had eaten nothing for the mid-day meal.

"Kitchen," she said, standing up.

In the kitchen, she organised tea, bread and cheese. Charlotte invited Mary and Deacon to join them. When Davie had taken the edge off his hunger, she asked him to tell her all the details of his encounters with the major.

"... and there was this note in the hut," he said, coming to the end of his tale. He got up and fished a soggy bit of paper from the coat he'd been wearing the day before.

Mantraps in woods. STAY ON THE PATH. Come to house, your mother is VERY WORRIED.

"Anything else?"

"He was angry with me for not telling him about the mantraps. He said his dog was nearly killed by one."

"Davie, did you see *who* set the traps? It sounds like Lord Tillson didn't do it, and Webb said the two of them only got to England from India last month."

"I don't know their names..."

"Have you seen them since the traps were set? Do you remember what they looked like?"

Davie shook his head.

"So this Lord Tillson really didn't know about them?"

"No, Mama."

Charlotte sighed. Lord Tillson may be a drunken wastrel, but it seemed she had done him an injustice by accusing him of setting the traps. And he had made Davie understand that lies did not necessarily have to be spoken untruths.

She would have to apologise.

CHAPTER 19

*C*harlotte set off for Birchanger Hall the next morning. She wasn't sure what she was going to say, but remembered with some embarrassment the way she had ranted at Lord Tillson two days ago. Habit took her through the woods, past the pile of posts ready to fence off the path. A fence there would mean an extra mile by road each way when she went to visit the squire. She frowned, her steps slowing.

Lord Tillson had made Davie understand what he had done wrong, and he *had* taken up some of the mantraps. On the other hand, he hadn't listened to her scold, standing and drinking from his flask instead. How much of an apology was really necessary? She shook her head. Somehow it was so much easier to like, or dislike, someone when everything was black and white and not shades of grey.

Unfortunately, all this thought was wasted when she reached the Hall, as Lord Tillson was away visiting the squire and not expected back until the afternoon. Mrs Jackson and Sally asked her into the kitchen for a cup of tea. She hadn't had any attention to spare for her surroundings the last time she had been here, so she looked around with interest now, taking in the old range with rusting turnspits, bare shelves, and grimy walls. The place was clean, but clearly hadn't been painted in many years. She felt a small twinge of sympathy for its absent owner.

Charlotte did not feel she should take a look at the rest of the house as Sally suggested, not without Lord Tillson's permission.

"Webb hasn't... bothered you?" Charlotte asked Sally.

"No, ma'am," Sally said. "He's bin polite enough."

"And I'll be keepin' an eye out to make sure he don't, nor any of the others!" Mrs Jackson added firmly.

Charlotte smiled to herself—this was a very different woman from the tearful one who had come to ask Mary's help not very long ago. Mrs Jackson didn't even seem to resent young Sally being given the more prestigious job of cook. Charlotte enjoyed a short chat, then said her farewells and set off for home, getting her pelisse and bonnet soaked as the heavens opened when she was only half-way to the cottage.

Back at home, she found Davie and Deacon sitting in the kitchen. Davie was asking Deacon about living on a ship, and how the ship worked. She went to change her gown, then joined them for tea and biscuits. They were still talking about life at sea, with Deacon explaining something that involved waving his arms around.

A notebook lay open on the table; she recognised it as the one Deacon used to make notes about repairs and their cost. The open page didn't contain notes, but two drawings. They both showed the gun deck of a warship, one with hammocks slung from the deck beams above, the other with the mess tables down between the guns. Unlike all of Charlotte's efforts to draw people, the men in these looked like real human beings.

"Mrs MacKinnon?"

Charlotte started. She must have been staring at the drawing for some time. "Deacon, do you have any more drawings?"

"There's more sketches in there, ma'am," Deacon said, a puzzled frown on his face. He leaned over and pushed the notebook towards her.

Charlotte turned the pages. There were technical drawings and pages of notes, but she stopped at a drawing showing Davie crouching by his model mill in the stream. It wasn't just a sketch, it was a detailed drawing with clean lines and correct proportions.

Charlotte felt rather dazed. Had the solution to one of her problems been here all along?

"Can you draw animals and plants as well?"

"I reckon so, ma'am."

"Would you come into my parlour, please, Deacon? I wish to discuss something with you."

Charlotte stood up. "Davie—you can peel potatoes for dinner while I'm talking to Deacon, please. And I know *exactly* how many biscuits there are left in the tin!"

Matthew leaned against a tree, steadying himself until the dizzy spell passed. He should not have stayed in the woods so long—Webb had clearly got the idea of what was wanted. The time spent yesterday helping the men search for the remaining traps probably hadn't helped either. Perhaps he just needed his lunch?

After a few minutes, the world stopped spinning, and he could see without blackness crowding the edges of his vision. His head still felt as it if were stuffed with wool, and his limbs ached. Stupid to feel like this after walking only a couple of miles. He shivered, wrapping his greatcoat more closely around his body to try to get warmer, but it didn't help. He took a deep breath. He should be able to manage the simple enough task of crossing the lawn.

He took the last few hundred yards to the Hall slowly, managing to reach the kitchen before having to sit down. Luckily there was a chair handy, but the floor would have done just as well. He fumbled in his pocket and found his flask, managing to get the stopper out without dropping it. The brandy warmed his insides, but made him cough.

He gradually became aware that young Sally was staring at him, eyes wide. He started to speak, but coughed again, a racking cough that hurt his throat and ribs. Skirts rustled as Sally disappeared. The next he knew, Mrs Jackson was standing in front of him, shaking his shoulder.

"I'm all right, leave me alone," he said feebly.

"You should be in bed, my lord," Mrs Jackson said.

"I'm warm enough here," he protested. He wasn't, but moving closer to the range or into his bedroom was too much effort. He took another swig of brandy, causing more coughing, and swore as the flask dropped out of his hands. He bent down to pick it up, but groaned aloud as a stabbing pain shot through his head.

"Tilly!" Mrs Jackson called, the stridency in her voice piercing his temples. She shook her head and moved away, saying something to Sally. Matthew was too tired to listen. He leaned his head against the back of the chair and was lost to the world.

"Stupid bugger," Webb muttered, looking at the major sprawled in his chair.

"Fire's warmed his room up a bit by now," Mrs Jackson said. "Sally warmed the bed as well."

"Let's get 'im in bed, then." Webb pulled one of the major's arms around his neck. "You'll 'ave to do the same," he said to Mrs Jackson. She hesitated, but then did as she was asked. It was a struggle to haul the major out of the chair, but he seemed to be conscious enough to try to walk, so at least his feet weren't dragging along the floor. Between the two of them, they managed to get him through the house and into his bedroom. The dog followed behind, settling herself down by the roaring fire.

"Pull the covers up, lass," Webb said to Sally, once he'd stopped wheezing from the effort of hauling the major. "We'll get 'is outdoor stuff off first so as not to dirty the sheets."

It wasn't easy wrestling him out of his boots and clothes, but eventually he was stripped down to his shirt and put between the warmed sheets. His face was flushed, shiny with sweat.

"Now what?" asked Webb, looking at Mrs Jackson. "I don't like the look of 'im."

"There's a doctor, but he lives all the way over in Dursley. And he might not come if he don't know you." She looked through the window at the scudding clouds. "Not nice weather to be coming a long way. There's an apothecary in the village. Halliton, his name is. He does surgeon's work too."

"It'll 'ave to be 'im, then. Where does 'e live?"

"His shop's on the High Street. Tilly knows. You can put her up on Daisy with you."

"All right," Webb said. "You'd better see if you can get an 'ot drink into 'im."

Hot—too hot. Thirsty. Dark. Can't escape, limbs hurt, can't move them. Get out! Push off the covers, unlock the door...

It took well over two hours to fetch Halliton back to the Hall, the man having insisted on finishing his luncheon before he would set out.

"Oh, Mr Webb, I'm so glad you're back," Sally said, hurrying into the kitchen where Halliton was removing his coat. "He's burnin' up, and shiverin' as well."

"Well, where is my patient?" Halliton asked impatiently. Webb led him into the major's bedroom. The light was dim, although it was broad daylight outside.

"Get me a lantern," Halliton ordered.

Webb moved over to the window to open the curtains instead.

"No, no. Leave those closed, keeps the air out, you know. Best to draw the bed curtains too."

"He don't normally like sleepin' closed in," Webb said, his tone uncertain.

"Nonsense. We need to keep bad air out." Halliton crossed to the bed where the major had thrown the covers off. He picked up one of the major's wrists to feel his pulse.

"Hmm. Tumultuous pulse, very thin." He put a hand to the major's forehead, only for his hand to be knocked away. "Feverish, restless."

"Can you do anything?" Mrs Jackson asked, anxiously.

"He's very ill," Halliton said. Webb muttered about not paying him to state the bleedin' obvious, but Halliton just looked around the room.

"Good, good, you've a fine fire going." He regarded his patient again. "Some laudanum to make him sleep properly, I think. And it looks as if he has some kind of wasting disease, to be so thin. Bad humours. He'll need to be bled. Yes, yes, letting a bit of blood out will help."

Webb frowned. That didn't sound like a good idea. His own experience of medical men was mostly limited to those dealing with bullet, sword or bayonet wounds, and the resulting fevers and infections. He did remember overhearing one army doctor saying that removing blood from someone who was already weak was not to be recommended.

Halliton turned and rummaged in the bag he had put down by the bed, pulling out a brown bottle. He looked around, spotting Sally waiting near the bed. "Get me a glass," he said. Sally ran to fetch one.

"You sure bleedin' 'im will 'elp, sir?" Webb asked doubtfully.

"We must expel the poisons causing this illness, and balance the humours," Halliton said impatiently. "Now, do you want me to treat him or not?"

Webb nodded reluctantly.

"Good, good. Now we'll give him some laudanum first. I can't bleed him while he's moving around like that. Prop him up on the pillows a bit, will you?"

Webb lifted the major up while Mrs Jackson pushed a couple of pillows behind his head. Halliton mixed some drops from his brown bottle into the glass Sally had filled with water, then held the glass to his patient's lips.

Poison! They're trying to poison me... so thirsty... that bitter stuff...the stuff of nightmares. No! Spit it out! Heathen bastards! They've already killed Benson and Stevens and Havers, and now...

Halliton narrowly escaped being hit in the face by the major's flailing arms, the glass flying across the bed and spilling its contents on the floor. Over by the fire, Reena sat up and whined.

"Don't think 'e likes laudanum, sir," Webb said.

"Nonsense. He's just out of his head. You must hold him down while I try again."

"I don't think that's a good idea, sir," Webb said, more urgently. Halliton ignored him, and started to mix another dose.

"I sent Jackson for Mrs Captain, or Mrs Sergeant," Mrs Jackson said quietly

Webb's anxiety abated a little—one of the Mrs MacKinnons could surely make the apothecary listen. Now he just needed to delay Halliton.

"Perhaps 'e'll quieten down, like, if you leave 'im be for a few minutes?" Webb suggested. "You'll need to tell us what to do when you've gone—mebbe you can do that now and I can write it down so I don't forget?"

"Oh, very well," Halliton said impatiently. "You can write, can you?"

Webb ignored the implied insult. He rummaged on the major's desk until he found a notebook and pencil.

"Ten drops of laudanum in water every four hours," Halliton said, tapping his foot impatiently.

Webb laboriously wrote the instructions out, forming the letters carefully and very slowly.

"Keep the windows tight shut and the bed curtains drawn." Halliton sighed as he waited again for Webb to finish writing his instructions.

"Keep the room warm. If he gets too hot, you may put a wet cloth on his forehead."

Webb gently shook his head as he wrote this down.

"Give him lemonade or barley water to drink, and a saline draught, or willow-bark tea. I will come back tomorrow, but if he is ready to eat before then, some thin gruel."

"He won't want gruel," Webb muttered.

"What the patient *wants* is immaterial. The patient should be given what I say, if you wish him to recover." Halliton looked over at his patient, who was now lying a little more quietly. "It's time to try again. Or perhaps I should just bleed him without—"

He paused as the door behind him opened and two people entered the room.

Webb saw with relief that Mrs MacKinnon had arrived.

CHAPTER 20

"What are you doing here?" Hallliton snapped.

"Good afternoon to you, too, Mr Halliton," Charlotte said, forcing herself to smile politely. "I was asked to come, just as I imagine you were."

She wasn't actually sure why—Jackson had said only that his lordship was ill. Charlotte had tried to get more information out of him, but all he said was that 'the missus' had sent him.

Lord Tillson was shifting restlessly in the bed, loosely covered by sheets and looking flushed. Even in the dim lighting in the room, she could see a sheen of sweat on his face. Lord Tillson's dog came over to sniff around her skirts, then went back to its place before the fire.

"Well, stay out of my way," Halliton said, and turned to Webb. "Now, you there, hold him down while I give him this..."

Webb didn't move. "It don't seem right."

"Are you *still* questioning my treatment?" Halliton demanded. "I've a good mind to leave you to it!"

"Very good, sir," Webb said. "Jackson will show you out..."

Halliton was at a momentary loss for words. Charlotte doubted that he'd ever been so summarily dismissed before. Mrs Jackson, though, looked relieved, even though the patient was moving restlessly.

Loud voices... angry voices... something's wrong? Something bad. If I could just get up or move; fight...

The argument paused as Lord Tillson started muttering to himself.

"Run, Benson, tell..."

"No!" he roared from the bed, startling everyone in the room. "Water! Give him water, you bastards!"

Charlotte stepped closer to the bed as Halliton waved his arm.

"You cannot just dismiss me like that!" Halliton said loudly. "If his lordship dies and you—"

"What seems to be the problem?" Charlotte asked, addressing her question to the middle of the room.

"'Is lordship don't like laudanum, ma'am," Webb explained. "Mr 'Alliton says 'e must be made to drink it, to keep 'im still enough to be bled."

"This man is—"

"Wally Jenkins looked just like this with the flu last year," Mrs Jackson interrupted. "But Mr Halliton never said—"

"The cases were not the same!" Halliton almost shouted.

"They look it to me," Mrs Jackson said, her jaw set. "Or are you just givin' his lordship laudanum and bleedin' 'im so you can charge more?"

"Perhaps you could just reassure Lord Tillson's people by explaining *why* you think the cases are different?" Charlotte suggested, keeping her voice calm.

"Lord Tillson has a wasting disease, Jenkins did not."

"Wally was real skinny, just like his lordship," Mrs Jackson said.

"That's because Wally Jenkins didn't get enough to eat. That isn't the case with his lordship! And he is delirious—out of his head!"

Charlotte frowned. Now she came to think of it, Lord Tillson did seem remarkably thin for one of his height. Not just slim, but gaunt. Losing weight would also explain why his clothes were so loose.

"Does his lordship eat regularly?" She'd seen him drink plenty, but she remembered one of Angus' friends who was too fond of the bottle —he'd never wanted to eat much.

"Plates allus come back empty," Mrs Jackson said.

"How much food do you give the dog?" Charlotte asked. "The dog looks a lot healthier than when I first saw it."

"Aye, she's fillin' out nicely, ma'am," Webb said.

"What's the dam... dratted dog got to do with anything?" Halliton asked. "Of *course* his lordship has enough to eat!"

"How much food do you give the dog?" Charlotte asked again.

Webb's eyes widened. "Oh, I see. She don't get food from me. Tilly —d'you feed her? Or Sally?"

"A bit," Tilly said. "But not much."

"So, perhaps Lord Tillson is not so different from Wally Jenkins?" Charlotte suggested. Beside her, Webb nodded his head.

"He still needs to rest, and the laudanum will do that!"

"Why don't you just give him some brandy if he won't take the laudanum?" Charlotte asked.

"If you are going to continually question my competence and ignore my instructions, I have better things to be doing," Halliton said stiffly, not actually answering Charlotte's question. He put away the bottle of laudanum. "I will send you my bill presently."

"I'd ask Mr Webb to pay you now, Mr Halliton," Charlotte said quietly. "Lord Tillson still owes money in the village, you know."

"Hmph." Halliton took a notepad out of his bag and started to write.

Webb opened his mouth to protest, but Charlotte caught his eye, giving him a slight shake of her head. She winced at the amount when Halliton handed over his bill, but showed it to Webb. "Do you have enough money to pay this now?" she asked. "Then Mr Halliton can sign it to say the money has been paid."

Webb frowned, but rifled through one of the desk drawers, pulling out a purse and handing the correct amount to Halliton.

"Thank you for your advice, Mr Halliton," Charlotte said politely. "I'm sure we'll hear nothing about what *your patient* has said here. Jackson will show you out."

"I explained about the money owed, ma'am," Webb said when Halliton had left.

"I know. But it is unprofessional for an apothecary to discuss his patients with others. Halliton is not a pleasant man, but now you have a signed piece of paper proving that Lord Tillson *was* his patient."

Webb's face cleared, and he produced the list of instructions.

"This is what 'e told us to do, ma'am. But 'is lordship don't like..." He stopped, pressing his lips together.

Charlotte looked round—Mrs Jackson, Sally, and Tilly were all watching and listening with interest, not nearly as worried now that someone they recognised as competent was in charge.

"Sally, could you see what you can make in the way of a hot drink? Some honey in hot water, or similar, please. Bring his lordship's flask too, if there is any brandy still in it."

Sally reluctantly left the room, and Charlotte turned to Mrs Jackson and her daughter. "Tilly, you can bring me a bowl of cold water and a cloth. Mrs Jackson, we will call if we need your assistance."

They trailed out of the room, taking a last look over their shoulders as they left.

"I think Mrs Jackson may be correct about it being influenza," Charlotte said. "But that is not all that is wrong, clearly. You will have to tell me *something*, Sergeant, if you wish me to advise you."

Webb still hesitated.

"I do not gossip," she added, even as her words to Letty Thompson about Lord Tillson's drunken fall came back to her. Any one of a dozen people could also have related that story, she reminded herself.

Webb considered for a moment. "'E don't sleep well, ma'am. Don't like bein' shut up. Gives 'im nightmares. Said once that laudanum makes 'em worse, so 'e don't use it no more."

Charlotte looked at Webb's list. "He *does* need to be kept warm, Sergeant."

"Reckon we could 'ave a window open, long as there's blankets and the fire is kept up."

"How much does he drink?"

"A lot." Webb's answer was reluctant.

"He may sleep better if you give him a little brandy now and then."

Webb frowned. "Give 'im *more* drink, ma'am?"

"If he normally drinks a lot, just stopping will make him feel ill even without the influenza. What else?"

"Gruel, 'orrid stuff, like prison food."

Prison food?

"I don't think we need to worry about that just yet, Sergeant."

Charlotte gestured towards the window. "Why don't you pull back the curtains and stoke up the fire? And tell Mrs Jackson to heat some bricks." She crossed to the bed and put a hand on Lord Tillson's fore-head—at the moment he felt too hot rather than too cold.

He looked dreadful, with dark circles under his eyes. His cheek-bones and nose appeared too prominent, and Charlotte could see in the opening in his shirt that his collar bones stuck out much more than they should. She picked up one bony wrist—his pulse was far too fast. There were also scars around his wrist that she couldn't make out clearly in the dim light, but she could feel faint ridges under her fingertips.

Voices... still the voices... but calm voices. Not asking me things... not telling me what to do. A woman's voice... thirsty...

"Help me sit him up a bit, Sergeant."

Webb put an arm behind Lord Tillson's shoulders and lifted so

Charlotte could rearrange the pillows. She held a cup to his lips, but he turned his head away, refusing to drink.

"It's only brandy, water, and honey," she said patiently, to little effect. "Come, my lord, you must drink something." But he did not seem to hear her, even when she repeated herself.

"'E ain't bin a lord long, ma'am," Webb said. "Mebbe 'e don't know you're talkin' to 'im?"

"What's he used to being called?" Charlotte asked.

"Major Southam."

"Come, Major, drink this!" Charlotte said, but those words seemed to make him more restless, and he struggled to get away from her.

"What's his Christian name?"

"Matthew."

Charlotte remembered the nurse she'd had as a child, and the way she'd ordered her charges. "Come, Master Matthew," she said sharply. "Just drink this, then you can go to sleep! It will do you no harm."

Nurse? Not my nurse... English... sweet... not the bitter drink of nightmares... good...

When Lord Tillson had drunk half a cup of the warm liquid, Charlotte put it down on a side table and turned to the bowl of water Tilly had brought, dipping the cloth into it.

"'E won't like that, ma'am." Webb warned. "Nearly drowned when 'e were a nipper—can't stand water bein' put on 'is face."

Lord Tillson was beginning to move around again. "We must try to make him cooler." Charlotte looked at the sergeant; she could see that he was really worried. She finished wringing out the cloth. "Be still, Master Matthew. You are too hot. This is a cold cloth I am going to put on your forehead. *Only* on your forehead. You have to trust me." She cautiously dabbed at his forehead—he moved a bit restlessly, but did not try knocking her hand away.

.   .   .

211

Trust? Damp, not wet... cool... Trust her...

"Good, good," Charlotte said. "Now, Master Matthew, take a little more drink, then sleep. We'll keep this cloth damp so it cools you."

He drank obediently, then they settled him down flat again.

Charlotte gestured Webb away from the bed, not wanting their voices to disturb the sick man. "Sergeant, I'm not qualified in any way to decide what to do with someone as ill as his lordship."

"Better'n that apothecary," Webb muttered.

"Nevertheless, we must consult a physician. Doctor Phelps, at Dursley, is just as likely as Halliton to want to bleed him. But I know a doctor in Bristol—would you be so kind as to ride there, if I give you a letter?"

"Bristol, ma'am?"

"I know it's a long way, Sergeant. Doctor Lorton was on the ship that brought Mrs Sergeant and me back from India after our husbands died. I spent a little time helping him with the sick and injured." Until they had both realised nausea that didn't seem to be related to the roughness of the sea was probably *not* sea sickness. He had banned her from approaching anyone who could possibly be infectious, to protect her unborn child.

"He is a very good doctor," Charlotte added. "And he listens to his patients."

"Very well, ma'am," Webb said. "If you think that's best."

Charlotte sat at the desk in the corner of the room and found some paper. "I will introduce you in the letter, and describe as much as I can about his lordship's condition." She put her spectacles on and started to write.

"Who'll see to things 'ere while I'm gone?" Webb asked. "Mrs Jackson didn't know what to do."

Charlotte considered him over her glasses. He seemed genuinely concerned, not just trying to get out of a long, cold ride. "I could ask Deacon to go, if you feel you cannot leave Birchanger. However, it may make it easier for Doctor Lorton to help if he knows *why* his lordship has nightmares and won't take laudanum. I think you know some of that, at least."

Webb said nothing.

"It is a very different matter telling a physician than if you were to confide in a stranger," Charlotte went on. "I leave it up to you how much to say. And I, or Mrs Sergeant, can stay here until you get back." She carried on writing. "You can read this, if you wish. I will not seal it."

She reached for another piece of paper. "If you could get Jackson to take a note to my house as well, I'd be grateful. Mary... Mrs Sergeant needs to know where I am and, if I am to be here all night, I will need some things."

"Very well, ma'am." He paused. "Thank you for 'elpin', ma'am."

Webb would not be back until this time tomorrow afternoon. He'd said he would get as far as he could before darkness fell, then try to find somewhere to stay and go on to Bristol in the morning. Charlotte sat by the bed, occasionally wringing out the damp cloth in cool water and placing it back on Lord Tillson's forehead. He seemed to have drifted off for the moment, his breathing slowing to the restful cadence of deep sleep.

Charlotte looked around the room with interest. It was sparsely furnished, but the bedding felt like good quality linen, and the curtains were heavy, with embroidered patterns. Wood panelling covered the walls to just above head height, with painted plaster above that. The wood was dark: a combination of both age and neglect, Charlotte surmised, judging by the little she had seen of the rest of the Hall.

Her perusal of the furnishings was interrupted when Lord Tillson began talking again, trying to throw off the covers and almost panting in distress. By the fire, the dog sat up and whined. Charlotte decided that even if he was sleeping, such a disturbed state could be doing him little good. She shook his shoulder gently, then more urgently when there was no response.

213

"You are safe at home, my lord," Charlotte said, as loudly as he was talking, but to little effect. "Master Matthew—wake up! You are safe with friends."

That seemed to get through. He opened his eyes for a moment while his breathing gradually returned to normal.

"Go back to sleep," she commanded. He blinked a couple of times, then his eyes closed. She looked around the room again, but there was little else to see; apart from the desk and the bed, there were only a couple of trunks standing by one wall. It did seem very odd to have so little in the way of furnishings.

In the bed, Lord Tillson was restless, but appeared to be sleeping without dreaming. Some of Webb's words came back to her as she watched—his lordship not liking being shut up, and the reference to prison food. Those scars around his wrists...

Charlotte rubbed her forehead. *Perhaps there's a reason he drinks so much?*

Nearly two hours later, Tilly came into the room with a basket. "Me dad come back with this, mum," she said. "He said Mr Deacon will be up later tonight." She cast a doubtful eye at the sick man. "Sally's gone home. Ma asked if you was wantin' anythin'."

"A cup of tea, please, Tilly. And whatever you are eating for an evening meal, when you have it. Oh, and a jug of hot water." She unpacked the basket to find the medicines she had asked for. There was also the article she was working on for Mr Berry, a newspaper, and a letter Mary must have brought up from Edgecombe.

She opened the letter, tilting it towards the lamp so she could see the writing clearly. It was from Ann—Charlotte was surprised to receive a reply so quickly. The note was rather short, saying merely that the new Lord Tillson had indeed only been confirmed in the last few weeks, after the executors had spent years trying to trace the heir. Ann was still trying to find out more about the man himself and his sergeant.

Charlotte didn't think she could concentrate on writing, so she picked up the newspaper. She wasn't able to read it for long, however. Lord Tillson started to talk in his sleep again, and he felt too hot when she laid a hand on his arm. She was kept busy renewing the wet cloth on his head, and she tried sponging down the rest of him. She did not feel she should remove his shirt, but it was so wet with sweat that dampening it with cold water couldn't make it any worse. He was talking, too, although nothing was coherent enough to be understood. Tilly had made some willow bark tea, but when she tried to make him drink it, his mind seemed to have gone back to the idea that 'they' were trying to poison him.

Deacon arrived late in the evening. "Mrs Sergeant sent me, ma'am, to let you get some rest. She'd have come, but she needs to be at the bakery in the morning."

Charlotte was glad to see him. Although she had done little physically, the worry of tending to the patient had worn her out. She had wanted to ask Mrs Jackson to sit with him, but the woman had looked so nervous when she brought Charlotte another cup of tea that it hadn't seemed a good idea.

She gave Deacon instructions, then went to see if she could rest somewhere for a while. She walked across the huge hall and through the passage to the kitchen, to find Mrs Jackson still sitting up.

"There be no beds but the ones we use," Mrs Jackson said.

"But there must be several bedrooms upstairs!" Charlotte took a deep breath, realising how sharp she had sounded. It was hardly Mrs Jackson's fault that she was tired, nor was it her fault that there were so few beds.

"Damp," Mrs Jackson said. "And no furniture."

"Oh, yes, Mrs Sergeant said something about that."

"You can have Tilly's bed, ma'am. I'll get the other kids to sleep in here."

Charlotte accepted this offer gratefully. Once in the small room, she only loosened her gown and stays before lying on the bed and pulling the covers over herself.

She slept for a few hours, but then tossed and turned for a while, listening to the noises of a strange house and wondering how the patient was going on. Giving up on the idea of further sleep, she righted her clothing and went to see how Deacon was coping.

Lord Tillson was much the same. Deacon reported that he'd managed to get a bit of brandy and water into the patient, but his lordship was still hot and restless, and still muttering incomprehensibly. While they were both there, she decided to try to make him drink some more willow bark tea in an attempt to bring his fever down. Deacon held him while Charlotte did her nurse impersonation again, managing to get nearly a full glass of the mixture into him. He seemed to settle a bit after that, and Charlotte sent Deacon off to rest for a few hours.

She was nodding off herself in a chair by the bed when Lord Tillson started to shout in his sleep again, loud enough to make the dog whine. Charlotte woke him up, dodging flailing arms. When he'd shaken off the nightmare, she offered the willow bark tea.

"You're not my nurse," he said, so faintly she had to bend her head near his to hear the words.

"No," she said, vastly relieved to hear words that made sense. She couldn't resist her next words. "I'm the old witch."

He blinked, and she thought he smiled very slightly.

"Drink this," she said, offering the cup again.

Lovely eyes...

He just stared at her through half-closed eyes.

Charlotte tried once more. "Come, drink this please. It will help you to feel a little better."

"What is it?"

"Willow bark tea—to reduce your fever. It should help your aches and pains, too, if you have them."

"No eye of frog and toe of newt?" he whispered, one corner of his mouth turning up, then obediently drank.

Charlotte tried not to laugh. He fell back to his pillows, exhausted by even that small effort. He still felt overly warm, but if he was well enough to make a joke, perhaps the crisis had passed.

CHAPTER 21

$\mathcal{C}$harlotte arrived home midway through the morning to find the house locked up and empty. Mary must have taken Davie with her to the bakery, as Deacon was up at Birchanger Hall.

Deacon had taken over again in the early hours while Charlotte rested, then she had sat with Lord Tillson for a while. His sleep was still disturbed, but although very weak and overly warm, he was lucid when awake. She had no qualms about leaving Deacon in charge.

Grateful for the peace of the empty house, Charlotte washed, put her nightgown on, and got into bed to try to sleep for a couple of hours. She didn't actually fall asleep, but drifted in a kind of in-between state, her thoughts wandering from Davie's clandestine activities, to worrying about his future, to further speculation about Birchanger Hall and its owner.

She must have finally slept, for a knock on her bedroom door jolted her awake.

"Mama?" When he got no reply, Davie poked his head around her door. "Are you ill?" he asked in sudden alarm.

"No, Davie." Charlotte sat up. "I was just very tired. Have you been with Mary at the bakery?"

"Yes. She sent me back home to tell you Sir Vincent is having a drink at the inn. She thinks he's going to come up here."

Bother! Over the last few years Sir Vincent had asked her to marry him at each annual Christmas party that his mother hosted, but Charlotte had just written to say she could not come this year. She wondered when Sir Vincent would give up—perhaps it had just become a habit with him? If he were seen to be courting her, his mother would not try to thrust other young women at him. Although courting did not really describe their occasional meetings at dinner parties.

"I'm getting up, Davie. Can you put the kettle on, please?"

"You're not going to say 'yes', are you, Mama?" Davie asked anxiously. "I don't *need* a father!"

"Should you dislike it so much?" she asked. "We'd have a lot more money—you could go to school, you could even have your own pony."

Davie shrugged. "I just don't like him much."

"Well, I'm not going to say 'yes' today."

She donned her dress, which was rather in need of a press after the night she'd had, and tidied her hair back into its usual knot. A cup of tea did much to revive her. She refilled the cup and took it into the parlour.

Davie helped her to exchange the landscape over the mantelpiece for the portrait of Captain MacKinnon in his regimentals that normally lived in a cupboard. She was just straightening it when Mary came into the room, slightly out of breath from walking up the hill.

"I put him off," she said. "I wasn't sure if you was back yet, so I told him you wasn't feeling well. He said he'd come back in a few days." She regarded the portrait critically. "You were going to tell him 'no' again? How long can you keep convincing him that you are still in love with your husband?"

Charlotte shrugged. "It just seems a kinder way of refusing him," she said. "Better for his ego than to be told that I don't need, or want, him. But…"

"But what?" Mary asked, when Charlotte didn't finish.

"School fees for Davie," Charlotte said.

"Oh. Hmm. But you are in mourning for your mother at the moment," Mary suggested. "It isn't the time to be deciding on things like marrying again. Put him off without saying 'no' if you really are considering it."

"I don't want to go to school," Davie said firmly. "And I don't want a father!"

Charlotte yawned, still tired. "I'm not going to argue now, Davie," she said. "Isn't Mr Hayes back yet?"

"I don't know, Mama," Davie said.

"Really? You're not just trying to avoid lessons?"

"No, Mama. I wouldn't do that again, honest!"

"Why don't you write a note for Mrs Thompson?" Mary suggested. "Davie can run over with it and fetch the answer."

"Good idea," Charlotte said. It would ensure that he didn't try to continue arguing about Sir Vincent. The note was ready by the time Davie had put his outdoor things on. "Straight there and straight back, Davie!" Charlotte said sternly as she wrapped his scarf around his neck.

Charlotte had been working for a couple of hours when there was a knock on the front door. Davie was not back yet, but she heard Mary answer, then come to knock on her parlour door.

"Sergeant Webb's back, wants to talk to you. I've put him in the kitchen—he looks like he needs feeding!"

"I'll come," Charlotte said, glad of the excuse to stop. Her mind was not working well at the moment, and she'd struggled to get anything done.

Webb sat at the table, looking both exhausted and worried, while Mary bustled about getting food and drink. Charlotte reassured him that Lord Tillson had seemed to be recovering when she left him that morning.

Webb looked happier at that news, then produced a letter for her. "From Doctor Lorton, ma'am."

Charlotte opened it, reading through it quickly. It was brief, but said she had probably done the right thing. Doctor Lorton also said he would try to visit in the next few days, both to see the patient, and to have a chance to catch up with Charlotte and Mary.

"Do you know what's in this?" Charlotte asked, holding the letter up.

"More or less, ma'am. Dunno if 'is lordship will want a doctor though, if 'e's recoverin'."

"Persuade him," Charlotte said firmly, and Webb sighed.

"Deacon is there at the moment," Charlotte went on. "But if his lordship is still improving you and Mrs Jackson should be able to manage, I think?"

Webb looked doubtful.

"Well, keep Deacon for tonight, and I'll come up in the morning to see how things are going."

"Thank you, ma'am."

Webb finished the food, then set off back to Birchanger.

Voices floated around Matthew as he drifted in and out of sleep. Different voices at different times, but all were quiet. They were soothing, not trying to make him do anything but drink some bitter liquid. He remembered seeing a pair of grey eyes looking at him with concern. Something about a witch? There was quiet, then voices again.

A cool breath of air brushed his face, although the room was warm. Too warm. He felt sticky, and he could smell sweat. The dull light of a winter's day illuminated the room. He was thirsty and hungry, his throat parched and stomach gnawing.

And he was not alone. All the bed curtains were drawn back, and a man he didn't recognise sat at his desk, bent over and concentrating on something.

"Who the hell are you?" He struggled upwards, resting on his elbows.

The man put down his pencil and came over to the bed.

"John Deacon, sir. My lord," he amended. "Mrs Captain asked me to sit with you."

Mrs Captain? Who..? Oh, never mind for now...

"How long—"

"You've been in bed since yesterday morning, sir."

"That's why I'm hungry." He was suddenly tired again, and collapsed back onto the pillows.

"I'll get you something to eat." Deacon went to the door. He called, then came back into the room. "Get you a drink as well. Coffee or tea?"

"Brandy," said Matthew tersely. He expected an argument if some managing female had given this man orders, so was surprised to see Deacon pour a small amount of amber liquid from Matthew's flask into a glass. As the man carried the glass to the bed, he noticed the bottom of one sleeve pinned up, and realised that Deacon had only one hand. Putting the glass down on the table beside the bed, Deacon helped him sit up, then adjusted the pillows behind him. Matthew drank the brandy, feeling the familiar, comforting fire spreading down his throat.

"More."

"No, my lord. You'll be needing some food first."

Matthew was about to protest, but Mrs Jackson came into the room carrying a tray with a small bowl of soup, some toast and jam, and a glass of barley water.

"That's not much," Matthew muttered grumpily.

"If you finish it you can have more," Deacon said patiently, helping to settle the tray across his lap.

Matthew couldn't finish it. He ate the toast, relishing the sweetness of the jam, but couldn't face the rest. Deacon made him drink the barley water, then gave him another sip of brandy before settling him back down.

His eyes closed almost immediately. When he awoke again it was dark outside, moonlight coming through the open curtains. Deacon fetched a tray of food himself this time, balancing the tray awkwardly across his handless arm. Matthew managed a bit more food before drifting off to sleep again.

The next time he awoke, it was daylight once more. A much nicer day, for there was a pale blue sky visible through the window, and a few wisps of white cloud. He slowly worked out that if the sun was not yet shining through the windows of this room it must be before noon. There was no-one around that he could see, so he struggled to disentangle himself from the sheets.

"Ah, woke up at last, 'ave you?" The voice came from the doorway.

"Webb?"

"Yessir. 'ow are you feelin'?"

"Like shit. How d'you bloody think?"

Webb grinned. "Feelin' better then, eh? You wasn't even up to cursin' at folks yesterday. Want some food?"

"Get me a drink, will you? And not that bloody barley water."

"Nossir."

"What?"

"Doctor's orders sir. No drink till you've ate summat."

"Who's in charge here, Webb?"

"Me, sir, for the moment."

Matthew lay back, tired by this brief outburst.

"'Course, you can get up and find some brandy yourself if you want, I ain't goin' to try an' stop you."

"Bugger off, Webb."

"Yessir."

Matthew closed his eyes, listening to Webb's heavy footsteps crossing the floor, after which there was only the noise of the fire crackling in the grate. Then the footsteps returned, and he opened his eyes to see another bowl of steaming soup and some bread. This time he managed to eat the lot, while Webb and Mrs Jackson brought in a bath and buckets of water.

He swung his legs off the bed and stood up, clutching one bed post when his legs almost gave way. Webb muttered a curse, leaving the screen he was setting up between the bath and the bed, and coming to help Matthew over to the bath.

Matthew sank into the hot water with relief, the warmth helping to ease the aches in his limbs. The sound of sheets snapping open indicated that Mrs Jackson was changing the bedding while he was out of the way.

"Soap, sir." Webb held out a bar of soap and he took it, washing away the smell of sweat from his skin and hair. Even that small effort exhausted him, and Webb had to help him out of the tub again. He insisted on drying himself, but was glad to be finally back in bed again, appreciating the feel of clean skin against clean sheets. The only thing missing was that soothing voice...

There were voices. Just normal, comfortable voices, discussing something quietly. Matthew could only hear the odd word or two, but they made no sense. Why would they be discussing hedgehogs?

He turned his head, opening his eyes slightly so he could see. There was the man he vaguely remembered speaking to before—Deacon, that was it. And the woman... the woman who was definitely *not* an old witch.

Deacon sat at the desk, with Miss MacKinnons leaning over to look at something he was showing her. All he could see was her black dress, and long hair pulled back in a tidy knot. Lots of rich brown hair, the colour of... of chestnuts. He wondered how long it was, and what it would look like when loose.

The fabric of the dress was flat, not reflecting any light—a mourning dress, then? And somewhat out of fashion—the officers' wives in India may have been a year behind the fashion in London, but even from the back, he could tell that the low waist and full skirt was much older than that.

His throat tickled and he coughed. Miss MacKinnons straightened up and the two of them looked towards him. Deacon left the room, and she came over to the bed.

"Back in the land of the living?" she asked, with a small smile.

He frowned—that remark was too close to some of his nightmares for comfort. *She can't know anything about that, can she?*

"May I?" she asked, but did not wait for an answer, her hand hovering near his head.

He gave a very small nod, then felt her hand on his forehead, cool and gentle.

"You still feel rather hot," she said. "Headache?"

"A little."

She picked up his wrist, and he turned his face away, not wanting to see the usual reaction to the scars there. But when he turned back, she wasn't looking at him at all. Instead, she concentrated on a man's watch she had taken out of a pocket. Taking his pulse?

"Well, doctor?" he joked, when she put the watch back into a pocket somewhere inside her skirts.

"I'm not a doctor," she said, her expression quite serious. "I have a doctor's instructions, though." She sat on the edge of the bed. "The eye of newt appears to have worked—you seem to be well on the mend."

He blinked at her forthright answer, the mention of newts seeming familiar. He abandoned his attempt to remember why when he saw her brows draw together.

"You wouldn't have been nearly as ill if you ate more!"

He closed his eyes. *Do all women nag?*

He felt her weight leave the mattress, and when he let his eyes crack open again she was back at the desk, bundling papers together and putting them into a bag. *Leaving?* He was about to say something, but Deacon came back into the room with Webb.

"I think his lordship is well enough to be left in your tender care now, Sergeant," Miss MacKinnons said.

"Very good, ma'am."

"You've got the list of Doctor Lorton's instructions?" she asked.

Webb patted a pocket.

Who the hell was Doctor Lorton? Had everyone been prodding and poking him while he was out of his head?

She returned to the bed.

"You need plenty of food and drink," she said, drawing the bedclothes up higher. "And that means tea or coffee or barley water, *not* brandy. You should be on your feet in a day or so."

He nodded weakly, head still on the pillow. She picked up the bag she'd packed, and left, Deacon following her out of the room.

"Get me a drink, will you, Webb?" he said when he was sure Miss MacKinnons was out of earshot. He was rather surprised when Webb handed him a small glass of wine.

"Disobeying orders, eh?" he said, swallowing it gratefully.

"Not exactly, sir. Mrs Captain said you could 'ave a bit, as long as you eat as well. So now you..."

"Who is Mrs Captain?"

Webb jerked his thumb towards the door. "Folks in the village call 'em that. Saves wonderin' about which of the Mrs MacKinnons someone's talkin' about." He pointed to his eye, still showing signs of black beneath it. "It were Mrs Sergeant what did this."

He supposed that made some kind of sense. "So who's this Doctor Lorton?"

"Lives in Bristol. Mrs Captain sent me with a note." Webb glanced away, clearing his throat. When he turned back he asked if Matthew was hungry.

"No. I'll have some more wine, though."

"Not without you eatin' first," Webb said firmly. Matthew swore at him, but Webb just stood at ease, hands behind his back, with the blank expression of a subordinate who was going to do what he wanted to, no matter what the bloody officer said.

"Webb, how many times have you been demoted?" Matthew asked, when it became apparent he was not going to get alcohol without having some food first.

"Only once, sir, officially."

"What do you mean, officially?"

"Well, I was due to be busted down to private again, but the stupid bugg... the lieutenant got 'isself killed before 'e did it official-like."

"Drunk and disorderly? Stealing?" Matthew remembered the ruby necklace.

"Nossir. Tellin' officers they was wrong, sir." He looked sad for a moment. "Would've saved some lives if they'd listened, sir."

Matthew stared at him. Maybe Webb really *was* that valuable asset —a soldier who knew what he was doing and had the courage to say so.

"Oh, very well. Bring me some dinner then."

∾

"Wake up, sir!"

Someone was shaking him; a dog was whining. Matthew was disorientated, waking from the dark and damp cell into a dimly lit room. He sat up, the abrupt movement sending a stabbing pain through his head.

"Shit!"

"Yessir." Webb waited until Matthew's breathing returned to near normal. "Funny thing, sir, but Mrs Captain and Deacon didn't say nothin' about nightmares after you was back to bein' yerself." Webb handed him a small glass of brandy without being asked.

"Are you still watching over me?" Matthew asked, seeing that Webb appeared to be dressed in a nightshirt.

"No, sir. Mrs Captain said it weren't needed. I was sleepin' in the kitchen—nice and warm by the range. Dog barked, woke me up."

Matthew rubbed his face. Perhaps earlier he'd known he was safe because someone had been with him, even though they hadn't said anything. The dog came and put her chin on the edge of the bed, still whining. She stopped when he absently scratched her head.

Webb left the room, returning a few minutes later dragging a mattress behind him. "Reckon I'll sleep in 'ere, sir, till you're up an' about." He didn't wait for a response from Matthew but lay down, wrapped his blanket around himself, and appeared to fall asleep straight away.

Matthew lay back and stared at the ceiling. It was pathetic, being afraid to sleep without someone there to stop the past haunting him. He thought of standing on the deck of the *Amathea*, watching those rolling waves, and wondered yet again why he hadn't just leaned over further. Webb's idea might work, but he was a grown man, not a child in need of a nurse. He couldn't spend the rest of his life this way.

His eyelids grew heavy and he fell asleep in spite of his reluctance to do so. This time, he did not dream.

CHAPTER 22

$\mathcal{M}$atthew sat in the window of his room, watching the Jacksons walk down the drive and into the woods. Mrs Jackson had asked permission to cut greenery from the grounds to decorate the kitchen for Christmas. Matthew had been vaguely surprised that Christmas was so close, having lost track of time while he'd been ill.

In India, Christmas had been celebrated with alcoholic enthusiasm by the army. He remembered the noisy revels in the mess, drowning out the wish to be home with wine and rowdy games.

Home? His lips twisted. The home he'd longed for had disappeared when his mother died. There had still been the smell of cut fir and roasting chestnuts, and the warmth of a good fire after snowball fights, but it wasn't the same after Serena arrived.

A spatter of rain hit the window, and his mouth turned down. Well, he'd got the fire and the cold weather, but just drizzle and mud so far. It fitted his current mood.

He swirled the wine around, watching the red drops run down the inside of the glass. Webb had persuaded him that drinking wine was better for him—well, slightly less bad for him—than swilling brandy. Webb had then pulled a low trick by hiding the supplies; Matthew suspected that they were stashed somewhere down in the far reaches of the cellars, where he would have to be really, really desperate to venture. A bottle came out as a reward for eating a meal. Just like being back in the bloody nursery. *"You can have your pudding when you've eaten your vegetables."*

Matthew studied the wine again, recalling the list of the apothecary's instructions Webb had shown him. He closed his eyes for a moment. Thank God Miss MacKinnons hadn't agreed with that regimen. He'd felt bad enough while he was ill—trying to manage on gruel and no drink would have been hellish indeed. *How did she come to be so wise?*

Turning to face into the room, he surveyed the gloomy panelling, the grimy outlines of pictures no longer there, the bare floor.

What must she think of this place? Of me?

She'd sat with him for... how long? He remembered waking several times to those grey eyes as she bent over him to help him drink, with that hair of hers, smelling faintly of lavender.

He took another mouthful of wine. Life couldn't be easy for a mother bringing up an illegitimate son alone; and doing it well, from what he had seen of the lad. He wondered about her family—he hadn't heard of her having any relatives nearby, apart from Mrs Sergeant, if she *was* a sister. Odd that the two women were called 'Mrs' Captain and Sergeant, but perhaps the villagers respected them in spite of Davie? They had been very helpful to Mrs Jackson and to Webb, after all. And she hadn't pried into the reasons for his nightmares.

The last time he'd seen her before he fell ill was when she was berating him—unjustly—for setting mantraps, and not searching for her son. She'd had a nice colour in her cheeks.

He rubbed his temples; he should not hold that rant against her. She was frightened for her son, and the assumptions she made were only natural. He should thank her for looking after him.

Matthew held his right hand out. He'd certainly eaten more food in the past couple of days than in the few weeks he'd been at Birchanger before his illness. He'd also drunk rather less than usual. His hand looked steady enough to risk a shave.

He put his glass of wine down. He'd visit this morning.

Once he'd found his gear and fetched a basin of hot water from the kitchen, he propped up his mirror on the mantelpiece. He winced when he saw his reflection. He hadn't shaved for a couple of days and this, combined with the dark circles under his eyes and the way his cheekbones stuck out, made him look like some creature out of a gothic novel.

He should still call to thank Miss MacKinnons—she hadn't actually cringed when she looked at him, after all. He took a deep breath and proceeded to make himself presentable.

Shaved and changed, Matthew was contemplating walking down to the village to call on the Misses MacKinnons when two thoughts struck him. He still wasn't feeling completely well and, more importantly, he had no idea where they lived. It probably wasn't in Edgecombe, because if that were the case their route to the squire's place at Northridge Hall would not lie through his woodland. In all likelihood they lived somewhere east of the village itself, but he didn't have the energy to wander around until he found the right place.

Out in the stables, he called for someone to saddle Daisy before remembering that the Jacksons were all out looking for holly and fir. He stood in the courtyard and shouted again for Webb, receiving only a bark from Reena in reply. Shrugging, he heaved the saddle onto the mare himself, leaning on her to catch his breath before fastening the girth. He hoisted himself into the saddle and set off down the drive. If he went into Edgecombe first, he could enquire there.

The fire in the taproom of the Hare and Hounds was warming so, after getting his directions, he sat and enjoyed a pint of ale. The inn was not busy in the middle of the day, and the only other customers were playing dice on the far side of the room, so he had no need to exert himself to talk to anyone.

His directions were to go up the lane to Upper Edgecombe. The landlord had described the end cottage of a row, a mile or so up a narrow lane from the village. Matthew had been told he 'couldn't miss it', and for a change this actually turned out to be true. The row of cottages was built of the same warm-coloured stone as Birchanger

Hall, but, unlike the Hall, their gardens were neat and their roofs intact.

He tied Daisy safely to the fence, then knocked on the door. It was opened by Davie, his eyes wide in surprise.

"Good afternoon," Matthew said. "I'd like to speak with your mother, if she is at home."

Davie nodded. "We're all in the kitchen, sir. My lord, I mean."

"Just 'sir' will be fine, Davie. Lead on!"

The kitchen was a haven of warmth and cheer after the gloomy drizzle outside. Evergreen branches—fir and holly—were arranged on the ledge above the range, and hanging in garlands on the walls; there was even a small kissing ball above his head in the doorway. The afternoon gloom was brightened by candles on the table. Matthew breathed in the pleasant aroma of gingerbread.

The two women of the house were sitting at the kitchen table. Miss MacKinnons sat with Deacon, her head bent over papers and drawings spread out in front of them. At the other end of the table, Webb appeared to be consulting another woman over a list. She must be the other Miss MacKinnons—Mrs Sergeant. They all stood up when Matthew followed Davie into the room. The middle of the table was littered with scraps of fir, pine cones, and lengths of ribbon, most of it in a part-made wreath.

A sudden knot of envy twisted inside him. Not that he wanted to be making decorations, but it struck him that the friendly domesticity of it all was something he had yearned for without realising.

"Please, don't get up," Matthew said. "I..." He hesitated. Interrupting what they were doing just to say thank you seemed an imposition.

"You lookin' for me, sir?" Webb asked.

"He wants to talk to you, Mama," Davie piped up, sitting down again with his fir twigs.

"Shall we go into the parlour?" Miss MacKinnons asked, standing up and removing her spectacles. Matthew nodded. She led the way back down the corridor and into another room.

"I'm sorry it's rather cold," she said. "I only have a fire lit when I'm working in here." She gestured him to one of the chairs by the fire place and they both sat down.

He looked around the small room with interest. There was greenery in here too, above the fireplace, along the tops of several bookcases, and even a bit draped over a mirror on the wall opposite the window. The table in the centre of the room held a pile of books, several small stacks of paper neatly arranged, and pencils and a bottle of ink lying ready. Not a dining table, then? The bookcases were full of books, with some of the shelves stacked two deep. It was quite unlike such items of furniture in his stepmother's house, which were full of ornaments. A faint scent of beeswax polish hung in the chill air, along with lavender and rose from a bowl of dried flowers on a side table.

"I'll light the fire," Miss MacKinnons said.

"No, don't bother, Miss MacKinnons. I won't interrupt you for long." Matthew noticed a quick frown before she spoke.

"Very well. How can I help you? You are looking much better than the last time I saw you."

"That's why I came—to say thank you for your help. Webb told me what the apothecary suggested."

"Indeed. I suspect it is the same list of instructions for every ailment."

"You sent all the way to Bristol for a doctor?" He realised this sounded like criticism. "I'm just curious, ma'am."

"I have known Doctor Lorton for a long time," she explained. "He is competent, and prescribes what is necessary, not what he can charge the most for. He also listens to his patients. I sent Webb with a note of your symptoms—he did not actually examine you himself."

He nodded. "Yes, Webb explained that. It seems to have worked."

She did have a lovely face—not beautiful, exactly, but with pleasing features and a clear complexion. Her skin wasn't as fashionably white as Serena's or Julia's, no doubt due to her frequent walks over to the squire's place, but the colour it gave to her cheeks was attractive.

As he gazed, her expression became quizzical, and he became uncomfortably aware that he had been staring.

He hastened into speech. "You must have given up a lot of your time, ma'am. Is there anything I can do?" Serena would have asked for money or jewellery—but then Serena wouldn't have helped someone voluntarily in the first place.

He glanced around the room again while he waited for an answer, noticing a portrait above the fireplace. A soldier, with a captain's insignia, his appearance that of a man in his mid twenties. And the greenery on the mantelpiece was arranged around a sword.

Mrs Captain...? *Mrs* MacKinnon? He glanced at her hands resting in her lap. How could he have missed her wedding ring? *Why did I assume she'd never had a husband?*

"My lord?" He became aware that she had been speaking. "Are you well?"

"I'm sorry. My wits were wandering." They had been wandering for some time, obviously. *What did I say to her? I didn't suggest Davie was illegitimate, did I?* He couldn't separate nightmares from reality while he was asleep—what if he was losing the ability to separate what was just in his head from what was reality in his waking hours too?

"I was explaining that I was grateful for the way you talked to Davie. You made him understand why he was wrong."

"My pleasure, ma'am," he said stiffly, standing up. He must leave before he said anything—or anything more—that might offend. "I'm afraid I must go. Excuse me." He nodded abruptly and left the parlour, passing Mrs Sergeant in the passageway on his way to the front door.

Mary closed the door behind Lord Tillson, then went into the parlour. "I came to see if he... if you wanted a drink," Mary said to Charlotte. "What did you do to him?"

"I have no idea," Charlotte said, puzzled at his abrupt departure. "He said he only came to thank me for seeing off Halliton." She shook her head. "Never mind. Just as well I didn't light the fire."

Half an hour later, Charlotte finished inspecting the drawings spread out on the kitchen table. Deacon had drawn the scenes for one of the hedgehog tales, managing to give all the hedgehog family distinct appearances without making their faces look too human. And the backgrounds… she shook her head in awe.

"These are brilliant, Deacon."

Deacon smiled, his face reddening. "They'll do, then?"

"More than—"

They heard a loud knock on the front door. Mary was still talking to Webb, so Davie went to see who it was.

"Hello, Sir Vincent. Have you come to see Mama?" Davie's voice carried clearly into the kitchen from the front door.

"Oh, no!" Charlotte patted her hair to check it was still tidy. "I could do without this!"

"I'll show him into the parlour," Mary said, getting up and taking a lighted taper with her.

"I'll be off, shall I, ma'am?" Webb asked, standing up too.

"No need, Sergeant, really. Unless you've finished?"

Charlotte thought Webb's eyes strayed to the kissing ball over the door, but perhaps she imagined it.

"Sir Vincent," she said as she entered the parlour, her voice as bright as she could make it. Her visitor turned away from the mirror where he had been checking the arrangement of his neckcloth. Mary was busy lighting the fire, so the room still had a distinct chill.

"I'm sorry it's so cold in here, Sir Vincent. We were busy in the kitchen, so I haven't had the fire on."

"That is quite all right, my dear Mrs MacKinnon." Sir Vincent bent over her hand, allowing her a view of his carefully pomaded hair, a few curls artfully arranged to fall forwards onto his forehead. He was dressed in riding gear, but it fitted beautifully around his wide shoulders and muscular thighs. Charlotte wondered how he managed to control his horse in such a tight-fitting coat. She was equally impressed by the lack of horse smell and mud after riding in this weather. Mary gave her a wink as she left the parlour, her cheeks dimpling with amusement.

"Do sit down, sir." Charlotte gestured towards the chair. "May I wish you and your family a happy Christmas?"

"Thank you, Mrs MacKinnon. I was disappointed to learn that you could not come to our Christmas party this year. We all missed you greatly."

She doubted that his sisters or mother had missed her—Lady Kinney did *not* approve of the prospect of having Charlotte for a daughter-in-law. "Well, I cannot keep myself in complete seclusion—" Charlotte began.

"Nor it is expected for the death of a parent," Sir Vincent put in earnestly.

"No, indeed. Nevertheless, I think to attend parties would be going well beyond what is acceptable. And now is not the time for making any important decisions," she added, hoping to head him off his predictable course.

"You know, Mrs MacKinnon, it is my earnest desire to relieve you of all your troubles and the *need* for you to make decisions." His eyes fell on her fingers, ink-stained as usual, and he pursed his lips. "You should only be worrying about which dress to wear, and what to order for dinner."

And whether such a life would drive me mad!

"You should not be having to earn your living, my dear. And David," he added, taking an as-yet untried tack. "He must be nearly old enough to go to school. I'm sure I could pull strings to get him a place at a good boarding school—perhaps even Harrow or Winchester."

Nicely out of the way.

"You needn't worry yourself about that kind of decision, my dear. Such things are best left to wiser minds—it is a big decision, after all, where to send your son."

"It's very kind of you to be concerned for me," Charlotte said. He started to speak again, but she ploughed on. "But I do feel I cannot even contemplate such a major decision at the moment." She left it to him to determine whether she was talking about Davie's schooling or his proposal. She fished a handkerchief out of a pocket and dabbed gently at her dry eyes, before looking up at the portrait over the mantelpiece.

"I do understand, my dear," Sir Vincent said gently, reaching over to pat her on the back of the hand. "I will call again in a month or two, and hope to find you feeling more the thing." He stood up. "Lady Kinney is beginning to worry about my future heir. I'm afraid she thinks I would be more suited to a younger woman, someone only just out."

Someone she can keep under her thumb.

"I do not wish…" Sir Vincent tailed off, glancing at the portrait over the fire again. "Er, perhaps I may persuade you to come to dinner, or for a picnic if the weather is warm enough in the spring? But I will leave you now, dear lady," he finished. "The season's greetings to you." He gave a small bow, and let himself out.

Charlotte slumped back in her chair, only now realising how tense she had been. It wasn't as if she hadn't been in this position before—but this was the first time she had refused him while wanting to make sure she did not burn her bridges. She didn't feel very happy with herself about it—in all fairness, she really should have told him she would never marry him years ago. And now she was only using him as insurance in case her father managed to stop the trust fund paying her.

She stood up and went over to the fireplace, reaching up to take the portrait off the wall.

"Well, Angus," she said to the painting. "You may have been unfaithful and a gambler, but you were more fun than Sir Vincent could ever be. You did save me from one truly hideous marriage prospect, and you are helping me to delay the inevitable now."

She brushed a few specks of dust from the painting, then put it back in its cupboard with Angus' sword. The landscape painting was put back in its place, and she straightened the greenery that would stay there until Twelfth Night.

CHAPTER 23

*M*atthew stabbed at the soil repeatedly with his spade, each thrust driven by a furious self-loathing that seemed to have no end.

That, for thinking that escaping the Indian heat, humidity, and smells would let him forget what he'd done.

That, for thinking that coming back to England would improve anything.

That, for not following the lure of the rolling waves on the ship and just leaning out further.

That, for thinking there could be any point to anything.

And *that...* for being so stupid as to assume that a respectable widow was some kind of lightskirt with a bastard son.

Feeling dizzy, he dropped his spade into the mud and leaned against the brick wall. He slid his back down the wet ivy leaves until he sat on the ground, resting his head in his hands. His back and hands hurt from digging, and moisture seeped through his breeches.

The exercise had not stopped his mind going over and over what a fool he'd very nearly made of himself with Mrs MacKinnon. He could see now how it had started. When Webb had mentioned the Mrs MacKinnons, he'd interpreted it as the Misses MacKinnons. How idiotic to be fooled by a plural and not just to ask Webb for more information! What had Davie said—he had no father? An adult might say that if they didn't know who their father was, but to a boy of his age, it was just a different way of saying that his father was dead.

And he, stupidly, had put the worst interpretation on it. Why? Because he resented her having seen him sprawl at her feet when he arrived in Edgecombe? That was his own fault for being a drunken ass.

Snow started to fall, the flakes grey in the dim light from the leaden sky. He thought about getting up and fetching a lantern to carry on, but the far wall was hardly visible in the gloom. There was still a vast area to clear. He should hire some men—God knows there were plenty of men around here needing work. He wasn't doing anything useful here, other than trying to avoid his own failings, his own feelings.

He sat until he couldn't feel his hands or feet, then reluctantly pushed himself up. He'd given everyone enough trouble, being ill. There was no need to put them all through that again. He left the spade in the mud and tramped out onto the drive and in through the front door of the Hall.

Inside, Mrs Jackson and the children had inexpertly draped fir branches and holly sprigs along any horizontal surfaces that would take them. The scent of the firs over the fireplace masked the faint smell of damp still lingering in the house. He shouted for hot water, and soon Webb and Jackson were carrying buckets into his room.

Webb looked disapprovingly at the muddy footprints Matthew had made across the floor, then asked him if he wanted any greenery to decorate his room. Matthew swore at him. Webb shrugged and took himself off.

Matthew sat by the fire until he felt a little warmer, then got into the bath, swearing again as he found he'd left it so long the water had got cold. He gave himself a cursory wash, dressed in dry clothes and shouted for Webb again.

"I were just goin' down to the village, sir," Webb said. "See some men in the inn. Thought I'd go to the midnight service."

"Bring me a bottle of brandy first," Matthew ordered, slumping into the chair by the fire. "No, make that two."

"Sir, I don't think—"

"Just bloody *do it* Webb! For God's sake, if we were still in the army I'd have you flogged." He remembered that technically he *was* still in the army. And he'd never really seen the use in flogging the men— even less so now.

"Just get me something to drink," he said wearily. He held his hands out—the blisters he'd remade were stinging and he ached all over, but although his body felt weary, his mind did not. Numbing it with alcohol might help. There was silence beside him for a moment, then he heard Webb's footsteps retreat. Some time later, a tray was put down beside him with food, a mug of coffee, a glass and a bottle of brandy. He ignored everything but the brandy, and didn't even bother with the glass.

The fortress walls shimmered in the heat, making an accurate assessment difficult. Matthew shifted uncomfortably, wiped the telescope lens and tried again. There was something odd about that section of wall, something that hadn't been there in '92, when he'd been in the fortress as a junior officer.

He sat up in bed, hands over his eyes, trying not to see, to relive, what his mind insisted on showing him.

...give it another day, see if we can find out more...

That had been his mistake.

Screwing up his eyes, he turned over, burying his face in the pillow, but the memories persisted through the pounding in his head: Stevens lying in the dust, looking almost restful apart from the pool of red spreading beneath him; a hand in his hair, forcing his head back; the triumph on the face of the turbaned soldier, holding the dispatch he'd sent off with Havers the day before.

Swearing, he flung the covers off the bed, ignoring the sudden yelp from Reena. More brandy was the only solution. He swore again as he tripped over his discarded clothing. There was still a glow from the dying fire, and he moved towards it, more carefully this time. He didn't see the brandy bottle until he kicked it over.

Empty.

My fault. How many men died?

He stumbled over to the window. The snow had stopped and the clouds cleared; he could see a couple of stars, fading now in the coming dawn.

Closing his eyes, he rested his forehead on the cold glass. Nothing had changed since he got home.

Home? He'd happily trade this whole mouldering pile, Farleton as well, for a cottage somewhere—a cottage with a family in it.

Who would want him, with that failure haunting him, with his nightmares, with this ruin he'd done nothing about in a month?

Shivering, he pulled a blanket from the bed and found a taper to light the lamp. He surveyed the trunks against the wall, then opened one, pulling the contents out and flinging them behind him until he came to what he wanted.

Snow blanketed the ground, glittering in the sunshine beneath a watery blue sky. The air was so still that the small fire Matthew had made in the hut provided enough heat to keep him from shivering, even with the icy temperatures. His breath misted, floating gently away.

The beauty of the day was an affront, not something to be admired or enjoyed. It *was* peaceful, though, away from the shouting of the Jackson children, excited at the Christmas gifts Webb had bought for them all.

His pistol had been a gift on the occasion of his promotion to major. One of a pair—he'd given the other one to Miss MacLeod during their trip to London. They had hardly been used, the elaborately chased silver mountings making them more for show, or duelling, rather than service in the field.

Breathing on the metal, he gave it a good polish with his handkerchief, then placed it on a stone on the ground in front of him and took another mouthful of brandy. He felt in his pocket for the balls he'd put there. He only needed one, but he arranged them in a neat row in front of the pistol, and set his powder flask next to them.

Such a small thing, really, a pistol ball. But quick. Better than rotting to death in a dungeon. Although if that had happened, he wouldn't have had to drag himself through the last six months, floating on a sea of alcohol and shame. No-one would miss him.

Matthew picked up the pistol, checking the flint was screwed in properly. Unstopping the flask, he tipped it to pour powder down the barrel.

Nothing came out.

He swore, peering into the flask, but the opening was too small to allow him to see inside. Putting the pistol down, he banged the mouth of the flask on the ground. Sodden lumps of wet powder fell out, and he stared at them in disbelief.

Amazing, Southam—the only thing you are really good at is being a failure. Can't even keep your damned powder dry.

He knocked the rest of the wet powder out of the flask, spreading it out on a flat stone, then wiped his fingers on his coat to get rid of the residue. It might dry out in front of the fire. If he was careful, he might get enough of it down the barrel to fire the pistol.

Matthew studied the powder flask, trying to work out how the powder had got wet. He'd had to pull hard with his teeth to get the stopper out, so water couldn't have got in that way. It had been fairly full—if there were a crack in it somewhere, surely much of the powder would have leaked out by now. There didn't seem to be anything wrong with the flask. But the fact remained that his powder was wet.

He gave up trying to think how it had happened, and considered his options. He had two options. Well, three, really, he managed to work out through the fuzziness in his head. He could wait for the powder to dry out, he could go back to the Hall and find some dry powder, or he could just sit here until he froze. He leaned back on the wall behind him and shut his eyes. It was actually quite restful here.

~

Charlotte surveyed the table with satisfaction, not able to eat another thing. Even Davie had declined a second helping of plum pudding. Mary had worked her usual wonders with the goose, and Deacon had a splendid recipe for mulled wine.

He'd brought that out last night—well, this morning, really, after they'd all walked back together from the midnight service. The air had been crisp and cold, their boots crunching in the thin layer of snow. Davie had been allowed a small sip of the wine before Charlotte took him off to bed.

She glanced down the table towards Mary, sitting at the far end. She was talking to Deacon, a smile on her face that Charlotte didn't recall seeing before.

Charlotte's eyes drifted to the kissing ball above the door. This year was the first time Mary had included a kissing ball with the Christmas decorations. Webb had been eyeing the ball a few days ago when she'd left the room to talk to Lord Tillson, and she suspected he'd managed to catch Mary under it—without earning a black eye this time.

When she'd come down from putting Davie to bed in the early hours of this morning, Mary and Deacon had been beneath it. Something about the way they were standing made her suspect that Mary had initiated a kiss this time.

Davie got up to fetch the box of spillikins.

"You play," Mary said. "We'll wash up."

Charlotte nodded, passing plates down the table to make space. Between them, Mary and Deacon carried the plates and bowls out to the scullery. Charlotte's eyes narrowed as she watched—they didn't speak, but there was something about the way they looked at each other, the way they moved.

She shook her head, turning back to Davie as he tipped the sticks into a heap in front of her. She'd find a time to catch Mary alone later, or tomorrow.

"You go first, Davie," she said, watching as he concentrated on pulling sticks from the pile, and suppressing a surprising pang of envy. She didn't *need* a man to run her life for her, but what if there were someone honourable and dependable…?

"Mama!"

"Sorry, Davie. Is it my turn?"

Matthew woke, forgetting where he was for a moment. The fire had gone out, and the cold was seeping into him. His head felt a little better, but the black cloud was still there, pointing out that it was all very well sleeping in the daytime, but normal men didn't have a past that made them afraid to sleep at night; normal men didn't panic in enclosed spaces or in the dark.

Beyond the hut, a harness clinked, and hooves crunched on dead sticks; the sounds must have woken him. Damn—what were other people doing here on Christmas Day? Perhaps they would just go past. The fire wasn't smoking any more to attract attention.

He shut his eyes, leaning back on the wall again, only to be roused a moment later by the sound of Webb swearing. He slowly opened his eyes again.

"Jesus! You're alive?" Webb exclaimed, the frown he'd been wearing suddenly clearing.

"What the hell are you doing here, Webb?" Matthew asked. "Bugger off back to your Christmas dinner."

Webb turned and walked out of the hut. Matthew heard a slap, followed by hooves moving off. Webb came back carrying a bag.

"Brought your dinner," he said, pulling out various packets wrapped in cloth. He dusted off a flat stone near the fire, pausing when Matthew exclaimed. He sniffed, tasted the black dust on his hand, then rubbed it on his coat.

Matthew stared at him. A soldier knew what powder tasted like, and Webb should have been surprised at tasting it here. But he looked satisfied, not puzzled.

"*You* put water in my powder flask?"

"'Ave some goose," Webb said, holding out a plate.

Matthew knocked it out of his hand, the plate cracking in half on a stone. "What bloody business is it of yours, what I do? Sod off and mind your own business. And get me some dry powder."

"Can't do both," Webb pointed out, calmly picking up the spilled food and sitting down opposite. "Get your own powder. But if you're goin' to do it, tell me first so I can clear up the mess before those lads find you, eh?"

"Damn you!" Matthew lunged towards him and grabbed the bag, searching through it frantically.

"Didn't bring none with me," Webb said calmly. "Turn out my pockets if you like?" He took another large piece of goose out of its wrappings and bit into it. "Sure you don't want some? It's good."

Matthew sagged back against the wall. "Why are you bothering, Webb? You don't need me—you've surely got more than that necklace we sold in Bath. Plenty to live on if you don't take to gambling."

"You don't 'ave to *need* someone to want to 'elp," Webb said simply.

"You think you're helping? Dammit, Webb, I've failed at everything. I couldn't even get word out about the mine in the fortress! Do you know what it's like to be *afraid* to go to sleep?" *And live with the shame of my failures.*

"No." Webb shook his head, looking down at the food on his plate. "But I know what it's like to listen to men with my mother, wonderin' if this one's goin' to beat 'er up after. And if 'e'll bother to pay. And when the last one beat 'er so bad she died, I was afraid they was goin' to pin it on me."

"Shit!"

"Yessir."

"Is that supposed to make me feel better somehow?"

"Nossir. Just that you ain't the only one with bad memories. I used to think I could 'ave stopped 'em. Or that I should'a bin earnin' money so she didn't 'ave to open her legs to any bastard what could pay."

"How old were you?" Matthew asked.

"Ten or so. Dunno exactly. Skinny little runt, I were, too."

"Ten? You couldn't have—"

"Right. I know that now. But it took a while before I worked it out."

Matthew took out his brandy flask, tilting it to drink the remaining drops. Webb got up and left the hut, returning after only a moment with two bottles of port. He opened one and handed it over, then gathered the last few bits of dry wood in the hut to get the fire going again.

"What did you do?" Matthew held the bottle in his hand without drinking. For now it was enough to know that there was more when he wanted it.

"Ran off. Stole food and money. Ended up gettin' arrested and took the King's shillin' 'stead of bein' sent to prison." He opened the other bottle of port and took a mouthful. "Hmm—I can see why the nobs like this stuff!"

"You liked the army?" Matthew asked, when Webb didn't continue.

Webb shrugged. "Only thing I know. The army was my family."

That made sense. The men watched out for each other, and took pride in their company, or their regiment. He doubted that most of them fought for king and country—what kept them together and fighting was loyalty to each other, and the sense of belonging to their own small unit. It wasn't quite the same for officers, but then officers had more choice in what they did; they could sell out whenever they wished.

"And now they've discharged you?"

Webb didn't meet his eyes. "Lookin' for a position, sir." He stared around him at the damp trees. "It'd be nice to belong somewhere."

"Yes, it would."

"You belong 'ere, sir." There was a faint question beneath the statement.

"Not really."

"What about your other place?"

"Farleton? I suppose I belong there—that's where I grew up. It belongs to me, of course, but that's not the same thing. I haven't seen it for ten years. It will have changed. Lord knows what my dear step-mother has done to the place."

"That's another reason not to do this," Webb said, nudging the pistol with his foot. "If you ain't made a will...?"

Matthew just shook his head.

"If you ain't got a will, then your brother and his mama 'ave won. They'll get just what they wanted."

"He'll get Birchanger even if I do make a will," Matthew said. He then had to explain entails to Webb.

"'E thought 'e already 'ad it," Webb said. "Was you declared missin' afore you turned up in that 'ospital?" Webb once again avoided Matthew's eyes as he asked the question.

"I don't know. It's possible. Why?"

"I reckon your brother got ahead of 'isself. That money the folks in Edgecombe said you owed?" Matthew nodded. "I reckon your brother came to see what 'is new place was like. Mebbe 'e found out you *were* comin' back after all, so 'e just left again."

"With what was left of the contents of the house." It made sense. "Mantraps?"

"I reckon so."

"Yes, it would be like him." Matthew contemplated his half-brother: Charles bullying his younger brother, Charles asking for more money for clothing, or for his gambling debts. "God knows what he's done at Farleton."

He took another drink—too many things to be decided. Just too many decisions. And not enough brain power. He rubbed his face, glancing at his pistol out of the corner of his eye.

"Sir?" Webb asked.

"What?"

"Just tell someone to sort it all out—like what most officers do."

"Who do I tell?"

"Me?" Webb hesitated a moment. "This place, it could be good. I'd like to belong to a bit o' land like this."

Matthew squinted at him. The sun had moved around far enough to shine into his little sheltered part of the hut. "You don't know anything about looking after land."

"Nossir. But I know about organisin' men, and that's 'alf of it. I can learn the rest."

"Are you serious?"

"Yessir. I can read and write and do numbers, too."

"All right. You're the land steward for Birchanger. Sort it out. That includes the Hall."

"Yessir. Thank you, sir."

"Webb?"

"Yessir?"

"If I forget I said it, remind me."

"Yessir. 'Ave some goose, sir."

This time Matthew took the offered plate and ate some of it. Webb rooted in the bag again, coming out with a couple of thick slices of plum pudding.

"It were better 'ot, with cream," he said, handing one over. Matthew ate some of that too.

"Did Mrs Jackson make this?" Matthew asked. "Or Sally?"

"Nossir. Mrs Wilton, at the bakery, she sells 'em. Mrs Sergeant told me to get one there." He looked slightly uncomfortable.

"You seem to have got your feet under the table there," Matthew commented. *More than I've managed.*

"Rather 'ave me shoes under the bed," Webb muttered, and Matthew almost laughed.

"I were just gettin' instructions for cookin' the goose," Webb explained. "Sally's at 'ome with 'er family, and Mrs Jackson wanted to do it proper, with all the trimmin's."

They ate in silence for a while, then Webb spoke again.

"Sir, about the dreams... I was thinkin' about the dog."

"Reena? What's she got to do with it?"

"I was thinkin' if she slept on your bed... I mean, it's not like someone sittin' with you, but..."

"Go on."

"Well, she woke up before me when you was shoutin' the other night. If she was on your bed… might you sleep easier if you knows you'll get woken up sharpish?"

Matthew thought about it. If he wasn't going to be able to use his pistol—for today at least—it was probably worth testing the idea.

"All right, Webb. We'll give it a try." He hoisted himself to his feet, then picked up his pistol, powder flask, and balls. If he was going to thwart his brother, he'd better start trying to eat a bit more.

"Do you think there'll be any hot food left?"

"Mrs Jackson made lots. She can heat it up again."

Webb had let Daisy loose, not knowing how long he would be there, so the walk back was at Webb's wheezingly slow pace. Matthew looked about him as he walked. With a covering of white snow sparkling in the sunshine, the place did indeed look beautiful. He should concentrate on that for now. After all, he still had his pistol. He should be able to get hold of some dry powder and keep it away from Webb. There was still that option.

But for now…

"Webb."

"Yessir?"

"Your first task as steward is to see to the construction of a snowman on the front lawn. You may employ the young Jacksons as labourers."

Webb's grin almost split his face. "Yessir!"

CHAPTER 24

Charlotte lay in bed on Boxing Day morning, lazily aware that it was already light outside. She was roused by a hesitant knock on the door.

"Come in," she called, thinking it was Davie.

"Are you decent, ma'am?" It was Deacon's voice.

"Yes, do come in." She pulled the covers up to her chin.

Deacon pushed the door open, and set a cup of tea on the table beside her bed. "Davie's up and about, ma'am."

"Thank you for looking after him," Charlotte said.

Deacon just nodded as he left the room, reddening slightly, then she heard knocking on Mary's door.

Now that's interesting. Charlotte sat up to sip her tea, her musings from the previous day coming back to her. She heard Deacon descending the stairs, and got out of bed. Slipping into her dressing gown, she took her half-finished cup of tea and a spare blanket into Mary's room. Mary, drinking her own tea, looked wary as Charlotte sat down on the edge of the bed—they had occasionally gossiped like this before, but not very often, and not recently.

"So, when did you decide on Deacon?" Charlotte asked. That was more likely to get an honest response than asking Mary what she thought of the man.

Mary blushed.

"*Have* you decided?"

Mary nodded, a smile widening on her face.

"Does *he* know yet?"

Mary laughed this time. "I think he's getting the idea," she said.

Charlotte studied her friend. Mary had a different look about her. She'd always been a fairly cheerful soul, concentrating on practicalities instead of worrying about the future. Now she almost glowed as she smiled.

"His hand… well, lack of hand, doesn't bother you?"

Mary shook her head. "No, why should it? I'm sure he can do what's necessary with one hand." The smirk accompanying this statement told Charlotte that Mary wasn't talking about household tasks.

"Mary MacKinnon! I'm shocked!"

Mary laughed. "No, you're not." She shuffled to one side, making space for Charlotte to sit next to her properly.

"He's a good man," she said seriously. "Taken advantage of by that one who called himself Smith. But when John first come here, there was something in his face…"

"Go on," Charlotte encouraged, when Mary didn't continue.

"Finding out he might be able to earn from his drawings made a big difference," Mary said. "Gave him back self-respect."

"We don't know yet if Mr Berry will buy them," Charlotte warned.

"That don't matter. He was a carpenter—a skilled man—and a warrant officer. And he's got a good head on him. I reckon, even if the drawings don't sell, he could earn a decent living organising building repairs, or some such."

"So when you said you'd walk out with Sergeant Webb if you had to, you meant to keep your options open?"

"No. Webb seems a good enough man, now he's learned to keep his hands to hisself, at least. But not for me. I thought I might have to show John he had a bit of competition, but I don't reckon I'll need to now."

"Has he got family?" Charlotte asked curiously.

"Parents, and brothers and sisters. He said he wasn't married—that it weren't fair on a woman to have her man gone for so long."

"He has a point." Then a mischievous grin crossed Charlotte's face. "But if I were to marry Sir Vincent, and he went to sea, I'm not sure I'd complain too much!"

Mary laughed. "Now then, don't worry about him today! Time to get up and have breakfast, then you get Davie to go and use up some of his energy so he don't run us all ragged! Jane's starting tomorrow, so you won't need to peel no more potatoes for a while!"

After breakfast had been eaten and cleared away, Charlotte decided to have a proper rest day. She settled herself in a chair by the kitchen range with a novel. Mary had gone out with Deacon to call on Emma Wilton, taking some small gifts for her two young children, and Davie was outside, happily working on his mill race.

She enjoyed her book for an hour before she was interrupted by knocking at the front door. Sighing, she put the book down and went to find out who was calling. She was pleasantly surprised to find one of Squire Thompson's footmen enquiring if it was convenient for his mistress to come in.

Letty was even bigger now, and needed helping out of the carriage. The footman gave her his arm along the short path to the door. Letty told her coachman to come back for her in an hour, and suggested the men wait in the inn in Edgecombe. Charlotte helped Letty into the kitchen and put the kettle on the range.

"We could sit in the parlour," Charlotte said, "but the fire's not lit."

"Oh, don't worry about that," Letty said, settling herself in a chair. "It's warm enough here. And it's a change for me—I feel as if I've been imprisoned in the house for an age."

"Why? You can go out visiting, can't you?"

"I suppose so," Letty said. "But I was at home with Mama so much before she died that I stopped calling on people. Most of the ladies I might visit now are all so much more fashionable than me."

"Letty," Charlotte said with a laugh, "you can't be fashionable when you are due to be confined within the month."

"I know," Letty said. "But Arthur doesn't want me to go too far from home, either. It took a lot of persuasion for him to allow me to come here!"

"Why did you? You could have sent a note if you wanted company. Not that I'm not pleased to see you, of course!"

"I did want to get out of the house," Letty said. "But I wanted to give you an invitation as well."

"You could—"

"No, I couldn't just send it. You would have declined."

"What kind of invitation?" Charlotte asked. "You know I can't attend parties while I'm in mourning."

"It's not a party exactly," Letty said. "I want to have a dinner on New Year's Eve. Arthur says he'll buy fireworks to celebrate—after all, it will be a new century."

"Have you been planning this for long?" Charlotte asked, surprised. Letty usually liked to discuss dinner parties and other events long before they happened.

Letty blushed. "No, not long." She hesitated a moment. "Sir Vincent came to call on Christmas Eve. He wanted to invite me and Arthur to a New Year's Eve party at Leverton Park. Arthur said I should not be travelling so far in my condition."

"So he let you have your own party instead?" Charlotte smiled. For all he was a bluff, heavy drinking, ride-to-hounds countryman, the squire did have a soft side to him.

"That's right," said Letty. "Bertie is looking forward to the fire-works, and I thought Davie might like them too. It's a dinner, not a party. There will be no dancing, so it should be all right if you come, shouldn't it?"

Charlotte was tempted. Davie certainly *would* enjoy the fireworks and, like Letty, Charlotte would appreciate a change of scenery.

"Who else is to attend?" Charlotte asked.

"Oh, just a few local people," Letty said vaguely. "I haven't sent the invitations out yet." She hesitated a moment. "Should you mind if

Arthur has his coachman drive you home afterwards? There aren't many guest rooms at Northridge, and they may be full with people who have further to come. I'll make sure you know before the day."

"It's only five days off, Letty!" Charlotte said, wondering how many people Letty was planning on inviting.

"Yes, I know. But Arthur says that doesn't matter. We don't need many people to accept the invitation to make up a friendly party. And I'd love to see fireworks too!"

"A lot of people would enjoy them," Charlotte said.

"Hmm. I thought about letting the servants have their own party, after dinner's finished. They can see the fireworks too. Do you think that would be all right?"

"Why not? It's a new century for them as well!"

"I'll let the housekeeper know," Letty said, nodding. "I wanted to ask you..."

She hesitated, and Charlotte wondered if the real point of Letty's visit was about to be revealed.

"I need to find a wet-nurse," Letty said. "How should I go about that, do you think?"

"I don't know," Charlotte admitted.

"Didn't you have one for Davie?"

"Yes," Charlotte said. "But I didn't find her. I wanted to feed him myself, but my father..."

It was one of the reasons she'd been so keen to move away from her father's home as soon as she could. He saw Davie as a hindrance to her next marriage, and he'd started planning a second marriage for her that would be advantageous to him even before Davie was born. If Charlotte hadn't escaped, she would hardly have seen her baby at all, and probably would have ended up married to an ancient lecher as bad as, or worse than, the one she'd escaped from by marrying Angus.

"Charlotte?" Letty sounded anxious.

"Sorry, Letty. Wool gathering..."

"I was wondering what it is like when..." Letty rubbed her abdomen, looking worried.

Charlotte concentrated on explaining what would happen and trying to reassure her.

It was a day for visitors. Letty had only been gone half an hour when there was another knock on the door. Charlotte put her book down again with a sigh, but again it was someone she was pleased to see.

"James! Do come in." She apologised again for the parlour being cold, but like her previous visitor, Doctor Lorton was happy to sit in the kitchen with tea and biscuits. She thanked him for seeing Webb and providing his advice.

"That's why I've come," he explained. "I thought I should see the patient for myself. I'm on my way up to the Hall. I was planning to stay at the inn tonight, so if his lordship isn't available today I could see him tomorrow. I take it he has recovered?"

"Yes—he came down on Christmas Eve to thank me for countering the apothecary's advice. I haven't seen him since, but I assume he's still on the mend. How is Martha?" James Lorton had been returning from India to be married when she and Mary had met him on the ship; since then, Charlotte had met his wife on a few occasions.

"Increasing again, I'm happy to say. And doing well." His smile said he was proud to be the prospective father of a fourth child. They spent some time chatting about his family and his practice, then Charlotte told him about her mother.

"May I ask a favour?" she asked, once condolences were over. "Davie is old enough for me to think about sending him to school. Is there a decent school in Bristol that is not too expensive? If so, would you be able to find out what they will expect him to know before he starts there? I wouldn't like him to be behind the other boys."

The doctor agreed to find out. He was just at the point of leaving when Mary and Deacon returned, so he stayed to catch up with Mary's news and be introduced to Deacon. Now she was aware of Mary's plans, Charlotte noticed the way they stood closely together, their little touches on passing, and small smiles when they caught each other's eye. Deacon wasn't just 'getting the idea', as Mary had said that morning, he was relishing it.

On hearing that the loss of Deacon's hand was relatively recent, the doctor asked to examine the stump.

"It looks a nice, tidy job," he said approvingly, when the brief examination was over. "It's certainly healed up well enough for you to get a hook for it—have you considered that?"

"I don't think I could afford that," Deacon said, not meeting the doctor's eyes.

"It shouldn't be very expensive," Doctor Lorton said. "I can get one sent, if you wish?"

"I… Yes, thank you, Doctor."

The doctor measured Deacon's arm, noting the numbers in a little book, then took his leave, promising to send details of schools to Charlotte as soon as he could find them.

"Someone to see you, sir," Webb said, showing a visitor into Matthew's room, then retreating to the kitchen. Matthew looked up from the map he was perusing. From his dress, the man was a professional of some kind.

"Good morning," the visitor said. "I hope I'm not interrupting anything. My name is Doctor James Lorton."

Matthew frowned, not immediately recognising the name.

"Mrs MacKinnon consulted me when you were unwell," the doctor added.

"Ah, yes. Matthew Southam. Er, Lord Tillson, I should say." Matthew did not immediately offer his hand.

"It is a trifle awkward, I'm afraid," Lorton said with a friendly smile. "After all, you did not choose to consult me. Nevertheless, I believe the advice I gave *was* followed, so I have come to check up on my patient."

"I'm perfectly well, thank you." Matthew realised he was being churlish. "Forgive me, Doctor. Do sit down." Lorton took the armchair and Matthew turned the chair he'd been using at his desk.

"It is also slightly difficult as you don't know me," Lorton went on. "You could trust Mrs MacKinnon's recommendation, but then I gather you don't know *her* well, either."

"At least you didn't get them to fill me with laudanum or stifle me," Matthew muttered.

The door opened and Mrs Jackson brought in a tray laden with coffee pot and cups, sugar, cream, and a large plate of cakes and biscuits. Matthew opened his mouth to say that he hadn't ordered refreshments and the doctor would not be staying long, but he caught Lorton's amused eye.

"Thank you, I will take some coffee," Lorton said. "Don't worry, I am used to seeing recalcitrant patients."

Matthew gave a reluctant laugh, and poured two cups of coffee. "Very well," he said, handing one to Lorton, then pushing the sugar and cream over to him. He took out his flask ready to add his usual slug of brandy to his own, but hesitated before pouring.

"Don't mind me," Lorton said. "I was consulted about influenza, not your addiction to the bottle."

Matthew, feeling a little like a defiant child, poured brandy into his cup, but not nearly as much as he normally did.

"Usually, at this point in the conversation, sufferers inform me that they can give up any time they wish to," Lorton said in neutral tones.

Matthew shrugged. "You wouldn't believe me if I said that."

"Do you think it?"

"Nice weather for the time of year," Matthew said, with a pointed glance at the world outside, once more grey and damp.

"Indeed. I am looking forward to my ride back to Bristol," Lorton said, straight-faced. "It was a pleasant ride over yesterday, as well, and it was good to see the Mrs MacKinnons again."

If the man was trying to make him feel guilty, he'd succeeded.

"Oh, very well," Matthew said. "What kind of examination do you intend?" It was many months since he had been poked and prodded by the medical profession; he didn't relish the prospect of another session.

"Are you truly feeling well? No racing heart, no dizziness?"

"No. Well, nothing that can't be explained by over-indulgence in the brandy." Matthew waved a hand at his flask. "I'm quite used to those symptoms."

Matthew was relieved when Lorton took a sip of his coffee, making no move to get up to take his pulse or peer into his eyes or mouth.

"Tell me, who is Benson?"

"What?" Matthew's eyes narrowed. "What makes you ask?" It was bad enough having Benson haunt his dreams, without being forced to explain himself to a stranger.

"You apparently mention his name in your sleep."

"It seems you have been given quite a comprehensive list of my failings," Matthew remarked bitterly.

"I wouldn't call them failings," Lorton stated.

"I would." The doctor didn't know everything.

There was silence for a while. Lorton took a piece of cake and started to eat it slowly.

Eventually, Matthew forced himself to speak. Lorton was clearly not going to be fobbed off by silence. "He was one of my men."

"Was, not is?"

"As far as I know." Matthew pressed his lips together, sliding his gaze towards the grey landscape outside. "I left him to die."

"In battle?"

"No."

Lorton finished his cake, carefully placing his plate and fork back on the table. "This is not an interrogation," he said.

Matthew winced at his final word.

"You may, of course, decline to answer my questions," the doctor went on. "However, in my experience, bottling everything up often makes things seem worse than they really are." He paused for a moment. "It does seem that Benson is haunting you."

"I'd haunt me too, if I'd done... Well, you know what I mean."

"So, what did you do?"

Matthew suppressed the temptation to tell the doctor to mind his own business and leave him alone. Talking about the past only brought more memories back. He took a deep breath. "We were taken prisoner," he stated. "It was my fault. Then I got out and left him there to rot."

"So you don't *know* he's dead?"

"He must be." Matthew stood abruptly and stalked over to the window, looking out but not seeing anything beyond the glass, with the familiar, unwelcome feelings of helplessness and fear washing through him. "He didn't appear afterwards, and he couldn't have lasted long. He must have died."

He turned back to face Lorton. "Died, alone in the dark with the rats. And he was so young." Matthew's voice nearly broke, but he swallowed the lump in his throat, Benson's pleading voice in his head again.

"Exactly *how* is this supposed to help?" he asked, controlling his voice with an effort.

"Bear with me just a little longer," Lorton requested. "Tell me how you escaped."

"I don't remember. But Benson was... *is...* still missing."

"You only just survived yourself, from what I heard."

"You *heard?*" He took a deep breath. He'd have Webb's guts for spilling all this to Lorton. "Mrs MacKinnon sent Webb to you, didn't she? Exactly how much did Webb tell you?"

"Webb was telling me *his* story, when I asked why he had difficulty breathing."

Matthew turned back to the window, shamed. He had never thought to ask Webb how he'd come by his breathing difficulties. He rubbed a hand down his face, his anger with Webb evaporating and leaving him feeling drained.

"He never told you?" Lorton asked.

"I just know he was set to watch me in hospital, and seems to have attached himself to me since."

"Encroaching?"

"Yes... no... I mean he's been very useful." He shut his eyes, remembering the incident in London. "Including knocking me out once or twice when my nightmares took control. I nearly throttled my brother's valet."

"You trust Webb?"

"Yes, I think so. At the moment, at least, our interests coincide." He told Lorton about Webb's idea for the dog to sleep by him.

"Is it working?"

"We're still training her, but she *has* woken me up once, when I was dreaming."

"It sounds as if it is worth persisting. You know, you have done very well to stay off the laudanum."

Matthew grimaced. "The nightmares were worse than the relief it gave. I climbed into a bottle instead."

"Nevertheless." The doctor's face held no trace of censure.

"You're not going to tell me to stop?"

Lorton shrugged. "You already know what any doctor's advice would be on the subject. If you do decide to stop, you will suffer less by reducing your intake gradually. However, many do not have enough self-control to do that, so must just stop completely."

The doctor brushed a few crumbs off his coat and stood up. "Thank you for talking to me, my lord. I'll be off now. I am not diminishing your experiences, and it may be little help to you at this moment, but the dreams *will* get less frequent with time. And I think you should ask Webb about Benson—if I'm interpreting both your stories correctly, you did *not* abandon him to die. Now, I'd like to give Webb a look over, if he's around."

Matthew came over and shook hands. "I'll think about what you said."

Lorton nodded. "Please do. It would be a shame to waste Webb's efforts."

Webb's efforts? He ran his hands through his hair. He needed brandy, not a talk with Webb.

~

Webb accompanied Doctor Lorton to the stables after the man had finished prodding him and listening to his chest. There were fewer listening ears there.

"Sir, did 'e tell you about Christmas Day?"

"No. What about it?"

Webb hesitated, not sure if he was betraying a confidence or not. Doctor Lorton waited patiently.

"I put water in 'is powder flask," Webb said eventually.

Lorton frowned, then his face cleared. "Ah! As far as you can tell, is it just the nightmares?"

Webb gestured to the damp patches on the stable wall. "It's this place as well, sir—a lot of things to fix. And 'is family—" He stopped as Jackson came into the stables, carrying a pitchfork.

"Sir, if I come down to the inn shortly, might you get a private parlour for 'alf an 'our or so?"

CHAPTER 25

"*L*etter for you," Mary said, sticking her head around the parlour door. "From Birchanger—Tilly brought it down."

Charlotte put her pencil down with relief. Now they were nearing the end of December, she had been trying to decide on February's *Cotswold Diary* article, but it was difficult to think of something she hadn't already written about.

In the kitchen, Davie sat at the table drawing a ship. Charlotte smiled wryly—at least he'd not inherited her poor drawing skills. Tilly sat next to him, warming her hands around a mug of hot milk. She jumped up when Charlotte came into the room, pulling a small, folded paper out of her pocket.

"Letter for you, mum," she said, holding it out.

The letter was addressed to Mrs MacKinnon in a bold, neat hand, definitely not Webb's scrawl. It must be from Lord Tillson; he was the only other person at the Hall who could write. The letter was short, merely saying that Davie's help with more surveying would be appreciated, if he was free.

Interesting—she thought she'd offended him when he called just before Christmas.

She handed the letter to Davie. "Do you want to go?"

Davie nodded eagerly.

"Get your coat, then."

Davie dashed off. Charlotte donned her own outdoor clothing, deciding that now was as good a time as any to get the apology over with. She wrapped up some bread and cheese for Davie's luncheon, putting it in a small satchel for him.

Mary handed the two children a biscuit each, then they set off. Tilly, energetic as always, skipped ahead towards the beginning of the footpath through the woods.

Charlotte frowned. The last time she walked this way there had been a pile of posts ready to fence the path off. Tilly must have come that way this morning, so perhaps the posts hadn't been for fencing? Charlotte's surmise was confirmed when she reached the stream and muddy slope. A simple bridge now spanned the stream, and wooden poles had been used to make steps up the slope beyond. She stopped on the bridge, looking up at the rise that had caused so many muddy hands and knees over the years; the steps would make getting up the slope so much easier than before.

She flushed with guilt, glad the two children were far enough ahead not to see her. Not only had she ranted at Lord Tillson about the mantraps, she'd also mentally castigated him for planning to fence off the path.

She caught up with Tilly and Davie by the time they reached the open ground in front of the Hall. Tilly led them all around to the back entrance and into the kitchen.

Lord Tillson sat at the table with a cup of coffee in front of him and a coat and shoulder bag hanging on the back of his chair.

He still looked rather gaunt, but appeared to be quite alert, and was definitely not the drunken wastrel of their first encounter. Taking a flask from his pocket, he added a dash to his coffee before noticing their arrival and standing up. Amused by the timing of her thought and his addition to his drink, she pursed her lips, trying not to laugh.

"Miss... Mrs MacKinnon," he said, making a small bow. He was about to say something else, but Davie got in first.

"Where are we going to measure today, sir?"

"I wanted to make a map to show the main paths through the woods," he explained to Davie, then looked at Charlotte. "As long as you have no objection, ma'am?"

"You have found all the traps, then, my lord?"

"I don't know," he admitted. "I don't know how many there were. I suspect my younger brother came and had them set while I was still in India." He broke off and rubbed a hand across this face. That wasn't relevant now. "Today's effort will be mapping only the well-trodden main paths. A map will help us to keep track of where we've searched when we go looking for any remaining traps."

"Why did you ask for Davie to help you?" Charlotte asked, tilting her head slightly as she looked at him. If all he needed was someone to hold the other end of a chain, there were several other people here he could use.

"Apart from Jackson, who is out checking for traps, I suspect Davie is the person who has the best knowledge of the paths through these woods."

Charlotte frowned, remembering how he had come by that knowledge. "Very well. I trust you will return him before dark."

"Thank you, Mrs MacKinnon."

Charlotte stood in the kitchen doorway watching them go. Was she wise to allow her son to go off with Lord Tillson? He drank too much, certainly, but he was showing no sign of being inebriated this morning. Her brow creased as she recalled his illness, and the things he had said in his delirium. *Is he drinking to forget something?*

She shook her head. It was none of her business, as long as he was not drunk when he was with Davie. She must not judge people without sound reasons—she'd thought badly of him twice already, and both times had been proven wrong.

And she had missed another opportunity to apologise, although doing so in front of an audience was not what she'd had in mind.

"Coffee, Mrs Captain?" Mrs Jackson offered, coming to the door.

"Thank you, yes." Charlotte accepted gratefully. While she was drinking the coffee, Webb came into the kitchen.

"Can I ask you about somethin', ma'am?" he said. "If you 'ave the time, o'course."

"By all means, Sergeant." Any excuse to avoid having to go back to the futile business of coming up with interesting things to say about the February countryside. They sat at the table.

Webb hesitated a moment, then spoke in a rush. "Lord Tillson has appointed me land steward for Birchanger."

"Congratulations!" Lord Tillson needed a steward, that was clear, but Webb seemed an odd choice.

"Thank you, ma'am. But the thing is, 'e said for me to sort the buildin' out as well. I don't know about managin' land or repairin' roofs and such, so I'm needin' some advice."

"I don't mean to be rude, but why did his lordship appoint you if you don't know how to do the job?"

"I... Well, I sort of told him to."

Charlotte laughed, recalling a comment Angus had often made about his men. "Good officers listen to their sergeants?"

"Yes, ma'am!" Webb grinned. "Even if the sergeant is sometimes talking bo— er, talkin' rubbish. I didn't expect 'im to take me seriously, but 'e'd been..."

"Drinking?" Charlotte asked, noticing Webb looked uncomfortable.

Webb nodded.

"Don't worry, I'm not his keeper. So, how can I help you?"

"Well, I reckon I can ask for 'elp about the land from the squire's man, if the major will put in a word. And I reckon there's not much to be done at this time of year anyhow. But gettin' this place fixed so it can be lived in proper, like, I should start with that. And there's the Jacksons livin' 'ere 'cause their place is fallin' to bits, and the other cottages need repairs too."

Charlotte's eyebrows rose during this catalogue of problems. Webb was going to have his work cut out for him.

"What does his lordship think is the most important?"

Webb looked uncomfortable again. "'E's not too good at... well, 'e'd rather I just saw to it, ma'am." He produced a list. "Me an' the major done this list when we first got 'ere," he explained.

Charlotte scanned the list quickly. "This looks expensive."

"Yes, ma'am. I asked in the village, and they've give me names of some folks what could do the repairs. Would you mind 'elpin' me to write letters?"

"You can write, Sergeant."

"Yes ma'am. But not neat, and not with the proper words for letters. I'll need to practise, but…"

"But you want to get things going." That made sense. Charlotte thought for a moment. "You'll need to keep a letters book."

"Letters book?"

"You keep a copy of letters you send in the book, so you have a record," Charlotte explained.

Webb nodded.

"If I write the letters for you, you can copy them into the book to practise your writing. You will also see how to compose your letters. Would that help?"

"Yes, thank you, ma'am."

Charlotte spent the next hour writing to builders, glaziers, and stonemasons, then toured the house with Webb, satisfying her curiosity about the interior of the Hall as well as checking and adding to the original list.

The Hall would be a lovely place when it was repaired and furnished properly, she thought. That would take time, not to mention a good deal of money. Fires in the rooms upstairs were warming the fabric of the building, but she could still smell damp in most of the rooms. No doubt that was why his lordship had set up one of the downstairs parlours as his bedroom.

When they finished their lists, Mrs Jackson gave them a late luncheon, then Charlotte asked to see the outbuildings and stables. The tour ended in the kitchen garden, where they stood regarding the small patch of partially cleared earth, and the much larger area yet to be dealt with.

"The major digs this 'isself," Webb said.

Charlotte's brows rose. It seemed an odd occupation for someone who apparently had enough money to start repairing the Hall. "You could hire some labourers to get it cleared more quickly," she suggested.

Webb shook his head. "I reckon I'll leave this for the major to do. We can buy in stuff if it don't get finished in time for plantin'."

"Do you have people to work the estate?" Charlotte asked. "Once you start on that, I mean."

"A few. But there's not many places for new workers to live." He shuffled his feet and cleared his throat.

There was something else he wanted?

"Just ask, Sergeant," Charlotte said. "The worst I can say is 'no'." She smiled, remembering how she had told him off when he came to apologise to Mary. "Well, the worst I can say to any proper suggestion!"

Webb looked shocked. "I would never, ma'am."

Charlotte just raised an eyebrow and waited for him to carry on.

"There's the cottages needin' repair too, ma'am. I can make a list, like the one for the 'All, but you'd be better at talkin' to the wives."

"I do have work to get on with, Sergeant."

"Yes, ma'am. I'm sorry…"

"No, don't worry. I can make the time. Tomorrow?" She could talk to the labourers about what they normally did for work in February while she was there, which might give her enough ideas for her next *Cotswold Diary*.

Matthew set off across the fields with Davie, his mood as grey as the weather. He'd been pleased Mrs MacKinnon wasn't so disgusted with him that she'd forbidden her son to come and help, but surprised to see her arrive with Davie. Then he had been so conscious of his mistake about her marital status he had actually started to call her Miss MacKinnons again. And she had pursed her lips in… anger?

Annoyance? Only the presence of Davie behind him, panting with the effort of keeping up, stopped him from cursing out loud.

"Sorry," he said, slowing down. "I forgot you have shorter legs."

"That's all right, sir. Thank you for asking me to come."

"You enjoyed it last time?" Matthew asked. He wasn't sure if Mrs MacKinnon had sent an unwilling victim. "Are you still in trouble for wandering around in the woods?"

"I don't think so, sir." Davie walked on, a frown on his face.

God, he hadn't managed to upset the lad as well, had he?

"I like *doing* something instead of just reading about it in books."

Ah, he'd just been thinking. Good.

"It's rather boring, and cold, standing around holding the chain, or taking bearings," Matthew said.

"It is a bit. But you have to be careful to do it right. And you can make a real map at the end!" He sounded quite awed by this. "Can I make one?"

"How did you get on with the numbers you took away before?"

Davie chattered on about what he'd done, complaining about the dents in the kitchen table spoiling his lines, and how he didn't have big enough pieces of paper.

Matthew made a mental note to invite him up to Birchanger Hall to help with the updating of maps of the estate and woods that Webb said was necessary. He wondered what he could do to mitigate the poor impression he'd made on Mrs MacKinnon this morning and convince her to let her lad help. That could be difficult; he didn't know what he'd done wrong.

Matthew started the mapping where the main path cut into the woods, taking measurements of distances and angles and making a sketch as they went along. He was amused to see Davie's writing becoming neater and his columns of numbers straighter as the morning went on; the lad clearly appreciated the need to be able to decipher his notes again later.

When it was time to eat their luncheon Davie led them to a small clearing, and Matthew managed a surreptitious pull at his flask. He realised, with surprise, that he'd got through several hours without a drink, not liking to have one in front of Davie.

"Sir, can you come and help me move this stone?" Davie's voice came from behind, and Matthew guiltily put the flask away.

"You haven't been into the woods, have you?" he asked, going over to Davie. "There might still be traps."

"No, sir. There's a little path with stones on it here. And I've been on this path since the traps were put down. There's a door—come and see!"

Matthew followed him, coming to a wooden door set in a small section of stone wall in a steep bank.

"I found this door with Bertie," Davie said. "But it doesn't go anywhere."

"It might be an ice house." Matthew tried the door. It was stuck. Parting the vegetation, he saw that it was held shut with a large stone.

"What's an ice house?"

"It stays cool, so if you put ice in it during the winter, it doesn't melt, and you can use it in the summer."

"Can we go inside? I couldn't move the stone when we came before."

God, no. Cold, dark, damp... enclosed.

Matthew looked at the lad's eager face. Davie's enthusiasm reminded him of the fun he'd had exploring the Farleton lands as a child, building his own dens and forts to defend against imaginary enemies.

He couldn't say 'no'. He was going to have to do it.

Not just yet, though. "All right," he said. "We'll finish these paths first."

Davie face fell, but he did not argue. They continued along the paths, measuring and noting, with Matthew trying to thrust images of airless dark from his mind.

"Is that right, sir?" Davie asked, noting down one distance.

Matthew looked at the numbers. No, it wasn't right. He'd given Davie the wrong number to write down. It was the third mistake he'd made since luncheon.

Just do it, Southam. It's not going to get any easier if you put it off.

"Time to stop for the day," Matthew suggested, one faint hope left.

"Oh, can we go in the ice house now?"

It *had* been a small hope. He sighed.

"Yes, Davie. Lead on."

The door itself was rotten at the bottom, hardly surprising in the damp and gloom on this north-facing slope. The last Lord Tillson must have used the place, or it would be even more dilapidated than it was. He managed to heave the stone to one side. Part of him was grateful that his weakened state didn't cause him to fail at this simple task in front of Davie, another part regretting there was to be no final reprieve.

They had to pull some weeds out of the way, but eventually the door creaked open, releasing dank and musty air. Matthew swallowed hard.

It's an ice house, not a cell.

"Don't dash in!" he said hurriedly, grabbing Davie's sleeve. "We've no light, and there may be steps."

Davie rooted around in the pockets of his coat, coming up with a short candle stub and a small tinder box. Resigned, Matthew waited while Davie lit the candle, then followed him in, firmly keeping a grip on the collar of Davie's coat. The darkness closed in, and he felt his heart pounding

Davie held the candle up and looked around. A short tunnel led away from the door, then there were indeed steps leading down into blackness. Above the top of the steps, a rusting pulley was fastened to the roof.

"What's that for?" Davie asked, pointing with his free hand.

"You can put a rope through it to help haul blocks of ice up," Matthew explained. Davie was going to want to go down the steps. What boy wouldn't?

There's an open door behind me. I can leave at any time.

269

Matthew took a deep breath. "Take one step at a time as you go down."

Logic and reason didn't work too well against irrational fears, and he concentrated on breathing steadily.

All went well for several steps, then Davie was startled by something dashing past his feet. He jumped, his foot slipped sideways, and he dropped the candle. There was a sudden flare of light as the flame lit something below, then it went out.

Davie's weight pulled Matthew off balance too, but in spite of his rising panic, the brief flash of light had been enough for him to see that the place was empty, with only straw below. He let go of Davie's collar, waving his arms to try to keep his balance.

The sound of Davie hitting the straw reached him at the same time as his own foot slipped, and he twisted as he fell to avoid landing on top of the lad.

He swore under his breath, propping himself on his hands and knees while he struggled to bring his breathing under control. The straw was wet. Very wet, and very muddy. Not to mention foul-smelling—it must have been mouldering here for years.

"Are you all right Davie?" He hoped his voice sounded normal.

"Yes, sir. Sorry, sir. Something startled me."

"Rat, probably."

"Oh."

Some part of Matthew's mind managed to be amused at Davie's subdued tone. Squelching noises indicated that Davie was moving about in the muck. At least it was only muddy straw and not animal droppings. Or dead animals. Perhaps he wouldn't mention that possibility.

He took more deep breaths.

"How are we going to get out?" Davie asked, his voice beginning to wobble. "I can't find the candle."

"If you wait a bit your eyes will adapt." The apprehension in Davie's voice helped to calm his own fears a little; hopefully the lad wouldn't want to linger. "We'll be able to see enough to find the steps, don't worry. We didn't fall very far."

"I think I can see where the door is," Davie said hesitantly.

"Up we go, then," Matthew said. He felt around for the bottom of the steps with one hand, then reached towards Davie with the other. The bottom step was a long way off the floor, so he lifted the lad up then scrambled up after him.

Outside, he looked up at the trees and the sky for a moment, then down at Davie, stupidly pleased that the lad hadn't noticed his fears.

"I don't think your mother is going to be pleased," he commented, looking from Davie to his own clothing. The pair of them were covered from head to toe in mud and bits of straw. "Fastest way back, I think, before we get too cold."

Charlotte was taking her leave of Webb when two muddy figures appeared in the stable yard. Davie looked the picture of guilt. Behind him was Lord Tillson, with the same expression. He looked so much like a child about to face a reprimand that Charlotte only just kept herself from laughing out loud.

Webb went back into the kitchen, then she heard him asking Mrs Jackson to heat water. Davie came straight up to her.

"I'm sorry Mama. I'm not hurt, just wet."

"And a little muddy? And cold?" He nodded, not saying anything else. "I think you need a hot bath." She glanced at Lord Tillson, who waved a hand in a 'carry on' gesture. "Then we'll see if Mrs Jackson can find you some dry clothes to go home in. I'll wait and walk with you."

Lord Tillson and Davie went indoors, Charlotte putting her hand to her mouth to hide her laughter as she followed them.

Matthew found dry clothes and changed, washing off as much mud as he could with warm water. He was cold, but it would take too long to heat water for a bath for him as well as Davie. He rubbed a wet towel through his hair to get the worst of the mud out, then went to see how Davie was getting on. The lad was sitting in a steaming tub by the kitchen range, with no sign of the women. A pot of tea stood on the table, so he poured two mugs and handed one to Davie, curling his hands appreciatively around the warmth.

"We're in for it now," Matthew said gloomily. "I should have taken better care of you." Borrowing a child and returning him cold, wet, and muddy was *not* the done thing. To his surprise, Davie grinned.

"I don't think Mama's really cross," he said. "That was her trying-not-to-laugh face."

"Her what?"

Davie pulled a face with pursed lips, mimicking very well the expression that had been on Mrs MacKinnon's face. "She looks like that when I've done something silly and she's trying not to laugh at me."

Matthew's gloom lightened. That was the same expression he'd seen this morning. She'd been laughing at him? Well, not-laughing at him. He didn't know what had amused her, but at least he hadn't upset her.

Charlotte took the old shirt gratefully—it was the best Mrs Jackson had been able to find for Davie and was better than leaving wet clothes on him. Armed with a towel and some blankets, she went back into the kitchen. Lord Tillson was talking to Davie, looking much more cheerful than when he'd returned to the Hall.

Charlotte concentrated on making sure Davie washed behind his ears and got all the mud out of his hair, then wrapped him in the towel and rubbed him down. She hadn't noticed Lord Tillson leave the room and come back, but as she was about to drape the blankets around Davie, he cleared his throat.

"Er, it will be rather large on him, Mrs MacKinnon, but this may help keep him warm on the way home? Webb's gone to put the horse to the wagon."

He offered Charlotte an old coat. She took it, and Davie held out his arms so she could pull it on. It was indeed large—Davie's hands came little more than half-way down the sleeves, and the bottom of the coat reached nearly to his knees. She pursed her lips, looking up at Lord Tillson.

His lips were turned up at the ends, the corners of his eyes crinkling slightly. When he caught her expression his smile widened a little, and she laughed.

"Far too big, my lord, but thank you."

CHAPTER 26

Benson cried for water again, whimpering and whining, and then licked his face. He felt hot breath in his ear.

Matthew sat up, heart hammering. A brief yelp accompanied his movement, and he realised Reena had woken him from a nightmare. His breathing gradually returned to normal, and he lay back, appreciating the warm bedding and the faint draught across his face. He knew a brief moment of regret that the warm body huddling up against him was only the dog.

His head hurt, unsurprisingly. He'd drunk rather too much the night before—again. At least he didn't feel the need to escape from the room, which was progress of a sort. He shut his eyes, hearing Reena's breathing become slow and regular.

The next thing he knew, Webb was shaking his shoulder.

"Go away, Webb." The bed was comfortable, and warm.

"Wake up, sir. Time to get up if you're comin' round the cottages with us."

"Coffee," he grunted, pulling the covers over his head.

"I brung some," Webb said, pulling the covers down again. He waved a steaming cup in front of Matthew's face.

Matthew groaned, but decided it was easier to do as he was told than to fight Webb. He sat up and sipped the coffee. "Who is 'us', Webb?"

"I asked Mrs Captain to 'elp me with writin' letters and such," Webb explained. "She agreed to come round the cottages today to see what needs doin'. She'll be better at talkin' to the womenfolk. Thought you could come along too."

Matthew grimaced.

"You don't need to do anythin', just say 'ello. But it would be good for your tenants to see—"

"All right, Webb, I'll come." He took a mouthful of coffee, then another. Webb was still talking, but Matthew had stopped listening.

Just ask.

"...'alf an hour..."

"Webb."

"...get some shavin' water..."

"Webb," Matthew repeated, more forcefully.

"Sir?"

"Before you start organising me again..."

"Yessir?"

"When Doctor Lorton came, he told me I should ask you about Benson."

Webb looked rather wary. "I don't know a Benson, sir."

"Then why did Doctor Lorton think you did? What exactly did you tell him when you went to Bristol to see him?"

"Just told him what Mrs Captain said to, sir."

"And you told him how you came to be wounded yourself?"

Webb just nodded.

"Well?"

"You really don't know, sir?"

"You never said." And *he'd* never thought to ask.

Webb took a deep breath. "We'd got into the town, and I was lookin' around and went into a prison. Found some keys and let some o' the poor sods out. Then I was carryin' one what couldn't walk when some bugger stabbed me in the back. Some mates found us before the bastard could finish us off, and we ended up in hospital. Got infected—buggered up me lungs summat proper, it did."

"We...?" Matthew was beginning to work out exactly what Webb meant by 'us' when the sergeant started talking again.

"No-one knowed who you was at first, then General Stuart come round the 'ospital and spotted you. Managed to get meself assigned to watch you."

Matthew stared at him. "*You* got me out of there?"

"Yessir."

"Why?"

"Couldn't leave anyone in that 'ell-'ole, sir."

"Why me and not Benson? Rescued the officer for a reward?"

"Nossir!" Webb shook his head, looking offended. "Couldn't tell you was an officer, sir. No-one did till the General spotted you. The bloke with you was dead." He paused. "Was 'e that Benson what you talk about in your sleep?"

"You are sure he was already dead?" *I need to know I didn't just abandon Benson there.*

"Yessir. No doubt about it."

Matthew didn't ask for details. He really didn't want to know. His imagination was enough.

"Sir?" Webb's voice brought him out of his abstraction.

"That's what Lorton meant about not wasting your efforts, I suppose. Thank you, Webb. I think..."

Webb shrugged. "Well, you got a choice now, sir. If you really wants some dry powder, you'll get it."

"At the moment, I don't want it." Most of the time, anyway. But he'd propped his pistol up on the mantelpiece in his bedroom to remind himself that he *did* have a choice.

"Why didn't you tell me all this before, Webb?"

Webb shrugged. "Didn't know you didn't know, at first," he said. "Then there didn't seem much point. Wouldn't make no difference to anythin'." He eyed Matthew warily.

"What? Spit it out, Webb."

"Well, some men—lords—might not like 'avin' someone around what's seen them in that state."

Matthew frowned. "I was in a pretty bad state in the hospital—which is the first I remember of you. That hasn't put me off having you around. How did you manage to stay in the officers' ward?" Not that he blamed him—Webb would have got better treatment.

Webb actually looked embarrassed.

"Told the general you rescued me?"

Webb nodded.

"Don't look like that, man! Anyone with any sense would have done the same." He wouldn't ask why Webb had been wandering around a prison in Seringapatam instead of helping to secure the fortress—he suspected that the ruby necklace was sufficient explanation.

"Sir?"

"Yes?"

"When we was talkin', on Christmas Day, when…"

"When you'd wet my powder? What about it?"

"You said summat about a mine. And not bein' able to tell."

"What of it?"

"Where was it, sir?"

Matthew closed his eyes, trying to fend off his imagination, but his mind saw again the explosion between high stone walls, the trapped British troops, their mangled and dying bodies strewn across the rubble.

Hell! I've been trying to keep my mind off that. So much for not wanting dry powder.

"Sir?"

Matthew rubbed his hand across his face. Bloody Webb would persist until he got an answer.

He took a deep breath. "I… we… thought there was something odd about the wall at the north-west corner—another wall behind the wall. A trap. I'd just sent word to avoid that bit of wall, but they caught Havers. I didn't do my bloody job."

He couldn't look at Webb, but he forced himself to continue. "I heard that's where the assault was." The sergeant was lucky *he* hadn't been one of the troops caught in the trap.

"Sir, there was a big explosion there a couple of days before the assault. Our major reckoned a shell hit some gunpowder or summat."

Matthew glanced at Webb, then back to the fire, the words percolating through his consciousness. He felt dazed, as if he'd dreamed the words.

"Sir?" Webb said, speaking more forcefully. "Sir, no-one died 'cos of a mine. Leastways, not the one you spotted."

Webb *had* said it.

"Thank you for telling me, Webb." *I really didn't cause—*

"Yessir. I'll get shavin' water sent in, sir."

"What?"

"Shavin' water, sir. The cottages. Mrs Captain."

Matthew stared at Webb for a moment, trying to understand what the man was blathering about.

"Oh, right. You don't really need me, do you?"

"Sir, it'd be better if you did come."

He *had* agreed. He'd have to think about what Webb had said some other time. "Oh, very well."

He didn't rise to dress immediately. If Webb was telling the truth— and there was no reason why he should not be—no-one had died because of his failure. Although it didn't really excuse the fact that he *hadn't* managed to get word back, perhaps that particular part of his nightmares might fade.

He took another deep breath and pushed the covers back. Only time would tell.

Matthew was still drinking his coffee in the kitchen when he heard the scrunch of footsteps across the yard, and Mrs MacKinnon came in, Davie following behind her. She had a rosy glow to her cheeks.

He stood. "Good morning, Mrs MacKinnon."

"Hello, sir," Davie piped up, before his mother could speak. "Are you coming with us?"

"Davie! Sorry, my lord—"

"No matter." He smiled. "Webb can be most persuasive," he added.

Her answering smile was wry. "He can indeed."

"All set, sir?" Webb spoke as he entered the kitchen. "Mornin', ma'am," he added cheerily. "Mrs Jackson's just comin'."

A minute or two longer would have been good, Webb.

"Mrs MacKinnon, would you care for some coffee before setting off again?"

She smiled, but shook her head. "Thank you, my lord, but I think we'd better get started. From Webb's account, there could be a lot to decide on."

Matthew finished his own coffee and donned his coat.

Mrs Jackson went with them to show them the best way through the woods. The terrace of ten houses was built of the local pale stone, with small windows and steep stone roofs. They looked much smaller than Matthew's memory of Mrs MacKinnon's cottage, but were otherwise of similar structure. These cottages, though, had cracked windows, slipped roofing slates, and overgrown gardens behind.

The Jacksons' cottage was on one end of the row. Mrs Jackson gave them a quick guided tour.

"Chimney's blocked," she said in the main living room, indicating the broken, basic cooking range and the blackened walls above it.

She pushed hard to open the door leading to a tiny scullery and pantry. "Damp makes the door swell."

The narrow staircase led to two bedrooms, one on either side of the stairs, with both low ceilings showing water stains and patches of mould. A couple of beds with rope bases had been moved from beneath the worst water stain; the sheets and blankets piled on them were damp.

Mrs MacKinnon pulled a notebook out of a pocket in her gown and started writing. Webb was doing the same, more laboriously. Matthew rubbed the back of his neck. Webb had been quite right to move the Jackson family into the Hall.

He looked out of the small casement; all he could see were the trees beyond the small gardens. He went through to the other bedroom, but trees blocked the view here too, making the room very dark and gloomy. The casement in this room was stuck—not that most people would want to open it in the middle of winter.

But the walls were too near, and the ceiling was closing in on him. The beginnings of panic rose from the hollow in his stomach. He took a few deep breaths in an attempt to control the fear, then started when he heard footsteps behind him.

Turning, he saw Mrs MacKinnon looking at him, a thoughtful expression on her face. He wondered if he could lie convincingly enough if she asked whether he was well, but she didn't ask.

"Davie," she called, and her son came in from the other room. "Why don't you and his lordship inspect the houses from the outside, and make a list of what needs to be done?" Davie nodded and dashed down the stairs.

"Good idea, ma'am," Matthew said, managing not to run as he followed the lad out of the house.

"I've got a notebook," Davie said proudly when they were outside, turning to a new page. Then he looked around him. "It's not a very nice place, is it, sir? At home, we have a garden behind the house."

"They do here, too." Matthew was beginning to feel better now he was out of doors again. He took his compass out of his pocket to check which way the fronts of the cottages faced. "The gardens here won't get much sunlight most of the year."

"Why not?"

Matthew glanced down at Davie, then waved one arm from south-east to south-west. "At this time of year, the sun rises that way and sets over there. The houses block the light."

"What about other times?"

"In the summer…" Matthew scratched his head. "Lend me your notebook."

Matthew and Davie looked up guiltily when Mrs MacKinnon and

Webb came out of the Jackson's house, twenty minutes later. Mrs MacKinnon glanced at her son's notebook, now full of diagrams, none of which had anything to do with repairing the cottages. Matthew saw her mouth purse and her eyes crinkle at the corners. He let out his breath, recognising the expression. She was amused, not annoyed.

"We... er, we were discussing the position of the gardens," he said. "Gardens at the front would be better."

Charlotte glanced up at the pale circle the sun made through the cloud, then back at the cottages, shaking her head at whoever had thought gardens *behind* the houses were a good idea in this location.

She turned as Mrs Jackson brought out the women from some of the other cottages, briefly introducing them. Most of them looked wary, but the stance of one reminded Charlotte so clearly of Mary on the warpath that she had to purse her lips again.

"Your lordship," the woman said, with a token bob of her head. "You come to get your back rent?"

Charlotte saw Lord Tillson's eyebrows rise slightly, but he took the rudeness in good part.

"No," he answered calmly. "I've come with my steward to see what repairs need doing." He indicated Webb. "And to ask if having gardens in front of the cottages would be helpful."

"You goin' to put the rent up if we get—"

· An elbow in the ribs from one of the other women stopped the complaint.

"Mr Webb will deal with that," Lord Tillson said. "He will discuss the situation with you, and work out a *fair* rent. That will be in a day or so, once he has decided what work needs to be done on your homes."

Charlotte glanced at Webb, catching a frown. She wondered again why Lord Tillson had given him a position he didn't seem qualified for. The cottagers, though, seemed happier, and began to discuss the benefits of having better gardens.

"It'd mean cuttin' down an awful lot of trees," Webb said doubtfully, looking at the woodland surrounding the cottages. "Not just where the gardens are to go, but more of 'em need to come down to let in more light."

"Perhaps you could sell the wood." Charlotte suggested.

Webb looked at Lord Tillson to see what he thought.

"You're the steward," Lord Tillson said unhelpfully.

"Why don't you ask Deacon?" Charlotte suggested. "He's a carpenter; he may know something about the value of the timber, at least." She looked at Webb's doubtful expression. "He's not your enemy, you know," she added.

Webb just grunted, and the discussion moved on to the most urgent repairs.

Lord Tillson really didn't like being in small spaces, Charlotte reflected as she walked home with Davie later that day. He'd made a good attempt at hiding it, but it was clear he'd been very uncomfortable in Mrs Jackson's upstairs rooms. Why, then, had he accompanied Davie into the ice house the day before? Because Davie wanted to go in?

"Were you really talking to Lord Tillson about gardens?" Charlotte asked, reminded of their sheepish look earlier.

"Not exactly, Mama. He was explaining about the sun rising in different places."

"Oh?"

That was all it took for Davie to launch into an explanation. As he chattered on, it occurred to Charlotte that she had, once again, forgotten to apologise to his lordship.

CHAPTER 27

*M*atthew dried his face and pulled the clean shirt over his head, wishing he hadn't let Webb talk him into accepting the squire's invitation. Webb had started with the argument that it would do the major good to meet his own kind now and then.

He picked up the neckcloth, using the mirror to help him tie a fancier knot than usual and trying to ignore the faint shadows under his eyes. Webb's revelations of a couple of days ago—about Benson's fate and the mine—hadn't, as he'd hoped, stopped his nightmares. Instead, having talked about it, the old dreams of regiments of redcoats dying in the explosion had replayed themselves repeatedly. Reena woke him, and each time he told himself that it *hadn't* happened, but that didn't stop his sleeping mind.

He eyed his uniform coat, lying ready over the back of a chair. He'd lost so much weight that none of his clothes fitted properly, but he was hoping the brightness of the red coat might help to disguise that. Mrs Jackson had aired it, managing to get rid of the smell of mothballs.

With a mental shrug, he put it on, pulling his cuffs down and buttoning it up. All this palaver made him want to give up, but he'd sent an acceptance. He couldn't back out now.

Webb—it was his fault. When his initial arguments hadn't worked, Webb had resorted to emotional blackmail.

"Tilly and the rest of 'em want to see the fireworks."

"They have an invitation too?"

"Not exactly, sir. But there's to be a servants' party after they've finished dinner, squire's bought a barrel of ale an' all. If the Jacksons take a bit of food from here, they could join in and stay for the fireworks. I don't reckon they can do that if you ain't going."

Matthew had given in after only a token protest. Perhaps it *would* be good for him to meet more of the local people. After all, he'd only really spoken to the squire and Mrs MacKinnon.

And perhaps he was spending too much time alone with his thoughts.

They arrived at seven, Matthew driving the wagon with Webb beside him on the seat, and the whole Jackson family in the back, their ride softened by straw and a pile of blankets.

The squire normally kept country hours but, as the fireworks were not due to be let off until midnight, dinner would be served late. It appeared that some of the grooms had already sampled the barrel of ale, for the man who came to show Webb where to put the horse was distinctly unsteady on his feet.

Webb and the Jacksons disappeared into the stables as a closed carriage swept into the yard. Matthew vaguely recognised it as one he had seen here before, and supposed the squire must have sent it to collect someone. He was surprised when Davie scrambled out, followed by his mother.

"Mrs MacKinnon," he said, bowing in greeting. She was wearing the same black dress he'd seen her in the day before—or one very like it, it was difficult to tell in the dark. He felt rather over-dressed in his regimentals, even though they were still hidden by his greatcoat.

"My lord," Mrs MacKinnon said, with a smile.

"May I escort you around to the front? I feel we should make a more formal entrance than creeping in through the kitchen."

"Thank you, but no. I need to get Davie settled upstairs with Bertie." She smiled, taking the sting out of her rejection, and headed for the back door. Matthew walked round to the front of the house.

A footman took his hat and coat before showing him into the parlour. Eight people were already in the room, the squire and his wife his only previous acquaintances. He bowed over Mrs Thompson's hand, and she introduced him to Sir Vincent Kinney, the local magistrate. The older lady present was Sir Vincent's mother, the three younger members of the party being his sisters and brother. Maria was the eldest, with blonde curls arranged in elaborate ringlets, and a dress revealing a startling amount of bosom. She was, perhaps, seventeen, and fluttered her eyelashes at him with a sweet smile. Isabella was a year or two younger, with chestnut curls arranged just as elaborately, but clad in a more modest gown. Samuel was introduced as Isabella's twin. The last member of the company was Mr Bretherton, the local vicar, a man of about his own age with thick, dark-blond hair and features appearing to be stuck in a perpetual frown.

"Welcome to the Cotswolds, Lord Tillson," Bretherton said. "We have not seen you at services—have you only just arrived in the area?"

"I'm afraid I've been busy," Matthew prevaricated.

Either the man was completely oblivious to happenings in his parish, and really did not know that Matthew had been at Birchanger since the end of November, or this was a thinly disguised reprimand for not attending church. Either way, Matthew decided that Bretherton was not one of the local gentry he wished to cultivate.

Drinks were offered, then Matthew was cornered by Lady Kinney. "Birchanger Hall has been empty for some time, my lord," she said. "How are you related to the previous incumbent?"

"Several generations back, Lady Kinney."

"Does your family come originally from these parts? Are any other members of your family to live at Birchanger?"

Matthew did not answer for a moment, but politeness forced him to respond. "My family's estate is in Somerset. I have no plans for any of my family to join me."

With a sinking feeling, Matthew recognised an expression of satisfaction cross her face; she had been asking if he was married.

Maria, standing just behind her mother and ostensibly talking to her sister, must have overheard, for a brief smile crossed her face at the same time. He had managed to avoid most of the formal dinner invitations in India, but he recognised the signs; matchmaking mamas and their daughters had been plentiful there, too. He wondered if the Kinneys had any idea they'd set their caps for such a failure.

His spirits lifted when Mrs MacKinnon finally entered the room. She stopped in the doorway with an expression of dismay. The squire hurried over to greet her.

"I thought it was only to be a small dinner," she said, her words easily heard in a lull in the conversation. Matthew saw her cheeks redden slightly.

"This *is* a small party, my dear," the squire said. "You must not worry about being in mourning, eh, Bretherton?" He looked around for support, and both Sir Vincent and Bretherton moved towards her.

"It is only dinner, not dancing or games, my dear Mrs MacKinnon," said Sir Vincent reassuringly, bending over her hand in greeting.

"Indeed. No impropriety, no impropriety at all," Bretherton added. Matthew's dislike of the man deepened.

By this time, Mrs Thompson had struggled up out of her chair and joined them. She said something too quietly for Matthew to hear, then turned to her husband.

"Time for dinner, eh?" the squire said. It would have been proper for him to lead Lady Kinney in, as the woman of highest rank, but he excused himself with a quiet word and offered his arm to his wife instead. Lady Kinney turned towards Matthew with an expectant look on her face. With an internal sigh, Matthew offered her his arm.

Thompson took the seat at the head of the table, with Lady Kinney on one side. Mrs Thompson sat at the foot of the table with Matthew and Sir Vincent either side of her. The seats either side of Mrs MacKinnon were quickly taken by Sir Vincent and the vicar. To Matthew's consternation, the flirtatious Maria was on his other side.

A large variety of dishes had been provided; Matthew accepted a selection of meats and vegetables, but then only toyed with the food on his plate. Watching Mrs MacKinnon across the table, he was unaccountably pleased to see that she didn't seem too keen to converse with the men either side of her. Her rather severe hairstyle contrasted with the elaborate curls and ringlets of the other women, but it framed her face nicely.

"So, how's the renovation work going, Tillson?" the squire said. Matthew gave a non-committal reply, managing to emphasise that the place was not yet ready to receive visitors, and turned his attention to his plate, hoping to avoid further conversation.

"Is it a very grand house?" Maria asked breathlessly, fluttering her eyelashes again and leaning towards him.

Odd, wouldn't the Kinneys have received invitations from the previous baron? Perhaps not, if he'd been the skinflint indicated by his letters.

"Not very grand, no," Matthew said.

"Is it as big as Leverton Park?" Maria asked, a small pout appearing at his abrupt answer.

"Not having visited Leverton Park, I couldn't say," Matthew said, irritated at her persistence. He was aware that most of the other guests were listening with interest.

"Perhaps we can visit when it is ready?"

"Maria!" her mother hissed.

"Perhaps I can help, my lord?" Mrs MacKinnon said. "I have the privilege of being invited to Leverton Park several times a year."

Maria pouted slightly. Matthew let out a breath of relief.

"Birchanger Hall is not as large as the house at Leverton Park," Mrs MacKinnon went on, addressing Maria. "I couldn't say about the size of the grounds. However, it is located near the top of the scarp, with a splendid view to the west, towards the Severn." She glanced at Matthew with a small smile. "So I would say honours are about even."

"You have visited his lordship?" Sir Vincent asked, putting down his fork and glancing between her and Matthew.

Who is Sir Vincent, to question Mrs MacKinnon's actions?

Mrs MacKinnon turned to Sir Vincent, eyebrows raised. "Is there any reason why I should not?"

Matthew suppressed a smile as Sir Vincent flushed slightly.

"No, no. Not at all, only—"

"How are you managing for outdoor staff, my lord?" Mrs Thompson put in hurriedly. "I believe Arthur could let you have a few of his men for a while if you need them—there isn't much work to be done here during January." She looked at her husband for support.

"Best check with Bateson—my steward, you know," the squire said. "But you're welcome, Tillson, if he can spare them."

"Thank you," Matthew said. "Some men to fell trees would be helpful."

"Clearing some woodland, are you?" Sir Vincent asked, accepting the change of subject. "Better for the game, I suppose?"

"Mainly clearing some land for gardens at some of the tenant cottages," Matthew said.

"Gardens?" Lady Kinney exclaimed. "You don't want to cosset the workers too much, you know! They'll get above themselves."

"It's not a matter of cosseting," Matthew said, irritated. "It's a matter of decent living conditions. They can grow some of their own food if a bit of land is cleared for gardens." He stopped there. Lady Kinney's expression indicated that this was not the sort of thing she expected in table conversation, or perhaps she was not used to being contradicted.

"Do you hunt?" Sir Vincent asked, filling the awkward silence that followed.

"Only for tigers, recently," Matthew said, then wished he had not. Young Samuel Kinney posed a stream of questions about tiger hunting; the squire and Sir Vincent joined in, completely ignoring the women present at the table.

Matthew cast an apologetic glance towards Mrs MacKinnon. She caught his eye then looked away again, but he thought he saw a trace of her trying-not-to-laugh expression.

"Oh, do tell me more about India," Maria breathed when her brother had finally run out of questions. "I've always been fascinated by the country. Such different customs." She tilted her head and looked up at him, eyelashes fluttering once again, and one finger toying with a ringlet.

Matthew, now he had started eating, was beginning to enjoy his food for once. He reluctantly put his fork down again.

"Maria, why ever didn't you ask me?" Mrs MacKinnon said. "I could have told you all about India years ago if I'd known how interested you were! We must have a talk next time I see you—after all, men wouldn't know all the things we women are interested in."

So, Mrs MacKinnon had lived in India, had she? Interesting. Was there even more to her that he hadn't yet seen?

She had completely taken the wind out of Maria's sails, thankfully, and Sir Vincent turned the talk back to hunting. He described the country around Leverton Park and runs he'd had so far this winter, the squire joining in the discussion enthusiastically. Although Matthew found their loud voices somewhat overpowering, it did have the advantage of preventing Maria Kinney from trying to start another conversation.

"You should join us one day, Tillson," Sir Vincent said, finally appearing to realise that he and the squire had been monopolising the table.

"My thanks, Kinney, but I've no suitable horse," Matthew replied, not wanting to commit himself to being in company for a whole day, even if most of it would be spent on horseback. "I'm rather out of practice at the moment, too. It was a long voyage from India."

"It's not healthy living in such heat," Lady Kinney announced. "And foreign food, too—you don't look well on it." Matthew bit back an impulse to thank her, wondering if she would even notice sarcasm.

Another awkward silence followed this comment, finally broken by the vicar. "Our troops are doing a grand job out there. Bringing civilisation and order to the natives, and spreading the word of God."

"They were pretty well ordered before the British arrived," Matthew said, gazing at Bretherton. Did the man really believe what he was saying?

"Nonsense—it takes the white man to truly bring order to a country," the squire said.

"If they didn't have order, Thompson, why would it take a large army to subdue them?" Matthew asked. "The English are in India for profit, nothing more."

"But it is also our duty to show them the true religion," Bretherton put in.

"That's not what the East India Company is doing," Matthew said. He couldn't resist trying to prick the man's complacency. "And they have their own religion. Who is to say which is the correct one?"

"Surely you cannot be serious, Lord Tillson?" Lady Kinney exclaimed.

"Lord Tillson, did Davie ever tell you about Maharajah?" Mrs MacKinnon asked. This abrupt change of subject silenced everyone.

"No, I don't think so, Mrs MacKinnon," Matthew said, puzzled, but willing to play along. He was sure she would have some reason for asking such an odd question. "Which Maharajah?"

"Oh, Maharajah was our pig." She gave a small laugh. It was an attractive laugh, not the high-pitched, annoying titter of Maria Kinney. Although it sounded forced to Matthew's ears, no-one else seemed to notice. "Davie tried to teach it to sing."

Matthew glanced around. Maria Kinney was staring open-mouthed, while Kinney and Bretherton were frowning. Suspecting what was coming, Matthew suppressed a smile.

"Did he succeed?" he asked.

"Oh, no, of course not. He didn't manage to teach it anything at all, but he did manage to annoy it considerably." She smiled at him, then turned to Lady Kinney. "How did your Christmas party go, Lady Kinney? So sorry I couldn't come."

"Oh, it was splendid!" Maria said, before her mother could answer. "I had a new gown, in silver gauze over white silk..."

Matthew kept his eyes on his plate as Maria babbled on, letting out a discreet sigh of relief when the talk turned once again to hunting and shooting. He was grateful for Mrs MacKinnon's warning; upsetting his new neighbours was no way to repay the Thompsons for their hospitality. The conversations flowed around him and he allowed himself to look up, catching Mrs MacKinnon's eye. She gave a wry smile, then turned her head to listen to Sir Vincent.

Matthew spent the rest of the meal exchanging bland remarks with Mrs Thompson about the weather, and where best to find tradesmen to work on Birchanger Hall, trying not to get drawn into discussions further up the table. He supposed he should be grateful to the squire, or his wife, for inviting him, but he couldn't say he had enjoyed the occasion so far.

At last, Mrs Thompson tapped a glass and announced that it was time for the ladies to leave the men to their port. Young Samuel Kinney hung his head in mortification when his mother declared he should join the ladies, and they withdrew.

Matthew felt in his pocket and pulled out a cigar.

"I'll just step outside," he said, waving the cigar as explanation, and escaped quickly before the squire said he could smoke indoors. He had eaten far more tonight than he had in months, and the food was sitting heavily on his stomach.

He circled the house, hearing sounds of revelry from the stables, but stopped before he reached the front door again.

The skies were beginning to clear, stars appearing in gaps in the clouds; breathing the cool air made him feel better. A few men moved around on the side lawn. Matthew wandered over to them, hurriedly extinguishing his cigar when he discovered they were setting up the fireworks. He enjoyed a short discussion about fuses and burning rates, before deciding he should probably, out of politeness, rejoin the men in the dining room.

"...good head on her shoulders, usually. For a woman, that is," the squire said. "Comes to discuss the newspapers with me every week."

Mrs MacKinnon?

"No logic, though, women," said Sir Vincent. "I mean, that story about the pig! What was all that about?"

Matthew went over to the sideboard to pour himself a glass of port, shaking his head slightly. A glance at his watch told him there were another two hours to get through before the fireworks. He sighed. Perhaps a discussion of game shooting, and whether deer in the woods caused problems, wouldn't be too tedious? However, he suspected that might lead on to poachers, where his opinions would once again be at odds with the consensus.

Then he wondered what Davie might be doing. Putting his glass on the sideboard, he excused himself and headed upstairs. Children were usually confined to the upper floors.

CHAPTER 28

*T*he door to the nursery was open when Matthew reached it, and he could hear the two boys arguing. Slipping quietly inside, he leaned against the wall by the door. The boys had regiments of toy soldiers lined up between them on the floor. They were arguing about the rules of the game so heatedly they didn't notice him enter the room.

Matthew, in turn, was listening to them closely and started when Mrs MacKinnon spoke.

"Davie—you were supposed to be having a nap!" Then a small "Oh!" as she spotted Matthew inside the room.

Davie scrambled to his feet. "I couldn't sleep. And Bertie... Oh, hello sir."

"I'm afraid I had to escape, ma'am," Matthew said. "The intellectual level of the conversation was a bit too much for me."

Her 'trying-not-to-laugh' expression appeared, then she gave in and laughed out loud. "You think it will be any better in the nursery, my lord?"

"No, but at least these two have the excuse of youth!" He paused for a moment, then continued too quietly for Davie to hear. "I wondered... that is, there are men outside setting up the fireworks. I thought Davie might be interested in seeing how it is done, as well as watching the display later."

She grimaced. "As long as they don't teach him how to *make* fireworks. And if they won't mind?"

"I think they were nearly finished. I'm sure I can find a little something to persuade them." He hastily checked his pocket, pleased to find he *did* have some coins.

Davie was enthusiastic when asked. It took only a few minutes to find his coat, hat, and gloves, then to make sure he was well wrapped up. Bertie, with ill grace, denied any interest, so they left him playing with his soldiers. As Matthew had thought, once the men were greased in the fist, they were happy to explain to Davie all the details of fuses and explosives.

"I wanted to ask Davie about the pig," Matthew said to Mrs MacKinnon as they stood together, watching. It was darker here, away from the lanterns the men were using. "I'm fascinated to know how he tried to teach it to sing."

"There wasn't a pig. I thought... of course, you *know* there wasn't a pig!"

Matthew laughed. "Thank you for warning me off, ma'am," he said. "Does it surprise you to know that neither our host, nor the other two gentlemen, took your meaning?"

"Not really," Mrs MacKinnon said, her sigh audible. She took a deep breath. "My lord, I must apologise for speaking to you so rudely when I thought Davie might have been caught in a mantrap. I realise now that you had nothing to do with setting them, and—"

"Think nothing of it, ma'am," Matthew said. "Your worry was quite understandable."

"Yes, but I was still very—"

"Before you reprimand yourself too much, ma'am, I have to admit to having misjudged you, too. You may wish to return to scolding me."

"Misjudged how?"

Matthew now wished he'd chosen a different way of diverting her apology, but had no choice but to carry on. Standing here in the dark, he could only judge the effect of his words by the tone of her voice.

"I... er... well, the first time I encountered Davie he said he had no father, and then—"

"Ah, I see," Mrs MacKinnon said, not letting him finish. "You are not the first to make that assumption, I must say."

"In my own defence, it is more usual that two ladies with the same surname are sisters rather than..." He paused, realising he did not know what the actual relationship was between the two women.

"Friends, my lord. Mary is the widow of my late husband's sergeant. Having a number of men with the same surname is not uncommon in Scottish regiments."

There was silence for a few moments, while he wondered how to keep the conversation going. He recalled something he'd wondered about when Sally started working at Birchanger. "I wonder if you could give me some advice about my staff. I understand you paid Sally five pounds a year, but that doesn't seem much for someone with her skills."

"You think I was exploiting her?" There was an odd note to her voice that he could not make out.

"It crossed my mind at one point. But that was when I thought..." He stopped, realising the hole he was digging for himself.

"When you thought I was an old witch and a fallen woman?" she asked sweetly.

"Er..." He felt his cheeks heat, grateful for the darkness to hide his embarrassment.

"Never mind. My first impression of you was a drunken wastrel," she said.

That was an amused note in her voice—it had to be. And she hadn't let him flounder for words to redeem his previous ideas.

"May I hope you no longer think so?" he asked. Her opinion *did* matter, but he managed a light-hearted tone.

"I don't think you're a wastrel," she said, "or a drunk."

Had there been a pause in there? He saw the turn of her head as she looked at him, but could not make out her expression in the dim light. *She isn't too sure about the drunk part, then.* With some justification, he had to admit. Why on earth had he started this line of conversation?

"I'm sorry, my lord, that was rather rude of me." Her voice was subdued now.

Take it lightly, Southam. "Not at all," he said calmly. "I no longer think you are old... or a witch." He'd intended his words to make light of her need to apologise to him, but he wasn't sure it had come out that way. Then, to his relief, she chuckled. His hand moved to the pocket that held his flask, but he thought better of it and clasped his hands behind his back instead. He wanted to continue the conversation, but didn't know how. Every time he opened his mouth he seemed to put his foot in it.

"Sally came to us completely untrained," Mrs MacKinnon said, answering his earlier question, her voice confident again. "Now she'll be able to pick and choose where she goes into service in the local area."

"You are a woman of many parts," Matthew said, grateful for the return to normal conversation.

"That 'part', as you put it, is mainly due to Mary."

Matthew, interested, glanced at her, mentally cursing the darkness that showed her face only as a pale oval against her hair and bonnet. He was about to ask more when Davie returned, arms clutched around his body and obviously shivering.

Mrs MacKinnon tutted, then led her son to the kitchen and seated him by the fire. Matthew followed them, regretting the termination of their conversation.

An elderly maid, the only servant not at the staff party, made Davie a cup of hot milk and started to assemble a tea tray. Mrs MacKinnon helped her, then Matthew carried the heavy tray until they reached the parlour door, Davie following with his glass of milk. Bobbing her thanks, the maid took the tray into the room.

Matthew followed Mrs MacKinnon and Davie in, seeing that the other men had already rejoined the women. Mrs MacKinnon settled Davie in a corner of the room with a book taken from her reticule. Matthew smiled when Davie's head soon dropped onto the arm of the chair, then surreptitiously looked at his watch. Only an hour to go... an hour that could have been enjoyably spent learning more about Mrs MacKinnon. He gave a mental sigh, resigning himself to more discussion of hunting or shooting.

The squire, his face flushed with drink, was in the middle of recounting the story of the mantraps, seemingly proud of his son for manipulating his way into a week or more without lessons.

"Thrashed him for telling lies, of course," he finished, his voice sounding over-loud to Matthew's ears. "Can't afford to spare the rod, eh?" He looked at Mrs MacKinnon pityingly. "Don't know how you manage, my dear, without a man about the house to deal with such things."

"I made him eat sprouts," she muttered under her breath.

Matthew suppressed a laugh.

"I will have a word with him for you next Sunday," the vicar said, picking up his glass and draining it, before signalling for a footman to replenish it.

"High time for both boys to be going off to school, I should think," Sir Vincent put in.

Matthew saw Mrs MacKinnon's lips tighten.

"Make a man of him, my dear," Sir Vincent went on. "He needs a man to learn from, to keep him from turning into a mother's boy, you know. School will be just the ticket. Davie going will allow you to give your attention to—"

"Thank you all for your advice," she said sharply, a flush rising on her cheeks. "But he is sharing Bertie's tutor. I'm sure that will suffice."

"Oh, I forgot to tell you, Charlotte," Mrs Thompson said. "I had a note from Mr Hayes yesterday. His father had a relapse and isn't well enough to be left alone. He doesn't know how long he will be needed, so he said it would be best if I found someone else."

"Oh well, no rush, eh?" the squire said. "Give the boys more time to play."

"Perhaps I could come for an hour or two a week, Mrs MacKinnon?" Bretherton said. "I can supervise his Latin."

She was almost frowning now. None of the cloth-heads trying to

297

run her life for her appeared to notice that their advice was not welcome.

"Nonsense," Sir Vincent put in. "I'm sure we can find someone for—"

"Thank you," Mrs MacKinnon said firmly. "I will think about this later. This is really not the best time to discuss the issue."

Sir Vincent sat forward in his chair, as if he were about to speak again, but Matthew spoke first.

"Thompson," Matthew addressed the squire. "Where's the best place near here to buy a decent horse? That talk of hunting earlier—I need to do more riding, but the slug I've got at the moment probably couldn't jump a fallen log, never mind a hedge."

"I know of a good hunter for sale," Sir Vincent put in. "Neighbour of mine. Come over one day and I'll introduce you."

Matthew thanked him, suddenly aware of a very slight slurring of the man's words. "Where's a good place to buy a curricle?" he went on, listening to the way Sir Vincent talked rather than what he said. The signs were slight, but the man was becoming the worse for drink.

"I'm going to need some decent plough horses too," Matthew said when the curricle discussion ended, toying with his glass but resolutely not drinking from it. His gaze slid sideways; Mrs MacKinnon was concentrating on her plate, her earlier flush beginning to subside.

He managed to keep the menfolk discussing such mundane practicalities until Mrs Thompson announced that it was time to go outside to see the fireworks.

Although the firework display did not last long, it *was* spectacular, as the squire had bought a good quantity to be let off in quick succession: fire fountains and rockets burst in the sky amid streams of coloured sparks. There were lots of 'oohs' and 'aahs' from where the servants stood, and even Maria Kinney forgot herself long enough to gasp in amazement.

Matthew received more pleasure from the expression of wonder on Davie's face than from the fireworks, as he'd seen far bigger displays. Mrs MacKinnon, too, was watching her son as much as she was the fireworks, and in the flickering light, Matthew thought she had a rather worried expression.

After the display it was time for Mrs MacKinnon and Davie to be taken home. The squire shouted for his coachman to bring the carriage round, but there was no response. Eventually the man was found to be too drunk to hitch up the horses, let alone drive them. Sir Vincent offered his own coach, but his coachman and groom, having expected to stay the night, were in no fit state either.

"If you don't mind an open wagon, ma'am, I can take you home," Matthew offered.

"Or you can stay the night here," Mrs Thompson said. "I'm sure we can find somewhere for you."

"Thank you, Letty," Mrs MacKinnon said. "I'd prefer to go home. That is, if you are sure you don't mind, my lord?"

"Not at all, ma'am."

Mrs MacKinnon borrowed thicker coats for herself and Davie, while Webb got the wagon sorted out. Matthew, eyeing the tired Jackson children, waved Webb round to the back. "The other Mrs MacKinnon did not come?"

"No. She preferred a quiet night at home."

"I'll drive," Matthew said. "Mrs MacKinnon, if you'd like to travel in front with me?" She nodded and scrambled up, followed by Davie. Matthew mounted and settled Davie snugly between the two of them, then set off slowly down the drive.

The chattering of the Jackson children soon quieted behind them. Feeling awkward in the silence, Matthew asked Mrs MacKinnon if she was warm enough.

"Just about."

Matthew hesitated, then fished his flask out and offered it to her. "Don't worry," he assured her. "You won't become a drunken wastrel with a few sips." He was rewarded with a faint chuckle, and she took a sip before handing it back.

"Tell me," he said, "was tonight a fair sample of local society?"

"A small sample, yes. There are also the Hetheringtons—Sir

Michael and Lady Sarah, a bit to the west, near the river. And Mr Sedgewick, who has a large estate on the way to Bath. But if you want assemblies or concerts, you'll have to go to Bath."

He was tempted to ask her if she patronised the city, but he suspected she didn't have the means. They continued in silence for a while. Matthew, his eyes on the road, wondered if she was dozing, but a glimpse of her face in the moonlight showed her eyes open and a frown creasing her brow. He took a guess at what might be worrying her.

"Wandering the woods while the tutor was away was Bertie Thompson's idea, not Davie's, as far as I can gather. Davie just went along with it."

She looked at him, her frown now indicating puzzlement.

"What I'm getting at," Matthew continued, "is that Bertie *does* have a father—the male influence those cloth-heads all seem to think is so essential. Yet he was the one who initiated the escapade."

"Oh, yes, I see what you mean. Thank you." She gave him an uncertain smile, but returned to her abstraction.

That wasn't the only problem then. He gave up, and concentrated on following the rutted lane to Upper Edgecombe.

Mrs MacKinnon woke Davie up as they approached the house, and he helped them both down.

"Good night, my lord, and thank you."

He touched his hat, then remounted and slapped the reins to take the wagon further up the lane to turn it. The evening had been far more enjoyable than he'd anticipated.

CHAPTER 29

*B*ack at Birchanger, Matthew retired to his room with a bottle of wine. He stoked up the fire and sat close to it. He was tired, but he had too much to think about and knew he would not sleep.

Twirling his glass, he watched the firelight make ruby sparks in the liquid. In his head, Mrs MacKinnon's words repeated themselves: not a wastrel, then the slight pause. He took a mouthful of wine. If she still thought him a drunkard, she was justified.

He screwed up his eyes as the memory of their first meeting came back to him, sprawling in the mud at her feet. It was a miracle she was even deigning to speak to him. A flush of shame heated his cheeks as he wondered what she'd really thought of him this evening. Had he been over-loud, like the squire? Face flushed, like Sir Vincent?

God, he hoped not. It was one thing to become the worse for drink in private, or in the mess with fellow officers, quite another to get in such a state in mixed company.

He reminded himself of Lorton's advice not to try to stop drinking suddenly. A first step would be to try harder not to drink in public.

Draining the glass he had poured, he pushed the cork back into the bottle and went to bed.

. . .

'...don't even know 'ow many bloody tenants 'e 'ad on 'is land...'

'...don't want to cosset the workers...'

'...you'd think a bloody major in the army could sort things out...'

Matthew's eyes flew open and he turned his head, seeing only patches of moonlight on the floor and shadows of the mullions in the windows. He rubbed his face. That hadn't been a dream from his past, not with Lady Kinney's voice mixed with Havers and Benson.

It was his conscience. He *didn't* know how many tenants he had. Birchanger was not a large estate, but there could well be many more than the row of ten cottages that he'd seen a couple of days ago. Probably in a similar state of dereliction.

Lying back, he tried to empty his mind and sleep, but it was no use. The same thoughts persisted, and eventually he gave up and got out of bed. Pulling on some clothes, he lit a lamp and found paper and a pencil. If he made a list, perhaps his brain would stop worrying him about it all until the morning.

Matthew went in search of coffee as the sky started to lighten. The kitchen was deserted, so he began feeding the fire in the ancient range. Once that was burning hot, he filled a kettle to make coffee.

Mrs Jackson appeared, looking both bleary-eyed and guilty. "I'm right sorry, my lord. I should 'a' bin up hours ago..."

"Never mind, Mrs Jackson. We were all very late to bed. Where's Webb?"

"Still a' bed, I think, my lord. You leave that now, sir, I'll have a proper breakfast done soon enough." She eyed him critically. "You going to eat it if I makes it?"

When had his entire staff started to nag him?

"No. I'm going for some air first. Just make coffee, would you?"

Matthew went back to his room for his coat, then took his coffee out to the kitchen garden. Making the list had *not* helped; all it had done was make him realise the enormity of the task in front of him. He'd drifted off to sleep once or twice, but woken to Reena's whining with a racing heart, not sure what he'd been dreaming.

The fine weather was soon to be over, he thought, looking at a bank of cloud to the west. Leaning on the garden wall just inside the door, he surveyed his progress to date. Not a lot, he had to admit, other than making him physically tired enough to get some sleep.

He finished his coffee and set the mug down, pulling the list he'd made out of his pocket. Turning to look up at what was visible of the Hall beyond the garden wall, he could easily make out slipped tiles and cracked panes. The Hall was in far better condition than those cottages, but that was no reason to put off the repairs.

You're a major in the army, for goodness sake. You should be able to deal with it!

He ran a hand through his hair, the helpless feeling of last night rushing back, and the shame. There was too much to do, too many decisions to make.

Just tell someone else to do it, Webb had said.

At least he could make sure that Webb *was* doing it, and had what he needed to get the work done.

Matthew had to wait some time, as Webb was still sleeping off his libations of the night before. Mrs Jackson put ham and eggs in front of him, and he felt a bit better after making himself eat some of it. Finally, he was in the steward's office, coffee in hand, sitting across from a bleary-eyed and yawning Webb. The sergeant looked as bad as Matthew felt.

"Everythin' all right, sir?" Webb asked, eyeing him warily.

"That's what I came to ask you, Webb."

Webb rubbed his eyes. "Sorry, sir, ain't much 'appened yet, I'm tryin'—"

"I'm only asking for a progress report," Matthew said, taking a mouthful of coffee.

"Well, I sent them letters Mrs Captain helped me with, and I got a couple of answers, but I ain't got no way of knowin' how much things *should* cost."

"Can't help you there, I'm afraid."

"Nossir. But I was wonderin' about them ledgers you got, if they say how much repairs cost, an' supplies and such."

"You're welcome to look in them," Matthew said. "They're probably still in the stables, unless you've brought them in?"

"Yessir. I know where they are." Webb rubbed his eyes, opened his mouth to speak, then closed it again.

"Go on," Matthew said, resigned.

"There's an awful lot to look through, sir, and the writin' ain't all that neat, and I'm not very—"

"Webb, the point of you being land steward was that I wouldn't have to do that kind of thing!"

"Yessir. That's not what I was goin' to say, sir. I wondered if Mrs Captain might 'elp."

Matthew waited.

"Thing is, sir, she's already spent near two days 'elpin' me, and she 'as her work to do. I don't reckon she can afford to spend more time unless she gets paid. But it don't seem right..." Webb shrugged.

"Work?"

No income from her late husband then? Or not enough.

"Yessir. She writes things for someone in London." Webb pressed his lips together, looking away. "Dunno as she'd want me to be tellin' things I 'eard when I was there," he went on, a moment later.

"Don't worry, Webb, I'm not expecting you to spy on people for me."

"Thank you, sir. But she might not be pleased..."

"To be asked to take work?"

Webb nodded.

Matthew mulled it over for a moment. "I see the problem. It's a good idea, but I'll have to think what to say."

～

Matthew knocked at the door of the cottage, hunching his shoulders against the sleet trying to get inside his collar. Although it was the middle of the day, the cloudy skies gave the impression of dusk. It wasn't long before the door opened a crack, but he could see no-one. Then the door was flung open and he realised he had been looking above Davie's head.

"Mama's not here, sir," he said. "But she won't be very long, I think. Do you want to come in and wait?"

Matthew nodded and followed him into the hall, shrugging off his wet greatcoat and putting his hat on a hook on the wall.

"You can wait in the parlour," Davie said doubtfully. "It's cold, though. But the kitchen is warm."

"Kitchen, please," Matthew said. He followed Davie into the welcoming brightness and warmth of the kitchen, taking a seat. Davie had been studying, for books were spread out across the table. The lad closed the books he had been using, then pulled a chair over to a shelf to take down a tin.

"Would you like a biscuit, sir?" he offered.

"No, thank you." He would like a large glass of brandy to warm his insides, but resisted the temptation to get his flask out. "Don't let me stop you," he added, seeing the boy's face fall.

Davie hesitated. "I'd better not," he said with regret, putting the tin back.

"What are you studying?" Matthew asked, not feeling comfortable sitting in silence.

"Latin."

The tone of disgust made Matthew smile. "How are you getting on?" he asked.

Davie pulled a face. "Mama's at Mrs Gilling's house, just down the lane," he said. "I'd better tell her you're here so she doesn't stay too long."

Matthew, suppressing a smile, interpreted this as Davie not wanting to show his skill—or lack of skill—with his Latin. When Davie had donned his coat and left, Matthew slumped in the chair. He'd ridden to Upper Edgecombe rather than walking, but he was still exhausted. The kitchen was warm, feeling cheerful even in this gloomy weather, with gleaming copper pans hanging above the range, and Davie's papers still spread out.

Feeling safe, surrounded by comforting domesticity, he decided to rest his head on his arms, just for a moment.

There was silence in the kitchen when Charlotte entered, Davie on her heels. Lord Tillson was sitting at the table with his arms crossed and his head resting on them.

"He didn't look very well when he came in, Mama," Davie whispered. "He's not dead, is he?"

"No, of course not," Charlotte said, but she went over to check anyway. When she was closer she could hear the sound of steady breathing. "He's asleep," she said.

"But it's the middle of the day!"

"Yes, I know. Davie, go and light the fire in the parlour, please." When he left, she took a closer look. Lord Tillson's short hair was damp near his collar, but dry where he had been wearing his hat. The collar of his coat was damp, but when she put a gentle hand to his forehead his skin felt normal. So he was just wet in places from the sleet. She relaxed in relief. Not much of his face was visible, but she could make out dark shadows under his eyes.

She quietly gathered up Davie's books and, as an afterthought, the biscuit tin, and took them into the parlour. Then she went upstairs for a blanket and draped it over Lord Tillson's shoulders before leaving him alone.

Davie complained about having to resume his lessons, but biscuits proved to be an adequate bribe for the moment and he carried on copying out lists of Latin nouns with little complaint. Charlotte put her cloak back on, then took Lord Tillson's mare around to the back of the cottage. They had no stable or shed big enough for a horse, but she loosened the saddle girth and led her to a spot beneath an apple tree next to the wall. The tree was bare, but between the branches and the wall the animal did have a little shelter from the wind.

Charlotte sat by the fire with a book while Davie studied his Latin, but she didn't read it. Instead, she re-read the letters that had arrived the day before. The first one—the easy one—was a short note from Ann saying she had been making enquiries about both Lord Tillson and Sergeant Webb at Horse Guards. She had also enquired at the East India Company offices, but wasn't getting very far. It concluded with the news that Thomas had taken lodgings for them at Plymouth; she was looking forward to moving down there next week, so she wouldn't be able to make any more enquires.

Charlotte put the letter aside. She was happy for Ann, both that she would see her husband more often, and that she had found someone she was so fond of. The lack of news about Lord Tillson and Webb didn't seem to matter so much now she knew both men a little better. She would write to Ann to thank her, and wish her well in her new home.

The other letters worried her more. Lady Henbury wrote with some general news, but the main reason for the letter was to say that Charlotte's father had finally discovered that the tiara had been removed from his house and was threatening to take legal action. However, Lord Meerbrook had convinced him that, as Lady Henbury had bought it, he would only make a fool of himself by persisting.

That was good news, in a way, although she suspected it would make her father more likely to contest the money from the trust fund; for revenge, if nothing else.

The third letter was from her father, writing to say that he'd obtained David a place at Harrow, at considerable expense to himself. The letter instructed her to bring his grandson to London. There he would be tutored, and found a place in a prep school until he was old enough to start at Harrow, ensuring he was not behind the other boys.

Harrow was one of the most prestigious schools in England; her father must have bribed someone to get Davie a place. As far as Charlotte knew, all such schools had a curriculum mainly devoted to Latin and Greek. Looking at her son, screwing up his face over his Latin, she wondered how the classical education of a gentleman would suit him. He was working, but not with the dedication he'd shown to his map-making efforts.

Her attention returned to the letter. Her father had said nothing about her own permanent return to London, but he must know that she would not send Davie away. He would have something planned for her that would be to his own advantage.

She resisted the temptation to throw the letter in the fire, folding it up instead and placing it on the mantelpiece. Perhaps she would talk it over with Mary when Davie wasn't around, although she wasn't certain it would help.

She shook her head. No, she would find some way of getting Davie an education without submitting to her father. His plans would make Davie unhappy as well as herself. She would write back, thanking him for his efforts but saying she would make her own arrangements.

As she returned to her chair, her thoughts turned to the enigma that was Lord Tillson. If she had only met him at last night's fireworks party, she would have described him as friendly and intelligent. He'd deflected attention from her when the other men were trying to tell her what to do, and there'd been those few moments of shared amusement during dinner.

On the other hand, he was drinking far more than was good for him and obviously eating, and sleeping, much less than he should be. So far, however, those failings seemed to be affecting only himself and not the people around him. And Davie seemed to like him.

Nearly an hour later, she heard the scrape of a chair from the kitchen. She went through to find Lord Tillson standing, folding the blanket and looking embarrassed. She bustled around, putting the kettle on, while he ran his hand through his hair.

"I do apologise, Mrs MacKinnon," he said, meeting her eyes only briefly. "I don't know what came over me."

"Exhaustion, by the look of you, my lord," she said candidly. She pursed her lips—compared to Sir Vincent or the vicar he was a welcome caller, even though falling asleep was not something her visitors normally did. He did indeed look exhausted.

"Davie said you had a trying-not-to-laugh expression, ma'am. Dare I hope that is it?"

"He said that?"

Lord Tillson nodded.

Charlotte smiled. "I'm afraid so."

"Please, just laugh—it is better than being offended. As I do seem to manage to make a complete fool of myself quite often, at least I may have the satisfaction of providing amusement."

Charlotte was about to smile at the friendly banter in his words, but something in his tone stopped her—a hint that he really did think many of his actions deserved ridicule.

"I wasn't laughing at *you*, my lord. I was just amused at the situation." She glanced away as his expression did not change. "I'm sorry if I have offended you, my lord. You did look tired, so I left you to sleep."

He was still standing, as she herself was not seated. "Would you care to talk in the parlour?"

She didn't wait for a reply, but hid her discomfort in assembling a tea tray with cups, milk, and sugar. Then she recalled her thoughts about him earlier, and took out the fruit cake Mary had brought back from the bakery the previous day. She cut three generous slices and placed one, with a mug of tea, on the table. She carried the tray into the parlour, and sent Davie back to the kitchen with his books.

"Now, my lord, how may I help you?" she asked, when they were finally seated by the fire with tea and cake. He was distracted, staring at the picture above the mantelpiece and frowning.

"Is something wrong, my lord?"

There was a bleak look in his eyes when he turned his head, and puzzlement as well.

"I don't know," was all he said. He rubbed a hand across his face. "I'm sorry—it appears my memory is playing tricks on me while I'm awake now, as well as…"

Charlotte looked at the painting of sunny fields and woods above the greenery on the mantelpiece. Of course, when he'd been here before she'd had Angus' portrait there. Why did the change of picture distress him so much? She could reassure him about that, at least. She got up and took the portrait out of its cupboard.

"This is what you remember?" she asked, showing it to him. "I think this was on the wall when you came before."

He looked at it, then back at her. "Yes." He put his tea cup down abruptly and stood up, walking over to the window and looking out. She got the impression he wasn't really seeing anything.

"My lord?"

"I'm sorry to have bothered you, Mrs MacKinnon. I'm obviously not in a fit state to—"

"Please, sit down, my lord. Have your tea and cake."

He looked around with a frown. She waited. He still seemed uneasy as he walked back to his chair and sat down again.

"Eat, my lord." When he hesitated, she added, "If you don't like fruit cake, I can get you something else."

He shook his head and took a bite of the cake. Charlotte kept her eyes on her own plate until she saw out of the corner of her eye that he'd managed to consume most of his slice.

"How may I help you?" she asked again.

Lord Tillson stared at the crumbs on his plate for a long moment, looked up at her and then looked away again.

"Please, my lord, just ask. The worst I can say is 'no'."

"It is a somewhat unusual request," he started, finally looking at her and frowning slightly.

She smiled encouragingly.

"Er, Webb told me how you helped him. With the letters and so on. He will need more help—looking through the old ledgers to check what we might expect from the estate, organising the repair work on the house, and so on."

"Pardon me, my lord, but why don't you just employ a competent steward? Someone who can do all this unassisted." She'd been wondering that since Webb first told her of his new position.

Lord Tillson hesitated again, opening his mouth without saying anything. Then he shrugged. "He'll be a good steward eventually. He wants to belong here, and he can handle men."

"Is he honest?"

This question seemed to amuse him, for his lips twitched. "Towards me, yes, I think so."

"So, you are asking me to be a kind of secretary?" Charlotte asked, returning to the topic.

"Webb said something about your work. I'm not asking you to work full time, if you wish or need to continue with your normal activities. But if you could spare one or two days a week it would be very helpful." He still seemed ill at ease, fiddling with a button on his coat.

"I suppose I'll not be going to the squire's so often now," she said, half to herself. She returned her gaze to Lord Tillson, realising that she'd spoken out loud.

"Mr Thompson gets a London paper delivered," she explained. "He liked me to go and discuss the news with him, and Davie shared Bertie's tutor."

Lord Tillson nodded, still fiddling with his button. "I... er, what I'm asking you to do is nothing I could not normally do for myself." He cleared his throat, his face reddening slightly. "The truth is, at the moment I find it very difficult to concentrate for long on anything other than mapping."

"Making maps seems a rather unusual pastime," Charlotte said, keeping her tone light.

"I did a lot of surveying in the Bombay Engineers, so it's familiar." He shrugged. "It takes concentration, but there are no significant or important decisions to be made." He looked away. "Davie seemed interested in it," he added.

"He has wondered if you've finished measuring. He said something about helping you to make the proper maps?"

"Yes, he seemed keen to help with that. I'm off to Bath tomorrow to order paper and so on. But if he's willing, I'd appreciate his help with the rest of the surveying."

He leaned forward in his chair a little, talking more confidently, now. "If you are still without a tutor for him, he can learn some mathematics while he's about it—he may not even realise he is having lessons."

"Would you really teach him?" Charlotte looked doubtfully out of the window at the sleet still coming down.

"We can draw up what measurements I already have if the weather does not improve. And I can always set him to work making a decent plan of the house."

"And quantities of paint needed?" Charlotte smiled, wondering what other hidden lessons she could find for Davie.

"Why not? And you must tell me what remuneration is appropriate."

Charlotte shook her head. "No, my lord. You will be teaching Davie—"

"Teaching Davie will be fair exchange for the help he will give me with the surveying," he said firmly.

"A child that age is truly helpful?" Charlotte did not quite believe it.

"Yes, he is."

Charlotte considered a moment. She was trying to write more articles for Mr Berry, but there was no guarantee he would take them all. She didn't want Davie to go to Harrow, mostly because her father *did* wish it, so she'd need as much money as she could earn. And perhaps concentrating on something other than her writing might be as good as a rest.

"Very well, my lord. Perhaps for a month to start with?"

"Thank you, Mrs MacKinnon." He *did* look relieved.

"Now, it is time for luncheon. You will stay and eat?"

Lord Tillson shook his head. "Thank you, but—"

"Good," she said, not letting him finish. "It's only soup and bread, but it'll warm you up before you ride back." She smiled as Lord Tillson looked quickly out of the window again. "Don't worry, my lord—I took her round behind the house while you were... resting."

"One more thing, Mrs MacKinnon—please could you stop 'my lording' me? I'm not used to it, and it makes me feel as if you aren't addressing me."

"Major?"

He nodded, but his smile did not quite reach his eyes.

Matthew followed Mrs MacKinnon into the kitchen, where she put a pot on the range and sent Davie into the pantry to get the bread and butter. He stood awkwardly in the doorway, wondering if would be rude to sit down while she was still working. She moved efficiently, fetching bowls and plates from a dresser, and finally looked his way.

"Oh. Do sit, please, my... Major."

He took the chair he'd used earlier and, wanting to do something to help, tidied Davie's books into a pile at one end of the table. He wasn't hungry, feeling the need of a drink more than anything else, but the soup was tasty and the bread fresh, and he managed to eat what was put in front of him. He couldn't think of much to say, but he needn't have worried, for Davie asked him about making more maps and where they were going next, and the meal passed quickly.

"Anyone for any more?" Mrs MacKinnon said, when all the bowls were empty, her eyes sliding in his direction for a moment. Davie accepted with alacrity, but Matthew was relieved when she did not press him to eat any more.

The meal over, he felt reluctant to leave the friendly warmth of the kitchen, but he felt he had already taken up too much of her time today.

"When do you wish me to start, my... Major?" she asked, after he had thanked her for the meal.

"As soon as is convenient for you, Mrs MacKinnon." The sooner the better.

"Tomorrow, perhaps?"

"That would be excellent. I will be away most of the day, but I will let Webb know to expect you. And thank you again for agreeing—"

"I will enjoy it, Major, I'm sure." She led the way through the scullery and out into the back garden, to where she'd tethered the mare.

Matthew looked with interest at the vegetable patches and flower

313

beds, mostly empty at this time of year, but he'd taken up enough of her time so he led the mare around to the lane. Mounting up, he gave a nod and smile of farewell, and rode off. He waited until he was well out of sight of the cottage before he pulled the flask from the pocket of his greatcoat.

CHAPTER 30

The following afternoon, Matthew rode home along the undulating road towards Edgecombe, leading a handsome chestnut gelding. The weather was still raw and damp, and he was looking forward to getting back to a fire.

He'd bought the paper and other things he needed in Bath, then found his way to Leverton Park to see Sir Vincent. The ladies of the house were—thankfully—out making calls, otherwise he might well have turned and run. As promised, Sir Vincent had introduced Matthew to the neighbour who had a hunter for sale. It was a fine-looking chestnut gelding and, after a brief ride, Matthew had bought it, together with its tack.

Sir Vincent had offered him a drink before he set off home, and then subjected Matthew to a quarter of an hour of boredom. He'd described the local hunts in tedious detail, but then suddenly changed the subject to ask how long Matthew was planning on staying in the area, and whether he was going up to London for the season if he wasn't posted back to his regiment before then.

"For there's not much society for you around here, you know," Sir Vincent had said. He'd then talked about marriage prospects in a vague way, until it had dawned on Matthew that Sir Vincent was trying to warn him off Mrs MacKinnon.

"Still mourning her husband, you know," he'd said. "Still in her blacks, after all these years. Keeps a portrait of him over the fire. Sword on the mantelpiece too." He shook his head; whether in sorrow or incomprehension, Matthew wasn't sure.

Matthew ran over the conversation again as the road climbed over the last rise before Edgecombe, wondering idly if he'd get the same kind of pointed conversation if he went to see the vicar. The two of them had seemed very keen to organise Mrs MacKinnon's life for her.

That landscape painting above her fireplace had confused him yesterday, but now the memory of it brought a smile to his face, then a laugh. The portrait of the late captain was *not* always over the fire in Mrs MacKinnon's parlour.

Davie was due to come to Birchanger tomorrow to help with the mapping—he might see if Davie could remember when Sir Vincent had last called on his mother.

As he rode into the stable yard, Jackson came out to see to the horses. Matthew let him deal with Daisy, and rubbed the new gelding down himself. He started the process of making friends with the animal by giving it an apple and a small lump of sugar.

Inside, Mrs Jackson made coffee and he sat at the kitchen table warming his hands on the mug. After a brief internal debate, he decided that his kitchen at the Hall did not count as being in public, and he added a hefty dash of brandy to speed the warming up process.

Webb found him there ten minutes later. "Took on a new man, sir, if that's all right," he said.

"One of the tenants?"

"Nossir. 'E come lookin' for work this afternoon."

"Did you have anything in particular in mind?" The man could always help with the kitchen garden, he supposed.

"Thought I could send 'im with Jackson to muck out the ice 'ouse, like you said. An' Jackson can tell me if 'e's any good."

Matthew nodded.

"And I asked Deacon about sellin' wood. 'E give me the direction of the navy shipyards in Portsmouth—said they might be int'rested in some of the oaks. Summat about the right shape for makin' bits o' ships."

Matthew nodded again.

"Said 'e'd ask around for someone what knows about managin' woods—reckons the woods need thinnin' out a bit. Mebbe some of the folks from them cottages could be used to do that? And cut down the trees for their gardens—"

"That all sounds fine to me. Webb—I don't need to know every detail."

Webb grinned. "Don't you worry, sir—I ain't *tellin'* you every detail!"

"Ha!"

"You goin' out measurin' again tomorrow, sir? Mrs Captain come up today, and said Davie can come up tomorrow if 'e's wanted."

"Yes, we're still working on the paths in the woods. We'll be out if the weather's dry."

"Blacksmith in the village asked around to see if 'e could find who set the traps, sir. 'E found a man 'alfway to Bath what reckons 'e sold ten to Lord Tillson."

"Ten? Damn."

"'Ow many did you find, sir?"

"Eight, including the one Reena set off." He sighed. "Never mind, I'll get these maps finished soon, then we can mark off all the places we've looked." It was something constructive to do. He could plan tomorrow's mapping now, in fact, with the aid of a bottle of wine.

Davie arrived before his mother the next morning. Although the skies were still cloudy, it was not raining, so Matthew collected the things he needed and they set off. They quickly settled into their routine of mapping the paths, talking now and then but mostly about what they were doing. They found themselves near the ruined hut at midday, and Davie brought out enough food for the two of them. Matthew ate a few mouthfuls then held out the rest towards Davie, saying he could have it if he wanted it.

Davie shook his head. "Mama said I was only to eat my own share," he said.

"She won't know," Matthew said.

Davie frowned, then shook his head again. "That would be an omission lie, wouldn't it sir?"

"I suppose it would, Davie. You are quite right."

Damn—sometimes total honesty could be a nuisance. Not to mention meddlesome women who took more upon themselves than they had been asked to! He wasn't hungry, but he managed to eat a bit more of the food.

"Do you remember your father?" he asked, as Davie was finishing.

"No, sir. He died before I was born."

Matthew raised his eyebrows. Sir Vincent had implied MacKinnon's death was more recent than Davie's nine or ten years. Or had he?

"Does your mama always wear black?" he asked.

Davie didn't seem surprised by the question—but then he asked plenty of random questions of his own. "Oh, no. Her mama died before Christmas, so she got her old black dresses out again."

Ah. Sir Vincent had been bending the facts somewhat then? Surely he didn't think *Matthew* was a threat to his chances? He couldn't imagine the quick-witted Mrs MacKinnon married happily to the worthy but dull Sir Vincent. On the other hand, the man was well turned out, he thought ruefully, looking at his own coat hanging loosely on him.

If you can't stop drinking, you could at least try to eat properly, even you don't feel like it.

He reached for the rest of his luncheon and forced it down.

The clouds had become thicker and darker during the morning, and showers of sleet started to fall as they finished their food.

Matthew decided to call it a day and introduce Davie to the details of transferring all their measurements to paper.

There was a strange horse in the stables when they returned, but no immediate sign of a visitor. Matthew asked Mrs Jackson to bring coffee, and set out his notes on the table in his room.

He asked to see the map Davie had made from their first surveying session several weeks before. The lad had made a surprisingly good job of it on his own, so Matthew corrected one or two errors and started Davie drawing a large map of all the woodlands to the north and east. He settled himself at the far end of the table and set about making a fair copy of the corrected map of the fields.

They were interrupted some time later by voices and footsteps, and what sounded like a small procession of people crossing the hall. Davie was still absorbed in his mapping, so Matthew left him to it and went to investigate.

The horse must belong to the thin man wearing a dark coat and a sour expression, just taking a seat at the kitchen table. There was also Webb, wheezing loudly, Mrs MacKinnon, and Deacon. All of them had traces of dust on their clothing. Deacon saw him loitering in the doorway and stood up again.

"Don't get up," Matthew said, waving a hand. He looked enquiringly at the stranger.

"This is Mr Worthington, my lord," Mrs MacKinnon said formally. "He has come to give us an estimate for the work needed to fix the roof."

"Do carry on," Matthew said, sitting down to listen.

"As I was saying, my lord," Mr Worthington said, running a hand over his balding head, "the best solution would be to replace all the timbers in the north wing, and reset the tiles over all the west-facing sections of roof as well."

"That would mean removing most of the tiles from the roof, didn't you say?" Mrs MacKinnon asked.

Worthington shrugged, looking at Matthew. "That is the best approach, my lord, if you want a proper job doing."

319

Mrs MacKinnon frowned, and Matthew's lips thinned. Worthington should be answering *her*, not talking to him.

"What about Deacon's suggestion of only replacing a few of the beams and reinforcing the others?" Mrs MacKinnon asked. "And just refixing the slipped tiles? That would be much quicker, and could be done at almost any time. The job you are proposing would have to wait for better weather in the summer, would it not?"

Worthington had glanced at Mrs MacKinnon while she talked, but returned his gaze to Matthew. "My lord, I was asked to give my opinion on the best way to fix your roof, and you have heard my reply. I will leave you a written estimate."

Matthew's annoyance grew as he noticed a flush rising on Mrs MacKinnon's face.

"Answer Mrs MacKinnon's question, Mr Worthington," Matthew said.

"My lord, this man," he waved a hand at Deacon, "who has no experience with buildings of this nature, suggests—"

"Mr Worthington." Matthew cut off the builder's rambling explanation, his voice curt. "I believe *Mrs MacKinnon* asked the questions. Please answer *her*."

Worthington grimaced and asked Mrs MacKinnon to repeat the question.

"What is wrong with Deacon's suggestion?"

"A roof is a complex structure, madam," he said stiffly. "It is best to replace all rotted timbers to avoid collapse. Deacon has no experience with roofing—he said so himself."

"What would happen if we followed his suggestion?" she persisted.

"I really do not recommend it, my lord," Worthington said, turning back to Matthew.

"Mr Worthington," Matthew said. "Mrs MacKinnon and Mr Webb will make the decision on this matter. If you cannot provide an answer to questions from them, addressed *to* them, then I'm afraid you have wasted your time coming here."

He glanced up the table at Mrs MacKinnon, the flush still on her cheeks and her lips pressed together. "Do you wish to employ this man, Mrs MacKinnon?"

"I think not, my lord."

"Very well. Good day, Mr Worthington."

"But you can't—"

Matthew stood, his patience at an end. "I *beg* your pardon, sir? Are *you* telling *me* what to do?"

"I mean, a woman doesn't—"

"I think you had better leave, Mr Worthington, before I become really angry. Send me a bill for a day's consultancy. A *reasonable* fee, Mr Worthington," he added.

"I'll help you with your horse," Webb said, and escorted Worthington out to the stables.

"I'm sorry," Mrs MacKinnon said, when Worthington was out of earshot.

"You have nothing to be sorry for," Matthew said. "An obnoxious man, and likely a greedy one too." He turned to Deacon.

"Deacon, I never thanked you for helping to look after me when I was ill," he started courteously.

"Mrs MacKinnon asked me to, my lord," Deacon said simply.

"What is your expertise?"

"Ship's carpenter, my lord, until this." He held up his hook.

"And my roof? The short version, if you please."

"Some rot, my lord, but with the rotten pieces cut out and the beams reinforced, and the roof made watertight and ventilated, there won't be more. As long as it's checked regularly, the repairs I've suggested will be fine for now. In the long run you may need part of the roof replacing, but that's best to wait until you've decided if you want to make any changes to the building."

"Mrs MacKinnon?"

"If Deacon can repair a warship so it holds together, I think he can be trusted with your roof."

That made sense to him. "Can you undertake the work, Deacon?" He saw Deacon glance at his missing hand. "I meant, are you capable of organising and supervising it?"

Deacon glanced at Mrs MacKinnon, who just waved a hand to indicate that he should answer. "Yes, my lord. But I—"

"You can sort out the details, Mrs MacKinnon?"

"I... er... well, yes, I... we will work out how much it will cost and—"

"Please, just go ahead and get it done."

Charlotte gaped as the major nodded at them and left the room. This was more than just helping Webb with the ledgers and letter writing —he'd just trusted her confidence in Deacon over the opinion of an expert, then told her to sort it out without giving her any limits on spending.

She met Deacon's eyes. He looked surprised, but pleased.

"Best draw up a proper plan, then, ma'am," he said carefully. "I'll need some skilled men..."

"You could start by asking at the Hare and Hounds this evening," Charlotte suggested, her lips curving.

"Yes, ma'am," Deacon said with a grin. "I'll be in the attics if I'm wanted!"

CHAPTER 31

"How's it goin' then, bein' a secretary?" Mary asked as they washed dishes after their evening meal.

Charlotte had hardly seen her over the past week, for Mary was spending a lot of time at the bakery now she was an official part-owner. Charlotte had spent three full days up at Birchanger the previous week, while today had been her second day this week.

"Different. Tiring."

"You enjoyin' it?"

Charlotte considered while she dried plates and pans. "Yes, I am," she said. "There's a lot to do, and organise…" She was beginning to feel a sense of satisfaction from her work, but a different kind of feeling from when she saw a story or article of hers in print. Strangely, on the days she worked at home, she seemed to write more efficiently than before.

"John said it's lookin' like he might have work up there for months —is that right?"

"If he wants it. Do we need him here, Mary?"

"I don't reckon so—not for workin', any road." Mary's expression could only be described as a satisfied smirk. "He's mended most of what needed seein' to."

~

Toby Minching's lad ran up the lane as Charlotte was leaving the house the next morning. He apologised—a letter for her had been dropped off by the carrier the day before, and Toby had forgotten to give it to Mary to bring up. Charlotte hurriedly thanked him and stuffed the letter into a pocket to look at later.

She took the path that passed by the row of tenant cottages, curious to see how the work was progressing. She did not expect too much, for Deacon had only found suitable workmen a few days ago. The repairs to the roof of the Hall itself had to wait until Deacon could organise some scaffolding, so he'd started the skilled men he'd recruited on the repairs to the cottages instead. The labourers the squire had lent had been set to clearing the trees in front of the cottages.

Coming up to the cottages, the change was astonishing, even after only a few days' work. The houses themselves no longer seemed gloomy now the trees in front of them had been cleared to let in light. All the chimneys had smoke coming from them, and the furthest cottage had men on the roof fixing the stone tiles. She didn't go any closer, not wanting to distract the workmen, but turned to continue up the path. Walking through the woods, she had an uneasy sense that someone else was following her, but when she looked round she only saw a flash of movement that could have been a shadow or a deer.

She put the incident out of her mind when she came out onto the drive to Birchanger Hall. Several wagons stood in front of the Hall, and men were unloading furniture. That was good. Once Webb had told her about the missing furniture, she'd decided that even if it all had to be stacked in the main hall, it would be best to let Mr Fulbeck have the use of his barn again. That way they could also take stock of what there was, and decide what needed to be bought.

She spent several hours making lists of the new furniture, measuring the larger items, and sorting out pieces needing mending and hangings and curtains in need of cleaning. Mrs Jackson helped her to bundle all the soft furnishings together and packed them into a couple of large chests. There were so many large pieces that she'd need to find a proper laundress to clean some of them.

Matthew followed Deacon and Jenkins, the man from the shipyard, through the woods. He found it quite relaxing to simply listen to the two experts discussing which trees to cut and bandying about terms such as keelsons, futtocks, and knees. He really must ask Deacon what a futtock was. Deacon certainly sounded as if he knew the subject, and Matthew was glad he'd taken Mrs MacKinnon's advice to let him deal with the roof.

Davie was proudly marking the locations of the first trees to be cut on a copy of the map he'd made himself, needing only minimal supervision. Matthew was amazed the lad hadn't got bored yet, but he suspected it might just be that mapping was more interesting than Latin.

Deacon had a pot of paint with him and was marking other trees for felling as they walked—the wood would be too green for burning well this winter, but it was time to start storing it ready for later in the year. He must remember to ask them to save thin straight branches for supports in the kitchen garden, assuming he ever won his battle with the brambles.

The experts were winding up their discussion, so Matthew left them inspecting a final patch of woodland and set off back to the Hall with Davie. It was a glorious winter's day—still and clear, with the smoke from all the Hall's chimneys going straight up into the pale blue sky. Today was one of Mrs MacKinnon's days up here—Matthew felt unusually content.

When they reached the Hall, Davie headed straight for the kitchen —in search of biscuits, most likely. Matthew went into the kitchen garden, thinking of spending a bit of time in there later, but most of it was still too muddy to be dug over at the moment. He stood contemplating his planned succession house until he was interrupted by a voice behind him.

"Excuse me, sir."

Matthew looked round. It was one of the new labourers, cap in hand, his blond hair ruffled.

"Yes? Aren't you supposed to be working at the cottages?"

"Got sent back for tools, my lord," the man said, not quite meeting Matthew's eyes. "I just thought you ought to know, my lord, about that man Deacon."

"What about him?"

"I served with him in the navy, my lord." The man glanced briefly at Matthew, then his gaze slid away again. "Thing is, my lord, he was discharged for thieving. Lucky not to get prison."

Matthew stared at him for a moment, and the man shuffled his feet. "Smith, isn't it?"

"Yes, my lord. I was worried now he's working on the Hall, my lord, in case he takes things of yours."

"Thank you for the warning, Smith. I'll ask Mr Webb to keep an eye on him." He nodded in dismissal and, after a moment the man tugged his forelock and walked away.

A very touching concern for his employer, Matthew thought, following Smith to the garden door and watching him walk down the drive. Or at least, it would be if it were genuine, which he very much doubted. He'd have a word with Webb later.

Being muddy, he went into the house round the back, so it wasn't until he'd taken his boots off and got himself a coffee that he tried to go through the hall on the way to his room.

"Good grief!" The place was crammed with furniture. Several beds were piled together, their dismantled posts and top frames lying next to the bases. He spotted one huge table and several smaller ones, and numerous chairs and sofas. Some of the furniture was stacked, and when he looked more closely he could see that there was a clear path around the edge of the room. Mrs MacKinnon appeared, her dress liberally streaked with dust.

"Good morning, Major."

"Mrs MacKinnon, good morning." He peered around the stacked furniture. "It appears I don't need to buy furniture after all."

"Oh, this won't go far," she said. "Really," she added, when he frowned. "I've made lists, if you want to—"

"No, no—I'm perfectly happy to leave it all in your hands." Especially as he had a bottle awaiting him in his room.

"Very well. Sally will have luncheon ready in half an hour."

"I don't want—"

"You should eat, Major."

Her tone was conversational, not nagging, but he felt defensive all the same. "Mrs MacKinnon, I asked you to help to organise the house, not me!"

"Well then, you should beware of employing managing females, Major!" She smiled. "Besides, I'm enjoying the work. I don't want to lose my job because my employer fades away!"

She didn't give him time to answer, disappearing back into the midst of the furniture pile. Matthew retreated to his room, debating whether or not to stay there, but then thought that avoiding luncheon would look too much like sulking. So, when Sally came to ask if he wanted a tray, he decided to join everyone else in the kitchen. He wasn't feeling hungry, but the rabbit stew Sally and Mrs Jackson had prepared was tasty; he ended up eating a reasonable amount— enough, at least, to stop Mrs MacKinnon from giving him disapproving looks.

Sally and Mrs Jackson appeared to be rather cowed by Matthew's presence at the table at first, but they were soon discussing something quietly between themselves. Mrs MacKinnon was absorbed in reading a letter, and Davie chattered to Deacon about something he was doing at home. Matthew watched them while he ate, recalling earlier discussions with Deacon. Unlike Smith, Deacon could meet a man's eyes when talking.

As he watched, he saw a smile spread across Mrs MacKinnon's face. She turned the paper over and read her letter again. Then she touched Deacon's arm to attract his attention, handing the letter to him.

Matthew frowned, wondering exactly how Deacon fitted into the MacKinnon household. Smith's words came back to his mind, but he dismissed them. He found it hard to believe that both the Mrs MacKinnons could have been fooled by a thief.

"Good news, Mrs MacKinnon?" he asked. Deacon was now smiling just as broadly.

"What is it, Mama?" Davie asked.

"Mr Berry wants to make a book from the animal stories," she said. "He wants more stories, and lots of Deacon's drawings."

Drawings?

"You are an artist as well, Deacon?" Matthew asked.

"Not really, my lord. I can draw well enough."

"That will keep you very busy then," he said. "You, too, I suppose, Mrs MacKinnon?"

She frowned, taking the letter back and reading it for a third time. He awaited her answer with some trepidation. Her presence for a few days each week had made a huge difference to Birchanger, and not just in terms of repairs. Deacon he didn't mind about so much—surely Webb, or Mrs MacKinnon, could find another carpenter.

"Busy enough, Major," she said absently, her fingers tapping the table one by one as if she were counting off days, then she gave a decisive nod.

"I can do the writing as well as a couple of days a week here, if that will be sufficient?"

"Of course," Matthew agreed, much relieved.

Deacon, too, said he thought he could manage both tasks. "Scaffolding can't come till next week, my lord," he said. "So there's not so much for me to do until then."

"Well, this calls for a bit of celebration!" Matthew said. He sent Webb for a bottle of wine, and poured all the adults a small glass. He felt a bit awkward leaving Davie and the young Jacksons out of it, but Mrs MacKinnon said in a stage whisper that perhaps the major would arrange for Mrs Wilton at the bakery to allow them to choose a cake for themselves. Matthew heard and nodded with a smile.

CHAPTER 32

$\mathcal{M}$atthew was digging the kitchen garden again when he heard the crunch of wheels on gravel. He ignored it, assuming Mrs MacKinnon or Webb would see to whatever was being delivered, but a moment later Tilly called him from the door in the garden wall. Hastily wiping his hands and donning his coat, he walked around to the front of the Hall. It was not the usual carrier's wagon, and there was only one crate on it. Four men dressed in normal winter clothing stood by it, but he could tell they were soldiers from the way they stood stiffly as they waited for him.

"Major Southam, sir?" one of them asked.

"Yes."

"Delivery for you, sir. And a letter." He handed over a small packet. "Need you to sign for it, sir."

Puzzled, Matthew resisted the temptation to ask what was in the crate, aware that the men were unlikely to know. He signed the receipt and directed them to carry the delivery into the Hall. They did so and took themselves off, leaving Matthew regarding the crate. It was firmly nailed shut, and the outside had only his name on it.

"Webb?" he shouted. After a few moments Webb appeared, wiping ink from his fingers.

"Sir?"

"Have we got a crowbar to get this open?"

"What is it, sir?"

"We'll find out when we get the crowbar, won't we?"

"Yessir," Webb said with a grin, and vanished in the direction of the stables. While he waited, Matthew broke the seal on the letter and read its contents, a frown gathering on his face.

"What does it say, sir?" Webb asked, returning with a hammer and chisel.

"Colonel Manningham wishes me to evaluate the four rifles provided, including a comparison with the standard muskets, two of which are also provided. There is to be a formal trial at Woolwich next month, but he would be grateful for an independent assessment without the presence of the manufacturers to make excuses for any failings."

"Colonel Manningham, sir?"

Matthew shrugged. "Never heard of him. I wonder why he thinks I'd be useful doing this?" He looked up at Webb, suspicion forming. Webb was wearing one of his bland expressions.

"Webb, do you know anything about this?"

"Never 'eard of Colonel Manningham, sir."

Matthew frowned, his suspicions deepening. "That wasn't the question, Webb. Do you know anything about why this was sent here?" he asked, kicking the crate.

"I didn't ask for them to..." Webb stopped as Matthew stepped closer to him.

"Do you know *anything* about this, Webb? Yes or no."

"I..."

"Yes or no!"

"Yessir."

"Explain."

Webb stood to attention and took a deep breath. "When Doctor Lorton came, 'e said it might do you good to have somethin' straightforward to do, not messy stuff like sortin' this place out." He eyed Matthew warily.

"Go on." Matthew said, back in control of his temper.

"So Doctor Lorton wrote a letter."

"Doctor Lorton knows Colonel Manningham?"

"Nossir."

"Webb!"

"Sir, General Stuart was worried about you, so 'e sent to the Earl of Marstone to see you was all right when you got back 'ere. I said the doctor should write to this Marstone bloke, and 'e must of talked to this colonel, or someone."

"Who the hell is the Earl of Marstone?"

"Dunno, sir, some toff. Er…"

"Just get on with it, Webb."

"That's it, sir."

"So you and Marstone were asked to play nursemaid to me, were you? Who else?"

"Kellet, sir," Webb said, avoiding Matthew's eyes.

"My solicitor?"

"Yessir. It weren't no accident, Mr Kellet… er, Mr Phineas Kellet meetin' you in town. 'E's secretary to the earl."

"Bloody hell, is there *anyone* not in some conspiracy?" Matthew realised he was shouting again.

"'E's a good bloke sir, I reckon," Web said earnestly. "Sir—you needed someone 'onest to 'elp with all the legal stuff, and now you got one."

"I don't seem to have one in you, Webb."

Webb looked hurt. "I ain't bin lyin' to you, sir."

"No—just not telling me things!"

"The last thing I told you didn't 'elp much, did it, sir? You 'ad more nightmares after you found out I dragged you out o' that prison!"

Matthew stared at him. Webb had a point, but he still didn't like it. He stalked over to the window and gazed out, taking a long pull from his flask. *Does it really matter? Does anything really matter?*

While he was staring, two of the Jackson children ran across the gravel in front of the Hall, laughing and shouting at each other. They were definitely getting plumper, and had warmer clothes. The Jacksons were better off, the tenants were getting their hovels turned back into houses, and Mrs MacKinnon seemed to like her job. He supposed he was the reason all this had happened, even if he hadn't actually done much of anything himself. He sighed, and turned around.

"Never mind for now. Let's see what they've sent."

By the time he'd used the hammer and chisel to take out his annoyance on the crate, he felt a little better. There were six weapons in there, two of which Matthew recognised as standard Brown Bess muskets. The other four were the new rifles, each one slightly different. There were no manufacturers' names on them, just a small plate on each with a number. There was also a large box containing several smaller boxes full of cartridges. Matthew tore one open to check—they appeared to be the standard kind that included the ball and a charge of powder.

Matthew stared at this for a good thirty seconds, then started to laugh. He laughed so hard his stomach hurt and he had to sit down. When he finally stopped, he discovered he had an audience, for not only was Webb standing gaping at him, but also Mrs Jackson, Mrs MacKinnon, Sally, and Tilly.

"I'm only laughing," he gasped, still short of breath. "You've never seen someone laugh before?"

"I don't think anyone has seen *you* laugh before, Major," Mrs MacKinnon said seriously. She smiled. "You should try it more often." She ushered the females in the audience away.

"What's so funny, sir, if you don't mind me askin'?" Webb looked puzzled.

"Webb, you got Lorton to write to Marstone after Christmas, yes?" Webb nodded. "Just after you'd put water in my powder flask? And as a result of that letter..." He started chuckling again, and pointed at the huge box of cartridges in the crate.

Webb frowned.

"Webb—you *will not* tamper with those cartridges!" Matthew said, suddenly serious. "If we're going to test those things, we need the powder to work!" Webb's eyes went to Matthew's pistol, still propped on the mantelpiece.

"Give me your word you won't use it for 'owt else, sir?" Webb asked warily.

Matthew's lips thinned for a moment.

"Oh, very well," he said at last. "The cartridges will only be used with the rifles." From Webb's frown, that wasn't quite as good a promise as he'd been hoping for, but it was all he was going to get.

"How many shots a minute could you get, Webb?"

"Four, sir, on a good day."

"Good shot, were you?" Matthew started to pack the weapons back into the crate.

"Not bad, sir. I weren't the best in the regiment."

"Very well. You will be taking part in the tests. Now clear off and let me decide how to go about it."

"Yessir!"

"Oh, before you go—how's that man Smith getting on? He came to me with some tale about Deacon."

"Lazy bugger, sir. Stops workin' soon as 'e's not bein' watched. Tried tellin' me the same story."

"Keep an eye on him."

"Yessir."

"Is everything all right, Sergeant?" Charlotte asked as Webb came back into the small room he was using as an office. She'd heard shouting, and then the laughter. When the women had left the room, they could still hear the sound of voices, even though they could not make out the words. The major had still sounded angry.

But Webb just grinned. "Nice to be given a good boll.... er, tellin' off, ma'am." He sat down and carried on copying a letter into his letter file.

Charlotte shook her head. And men said women were incomprehensible!

333

Sleet was turning to snow as the curricle approached Birchanger Hall. Matthew was sitting in a window seat looking gloomily out through the half-erected scaffolding poles. He could just make out two figures in the vehicle, pulled by a matched pair of grey horses. A few gleams of red and gold were visible through the snow, jogging Matthew's memory. What did that remind him of? Ah—the curricle in the mews behind the town house. He squinted, trying to make out more detail through the swirling flakes. Was that Charles driving?

All I need to make the day perfect!

Matthew stood up and found a neckcloth to put on. If this was Charles, there was likely to be a confrontation; he didn't want to give his half-brother grounds to criticise him for being only half dressed. The curricle had disappeared around the side of the Hall, heading straight for stable yard, so Matthew made his way through the kitchen to the back entrance. He stood in the doorway waiting for the two men to emerge from the stables. Whoever they were, he'd have to put them up for the night.

He stood while the snow refilled the tracks made by the curricle and horses. They were taking their time—surely Webb or someone would be dealing with the horses for them? But Webb came up behind him, and muttered something about Jackson being down at the cottages. Did that mean Charles was actually unharnessing the horses himself?

"I'd best go and give a hand, sir," Webb said, and hurried across the yard. It wasn't long before the two travellers appeared, snowflakes settling on the shoulders of their coats. One of them was walking with the aid of a stick. As they drew closer Matthew frowned—definitely not Charles, this man was too tall. And not dressed as nattily as Charles, either. He stood back to let them enter, and came face to face with a pair of blue-grey eyes like his own, set in a face with hints of Serena's rather sharp features, but softened by lines that indicated frequent smiling. It took him a few moments to work out who this was.

"Richard?"

The newcomer grinned. "The very same." Then he frowned. "Good grief, Matt—what in hell's name has happened to you?"

Matthew stiffened, but relaxed again when he realised the words had been said with concern, not derision. Richard gazed at him for a few moments then looked away, appearing slightly embarrassed to have been staring.

"It's good to see you, Rich," Matthew said. And it was. Never mind Kellet's tales of the whole family overspending—this looked like the younger brother he remembered. Well, ten years older and no longer a child, but still his younger brother. "Come in—what possessed you to travel in this weather?"

"It wasn't snowing when we set out." Richard took off his sodden coat. Not finding anyone ready to take it, he was about to drape it over the back of one of the kitchen chairs when the figure behind spoke.

"I'll take it, sir."

Matthew looked more carefully, Richard having taken all his attention until now. "Baldwin?"

"Yes, sir."

"He's come for that job you promised him," Richard said, with another grin. "Any chance of a hot drink?"

Mrs Jackson appeared, and was soon bustling about with the kettle. "I'll bring it through, my lord," she said.

Matthew led his brother through to his own room. Richard looked at the furniture stacked in the large central hall with interest, then at the scattering of maps and plans on the table in Matthew's room.

"Lots of work to be done?"

Matthew nodded, clearing the papers to one side to make space for the tray when it arrived, and sat down. Richard remained standing, rolling his shoulders and stretching his arms out.

"Long journey?" Matthew asked.

"Stayed one night on the road."

"A curricle? At this time of year?" He glanced towards the swirling snow in the gathering dusk. "Did Charles lend it to you?"

"There *is* a reason for that," Richard said. He finished stretching and sat down at the table, resting his stick on the floor.

"Charles said you were involved at Bergen—bit of a disaster from what I gather?"

Richard frowned. "Don't get me started on that," he said. "Bloody incompetence lost us that battle." He wriggled his ankle. "Broke my ankle and took a ball in the arm. Ankle still isn't right, although the sawbones says it should mend in time. Hurts to ride." He shrugged, and broke off as Mrs Jackson entered, bringing a tray of coffee and cakes. Matthew reached behind him for brandy and added a good measure to his own cup. He offered it to Richard.

"Don't mind if I do. I might just about thaw out by the end of the month at this rate."

Matthew got up to put more wood on the fire, and asked Mrs Jackson to sort out somewhere for the two men to sleep.

"What brings you here now?" Matthew asked, when Mrs Jackson had gone. "Don't mistake me—I'm very glad to see you. But the weather..."

"I'm afraid I let the cat out of the bag," Richard said. "Mama found out you *had* been corresponding with Father, and that Baldwin had been instrumental. So he's out of a job, without a character. And I'm in her black books too, so driving here in this weather was a more pleasant prospect than staying in London to be nagged and complained at."

"He's welcome here, of course," Matthew said. He ran his hand through his hair. Trust Serena to take revenge on a servant if no-one else was available.

Richard nodded. "That's what he said—glad to find it's true."

"Why wouldn't it be?"

"No reason—except there've been so many half-truths bandied around in the last couple of weeks, I'm even beginning to doubt myself."

They were interrupted again as Mrs Jackson brought in plates of stew with bread, apologising for the simple food.

Richard waved a hand. "No matter—anything warm is good."

Webb had also fetched a bottle of decent wine from the cellar and sent it in with a couple of glasses. Matthew sat back in his chair, toying with his wineglass as he watched his brother eat. A warm feeling started somewhere inside him, having nothing to do with the wine or the bit of stew he'd eaten. Here was one member of the family who'd greeted him with no snide comments, and had seemed genuinely pleased to see him. A novel experience, in recent years.

"What did you mean about untruths?" Matthew prompted Richard when he'd finished eating.

"Yes. Bear with me, Matt. You can tell me which bits are wrong afterwards." He refilled his glass. "It took me a while to get home after Bergen—had to make sure the wounded men got seen to properly." Matthew nodded in approval. "Then I went to stay with Mountjoy for a while. He took a sword slash across the shoulder—went deep. He should get back most of the use of his arm, but he was very low."

Matthew frowned.

"You know Mountjoy?" Richard asked.

"George Mountjoy?" Matthew asked, and his brother nodded. "I did know him once, yes. But that can wait."

Richard shrugged and carried on. "Well, I finally got to London and went to see the solicitor to ask if I could have an allowance, now I was on half pay for a while. Dear Charles told me a couple of years ago that you'd stopped my allowance—"

"What?"

"No, I know now that's not true. I didn't really believe it at the time. I wrote to ask you about it, but I imagine the letter didn't get through. I've been moving around a lot, and mail rarely catches up." He shrugged again. "Regardless, I wasn't spending a great deal at the time, so it didn't matter too much."

"After Father died, I sent my letters to you care of Horse Guards." Serena couldn't have intercepted those.

Richard shook his head. "I got one letter, I think." He shrugged. "Thought you must be all right as long as I didn't hear anything. Luckily, word that you were returning wasn't long behind a letter saying you were missing. Dear Mama didn't hesitate in passing on the first message."

"She's still your mother," Matthew said, wondering at the sarcasm in his tone.

Richard grimaced. "And our father was still our father—and he would have been horrified if he'd known she was trying to destroy your letters, and more so if she had succeeded." He shook his head. "I never understood what she had against you."

"I was born," Matthew said dryly.

"I know—what I mean is, I can't understand *why* she was like that. She knew you existed before she married Father." He was silent for a moment, then reached for the bottle and refilled their glasses.

"Anyway, I was making ends meet until they put me on half pay."

"Not a gambler like Charles, then?"

Richard laughed. "I do gamble, but *I* do it sober, so I generally come out ahead. I went to Mayhews', but they told me they were no longer dealing with things, and sent me to your man, Kellet. We had a very interesting discussion once we'd sorted out the misunderstandings." He paused, but Matthew just nodded and let him carry on.

"It seems the books show that not only have I been drawing my allowance since Charles said you'd stopped it, but that I have been overspending. Somewhere in my bag I've got a sheaf of receipts, made out in my name, for things like that curricle out there, and the greys. Fine animals, those."

"You chose well, Rich." Matthew said, straight-faced.

Richard laughed. "So," he carried on. "What with Charlie being off at a house party somewhere, and Kellet giving me the receipts for things I'd apparently bought, I decided to use 'my' belongings and come and see you!" He grinned. "Poetic justice, eh?"

Matthew smiled, but he didn't feel like laughing. He was thankful to have one honest and friendly member of his family. The evidence that Charles had not only stolen from the Birchanger estate, but had cheated other members of his family—his own full brother—was depressing.

Soon Richard would ask what had happened in India, and he didn't want to go through all that. It would only end with more nightmares.

"So, tell me about Bergen," Matthew said.

CHAPTER 33

The snow continued for most of the night, covering the garden and lane in a thick blanket by morning. Charlotte awoke to a white glow coming through the curtains. Rubbing frost from the inside of the window, she saw that the sky was a pale blue, with watery sunshine reflecting off the white landscape. The front path had been cleared, but two sets of footsteps led from the gate out of sight down the lane. There were none coming back, so Deacon had either stayed to help Mary at the bakery after escorting her down, or he'd gone directly up to Birchanger from the village. That meant Jane hadn't arrived yet either, so she'd be making her own breakfast. But, she smiled in relief, it also meant the snow wasn't deep enough to prevent her going up to Birchanger today.

The air was crisp when Charlotte and Davie set off, their breath fogging the air around them. Despite the cloudless sky, it was cold enough to stop the snow melting. Their footsteps crunched as they went down the lane to the beginning of the path, then up through the Birchanger woods. There was less snow under the trees, so they reached the Hall in good time.

A wagon stood in front of the building, workmen unloading more long poles. Charlotte nodded in satisfaction; once they finished erecting the scaffolding, the roof repairs could begin.

They went in through the kitchen, as usual. Mrs Jackson was clearing away the servants' breakfast, and put the kettle on the range again when she saw them arrive.

"His lordship's brother turned up last night," Mrs Jackson said as she set out the mugs and milk for their tea. "They've not got up yet."

Charlotte raised her eyebrows but did not comment. That was not good news.

"Had another man with him," Mrs Jackson went on. "Butler from the town house, from what I heard. Come to work here. Webb ain't happy."

"Why not?"

"Didn't say. But I reckon he thinks this new man, Baldwin, is out to take over here."

Charlotte sighed, hoping the major could sort it out. She liked Webb. He was the most unconventional land steward she had ever come across—not that she'd met many—but she was beginning to think he'd be good at it. He certainly *wanted* to belong here.

Davie's task for the day, and his hidden mathematics lesson, was to work out the amount of paint needed by calculating the wall areas in the various rooms. Charlotte smiled to herself at his keen expression as she explained what to do. She sent him off to the servants' quarters on the second floor with a notebook, pencil, and measuring tape, along with Tilly to hold the other end of the tape for him. She'd go and check in ten minutes to make sure he was taking the measurements correctly.

Charlotte's own plan for the day included continuing to glean what information she could from the old estate ledgers, and planning the renovation of the inside of the house. Hopefully, no more damp would get in once the roof was fixed. She poured herself another mug of tea and took it through to the room that would eventually be the dining room. She was thinking about colours for the wall above the wainscoting, and for the curtains, now she knew how the seats of the dining chairs were upholstered.

She stopped in the doorway. A couple of used glasses rested on the floor, together with several empty bottles and plates, bits of string arranged in lines, and rows of small pebbles and coins. Charlotte frowned—it looked as if the major had been playing soldiers, with coins and pebbles instead of men. She was still wondering about it when she heard footsteps crossing the hall. The door opened behind her. She turned, expecting to see Webb or the major, but it was a stranger.

Not quite a stranger in appearance, though. This must be the brother.

"Good morning, ma'am," he said cheerfully, sounding very like the major. Charlotte stared at him for a moment, then tore her gaze away. She could see the family resemblance. She could also see in him a shadow of what the major *should* look like, if he filled his clothes out properly and smiled more often. He wasn't what she had expected from the major's comments about his half-brother. He looked far too friendly and cheerful.

"Mr Southam," she said frostily, giving a small nod.

He regarded her quizzically, leaning on a cane. "I'm the *other* brother, ma'am," he said. "The nice one!"

"I'm sorry, sir," Charlotte said, realising she'd been frowning at him.

"Lieutenant Richard Southam, at your service, ma'am." He clicked his heels and gave a small bow, a grin on his face. "If you've heard bad things about a Southam, they will have been talking about my older brother, Charles."

Charlotte had to smile. "Charlotte MacKinnon," she said. "Mrs MacKinnon. I'm... well, the major is employing me as a kind of secretary, to make the Hall habitable." To his credit he hardly blinked at this —unlike the kind of reaction she'd expect from the vicar or Sir Vincent.

"Battle of Bergen, ma'am," Lieutenant Southam said, nodding at the things on the floor. He stood straighter and waved the stick at the pebbles and coins. "British, Russians, French, Dutch," he said, pointing at different parts of the floor.

Charlotte recalled discussing the campaign with the squire, back in September. "The Gazette reports seemed to blame the difficulties caused by the canals," she said. "A great many losses for the army to end up in the same—" She broke off as he frowned. "I'm sorry, Lieutenant—"

"Eh? Oh, no, ma'am," he interrupted with a wry smile. "The terrain was difficult, but that should not have been a surprise. Planning, proper planning, that would have helped." He shrugged. "It still annoys me."

"I hope Mrs Jackson found you somewhere suitable to sleep, last night, sir," Charlotte said, deciding that a change of subject was wise. "I'm afraid it will be some time before the Hall is fit for visitors."

"Room on the servants' floor," he said.

Charlotte frowned.

"Don't worry about that, ma'am," he added with a laugh. "A great improvement on campaign accommodation."

"We can at least offer you a decent breakfast, Lieutenant," Charlotte said. *That laugh, that smile—if only the major looked like that sometimes.*

The lieutenant followed her back to the kitchen, where Mrs Jackson fussed over him, making him coffee and asking what he'd like for breakfast.

"Whatever my brother has," he said.

"You'll go hungry, then," Charlotte muttered as she put her mug down and went to find Davie in the upper rooms. She smiled as she heard him change his mind and ask Mrs Jackson for two large servings of ham and eggs, to eat in his brother's room.

Charlotte found Davie making good progress with his measurements. She watched for a few minutes, then left him with the instruction to come downstairs once he'd measured all the rooms on the top floor so she could show him how to do the calculations.

Back downstairs, she found Webb in his little office, and got out the old estate books to continue looking through them. It didn't take her long to notice Webb staring into space, frowning, rather than working on his latest set of letters.

"Is something wrong, Sergeant?"

He started, looking over at her.

"Dunno, ma'am. I were just wonderin' about that Baldwin."

"I haven't seen him yet. Who is he?"

"'E's the butler in the 'ouse in London. Went to see if 'e could sort out a better place for the lieutenant to sleep. Seemed to think 'e'd be stayin' 'ere."

"That's good, isn't it? It saves us having to find a butler once the Hall is ready."

Webb was still frowning, but she could see that this aspect of the situation hadn't occurred to him.

"You've got a lot to learn about managing the land, Sergeant," Charlotte went on. "You'll be busy enough looking after the outdoor staff once this place is working properly again. You don't want to be bothered with supervising indoor staff."

That seemed to cheer him up, and he turned to his letters again. He showed Charlotte the draft of a letter he'd written enquiring about the price and availability of stable supplies. Charlotte made a couple of minor changes, and dutifully admired the improvement in his handwriting. It still resembled the tracks from a drunken spider trailing through ink, but it *was* legible.

Charlotte was busy summarising the estate's agricultural expenses when Tilly knocked and put her head around the door.

"The major says will you come to his room, mum," she said. Charlotte put her pen down with relief, taking off her glasses and rubbing her eyes. The handwriting in the ledgers was little better than Webb's.

Matthew and Richard stood when Mrs MacKinnon entered the room. Matthew saw her eyes flick to the plates on the table—an empty one in front of Richard, his own still half-full.

"Ah, sorry, Major," Mrs MacKinnon said. "I'll come back when you've finished breakfast."

There was a snort of laughter from Richard, hastily suppressed. Matthew grimaced.

"No, please sit down, Mrs MacKinnon. I wanted you to listen to what Richard has to say."

"You can finish your breakfast while I'm talking then, Matt," Richard said.

Matthew saw Mrs MacKinnon wearing her trying-not-to-laugh expression. He had to smile, contenting himself with muttering quietly about a conspiracy, and started to force down the rest of the food on his plate.

"I went to see Kellet, Matt's solicitor," Richard explained.

"Isn't this private family business?" Mrs MacKinnon asked, before Richard could carry on.

"You already know most of it, Mrs MacKinnon," Matthew said. "If you're going to continue to act as a secretary, which I hope you will, you'll be involved at some point."

"Very well." She still looked doubtful, but sat back in her chair, ready to listen.

"It seems my brother, Charles—Matt's half-brother—has been spending far more than his allowance from the estate, the Farleton estate, that is. And spending my allowance while telling me that Matt had stopped it."

"Where did the extra money come from?" she asked

"Kellet suspected some fraud in the books he was sent from Farleton," Richard went on. "The most likely fraud is recording payments for repairs that were never actually done."

So, dear Charles has been cheating the Farleton tenants as well, in effect. Matthew pressed his lips together, angry again at Charles' deceit, and surprised that Richard didn't seem to mind.

"Kellet came here before Christmas," Matthew said. "At that time he thought I should concentrate on stopping this place deteriorating any further." He pointed to the window, scaffolding poles now obscuring the view. "You and Webb are well on the way to dealing with all that. Now we've found out that Charles has been cheating Rich as well, Kellet recommends I go and see for myself." He ran a hand through his hair. It was not something he wanted to do; it would mean more confrontations, more decisions to be made.

Mrs MacKinnon tilted her head to one side. "Your brother must have several people in league with him. At least one person at Farleton."

"Yes, and the solicitors," Matthew said bitterly. "The family's *former* solicitors."

"Why don't we both go?" Richard suggested. "I'm on half pay until my ankle's fit for use again." He looked around the room. "Anyway, Matt, why are you still here instead of at Farleton? It can't be fun living with the house at sixes and sevens. You could just move there until this place is sorted out."

Matthew followed his brother's gaze, noting the grubby and flaking paint above the wainscoting, the missing diamond of glass in the window, the sparse furnishings. Somehow, his mental list of the deficiencies of the Hall didn't seem nearly as depressing as they had when he first arrived here.

"As far as I know it's still staffed," Richard went on. "In fact, Mama was talking about having a small house party there."

"Good heavens! Well that's enough reason *not* to stay there, if she might turn up!" Matthew hadn't thought much about Farleton recently, but Richard's question made sense. His gaze drifted to Mrs MacKinnon, then he looked away hastily, blinking at the abrupt realisation that he wanted to live here, not to move permanently to Farleton.

Why? Farleton was my home.

"This place is entailed," he said, at last, needing to fill the silence. "So I'm saddled with it. Apart from dear Charles stealing the furniture and setting the mantraps here, this place doesn't have any associations with him, or your mother." He eyed his almost-finished breakfast. "There are enough people here harassing me, without adding old family retainers to their numbers. No doubt there'll still be a few at Farleton who remember me as a child and will tell me so."

Richard shook his head. "Not as many as you might hope," he said. "Mama got rid of a lot of them after Father died. Baldwin was lucky to have kept his job as long as he did."

"You could take Baldwin with you," Mrs MacKinnon suggested.

"You'd have one member of staff there who you know is loyal. When were you thinking of going?"

"I've got the rifles to trial. That crate that came a couple of days ago..." He explained the request from Colonel Manningham.

"You could start testing them here, but there's no reason we can't take them with us," Richard commented as Matthew finally cleared his plate. "I can help, if you like."

Matthew pushed his empty plate away. "I've only got a wagon," he said, addressing his brother. "You'll have to drive Baldwin in the curricle; I'll ride. The rifles are too big and heavy to take with us if we're travelling that way, so how about going at the end of the month? That will give us a couple of weeks to trial them, which should be plenty of time."

Richard's agreement was interrupted as Davie entered the room. "Mama, Mrs Jackson said—"

"Davie—how many times have I told you to knock before coming into a room?"

"Sorry, Mama. I've done the measurements, though." He held out his notebook. "Tilly's gone to make a snowman," he added, and gazed longingly out of the window.

"A snowman, eh?" Richard said. "I haven't built one of those in years."

Mrs MacKinnon sighed. "Go on, then," she said to Davie. Then, as Matthew was about to say he would join them, she said "Major, could you come around the house with me, please? It won't take long."

"I'm sure whatever you decide will be fine, Mrs MacKinnon," Matthew said. He really was perfectly content to leave all the decisions up to her.

"No, my lord," she said firmly.

Matthew rubbed the back of his head. If she was 'my lording' him, she was serious.

"It's your house and you need to make some decisions. Or at least, listen to what I've decided and agree to it!"

Matthew was pleased to see her lips pursed in her trying-not-to-laugh expression again.

Richard grinned and abandoned them.

Charlotte started in the room that still had the Battle of Bergen on the floor, pleased to see that someone had tidied away the bottles and glasses.

"The sun won't be in here until the afternoon," she said. "It will be quite dark for breakfast, particularly with the wood panelling."

The major touched a lighter patch on one panel.

"That's where Deacon was trying out some cleaning methods," Charlotte explained. "The wood should come up lighter than this, and light coloured paint and curtains will help as well."

"That sounds sensible," he agreed.

"There's enough furniture for this room," Charlotte went on, then led the way across the hall back into the room he was using for his bedroom and office. "This will be a parlour, and the next room a study and library, if you get any books. Darker curtains and carpets in here, I think?"

"There should be plenty of books at Farleton," the major said. "I'll get the ones I want sent back."

Charlotte suddenly felt happier—that did sound as if he was intending to stay here. She could keep this job for a little longer. It wasn't just the extra income; she was enjoying the challenge.

"In the main hall you could have seating round the fireplaces. It's big enough to hold a small ball—"

He shook his head, frowning. "Don't even *think* about that. That evening at the squire's was bad enough!"

Charlotte laughed. "You'll want one of the front rooms upstairs for your bedroom—the one with the biggest windows?"

"I think so, yes." He glanced at the notebook in her hand. "Mrs MacKinnon, I really am quite happy for you to make the decisions, as long as you don't inflict frills on any of the rooms. And no floral wallpaper," he added.

"Lace, then?" she asked, managing to sound serious, then laughed again when he pulled a face. "Very well—no lace, and no more decisions from you. As long as you promise not to complain when it's done!"

"It's a deal, ma'am." He glanced out of the window, then opened the casement to peer out. "I thought they were building snowmen?" Charlotte moved over to look.

"That looks more like a fort," she said, just as a snowball hit one of the stone mullions in the window, showering the major with bits of snow. On the lawn, Richard dusted off his hands, a triumphant grin on his face. Davie was laughing, bending to make his own snowball.

"You're not going to let him get away with that, are you?" Charlotte asked.

The major grinned, grabbing his coat as he left the room.

Five minutes later Charlotte and Mrs Jackson stood in the front doorway watching the battle in progress. The major had recruited Webb and Tilly, and the three of them were throwing snowballs as fast as they could towards Richard, Baldwin, and Davie.

"They be nothing but taller children," Mrs Jackson said, with no censure in her voice. "Best get some soup on for when they come in cold and wet."

The good weather lasted all day, allowing the workmen to almost finish erecting the scaffolding. They promised to come back the following day to assemble the final sections, so that the work on the roof could start. The sun was low in the sky to the south-west as they left, and Matthew had a sudden impulse to climb up. He'd not ventured into the attics at all, and he'd spent very little time in the small rooms on the second floor for fear of the walls closing in on him. At least he could inspect his roof from the outside.

With the sun almost set the air became much colder, frosting Matthew's breath as he clambered up the ladders. He didn't spend long inspecting the loose tiles, but instead sat and watched the sun gradually sink towards the horizon.

It was wonderfully peaceful up here with no-one to bother him, no sounds from the still landscape below. He thought back to that morning's question about why he was here rather than at Farleton. At the time, he'd said what came into his head as a plausible reason. Despite the fact that he'd not yet been here two months, this place now felt as much like home as Farleton.

More so. This is my home.

Beyond the Vale of Berkeley, the Severn glittered in the setting sun, backed by the shadowed mass that was the Forest of Dean. To the north-west he could make out a vague hint of the Black Mountains on the horizon. The view from here was far better than anything at Farleton, situated as it was in the flat lands just east of the Somerset Levels. Birchanger Hall itself would be lovely, too, once the roof was fixed and Mrs MacKinnon had organised the decoration.

Farleton Manor held some good memories, mainly from his childhood when his mother was still alive, but it was also the scene of numerous disputes with Serena and, later, with Charles. From what Richard had said, he wouldn't know most of the staff there, and he'd never really known the neighbours. He'd played with the children of the local gentry, but most of them would have moved on by now. Once he was grown, he'd joined the army and left for India. Birchanger, on the other hand, could be what he made of it. Perhaps it could even be a new start?

If the past will let me go.

He sat there as the sky turned from dusky blue, through pink to dark purple. The moon rose behind him and the first stars twinkled. Too cold to watch the final darkening into night, he shuffled back to the edge of the platform and carefully descended the ladders. It was time for a hot toddy. Or two...

CHAPTER 34

*H*edgehogs, Charlotte thought. Lady Meerbrook had said her children wanted more stories about Mr and Mrs Hedgehog. But it was difficult to think about them with snow on the ground—hedgehogs hibernated at this time of year. Charlotte leaned back in her chair and closed her eyes, trying to picture a hedgehog family waking up in spring, when the earth warmed and things started to grow. What would happen if they woke up early, when snow was still on the ground? What if they'd never seen snow before?

Charlotte had scribbled a couple of pages of notes before she was interrupted by a knock on the parlour door.

"Mama?" It was Davie. "The lieutenant has come to see you."

She glanced out of the window to see a curricle and pair being led up the lane. She'd been so wrapped up in her imaginary world that she hadn't heard anyone arrive.

"Send him in, Davie."

Davie ushered her visitor in, and she offered him a chair by the fire. He declined tea.

"I won't stay long, ma'am," Richard Southam said. "I've roped in poor old Baldwin to walk the horses so they don't get too cold. Would have walked down, but…" He tapped his bad ankle with his cane. "I hope I'm not interrupting," he added, noticing the papers spread out on the table.

"You are, but that doesn't mean you are unwelcome," she said.

He grinned. "I do hope you'd just tell me to go away if I were?"

She shook her head. "How can I help you?"

"Matt wanted me to ask if you would allow Davie to help with these rifle trials. I volunteered to drive down and enquire."

Charlotte frowned. "I'm not sure I like that idea. There are too many broken soldiers around here as it is, without encouraging my son to join them."

"You mean me, ma'am?" He slapped his leg again. "This will mend."

"That's good to hear."

"Webb, I suppose," Richard said.

"There's Deacon, too. You may not have met him—he was in the navy, not the army."

"Chap with one hand?"

Charlotte nodded.

"Three's not that many, considering there's a war on!"

Charlotte's brows drew together. Could he really not see that the major...?

She gave a small shake of her head, realising she had been staring at him. "Never mind," she said at last. "I suppose telling Davie he's not to take part will only make him more interested. What do you need him for? He must be too young to handle a rifle."

"Matt said something about timing, keeping records, and the like."

"Very well, when do you need him?"

"Tomorrow, if possible."

Charlotte nodded in agreement, expecting that he would take his leave, but he didn't move.

"Can I help you with anything else?" she asked.

"I... I was wondering what was wrong with Matt," he said at last. "He said he'd *been* ill, but he still looks dreadful. He's not eating..." Richard's gaze slid away, as if he were embarrassed to be making such an enquiry.

"Does he know you're asking me?" Charlotte asked cautiously.

"No." Richard shrugged. "I'm his brother—I want to help, even if he doesn't seem to want any help. What was the illness that made him so thin?"

Charlotte considered a moment—Webb knew, and if Webb knew it would surely do no harm for the major's brother to know. *This* brother, at least.

"Influenza, not long before Christmas," she said. "Although I suspect he fell ill so badly as a *result* of not eating." She closed her eyes for a moment, picturing the major's gaunt appearance as he lay in his bed. "Believe me, Lieutenant, he's looking better now than when he arrived at Birchanger."

Richard's eyes widened, then he frowned. "D'you mean Matt's another broken soldier?"

"You don't think so?"

"I just thought he'd been ill."

"He has nightmares, but I don't know what they are about or what causes them. That could be why he drinks so much. I think Webb knows a lot more about it, and possibly the doctor who came to see him after the influenza."

"You haven't winkled it out of him then?"

"It's not my business to pry, Lieutenant." She rubbed her forehead, recalling some of the things Webb had said about the major. "I don't think he *told* Webb anything about it—Webb knows for some other reason. He may or may not have told the doctor the details—but it is not for me to find out such personal information."

Richard sighed. "You're right, of course. Perhaps I can find out."

"For what purpose? It may be best to let sleeping dogs lie."

"It seems wrong to do nothing."

"Getting him to eat more might be a better goal."

Richard nodded. "Very well." He stood. "Davie will come up in the morning, then?"

Charlotte ushered him to the door, and watched as he walked out to the waiting curricle, leaning heavily on his stick. He drove off at a fast pace, and Charlotte wondered how many small animals got trampled beneath hooves on the roads. Or if cows ever stepped on smaller animals? She went back into the parlour and sat at the table, but she had only got a few ideas down when she was interrupted by Davie again, clutching a letter this time.

"Is that for me?" Charlotte asked, reaching for it but drawing back when she saw that it had been opened.

Davie shook his head. "It's for me," he said. "From Grandfather."

Charlotte stared at him for a moment. "From *my* father?" she asked —stupidly, as Angus' father was dead.

Davie nodded.

"You want me to read it?"

He nodded again, and held the letter out.

She tried to keep a neutral expression as she read. It was a master-piece, she had to admit. Without actually saying so directly, it managed to imply that it was Charlotte's fault that Davie had never seen his grandfather and that his grandfather Metcalf would love to have a grandson, totally ignoring the fact that Beatrice and Augusta had both provided him with grandsons. The letter further implied that Davie was being denied treats such as visits to Astley's amphitheatre. It ended with the hope that his mother would let him see *this* letter, and might allow him to come to London this time.

She looked up. Davie stood shuffling his feet, a frown on his face.

She pulled another chair up to the table. "Come and sit down, Davie," she said.

"Mama, why does he say he's sent me other letters?"

"He never has—"

"I know that," Davie said impatiently. "I bring the post up from the village quite often, I'd know if there was some for me, wouldn't I?"

Charlotte closed her eyes in relief. Her father had underestimated Davie's intelligence.

"This is not a very nice thing for me to have to say about my father, Davie, but I think he is trying to make trouble between us."

"Why have I never seen him? Or any of my other grandparents? I mean, I know your mama died, but—"

"It's a long story, Davie. Perhaps I should have told you before, but I didn't think you would have understood all of it."

He nodded solemnly.

"*My* grandfather, your great grandfather, was Lord Meriden. He was a baron, like the major." Davie nodded again. "But my father hasn't got a title because he's got an older brother. His father died, so that brother is now Lord Meriden."

She paused, wondering how much detail to give Davie, but in the end decided not to try to hide any of the relevant facts.

"My father wanted me to marry a viscount, which is more important than a baron."

"But your father isn't a lord."

"He wanted to be. He wants to be important," Charlotte said, not trying to hide the contempt she felt. "That viscount was quite old, and not a nice man."

Just talking about it brought back memories of his leering expression, and the way his hands lingered over-long on hers when he greeted her or took his leave. And then there were the rumours about his previous wives...

"Mama?"

"Sorry, Davie. That lord would have given my father a lot of money, and my father would have been able to call lots of other lords his friends. But the viscount was horrible."

"So you married my father instead?"

"Yes. We had to run away and get married in Jersey." The trip in the boat across the channel and then managing to get the two of them onto Angus' booked voyage to India were another story. Thankfully Davie didn't seem particularly interested in details of that at the moment.

"And then he died, and you had me."

"That's right. I didn't know I was going to have you until I was on the ship on the way home, and you were born in my sister's house in London."

She'd arrived at Augusta's home, still rankling under her father's insistence that she should not damage Beatrice's chance of a good marriage. She'd persuaded Augusta that she wanted to feed Davie herself, but her father had put his foot down. She remembered the agonising wrench of being forced to hand Davie over to a wet nurse, only seeing him for a short time each day. She was *not* going to place herself in her father's power again.

"Mama?"

Charlotte took a deep breath. "My father wanted me to get married again, but I didn't want to." She moved her chair closer to his, putting her arm around his shoulders. "Even if he found someone nice, most men don't want somebody else's son to look after. They would have sent you away to school as soon as they could. I wanted to keep you to myself, so I came to live here with Mary. It made my father very angry."

"He didn't come to see you? Or me?"

Charlotte shook her head. "No. My mama would have loved to see you. She wanted to, very much, but she had to do what my father said. I didn't take you to London when I went to see her, in case my father found out and tried to keep you there. He never tried to come and see you here."

"What about my other grandfather?"

"He died quite a long time ago, before I met your father, and your other grandmother had a new husband who didn't want us to live with them. They gave me a little bit of money."

They'd been the most joyless couple Charlotte had ever encountered. She'd not met Angus' mother until she visited with a very young Davie, but after half a day in her company she could understand why Angus had turned out so wild and rebellious.

Davie looked at his letter again, the scowl still on his face. "Why has he written now?"

"He thinks I should get married again. He wants to find another rich—"

Davie's face screwed up in distress. "I don't want you to get married, Mama. I don't want to be sent away!"

Charlotte pulled him off the chair and into her lap. "I don't want you to be sent away either," she said. "Don't worry."

"But you want to send me to school!" She could see tears forming in his eyes.

"Davie." She waited until his breathing had calmed a little bit. "Davie, I love you, and I don't want to send you away. Be sure of that."

He sniffed and eventually nodded.

"I want to find a school nearer to home so you can come home at weekends."

"Will I like it at school?"

"You'll have other boys to work with and play with. I don't know what it's like really, because girls don't go to the same kinds of school." She hesitated a moment. "You could ask the major what it's like, perhaps?" The major wouldn't say anything that would turn Davie against the idea.

Davie looked thoughtful, but at least a bit more cheerful. "What shall I do with this?" he asked eventually, holding the letter out.

"Do you want to answer it?"

"Not really. Do I have to?"

"You don't want to visit him in London?"

Davie shook his head firmly. "I don't think he really wants *me* to go, does he?"

"No, I don't think so," Charlotte said rather sadly. She wondered, with no little apprehension, what her father might decide to do when he got no reply from Davie.

CHAPTER 35

Charlotte could hear the sounds of rifle fire as she turned up the drive to Birchanger five days later. She'd sent Davie on ahead this morning, wanting to finish her final draft of the hedgehog story so Mary could take it into Edgecombe to be posted the next day.

She had managed to concentrate on the story that morning, but during the walk her mind had returned to the most recent letter from her father. It was less than a week since Davie's letter had arrived, so it must not be obvious yet that Davie was not going to reply. In the latest letter, he reiterated the trouble and expense he had been to for her benefit, and said that if he did not hear from her very soon with a date on which she would be arriving in London with her son, he would travel to Edgecombe to see her.

Pausing in the sunshine as she came out of the woods, she tried to put her father out of her mind, looking towards the targets set up on the lawn beyond the walls of the kitchen garden. Davie sat at a table with his record book and a watch. He gave her a wave, then returned to his task. From his chatter in the evenings, he was enjoying being part of the trial and, she suspected, unwittingly learning more mathematics.

She walked on with a smile, feeling grateful once again for Mary's

357

friendship. Without Mary she may not have managed to escape her father all those years ago. Grateful, too, for this job—it not only helped financially, but she was enjoying bringing order out of chaos and having something to do other than write. As she approached the Hall, she could see the workmen moving around on the bare sections of roof, making the most of the dry spell. With any luck, the major beams would be repaired by the end of the day, leaving only loose tiles to be found and refixed—a job that could be done in the rain, if necessary.

She left her coat in the kitchen, which looked brighter and more cheerful now that a coat of whitewash had been applied to the walls, and pots, pans, and dishes arranged in orderly fashion on the shelves. She went on into the steward's office. Webb was taking part in the rifle testing, so she had their little shared room to herself. She opened her notebook, thinking what to do first.

Half an hour later, she was part way through totalling a column of expenses when she heard a faint scream. She frowned—it sounded too high-pitched for Mrs Jackson, but not high enough to be Tilly. That left only Sally, who should be in the kitchen. She went to investigate.

In the kitchen, Mrs Jackson was already heading for the back door. "Came from outside," she called as Charlotte ran out after her.

"Sally?"

Mrs Jackson picked up her skirts and ran across the yard. "She was going to clean out the stable office. It better not just be a spider!"

When they reached the little office room, they saw a man shoving Sally against the wall, his hand pulling up her skirts as she tried to hit him.

"Get off her!" Charlotte shouted, looking around for something to use as a weapon. Mrs Jackson beat her to it. A stool crashed down on the man's shoulders, and he let go of Sally with a curse. Turning, his frown turned to a leer as he stared at Charlotte, his gaze running from her face down to her chest. He licked his lips and started forwards.

Charlotte swallowed, backing away. She recognised him now—the man who'd been with Deacon when he first arrived. He advanced on her, the expression on his face making her stomach knot. Behind her, she heard Mrs Jackson break into a run. Sally dodged around them and ran out into the yard, shrieking for help.

The man swore again, still moving forwards. Charlotte had backed into the yard by now, and she spun around, grabbed a handful of skirt, and ran. She heard his footsteps close behind her, almost drowned by Sally's shrieks. Breath coming in gasps, she ran on until she saw a couple of workmen round the corner of the Hall. She heard another curse from behind, and slowed to a stop as she saw Smith making for the drive, dodging around the approaching men.

Shaken, Charlotte took several deep breaths, waiting for the trembling in her knees to ease. Rubbing her forehead with a shaking hand, she pulled herself together and walked over to Sally, now slumped down with her back against a wall. Mrs Jackson stood next to her, hands on hips, staring in the direction Smith had taken

"See to Sally," Charlotte said. "Best take her inside and make some tea?" Mrs Jackson nodded. Charlotte, beginning to feel a little calmer now the danger appeared to be over, went to see what had happened to Smith. She found him being held by two of the workman, protesting loudly that he'd done nothing wrong.

Matthew squinted at the target and put the rifle down. Another shot near the centre. It was at least a year since he'd tried target shooting, and then only with the less-accurate muskets. He was rather pleased he was just about beating his brother, although neither of them could match Webb, either in accuracy or rate of fire. He felt a pang of regret that he'd not come across Webb when he was serving—he would have been an excellent sergeant.

Davie trotted off across the field to retrieve the targets, and Matthew was just wishing for a mug of ale to take the taste of powder from his mouth when shouts and screams came from the house. Running, Matthew rounded the corner of the garden wall to see a man struggling in the grip of two of the roofers.

Mrs MacKinnon stood near them. Anger stirred as he took in her white face and the way her arms were crossed around her chest.

"What happened?" he asked, glancing from Mrs MacKinnon to the prisoner. Smith, he recalled. The man Webb said needed watching—the one who had accused Deacon of being a thief.

"Dunno what's wrong, my lord," Smith said, bowing his head slightly. "I was just workin' in the stables when that woman came and attacked me…"

Smith's voice tailed off and his eyes widened. Footsteps crunched on the gravel behind, and Matthew turned to see Deacon standing beside Richard, with Webb and more of the roofers behind him.

"Mrs MacKinnon?"

"We heard Sally scream," Mrs MacKinnon said. Her voice sounded calm, and a little colour was coming back to her cheeks. "When we got to the stables he had one hand over her mouth and the other up her skirts."

"Where is Sally?"

"Mrs Jackson took her inside."

Matthew turned to glare at Smith.

"She asked for a kiss," Smith said, attempting a smile. "There weren't no screamin'."

Matthew didn't know Sally well, but she'd been working for the Mrs MacKinnons for a year or so, and he didn't think they would have recommended her if she'd been that kind of girl. His lips thinned—Smith had assaulted one of his staff, and now was blatantly lying about it. Did the man take him for a complete fool?

"I'll see what Sally says," Matthew said, controlling his anger with an effort. "Deacon, is there somewhere to lock him up until I can talk to Sally?"

"Storeroom has a door that can be—"

"Johnny, boy, tell them I wouldn't hurt anyone!" Smith said, turning to Deacon. "Best mates, we were, my lord. Served together in the navy until we was discharged."

Deacon shook his head, his frown deepening. "I never served with you, you know that. I never saw you till I was being sent home after this." He waved his hook.

"But we was good friends, Johnny. I looked after you—"

"Drank all my money, more like," Deacon said.

"You can't believe him, my lord," Smith said, turning his gaze back to Matthew. "Why, he's fooled them women into taking him in." Smith's eyes flicked towards Mrs MacKinnon for a moment. "Not right, it ain't; a man living with two single women like that."

Matthew stiffened.

"Can't trust women like that, my lord," Smith went on.

"Women like what?" Matthew said, quietly.

Smith produced one of his ingratiating smiles again. "All women want it, don't they? Askin' for it. Then they lie about—"

His words were cut short by Matthew's fist in his face. Surprised, the men holding Smith let go of him, and he staggered backwards a couple of paces. He muttered something below his breath, and Matthew took a step towards him, one hand rubbing the knuckles of the other.

"Sir!" Webb's hand on his arm stopped Matthew from taking another step. Smith was running, yards away by now, but Deacon wasn't far behind him.

"Hold him, lads," Deacon shouted, and two of the workmen intercepted Smith and tackled him to the ground.

"Sir, it don't seem right, you attackin' a labourer," Webb said. "Sounds like Deacon has reason to."

Matthew stood rigid for a moment, then gradually relaxed. "Thank you, Webb."

Smith was trying to wriggle free from the men holding him. "'Ere —that ain't fair, all you against one!" he protested.

"It was fair, was it, when you attacked Sally?" Deacon said, closing the gap. "Was it fair when I was out of my head 'cos my hand hurt, and you took charge of our money—which was mostly *my* money? Was it fair when you stole that ham and tried to get me blamed for it?"

"It were only a joke..." Smith said weakly, glancing around to see if there was any sympathy. "It still ain't fair, all you against one!"

"Oh, they won't fight you," Deacon said. "I reckon I'll manage that on my own. They'll just stop you running away before I've finished with you. And if you're very lucky, maybe they'll stop *me* before I kill you."

Smith desperately twisted free from the men holding him and turned to run, but he wasn't fast enough. Deacon ran after him and tripped him so that the two men fell to the ground.

Matthew belatedly remembered that Mrs MacKinnon was standing near him and turned round, but she was walking back towards the stable yard.

"Don't let Davie get too close," he said to Richard, and followed Mrs MacKinnon towards the kitchen. His anger still simmered, thoughts of other possibilities flitting through his mind. What if Smith had trapped Mrs MacKinnon in the stables? What if no-one had heard her?

Inside, Sally sat with her hands around a mug of tea, tracks of tears showing she had been crying. Mrs MacKinnon sat next to her, while Mrs Jackson was stirring something on the range.

"I'm sorry you had to see that," he said to Mrs MacKinnon. Sorry she'd had to hear what that man had said, as well.

"It wasn't my fault, my lord!" Sally protested, seeing Matthew standing over her. "I never asked him—"

"No, I'm sure you did not," Mrs MacKinnon said soothingly. "Major, would you sit down, please?" she added. "You probably appear quite threatening to her at the moment!"

Matthew frowned. Recognising the truth in what she'd said, he sat down across the table from Sally.

"Mrs MacKinnon said you screamed," he said. Sally nodded. "That was exactly the right thing to do," he said encouragingly. "I'm sorry one of the workmen frightened you. He will not be working here any more. I will not tolerate that kind of behaviour from anyone working for me."

"He won't come back?" Sally asked, her voice wobbling a little.

"No. If I have my way he won't even stay in the county."

Sally looked down at the table. "Constable won't believe me over him."

"I believe you, Sally. I doubt a magistrate would do anything about it, but by the time Deacon has finished with him I don't think he'll want to stay around. Now you sit there and let Mrs Jackson give you more tea and cake until you feel better. Mrs MacKinnon—if you will come with me?"

Charlotte turned to face the major when they reached the hall. He still looked angry, his lips compressed.

"Sally wouldn't—"

"No, I know." He shook his head, and ran a hand through his hair. "I'm sorry to have resorted to hitting Smith in front of you."

"I don't approve of men who use violence towards their employees," Charlotte said, a flush coming to her face as she recalled what Smith had said. "However, in this case, I don't think any amount of reasoning would have worked. I can't blame Deacon for wanting to have it out with him, either."

The major was looking more relaxed now. "What was Deacon saying about Smith?" he asked.

Charlotte explained what had happened when Mary took on the two men for a day's work in the garden.

"So Deacon was discharged wounded?"

"I haven't seen any paperwork, but I've no reason to doubt him. He said he served on the *Wessex*. You could check if you wished."

The major shook his head. "If you trust him, Mrs MacKinnon, that will do. From what I have seen of him and his work, he seems trustworthy."

"I assumed Smith left the area after Mary reported him to the constable for stealing," Charlotte went on. "That was back at the beginning of December."

"He's only been here a few weeks," the major said, frowning again. "I will make enquiries about him. It is quite possible he deserted the navy. Could you ask Deacon for the details of exactly where and when he first met Smith?"

She nodded.

"Thank you." He rubbed his hand through his hair again. "Mrs MacKinnon, are *you* all right?"

"I… yes, I am now, thank you." He *did* look concerned. "I'm fine, Major. I'll just check on Sally, then get back to work."

He followed her back to the kitchen, carrying on out to the yard. Sally was recovering, sitting at the table and peeling a large bowl of potatoes.

Charlotte collected a mug of tea and took it back to the steward's office. The major and his brother were due to depart for Farleton in two days. She wanted her army of cleaners and painters ready to move in as soon as they left.

CHAPTER 36

$\mathcal{M}$atthew rode behind the curricle, following its climb up the slight rise towards the gates of Farleton Manor. The weather had been fine, if cold, as they travelled over the Mendips and down into the valley of the River Axe. The rhynes and other drainage ditches they crossed were full after recent rain, and glittered in the setting sun. The drains seemed to be keeping the fields as dry as could be expected for this time of year. The gates, unlike the ones at Birchanger, were still attached to their hinges and moved easily when pushed. The drive, too, had been weeded within the last few months and the gravel was tidily raked.

Matthew recollected that the cottages they'd passed also belonged to Farleton, and their condition was not so impressive. They were nowhere near as dilapidated as the Birchanger cottages, but were still in need of a little care and attention.

Richard pulled the curricle to a halt in the circle at the front of the house, and Reena jumped down eagerly. Farleton Manor had been built much more recently than Birchanger Hall. It was a solid, square Georgian building with graceful proportions, but no false pillars, porticoes or pediments. Matthew remembered arguments between his father and stepmother when the latter wanted to rebuild the facade. His father had remained adamant. Thankfully such a project was far too expensive for even Charles' larcenous endeavours to fund, if he ever spent money on anything but himself. Perhaps Serena had lost interest in making the country estate look more fashionable if she spent most of her time in town.

Matthew hadn't written to announce his arrival, so when Baldwin knocked at the door it was some time before it was opened by an ageing butler. The man was almost knocked off his feet by Reena dashing past him into the relative warmth of the entrance hall.

"Featherstone?" Matthew asked Richard in a low voice.

Richard nodded. "Time he was pensioned off, really, but he doesn't seem to want to go. There's not much to do here most of the time, from what I gather. Just the odd mad month when dear Charles, or Mama, fancies holding a house party."

Featherstone was slow and a trifle bent, but still had all his faculties. He greeted Richard and Matthew warmly, ignored Reena sniffing around his feet, and summoned a footman to take their small valises. A groom came to take the curricle and Matthew's horse.

"I'm afraid your rooms need airing, Major, Lieutenant," he said. "Er, my lord, I should say!"

"Major will be fine, Featherstone. If you can arrange refreshments I'm sure Mrs..."

"Mrs Summers is housekeeper now, sir. You won't recall her."

"There is time for Mrs Summers to have fires lit and the beds aired before we need to use them. A simple dinner will suffice."

Featherstone glanced uncertainly at Baldwin, standing respectfully behind them.

"Baldwin hasn't come to replace you, Featherstone," Matthew said, wondering if the old man needed reassurance. "Unless you *wish* to retire, that is. He is in my employ now, rather than Mrs Southam's."

"Very good, sir."

Featherstone showed them into the library, where there was already a small fire burning. As they entered, a maid left the room with a tray containing empty plates and a wine glass. Matthew wandered along the shelves, gently running his fingers along the rows of leather-bound volumes, while Richard put more wood on the fire. Reena sniffed around the room for a while before settling herself by the hearth.

"They were expecting us?" Matthew asked.

Richard suppressed a grin. "I suspect Featherstone has been using this room for his own recreation," he said, pointing to a pair of spectacles on the table that the maid had missed. "I can't blame him, it's more pleasant than the servants' quarters, and there's no-one else here to use it, normally. If he's kept the room warm, it will have helped keep all these books in good condition."

"Not the steward?"

"Staines? I think he lives out." Richard shrugged. "It doesn't really matter, does it?"

"No," Matthew said. "You don't think it's Featherstone who's been fiddling the books?"

"It's possible, I suppose. Although it's just as likely to be Staines. Best get Featherstone to let him know you want to see him." He glanced at the clock on the mantelpiece. "Tomorrow, now, I suppose."

"Yes, tomorrow," Matthew said, stretching to ease the aches from spending all day in the saddle. "You'll see him with me?"

Richard raised his eyebrows. "It's your estate, you don't need me."

"You get an allowance from it—it's in your interest as well to make sure things run well." Matthew hesitated. "And, to be frank, I'm not always as clear-headed as I should be these days. Another head would be useful."

"If you wish," Richard said, making no comment on the reasons Matthew had given him.

Matthew, embarrassed at having to make such an admission, returned to his perusal of the shelves, pulling out a few books he remembered being fascinated by as a lad. He turned at a knock on the door. A woman entered; from her clothing, this must be the housekeeper. She was followed by a footman with a tray loaded with tea, a plate of sandwiches, and decanters of wine and brandy.

"Ah, Mrs Summers," Richard said. "Thank you."

"You're welcome, sir. My lord." She bobbed a curtsey, glancing at the dog. "I'll take the dog to the kitchen to be fed, my lord, I don't hold with animals eating in the rooms."

Matthew nodded, about to thank her, but she was still talking.

"Baths will be ready in your rooms in half an hour, I'm preparing your old rooms for both of you, if that is all right, Mr Featherstone told me which one you used to have, my lord. Mr Baldwin says he can act as valet while you're here, for we've no-one else suitable as Mr Charles brings his own man with him when he comes, of course. Dinner will be ready at seven, if that suits you, my lord. Will you wish to eat in the dining room or here? Only the dining room's a bit cold at the moment, not having had a fire lit for some time."

Matthew stared at her, still trying to take in everything she had said—without breathing, it seemed.

Richard laughed. "We'll eat in here, Mrs Summers," he said. "Thank you."

She bobbed another curtsey and left.

"Good grief," Matthew said, reaching for the brandy. At the last minute he changed his mind and decided that he would have food and tea first. *Then* a nice big glass of brandy with his bath.

"She takes a bit of getting used to," Richard said, "but she's efficient."

An hour later Matthew was soaking in the promised bath, a glass of brandy in one hand. He leaned his head against the tub, looking around the parts of the room he could see without twisting round.

The room had been redecorated since he left for India, and he didn't recognise anything in it. The decoration wasn't recent, he thought, seeing scuff marks on the painted walls. That reminded him of Birchanger, and he wondered how the work there was progressing.

Mrs MacKinnon had seemed in a hurry to see the back of them yesterday. He'd felt reluctant to leave, even suggesting he should stay another day or two to check more of the woods for the remaining two mantraps, but she'd said that could wait.

His argument that he needed to find the traps before too much vegetation covered the ground hadn't worked. She'd tilted her head to one side a little, as she did when she was thinking, then pointed out that he had several months before the undergrowth started growing again. She was right.

She usually is. He smiled, swirling the glass in his hand and watching the warm reflection of the fire in the amber liquid. He recalled the unusual number of people they had passed on the road between Birchanger and Edgecombe, and Mrs MacKinnon's comment that she'd recruited people from the nearby villages to clean and decorate the whole house.

The only sounds in the room were the crackling of the fire and the quiet slosh of the water as he moved in the bath. Birchanger would be full of chatter and noise most of the day. She'd been correct again, of course, to tell him he'd be better off at Farleton for the next week or so.

A knock on the door interrupted his thoughts, and Baldwin asked if he wanted his shaving water yet. He put the glass down, surprised to find he'd only drunk half of what he'd poured, and rinsed himself off.

He shaved while a couple of footmen emptied the bath, looking around the room as he towelled his face dry. His bookcase had been over there, by the window, where a small chest now stood. He wondered if his old childhood books and toys were still around—but wasn't sure he was interested enough to find them if they'd been banished to the attics.

Baldwin had taken the clothes from his small valise away for brushing and pressing, and now laid out a clean set ready for dinner.

"Any gossip amongst the staff, Baldwin?"

"Nothing in particular, my lord," Baldwin said, handing a starched neckcloth to Matthew. "I've been asked about Birchanger, and whether you'll be staying here long."

"Do they regret my return, do you think?" Matthew raised his chin to tie the knot.

"Not the few who remember you, my lord. The others are used to

Mrs Southam and Mr Charles, so they are worried in case you wish to change things too much."

"The steward?"

"Not here at the moment, my lord. He lives out—about half a mile away—with his family." Baldwin picked up the waistcoat, holding it out ready.

"See what you can find out about him, can you? Subtly, Baldwin."

"I'll see what I can do, sir."

Matthew took the coat Baldwin held out and pulled it on. "Did you find any other signs of... well, irregularities, I suppose?"

"Sir?"

"Financial irregularities."

"Cooked accounts, sir?"

Matthew nodded.

"I doubt it's Mr Featherstone," Baldwin said, brushing a few specks of dust from Matthew's shoulders. "I'll see what I can find out." He moved around the room, collecting up Matthew's riding gear. "You'll want these tomorrow, sir?"

"Yes—we'll have a quick tour of the estate in the morning, before I meet with Mr Staines." He thought for a moment, an idea forming, and wondered how far he could trust Baldwin. He had to trust *some* people, and Baldwin had shown his loyalty over the years.

"I'd like you to come along as well, Baldwin," Matthew said.

"Me, sir?" Baldwin said, surprised.

"You must know the estate well. Better than I—I've been away for ten years! How long is it since you lived here?"

"Around five years, sir. After Mrs Southam was out of mourning for your father, she moved to London. They only come here for a month or so in the summer, and not always then if she manages to get... that is, if she is invited to a house party."

"Very well. I don't suppose you ride?"

"No, sir."

"Well, you can share the curricle with my brother again."

"Very good, sir."

.   .   .

The following morning was windy and grey, with the threat of rain. Richard drove Baldwin around part of the estate in the curricle, while Matthew rode. The dreary and raw weather meant that they didn't tarry. They noted various repairs that needed to be addressed before heading back to the Manor.

Matthew was relieved by their findings. There *were* outstanding repairs, but nothing on the scale of what was needed at Birchanger. Just as well, he thought, as the revenues from Farleton would have to subsidise Birchanger for some years to come.

They dropped Baldwin off at the Manor and handed the horses over to a groom. Matthew followed the man into the stables to have a look around, Richard behind him.

"Would it be all right if I invited Mountjoy to stay for a few weeks?" Richard asked, absently stroking the nose of one of the greys.

"Of course, you don't need to ask."

"Well, it is your place now—"

"It's your home, too."

Richard shrugged. "I never had any expectation of it becoming mine, though," he said. "Unlike Charlie."

"He was *expecting* to inherit?"

"Hoping might be more accurate," Richard said. "There was a lot of talk about the dangers of being in the army, tropical diseases, and so forth."

Matthew's lips thinned. Even though he and Charles had never got on well together, it wasn't pleasant to hear that his half-brother had wished him dead. He suppressed the thought that Charles had very nearly got his wish.

Richard must have noticed Matthew's expression. "Sorry, Matt, but there's no getting around it—my side of the family are not very nice people."

"Father must have been proud of *you*." Matthew remarked.

Richard looked round sharply, searching Matthew's face, then smiled. "I was still finishing school when he died," he said. "But he'd already arranged to buy my colours. Anyway, Mountjoy's family are nice enough, but they're a bit much when he's stuck indoors with them. They fuss over him endlessly—poor chap never gets a moment's peace!"

"Bit of a coincidence, you ending up in the same regiment as someone I knew at school," Matthew said.

"Not really, he got me transferred in. We were friends at school—for some reason he took me under his wing when I started, kept dear Charlie from doing at school what Father had stopped him from doing at home. How do you know him, anyway? He must have been just starting the year you left..."

Richard's voice trailed off, and he stared at his brother for a moment. "He didn't take to my sunny nature or youthful wit, did he?"

"He must have, if you are still friends."

"Come on, Matt. You were being the big brother?"

Matthew shrugged. "I did the same for him when he started school. Asked him to pass on the favour when you started, as I'd be long gone by then. I didn't know if he'd keep his word. Glad to know that he did."

Matthew wondered if Richard was offended by his interference. "Do you mind?"

"That my big brother helped me? Not at all. I was only a child. In fact, I hope I'm not so stupid as to reject help when it's offered now I'm grown. Accepting help isn't a sign of failure."

It is when you need as much help as I seem to. Matthew realised Richard was staring at him. "I do accept help," he protested. "You're here, aren't you?"

"True—but I'll bet money you think you should have sorted this mess out on your own."

Matthew shrugged again, not meeting his brother's eyes.

"Bloody idiot!" Richard said. "It's no different from you setting Mountjoy to watch me."

"You were a child. I'm a major in the army."

"Someone must think you're capable or you wouldn't have made it to major." He hesitated. "You didn't buy the rank, did you?"

"It goes by seniority in the East India Company army, not purchase."

"Well then."

"That was before I made a complete shambles of everything."

"How did you manage that?"

Matthew turned away and set off across the stable yard towards the main house. He was *not* going to drag all the details of Seringapatam back into his memory again.

"Come on, Matt—talking about things can help, you know."

"It doesn't." Every time he talked to someone about it, his nightmares got worse.

Richard followed him. Matthew kept walking, and when Richard put a hand on his arm, Matthew shook him off.

"Come on, Matt," Richard said again.

Matthew abruptly turned and pushed him away. It wasn't a hard push, but it caught Richard off-balance. Matthew saw him wince as his ankle gave way, sending him sprawling on the wet cobbles.

"Damn—I'm sorry, Richard, but just leave me alone, will you?"

"Give me a hand up." Richard held up one arm, and after a moment Matthew grasped it and hauled him to his feet. "You caught me by surprise," Richard said. "I could take you in a fair fight, dodgy ankle or not!"

Matthew looked at him. "I'm sure you could," he said, his expression bleak.

"Come with me," Richard said, heading back towards the far end of the stables.

"I believe you, Richard—you don't need to prove it."

"Shut up, you idiot, and come along."

Matthew just stood there, wondering what Richard wanted. He'd enjoyed working with his brother testing the rifles, but now he was acting more like Charles.

Richard turned and beckoned again from the far side of the yard, a quizzical smile on his face.

Don't let Charles poison things with Richard.

Matthew sighed and followed, to find his brother searching through a pile of debris at the back of a store-room. Eventually Richard grunted with satisfaction and pulled a large leather bag out, dragging it along the floor.

"Give me a hand, will you?" Richard asked. "There should be a pulley in the ceiling out there somewhere. Get some rope."

Matthew found a length of rope thin enough to go through the pulley, and Richard fastened it to the top of the bag. As he hauled on the other end of the rope, Matthew could see it was a punch bag for boxing training. It gently swung to and fro, twisting on its rope and revealing writing, done in white paint. Some of the letters were worn, and they were unevenly drawn, but the name still clearly said 'Charles'.

"I never would have thought of Charles using something like this," Matthew said, surprised.

"It's mine, not his."

Matthew laughed.

"It's no worse than you calling your dog after my mother," Richard said, slightly defensively.

"I don't hit Reena."

"The bag doesn't have feelings! Now hit it."

Matthew's fist hit the bag.

"No, put some effort in. Pretend it's that deserter your man Deacon saw off last week."

Richard steadied the bag from behind, and Matthew attacked it again. He managed several good, hard hits before his hands and arms started to hurt. The time he'd spent digging the kitchen garden over the last couple of months had obviously not been developing the right muscles. Or any muscles, possibly.

"You big molly!" Richard laughed.

Matthew's lips thinned and he looked away.

"Matt? Matt—I was joking! You just need to eat more and spend a bit of time working at it."

"Mind your own business." Matthew set off for the house again, the fact that Richard was right only exacerbating his feelings.

Richard struggled to keep up with him. "You *are* my business," he protested. "If our positions were reversed, what would you do?"

"Leave you alone if you asked me to."

"Would you really?"

Matthew didn't answer.

Richard clapped him on the shoulder and walked off. "See you for luncheon in an hour. If you don't turn up, I'll come and find you!"

Staines arrived on time, half an hour after Matthew and Richard had finished eating, and presented himself in the estate office.

Matthew waved him to a seat, wondering how old he was. He wore his hair unpowdered, showing a few threads of grey, but his face was lined with strain, and he had bags under his eyes. He clutched several large ledgers to his chest.

Instead of sitting down, Staines went straight to the desk and set the ledgers on it, opening two of them to marked pages, then standing back.

Matthew glanced at Richard, eyebrows rising in surprise, then the two men turned their attention to the rows of figures. It soon became clear that the two ledgers referred to the same amounts of money, differing only in the destination of outgoing sums. The money spent on repairs and general maintenance shown by one ledger had, according to the other, mostly been transferred to either Charles Southam or Mrs Southam.

Matthew turned to Staines. "Why?"

"Mr Charles threatened to accuse me of taking money from the estate," Staines said, wearing the expression of a man about to be sent to the gallows. "Even if he failed to make the charges stick, I'd never get another job."

"So my brother doesn't know these ledgers exist?" Matthew asked, placing a finger on the one showing payments to Charles. Staines shook his head.

"Very well. Report back here tomorrow morning, Mr Staines."

The man bobbed his head and left the room.

Matthew looked at Richard. "I can't help having some admiration for him owning up," he said.

"Agreed." Richard looked at the ledgers still spread out on the desk. "D'you really want me to go through those with you, Matt?"

Matthew sighed. "No. My responsibility." He waved a hand. Richard clapped him on the shoulder and left.

He spent an hour looking through both sets of books, then the ache behind his eyes from trying to make out Staines' crabbed handwriting threatened to turn into a proper headache. He marked his place, closed the books, and went outside for a brisk walk around the grounds in the gathering dusk. It was a pity he couldn't have brought Mrs MacKinnon along to help.

The walk gave Matthew an appetite for dinner. Mrs Summers had organised a substantial meal with a variety of dishes—a meat pie solid with beef and a leg of lamb, all served with crispy roast potatoes and vegetables, followed by a pudding. None of it resembled the fancy dishes with little substance he'd been served when he was at the town house with Serena.

They retired to the library with a bottle of port after the meal.

"How well do you know Staines?" Matthew asked, taking a mouthful of port. He'd learned from Baldwin that Staines had an ageing mother and a sickly wife to support. That Staines hadn't mentioned these facts in mitigation made him respect the man.

Richard was sprawled on a chair on the other side of the roaring fire. "I know *of* him—he started here some time ago, when I was at school. He would have been here when I came for holidays. But I never had anything to do with him."

"Did you believe him?"

"I think so," Richard said. "Although I don't know Staines, it's also a matter of believing that Charles *would* do such a thing. If you and Charles had been reversed, then Staines would be lying. But as it is…" He shrugged, not looking happy. "What are you going to do?"

"I'm thinking of keeping him on. I don't think I can legally take

Charles to task without getting Staines convicted as well. Nor do I want to have our family problems made public. It wouldn't do your career any good."

"Or yours."

Matthew gave a dismissive shrug. "That's no matter." He should have already resigned his commission, really. He brought his mind back to the present.

"I don't see that Staines could have done anything to stop it," he said. "Refusing would have cost him his job."

"How d'you know he won't do it again?" Richard asked.

"Make it clear that he works for me, not Charles, and take a copy of one of his honest ledgers." Matthew took another mouthful of port. "I was thinking of leaving Baldwin here."

"Featherstone will be—"

Matthew shook his head. "Baldwin will be a kind of indoor steward, in title at least. He's to oversee and sign off Staines' accounts and spending. Perhaps gradually take over from Featherstone." He looked back at his brother. "Does that make sense?"

"Sounds like an excellent plan to me," Richard said. "I take it that Baldwin's extra responsibility will bring an increase in salary."

"Naturally." It was a way of rewarding him for his loyalty without handing him a gift of money.

"What's the plan for tomorrow?"

"Tell Staines and Baldwin about their new positions, then more touring the estate, I suppose."

Richard grimaced. "What fun." He refilled his glass, then held the bottle out to Matthew.

"Not just yet," Matthew said. "D'you fancy a game of piquet to pass the time?"

"Why not?" Richard got up to find the cards, and Matthew brought a table over to set between their chairs.

Richard cut the deck. "Matt?"

"Hmm?" Matthew's card was higher, and he picked up the pack to start dealing.

"If you *do* want—or need—to talk about anything…"

Matthew looked up, meeting his brother's eyes for a moment.

Accepting help isn't a sign of failure.

He gave a small nod. "I will. Now, are we going to play?"

CHAPTER 37

Charlotte inspected the room that would become the major's bedroom, admiring the changes. Deacon's foul-smelling turpentine mixture had stripped centuries of old varnish and grime from the wood panelling, and after a few coats of beeswax the lighter colour of the oak showed up beautifully. The painters were due to arrive today, and soon the walls above the panelling would be a deep red, the colour picking out some of the embroidery in the bed curtains Mr Fulbeck had returned. The burgundy-coloured carpet had been taken out to the stable yard a couple of days ago when the weather was fine and beaten thoroughly. It was now rolled up in the hall waiting to be put down when the paint was dry.

The unpleasant smell of the cleaning solution still lingered. She'd had the panelling in here and the parlour done first, to allow plenty of time for the odour to dissipate before the major returned. The cleaners had worked in short spells on the panelling, spending the rest of their time scrubbing the floors and cleaning the windows in the servants' rooms on the upper floor.

Pulling the door closed behind her, she went on up the stairs. These small rooms all looked much better now, clean, and with fresh whitewash on the walls. She had ordered a large bolt of printed calico, and some of the women were sewing curtains, sitting together in a room further along the corridor, gossiping as they worked. Snippets of different conversations came to her as voices rose and fell.

"...not seen much of Lord Tillson in the village..."

"...bit of talk from that apothecary about him—didn't say much, just that 'e was..."

Charlotte frowned. It sounded as though Halliton had not resisted the temptation to pass on something of what he'd seen and heard when the major had been ill.

"...don't mind him, sour grapes if you ask me..."

"...ain't complaining about someone who's payin' us for sittin' in the warm havin' a good gossip..."

She smiled at that. Halliton was not popular amongst the local working people. Hopefully they would not give too much credence to anything he said. The major had come a long way since then, too. She rarely saw his flask out, for one thing.

"... house ain't as big as I thought..."

"... nice when it be finished. Mrs Captain do seem to be..."

That raised another smile. She suspected that not everyone who had turned up the first day actually wanted the work—some were just curious to see the inside of the Hall, and they had not returned the next day. The rest appreciated the work, as there were few agricultural jobs in the winter.

She shut the door of the room she had just inspected, making as much noise as possible, and by the time she reached the sewing room the women had stopped talking. After checking that they had everything they needed, she went back downstairs.

The men with the new kitchen range arrived mid-morning, just as the scaffolders were dismantling the final sections. Charlotte showed them into the kitchen, and they got to work straight away, demolishing the old one.

To her surprise, a woman had arrived with them. At first, Charlotte assumed she was the wife of one of the men, for she looked to be a similar age, although rather better dressed. Charlotte was about to go outside to talk to the scaffolders when she noticed that the woman was still standing by the kitchen door, next to a small trunk. She frowned. Had the men just given her a ride up from the village on their cart?

"May I help you?" Charlotte asked, looking at her more closely. She had on the neat but drab-coloured clothing of an upper servant, with a white cap beneath her bonnet. Charlotte guessed she was in her early thirties, although the worried expression might have made her look older than her years.

"I wondered if... er... is Lord Tillson here, ma'am?"

"I'm afraid he is away at the moment."

The woman looked even more uncertain. "Is there a Mr Baldwin here?"

"I'm afraid not. You look tired—have you come far?"

"From London, ma'am."

"Come in," Charlotte said. "I'm afraid there are no hot drinks to be had at the moment..." She gestured towards the two men working on the range. "I'm Mrs MacKinnon. I'm... well, I'm a sort of secretary here."

"Mrs Malplass. Well, Miss Malplass really, but everyone calls me Mrs." She left her trunk by the door and followed Charlotte through into the steward's office.

"Now, how may I help you?"

"I... Mr Kellet said..."

Charlotte waited patiently.

"Well, I was hoping Lord Tillson might be able to find me employment," the woman finally said.

"What was your previous post?"

"I was housekeeper for Mrs Southam. She turned me off without a reference."

"As she did to Baldwin?"

Mrs Malplass nodded. "Baldwin thought his lordship might give him a job, but if he hasn't—"

"He did," Charlotte interrupted, thinking this would help set the woman at ease. "Baldwin is not here because he accompanied Lord Tillson to Farleton Manor."

The woman looked less anxious. "Is his lordship expected back soon?" she asked hopefully.

Charlotte shook her head. "It could be a couple of weeks, but don't worry, you can stay here until he returns. If you don't mind turning your hand to cleaning, there's a lot to be done, and you'll be paid. I'm not sure I have the authority to offer you a permanent job, but his lordship will need a proper housekeeper. He can discuss that with you when he returns." She hesitated a moment. "As long as you weren't turned off for stealing?" She made the last a question.

Mrs Malplass shook her head.

"Why *were* you turned off?"

"Mrs Southam said I was spending too much."

Charlotte looked encouraging, hoping the woman would elaborate. It really wasn't her business, but she couldn't help being interested.

"It was that Mr Kellet," Mrs Malplass said. "He said Mrs Southam had to stick to her proper allowance, so she couldn't spend so much on food and the like, but she wanted everything to be like it was before, just with less money."

"An impossible task," Charlotte said reassuringly.

This time Mrs Malplass ventured a smile.

"Did you know Lord Tillson before he went to India?" Charlotte asked.

"No, ma'am. I was taken on when Mrs Southam moved to London permanently. But I heard from Mr Baldwin that he was likely to be a good master to work for."

Charlotte sat for a moment, thinking. This woman could be very useful. She would know things like the number of sets of bedding needed, and how many maids and footmen were required to run a house this size. Charlotte could estimate some these things, but she had never taken an interest in how her mother ran her own home. The only household she'd lived in since then consisted simply of herself, Mary and one daily girl. Although butlers were not normally asked to give references for housekeepers, in the current circumstances she thought asking Baldwin might be the best plan.

"Let me show you around the house," she said, getting to her feet.

The rain pattered against the library windows, but the fire kept the chill off. Matthew looked at the shelves full of books, trying to decide which ones to send to Birchanger. Birchanger had a library, and libraries should have books.

He had found some bound copies of an agricultural journal, and several books on horticulture and the growing of fruit and vegetables —they would be useful, so they joined the growing pile on the floor. There was a copy of Repton's book with hints on landscape gardening, and Matthew even found a Red Book that Repton had done for Farleton with suggestions for landscape improvements. He glanced at the watercolours in it, then squinted out through the rain running down the windows. Serena may have managed to persuade his father to pay for a Red Book, but it appeared that she hadn't been successful in persuading him to undertake the landscape work it suggested. He studied the drawings. The ideas for landscaping near the house could possibly be adapted for Birchanger when he had the time, so he added it to the pile. In any case, Davie would be interested in how the Red Book used overlays to show ideas. That reminded him of the books still upstairs in the nursery, so he went in search of the stories he remembered reading as a child.

An hour later, Richard found him in the nursery, flicking through a book on forts and guns, with piles of books stacked on the floor around him.

"Planning on setting up your own nursery soon?" Richard asked.

Matthew looked away, embarrassed. While thinking Davie would enjoy the books, it had crossed his mind that Mrs MacKinnon would also be pleased if Davie had more books to read.

"I thought Davie might enjoy them," he said, trying not to sound defensive.

"*Basics of Latin?*" Richard raised a brow, then picked up another one. "*Forts and Fortifications?*"

"He might be interested in the forts one," Matthew said.

"You'll have to get leg-shackled at some point, Matt, unless you want Charlie to end up with everything."

"If I get around to making a will, he'll only end up with Birchanger," Matthew said, ignoring the first part of Richard's comment. "Anyway, are you so sure he'll outlive me?"

"Unless an irate husband gets to him, he's looking healthier than you. You still look as if you could fade away at any moment."

"Thank you for those few, kind words."

"Any time, brother!"

Matthew had to smile. "Mrs Summers seems to be doing her best to fatten me up."

"And you will get fat, if you just sit around with your nose in books all day. Haven't you noticed the rain's stopped?"

He hadn't.

"How about half an hour with the punch bag before luncheon?" Richard said. "Then we can do something out of doors afterwards."

Matthew agreed, tidying the books before going to change his clothing.

After luncheon, Richard decided to test the progress of his ankle by having a gentle hack around the estate. Matthew went in search of the head gardener.

The man Matthew remembered from his childhood had retired some years ago, and Yardley, the current head gardener, was a man not much older than Matthew himself. Pleased someone was taking an interest in 'his' gardens, Yardley showed Matthew around the kitchen garden, explaining what they were growing, and how, in great detail. Matthew had taken little interest in gardens since his boyhood, but now that early fascination rekindled.

"What happens to all the produce?" he asked eventually. "You must be growing more than enough to feed the staff here."

"We... er... Well, Mr Southam—Mr Charles, that is—says we've to sell it."

"And what do you *actually* do with it?" Matthew asked.

"We're quite a long way from market, my lord, and without a *regular* presence..." Yardley shuffled his feet, not meeting Matthew's eyes.

"Mr Yardley—I was merely asking for information, not criticising."

"Give some to the workhouse, my lord, and some to the older tenants on the estate."

"Very good." Matthew walked on, pleased that not *all* the staff here had been cowed by Charles.

After a moment Yardley closed his mouth and followed. Matthew compared this garden with the one at Birchanger. Although the kitchen garden at Birchanger was not yet cleared, he was aware that he'd need to organise the planting carefully if it was going to produce enough food for himself and the staff. As he looked at the gardens here, having a blank canvas to work with at Birchanger was beginning to feel rather daunting. He realised how little he knew about anything to do with running an estate of this size. With Webb as steward, he would not get any knowledgeable help from his staff.

He wondered about moving Yardley to Birchanger—either temporarily or permanently—but the man had lived here on the levels all his life, and wasn't likely to be happy at being moved nearly fifty miles away. Instead, after they had finished the tour of the gardens, he asked Yardley if he would be interested in helping to plan the gardens at Birchanger. Matthew even told him about his ideas for a succession house, but he needed to know the measurements before Yardley could help him with the details.

By the time he'd finished talking to the head gardener it was raining again, so he didn't bother with his ride. Instead, he ventured into the attic to see what Serena had banished there. He made a list of quite a few items of furniture he remembered and liked. Looking at his watch, he was surprised to realise he had managed to stay up there for over an hour in the dark. Even the lack of windows hadn't bothered him.

. . .

After dinner he wrote a letter to Mrs MacKinnon that would be sent off with the boxes of books the next day. He listed, in detail, the items of furniture in the attic, as there was no point in sending them if they weren't going to fit. He also wrote a letter to Davie, explaining the measurements of the kitchen garden he needed. The lad would be pleased to do something other than his Latin. A grin spread across his face as he had an idea, and he went off to the library to find a Latin dictionary and grammar.

CHAPTER 38

The welcome aroma of coffee greeted Charlotte when she arrived at the Hall. The men had taken two days to fit the new range and had just been finishing the day before when she set off for home. The aroma told her, even before she set foot in the kitchen, that the new range was not only working but had already been put to use.

As she took off her cloak, she was pleased to see that Webb had returned from his trip to London with the rifles. He was just finishing his breakfast, so she invited him to look around and see what had been achieved so far. He was suitably impressed, and agreed to her request to move his office into one of the upstairs rooms so the steward's office on the ground floor could be redecorated.

Later that morning Charlotte was checking progress in the library when Tilly came into the room to tell her that a wagon had arrived.

"Man wants to know where to put the boxes, mum," the girl said.

"Boxes?"

"Yes, mum. Lots of them!"

Charlotte frowned—she didn't think any more deliveries were due this week, but she went downstairs to check. When she reached the yard, the man driving said he'd come from Farleton.

387

"There's a letter, ma'am," the driver said, handing her a fat packet. "I'm to stay until tomorrow, and take any reply back."

"Very good. Tilly will show you the stables. Tilly—please show him where to take the horses, and then ask your mother to sort out somewhere for him to sleep."

"Yes, mum," Tilly said, and scampered off. Charlotte took the letter into the kitchen and unsealed it. Several smaller packets fell out. She was surprised to see two of them addressed to Davie but she put those aside, hoping one of the other letters would explain.

She read the letter addressed to her. The final part of it raised a smile, and she examined the two letters to Davie again. She tucked one of them into the back of her notebook. The list of furniture she would give to Mrs Malplass to take a look at. The boxes contained books, but they could stay in the stables for a day or two until the painting in the library was completed. She hadn't seen Davie for a while, but when Tilly reappeared she was sent off to look for him.

Charlotte went to find Webb, and asked him to accompany her to the kitchen garden. They stood just inside the door, looking at the expanse of bramble and weeds, with only a narrow strip dug and cleared of roots.

"The letter says he wants it dug over, ma'am?" Webb sounded doubtful.

"Yes. Is that a problem?"

"Well, he was doin' it hisself. Summat to take his mind off things."

"He seems to have changed his mind."

Webb nodded.

"Some of the men who came to start work didn't take to the indoor tasks," Charlotte went on. "You could see if they want outdoor work instead."

"Right you are, ma'am. I reckon I'll need to use them as has their own tools."

"Try asking the squire's man to lend you some tools, if you're short of them." She paused. "You could probably start by asking at the inn."

Webb grinned. "Splendid idea, ma'am." He stood and reached for his coat.

"Could you call at my house at some point and ask Deacon if he can spare the afternoon to come up here?" Charlotte asked.

Webb nodded, and set off for ale and a chat.

Davie was waiting in the kitchen when Charlotte went back indoors.

"The major sent a letter to you," she said, handing it over. He opened it, and she had to bite her lip to keep from laughing as his expression changed from interest, to puzzlement, and then consternation.

"What does it say?" she asked, attempting a tone of innocent enquiry. Davie handed it to her wordlessly.

"Southam D. MacKinnon dicit," she read out, straight-faced. "Metire horto, etiam altitudines muros..." She stopped, still trying not to laugh. "I think it is a job he wishes you to do for him."

"But I can't read it!"

"You've been having lessons in Latin for at least a year."

Davie hung his head. "Bertie never liked Latin lessons, so we..." He looked at his shoes.

"Hmm. Well, if you go to the stables and find the box with an L marked on it, you may find something to help you."

He looked doubtful, but went off anyway. Charlotte grinned—it was thoughtful of the major to send a Latin dictionary and grammar book as well.

She let Davie struggle with his translation for an hour before giving him the version in English. He should have the kitchen garden measured by tomorrow. Deacon could check his results, then the man from Farleton would take the details back with him.

After luncheon, Charlotte went to inspect the finished paintwork in the major's bedroom, and check that the bed had been placed correctly. Webb reappeared as she was contemplating which of the paintings should hang over the mantelpiece.

"Got 'alf a dozen men to start diggin' tomorrow," he reported.

"Reckon they can be put to diggin' drains in some of the fields after they've..." His voice tailed off as his attention turned to the scene beyond the window.

Crossing the room to stand next to him, Charlotte saw a coach and four emerging from the trees.

Webb tutted.

"What is it, Sergeant?"

Webb opened the window for a better look. The coach pulled to a stop in front of the Hall, and a footman jumped down and opened the door, letting down the steps. A woman emerged, expensively dressed with a fur collar to her redingote and several plumes on her hat.

"It's 'is lordship's mother," Webb announced. "'Is stepmother, I should say."

"Ah!" Charlotte thought for a moment. "Sergeant, could you find Mrs Malplass? She's on the top floor somewhere. Warn her to keep out of the way." That would be one less argument to have with Mrs Southam, and it would save Mrs Malplass some distress.

"This room is almost habitable—perhaps you could get a few jars of Deacon's turpentine mixture to stand near the fire for a while?"

Webb looked puzzled for a moment, then a grin spread over his face.

"In case she wants to stay?"

"Exactly!"

She could hear him chortling as he set off up to the top floor. Squaring her shoulders, she went down to meet the monster she'd heard so much about.

The groom with the wagon arrived back at Farleton as dusk fell. Matthew and Richard had ridden around the estate again, making the most of the February sunshine. Now Richard had retired to the parlour to rest his aching ankle.

"No problems?" Matthew asked as the man unhitched the horse.

"No, my lord. Well..."

"What?"

"Mrs Southam arrived." The man shuffled his feet. "Er, Mrs MacKinnon sent you a letter, my lord."

Matthew took the proffered letter and went to join Richard in the parlour. Ten minutes later, and with an untouched glass of brandy beside him, he was laughing.

"Share the joke?" Richard asked, curious. "Who's the letter from?"

"Mrs MacKinnon. You may not find it as amusing..." Matthew said.

Richard raised his eyebrows enquiringly.

"Oh, very well." Matthew started reading aloud partway through the letter.

We had a visitor yesterday—a Lady Tillson called. It took some time to ascertain, firstly, that she was not an as-yet-unknown relict of the late Lord Tillson and, secondly, that she was probably too old to be the wife of the current Lord Tillson—this part of the discussion was not appreciated by the so-called Lady Tillson. Further, she was not the current Lord's mother, nor had her late husband ever been Lord Tillson, having pre-deceased the previous incumbent.

Her identity thus clarified, it was further established, much to her dismay, that Birchanger Hall was not her property, nor ever had been, and she had no authority to terminate the employment of any persons on the premises. I stated that she was welcome to stay, if she would be satisfied with one of the beds in the servants' rooms on the top floor. She could, of course, have occupied your lordship's room which was ready for use, except for the regrettable fact that someone had left several open containers of the turpentine-based cleaning solution standing near the fire, which had given a distinct and nausea-inducing aroma to the chamber.

It was also regrettable that the landlord of the inn in the village, where she had stopped for directions, had neglected to tell her that the Hall was not fit for visitors—a fact known to all in the immediate area. This would have saved her staff the effort of unloading her baggage and then having to load it up again. Perhaps Mr Minching's omission was due to her pleasant manner, dazzling him with her charms and so quite putting practicalities such as that out of his head. It is to be hoped that Mr Minching did, in fact, have a room suitable for her occupation, otherwise she would have had a long drive in the dark to the next village. This would probably have been a very long drive indeed if Mr Minching gave her driver directions.

Unfortunately, no-one at Birchanger had authority to pay for her accommodation elsewhere. She was offered refreshments, but considered tripe and onions was not suitable fare, nor pig's trotters, and so took her leave.

She also thanked him for Davie's two letters. Davie might not have learned much more Latin than he knew before, but he'd certainly had plenty of practice using the dictionary. Matthew didn't read that part out.

It was a few minutes before Richard could speak. Eventually he dried his eyes. "She really offered Mama tripe and onions?" he asked, still a little breathless. "And *pig's trotters?*"

"I have no idea," Matthew said, still chuckling. "But I like to think so. It seems that Serena has finally met her match."

"God, I wish I'd witnessed that encounter," Richard said. Matthew did too—Mrs MacKinnon would have been wearing her trying-not-to-laugh expression, and he could imagine her laughing out loud as soon as Serena was out of earshot, grey eyes sparkling…

"If she was looking for you, she could turn up here. Matt? Are you listening?"

Matthew tried to put the grey eyes out of his mind.

"If she was coming I'd have thought she'd be here by now." He checked the letter again. "My man didn't set off until the afternoon of the day after she called. She would have been at least as fast in a coach as he was with the wagon."

"What do you think she wants?"

"Money," Matthew said shortly. "Kellet was going to keep her within her allowance."

"That wouldn't have gone down well." Richard eyed the letter Matthew was still holding. "Is there more?"

"The rest isn't as amusing, I'm afraid. You recall Mrs Malplass?"

"Housekeeper at the London house?"

"No more, it would seem. She arrived in search of me, hoping I might give her employment—she must have known where Baldwin was headed. What's she like, any idea?"

Richard shook his head. "As far as I could tell, the place ran smoothly. You'd be better asking Baldwin what he thinks. Are you staying here?"

"I'm not going to run away from her," Matthew said. "We'll have to straighten things out at some point—may as well get it over with. Besides, I've not finished here. I need another few days, at least." He looked back at his brother. "Will you come back to Birchanger with me?"

"Do you need me to?"

Matthew shook his head. "Not need, no. But you are always welcome."

"I'll stay on for a while then. Perhaps I'll come up to Birchanger for a day or two once the place is in order."

Serena did not arrive at Farleton. Matthew, slightly uneasy about it, could only speculate. Eventually, he put her out of his mind, and concentrated on planning the kitchen garden, using the measurements Davie had sent. He looked in detail at the way Farleton's succession house was constructed, filling pages of his notebook with sketches of the structure and heating arrangements. He spent some time with Staines, learning about land management. He got Baldwin to send off the items of furniture Mrs MacKinnon said would be useful, and several boxes of linens Mrs Summers had sorted out.

He also developed a routine, spending a couple of hours a day digging with Yardley or hitting the punch bag. By the time he left for Birchanger, he was managing a respectable amount of time at these exercises without feeling too much pain afterwards.

On the day he left, he sent the wagon off early with Reena and more boxes of books. He couldn't take the dog with him on horseback, and he was planning on stopping in Bristol on the way back to call on Doctor Lorton, and see if the man could help him to find Benson's family.

It would be good to be home again afterwards, and to have Mrs MacKinnon show him what she'd achieved in his absence.

~

Matthew turned the horse up the drive to Birchanger, looking forward to warming up and getting indoors out of the damp and dreary weather. He'd found Lorton the evening before, and the doctor had promised to see what he could do. Without Reena, Matthew hadn't slept very well, and had set off early. He rode straight round to the stables without announcing his arrival, but someone must have been watching because Jackson was waiting to take his horse as he dismounted.

The kitchen looked different—brighter, but full of people. The long table appeared to have become the servants' dining table, for it was crowded with people in working clothes, most of whom he didn't recognise.

"Welcome back, sir," Webb said, getting up from his place. The rest of the people stood, most shuffling their feet or glancing at him uncertainly.

"This is 'is lordship," Webb announced, and there were various bobbings of heads. "If you'd come this way, sir?" Webb led the way into the main hall, and Matthew heard chairs and stools scraping again as the meal was resumed.

"Who *are* all those people, Webb?" Matthew asked, then stopped again as he took in the hall. The windows had curtains, and fires in both fireplaces gave the place a welcoming feel. He dropped his saddle bags and turned, taking in the rest of his surroundings. The panelling glowed—surely it was paler than before. New rugs lay in front of the fires, with chairs and sofas around them.

Webb jerked his head towards the kitchen. "Men diggin' the kitchen garden, sir. Some of 'em come from a fair few miles away, so Mrs Captain said they could 'ave bed and board if they wanted it. The ones what only work for the day get proper food as well—Mrs Captain reckons they work 'arder."

"Do you?"

Webb grinned. "I reckon she's right, sir. The women, they're still 'elpin' sort out some of the bedrooms. But your room is done, and the library and parlour. Mrs Captain thought you wouldn't mind eatin' in the parlour until the dinin' room is finished."

Some of Matthew's pleasure at being home disappeared as he realised Webb wouldn't be talking about Mrs Captain like that if she were here. He'd been looking forward to having her show him the progress on the house.

"I'll get bath water sent up, sir."

"No need. Not until this evening. I don't want to interrupt their meal," Matthew said, "Can you get Mrs Jackson to send me a tray?"

"Yessir."

Crossing the hall, Matthew entered the room he'd been using as his bedroom. His things had been replaced with a small dining table and various chairs, sofas, and side tables. He vaguely remembered Mrs MacKinnon saying this room would be done in dark colours, but she must have changed her mind. The carpet was deep green but the walls were a very pale green, with cream, light green and gold patterns on the chairs and in the curtains. In spite of the gloomy weather, the room felt light and airy.

He moved on to the library. Here, the walls were darker above the shelves. The shelves themselves had been cleaned and polished and, like the panelling in the other rooms, contributed to a more cheerful appearance. The books he'd sent had been unpacked and placed on the shelves as they had come out of the boxes. He smiled; organising his library would be a pleasant task for a winter's day.

His desk was below one of the windows, with his pens and drawing instruments more or less as he had left them. He sniffed—the place smelled vaguely floral and spicy, and he noticed bowls of pot pourri on a couple of small tables, mingling with the aroma of wood smoke drifting in from the hall. The all-pervading smell of damp he remembered seemed to have gone.

By the time he reached his bedroom upstairs, someone had brought a jug of hot water, lit the fire and left a tray with stew, bread, and ale. He sat down to eat it before it went cold, then examined the room. The bed hangings were the same, but must have been washed, as they looked brighter than before. The walls were painted in a dark red above the panelling, making the room cosy and inviting. He had a fleeting thought that a bed that size was wasted on just one occupant. Trying to ignore the idea of the particular additional occupant he had in mind, he unpacked the change of clothes he'd brought in his saddle bags. Then he went back out to the stables to see about setting up the punch bag somewhere under cover where he could continue to use it regularly.

CHAPTER 39

*C*harlotte had intended to be at Birchanger when the major returned. She wanted to show him what had been achieved while he was away, hoping he would be pleased enough not to mind the rather large bill for labour; although the money would have been spent eventually, it did seem rather a lot when all spent at once.

When the final wagon-load of boxes arrived with the major's note saying he would be back the following day, she checked that Mrs Malplass knew where the things were to be put and set off home early to get her final batch of articles ready to send to Mr Berry. This took longer than she expected, and she had to finish work on them the next morning. It was nearly lunchtime before she finished her manuscript. She carefully wrapped it with Deacon's latest batch of drawings and addressed the parcel. She and Davie ate a quick luncheon before setting off together into Edgecombe to drop off the parcel before going up to Birchanger.

Charlotte hesitated as they approached the Hare and Hounds. A coach and four was drawn up outside the inn. It looked like a hired coach, but the sight of it made her uneasy—her father had said he would come to Edgecombe. She debated going around to the kitchen door and giving her parcel to Mrs Minching, but she couldn't avoid her father for ever.

Squaring her shoulders, she walked into the taproom and handed the parcel over to Toby Minching. There were only villagers in the room as she handed it over, but she could hear her father's voice in the private parlour across the entrance hall. He came to the parlour door.

"Ah, Charlotte, my dear!" He gave a passable imitation of someone who was pleased to see his dearest daughter—it would fool anyone who did not know him. "Perhaps you can direct my coachman to your home."

"Why?" Charlotte made no move towards him. The villagers in the taproom, while not actually looking at her and her father, had stopped talking. Davie wasn't here, but she'd seen him go to look at the carriage as she walked into the inn.

"Why?" her father repeated, sounding surprised. "So I can freshen up in my room, then we can have a nice talk. I *have* travelled a long way to see you."

"I haven't got a spare room," she replied. "You'll have to take a room here."

Her father frowned. "Very well," he said, making an obvious effort to speak politely. "I'll make the arrangements, then we will go to your house to talk."

"I'm already late for an appointment," Charlotte said, shaking her head. This wasn't quite true, as the major wouldn't mind what time she turned up.

Andrew Metcalf's eyes narrowed for a moment, then relaxed again as he gazed beyond her.

"Mama?" Davie, unfortunately, had finished inspecting the carriage.

"You must be David?" her father said, with a wide, insincere smile. "I'm so pleased to be allowed to meet you at last. I'm your grandfather Metcalf."

Charlotte wished she'd had chance to talk to Davie about how to behave with her father—she really should have warned him that they might be getting a visit. But Davie didn't fail her.

"I am pleased to meet you, sir," he said politely, but without feeling. He moved closer to Charlotte, and she put a hand on his shoulder.

"Landlord!"

Toby Minching appeared promptly at Metcalf's call.

"Prepare a room for me, and see to the horses. Send my valet up."

Charlotte could see Toby's eyebrows rising at her father's manner. Toby glanced at her for confirmation, and she gave an almost imperceptible nod.

"I'll be using this parlour as well," Metcalf added. "Send in ale." He hesitated, glancing at Davie. "And something for the boy." He went into the parlour, leaving Charlotte and Davie to follow him.

Charlotte took off her cloak and draped it over the back of a chair. The room was warm, and this was going to take more than a few minutes. Davie sat down near her, as her father took up a position in front of the fire. He was about to speak when the door was pushed open and Mrs Minching appeared with a tray.

Bless them, Charlotte thought, as she spied a teapot and three cups, as well as the ale her father had ordered. Davie's eyes lit up for a moment as he spotted the plate of cakes, then he resumed his blank expression.

Metcalf waited while Charlotte poured tea for herself and Davie, then he picked up the plate of cakes and offered it to Davie.

"No, thank you, sir," Davie said stiffly.

"Come, my boy, everyone likes cake."

"I've just had my luncheon, sir," Davie replied.

"Well, well—you may wish to have some later." He drew up a chair, asking Davie about his lessons and his friends and managing a far friendlier tone than he had when speaking to his daughter.

Charlotte clenched her hands as she listened. She wanted Davie to give a good impression, so her father could not complain that he was receiving an inadequate education. Davie answered politely but briefly. He did glance uncertainly at her when he answered his grandfather's questions about his tutor in a way that implied he was still having the lessons, but Charlotte gave a small, reassuring smile. She'd need to have another talk with him about when lies might possibly be justified.

When her father started to talk about schools and the proper social contacts for a young gentleman, Charlotte interrupted.

"Excuse me, Father, but Davie is late for his mathematics lesson. Perhaps you and I could discuss this privately?" Luckily Metcalf was looking at her, not Davie, and so missed the momentary puzzlement on her son's face. "I'll see you there later, Davie," she said. His face cleared, and he stood up.

"Excuse me, sir," he said, and walked out of the room without a backwards look.

"Perhaps I should see this tutor of his," Metcalf said.

"Why?" Charlotte asked, resisting the impulse to fold her arms around her chest.

"To judge whether he is a suitable person to teach my grandson, of course." Metcalf looked down his nose at her. "Only a gentleman can judge the suitability of a tutor for educating gentlemen."

"Davie uses the same tutor as the squire's son," Charlotte said. "He will go to school when Mama's five thousand pounds is made available to me."

"Five thousand pounds won't go far enough to put him comfortably through university as well," her father said, through stiff lips. His face was reddening; it was clearly a struggle to maintain a polite tone.

"There's nothing stopping you settling some money on him for his education," Charlotte said.

"I'd want to make sure it was spent properly," Metcalf said. "He *is* my grandson, after all."

"He's *my* son," Charlotte said sharply. "It's taken you ten years to take an interest in him."

"Come now, Charlotte, my dear. Wouldn't *you* enjoy returning to London and taking up the social life your class warrants?"

"No," Charlotte said shortly. His attempt at being friendly would have made her laugh if she hadn't been so worried about what he might do.

"Now then, every woman enjoys balls and parties!"

"I do not."

"You would sacrifice your son's education to stay here?" Metcalf said incredulously. "Here, in this miserable little village, in a house so small you cannot even accommodate your own father!"

"I am not sacrificing his education." Charlotte's nails dug into her palms as she tried to control her own temper. She *would* find the money for Davie's education somehow, without sacrificing herself to her father's ambitions.

"Do you at least have servants?" he asked. "Or are you doing your own cooking and cleaning? A fine experience for my grandson!"

"I have a maid and an outdoor man," Charlotte said, knowing Mary and Deacon would not mind her bending the truth in this way. "And another girl who comes in by the day. Is that not sufficient for one woman and her son?"

"Any boy who is to grow up to be a gentleman needs a man to guide him," Metcalf said.

"That is why he has a tutor," Charlotte stated. She stood, picking up her cloak. "If you have nothing new to say, this interview is at an end. I am late for an appointment."

"But—"

"If you are concerned about *my* son's education, do feel free to pay for a good school for him." Charlotte donned her cloak and started pulling on her gloves. "You have yet to explain why his education needs to be tied to my return to London. Until you can explain that, we have no reason to speak further." She stalked towards the door.

"You haven't heard the last of this," Metcalf threatened. "You have flouted my authority too often—"

Charlotte turned to look at him, her hand still on the door latch. "Your authority over me ceased when I married," she said. There was a faint scuffling from beyond the door, but under the circumstances Charlotte was quite happy for Toby Minching or his wife to eavesdrop. She hoped her father had shown his true colours well enough to make them reluctant to answer any questions he might ask.

She marched out, too angry and upset to exchange words with anyone, and set off for Birchanger at a blistering pace.

Charlotte took her usual route into the Hall via the stable yard. There was an odd, thudding noise coming from the stable building, so she didn't head directly for the back door, but went partway across the yard to investigate.

A large bag hung from the rafters just inside the stable entrance. The major was standing with his back to her, hitting it repeatedly. He wore his normal boots and breeches, his shirt tucked in but no waistcoat or coat.

He must have been eating well while he was away, as he seemed to be filling his breeches better than before. *Much* better.

As she watched, he stopped and stretched his arms out, then pulled his shirt out of his breeches and over his head, using it to wipe his face. Charlotte felt heat rise to her face as she took in his bare back, dark lines criss crossing it. His ribs were no longer showing, and muscles moved as he rubbed his hair with part of the shirt.

A flood of heat spread through her body, a wave of longing. She missed the comfort of being held, but she also wanted the feel of skin on skin, and all the rest of the sensations that went with being intimate.

He lowered the shirt, and Charlotte spun on her heel, walking briskly to the kitchen. She could *not* be caught staring at her employer like that. She paused inside the kitchen door, her face flushed and pulse racing.

"You all right, ma'am?" Mrs Jackson asked, seeing her expression.

"Yes, I'm fine, thank you." Charlotte managed to sound normal—she hoped—in spite of the breathless feeling in her chest. "Just hot from walking up here too fast." Taking off her cloak, accepted the glass of water Mrs Jackson offered her. "Is Davie here?"

"Yes. He's looking at books in the library."

"I'll just go and check on him," Charlotte said, but she only went as far as the hall. She sank onto one of the sofas.

Good grief, what came over me?

She had seen the man partly dressed before, when he was ill. He wasn't ill now—far from it.

Why now, for heaven's sake? She took a deep breath, trying to calm herself. *He's my employer!*

"Mrs MacKinnon?"

Charlotte jumped at the major's voice, not having heard him approach. She put her hands up to hide her flushed cheeks.

"Major. Welcome back." She was pleased the words came out normally.

"Are you feeling quite well?" He stood in front of her, a small frown on his face. He was dressed once more, but with his neckcloth undone and hanging loosely around his neck. The bundle of cloth in one hand must be the shirt he'd been exercising in.

Charlotte averted her eyes, the sight of the shirt in his hand bringing to mind the body beneath his clothes.

"I... yes, I'm perfectly well, thank you. Excuse me, I was just going to check on Davie. Make sure he is not getting up to mischief."

"I sent him to the library when he arrived. He seemed rather... subdued. Worried, even?"

"His grandfather... my father, that is... he was..." Charlotte cleared her throat and gave her head a small shake.

Concentrate!

"Davie is worried about being sent away to school," she explained. That was enough—he didn't need to know the details of her unpleasant relationship with her father.

"You are worried too?" he asked.

Charlotte looked up, then away again, the concern on his face bringing a lump to her throat.

"I would miss him," Charlotte said, aware of his eyes on her face. "This is just a decision I have to make," she added when he did not speak, horrified to find that her voice was starting to wobble.

"If there is anything I can do to help, you would ask, would you not?"

Charlotte felt tears prick her eyes at the kindness in his voice. So many people came to her for advice, or for help—it seemed so long since anyone had offered her help in return. And he'd not tried to *tell* her what she should be doing.

She tried to stop them, but a couple of tears began to run down her cheeks. She dashed her hands angrily across her eyes, looking anywhere but at the major. She had a sudden need to tell him everything and ask him what to do, but it was not his problem.

"It's nothing. Now you're back, Major, I need to show you what I've spent on the renovations..." Her attempt to change the subject was spoiled when she sniffed.

"Mrs MacKinnon?" the major said again, tipping his head and bending forwards so his face was level with hers. "The accounts can wait. That is not what is worrying you, is it?"

Charlotte sniffed again, then blew her nose.

"Sometimes talking about a problem can help you to see your way through it," the major said gently. "Perhaps talk to Mrs Thompson, or even Mrs Sergeant, if it is not something you can share with... anyone else?"

"I'll talk to Mary," Charlotte said, although Mary didn't really understand.

"Can I get you something? A drink? Brandy?"

She shook her head, taking deep breaths. A noise came from the library door, and she hurriedly wiped her eyes.

"Oh—I don't want Davie to see me crying," she said. "He's worried enough... besides, I never cry," she finished firmly, taking another deep breath.

"Of course not," A brief smile crossed his face. "I'll keep him busy for a few minutes. Go into the parlour until you are feeling more the thing."

"Thank you." Charlotte whisked herself into the parlour just as Davie came out of the library. She heard the major say something to him, then the door shut again behind them.

Damn the man! It would be easier to ignore the desperate wish to let him solve all her problems if he hadn't been so kind to her. She breathed deeply, calm gradually returning in the now-familiar surroundings of the parlour. Her father could not touch her here. It was harder to dismiss her need to be held, her desire for physical—

Stop it!

The clock on the mantelpiece struck two, and she resolutely got to her feet. She could not spend the day hiding. Back in the hall, she heard voices coming from the library; the major was still talking to Davie.

She hesitated. She wouldn't be able to concentrate on much if she stayed here, worrying about what her father would do as well as being distracted by the presence of the major. She had to know if her father was still in Edgecombe.

Taking a deep breath, she opened the library door. Davie stood with the major at a table near the window, looking at a large sheet of paper spread out there. They both looked round as she entered, and both smiled.

Charlotte swallowed. The major did have an attractive smile, when he used it.

"I… er…" Pulling her mind back to why she was here, she remembered that Davie was not to know she'd been upset. "I'm afraid I've just remembered something I forgot to put in my letter to Mr Berry," she said, crossing her fingers, her hand hidden in her skirts. "I need to hurry back to Edgecombe before the carrier collects the parcel."

Thankfully, neither of them questioned this. Davie's face fell, as his gaze turned back to the table.

"You don't need to come with me," Charlotte added, then glanced at the major. "As long as the major doesn't mind you staying?"

"Not at all. I was showing Davie the plans for the kitchen garden."

"Thank you," she said, managing a small smile as she turned and left. It was rude to rush off so quickly, but she didn't trust herself to remain calm if she stayed to make conversation.

Once in Edgecombe, she walked slowly towards the inn. There was no sign of her father's coach, but that did not necessarily mean he'd gone. She crept around to the back of the building, slipping into the kitchen. A scullery maid was washing dishes, and Mrs Minching was sitting at the table with a book of accounts open in front of her.

"Mrs Captain?"

"Mrs Minching. I... I wondered if—"

"'E's gone," Mrs Minching said, without ceremony.

Charlotte released a breath she didn't know she'd been holding.

"Funny thing," Mrs Minching went on, "Toby found 'e didn't 'ave a room free after all." She smiled, raising an eyebrow. "And no-one in the inn knowed exactly where you live."

"Thank you, Mrs Minching. He's really gone?"

"Toby sent Ben after 'im. Followed 'im most of the way to Wickwar."

That was a relief. He wouldn't give up, but she needn't worry about him at the moment.

CHAPTER 40

*M*atthew spent the next morning sorting out some of the books he'd sent from Farleton and arranging them by subject. He resisted the temptation to dip into them and so waste half the morning reading. Keeping his mind entirely on the task proved more difficult, as Mrs MacKinnon's brief tears the previous day kept coming back to him.

Although she'd said she was upset because of her father, he couldn't help wondering if *he'd* done something to upset her. He'd felt a strong urge to put his arm around her to offer some comfort, but she had regained her control very quickly, turning down all the help he'd tried to offer. Of course, there was no reason why she *should* wish to confide in him, was there?

He shook his head, turning to the next set of books.

Mrs Jackson brought a tray at lunchtime, and he realised his days of informal meals with Webb and the Jacksons were over now Birchanger had more staff. He wondered if Mrs MacKinnon still ate in the kitchen when she was here.

He ate his luncheon in the library, a book propped up in front of him, then went back to arranging his books. They only filled a few of the shelves, but he could write to Richard with a list of more to be sent. He'd do that later.

Finished in the library for the moment, Matthew wandered over to the dining room. The panelling and floor had been cleaned in here, and gleamed softly, but the walls above the panelling still had to be painted and there were no curtains at the windows. He could ask Mrs MacKinnon what colours she'd chosen next time she came, and perhaps she would still eat luncheon with him.

A knot formed in his insides as he wondered how much longer she would continue coming to Birchanger. Mrs Malplass didn't need any supervision, and the redecoration was almost finished. He needed to think up some other inducements.

Back in the library, he unrolled the plan of the kitchen garden he'd been looking at with Davie the previous day. Marking out the paths and beds would be a good geometry lesson for the lad.

He grinned—that would be a good start. Perhaps he'd ride over to see Squire Thompson later, and borrow the latest newspapers. He should really subscribe himself, so he sat down to write to Kellet. He'd take the letter into Edgecombe and ride to Northridge Hall from there.

Charlotte stood in her parlour window with a cup of tea. She should be working on the next batch of stories, but the words would not come today. Every time she tried, images of her father's angry face got in the way, or images of the major. Both set her pulse racing—for very different reasons.

She put her cup down and wrapped her arms around her body. Going back to Edgecombe yesterday to check whether her father had gone had just been an excuse to leave Birchanger, to escape from her tangled emotions. She could easily have asked Mary or Deacon to go.

As if the thought had conjured them up, Charlotte saw Mary and Deacon approaching up the lane, Mary's hand on Deacon's arm. Leaning closer to the window, she frowned, then raised an eyebrow.

Taking a man's arm was not unusual, although Mary wasn't the type to need such support. Walking so close that their shoulders were in contact was less usual. The two of them shared a smile as they approached the gate, a smile so intimate that Charlotte's breath caught. She turned away from the window, feeling she had intruded on something private.

Something I want.

She sat down again, determined to get at least a little work done, to concentrate hard enough to stop the thoughts spinning in her head. If she couldn't manage a story, she could at least list ideas for the next few instalments of the *Cotswold Diary*. There had been some agricultural journals in the boxes of books the major had sent from Farleton; perhaps he would allow her to borrow some to look for ideas.

That thought brought a pang of guilt. She should be at Birchanger today, organising things ready for the painters to start on the remaining rooms and helping Webb with the old ledgers. She would go tomorrow—hopefully she'd be in more control of her feelings by then.

Davie would be pleased; he'd protested at being made to sit in the kitchen with his Latin all morning.

Charlotte managed a few notes by lunchtime, but was pleased when the clock chiming one gave her an excuse to go into the kitchen. Davie had gone off somewhere, leaving his books stacked neatly at one end of the table.

Mary and Deacon sat together. A bottle of wine and three glasses stood on the table in front of them, but Charlotte didn't need that hint to know they had news to impart.

"We're calling the banns," Mary said, a huge grin on her face.

"Congratulations!" Charlotte said, pleased for them both. She swallowed, suppressing a sudden feeling of envy for their obvious closeness. "When are you planning on tying the knot?"

"In three weeks," Deacon said, his grin almost as wide as Mary's.

"This calls for a celebration," he added, pointing at the bottle. "Got this from Toby Minching."

He had the corkscrew ready and soon they were toasting the forthcoming marriage.

"We need to find somewhere to rent in the village," Mary said afterwards. "Closer to the bakery."

Charlotte nodded. That made sense. "You'll stay here as long as you need to," she said. "No point in rushing into a decision on where to live." She'd have to check her finances; the remaining tiara money wouldn't be enough to buy Mary out of her share of this house, but she should offer it. However, business matters could come later.

"Will your family be coming, John?" Charlotte asked. Mary had no-one else, she knew.

"I'm going to visit my family in Lancashire, ma'am," Deacon said. "Tell them the news in person. Some of them might want to travel down for the ceremony."

They talked for a while about possible places to rent, then Mary changed the subject. "There was one odd thing," she said. "The clerk who took the notice said he'd been asked to let a solicitor in London know if I called the banns. What would that be for?"

"Who wanted to know?" Charlotte asked.

"He didn't say. He wouldn't let me see the address."

"That's not normal, is it ma'am?" Deacon asked.

"I don't know. There's no reason why you cannot marry, is there?" Mary shook her head.

"Did he say *when* he'd been asked this?"

"About a week ago," Deacon said. "I reckon someone paid him, but I couldn't make him say who. He must be feeling guilty or he wouldn't have said anything at all."

"A week ago...?" Charlotte mentally counted back the days. Mrs Southam had called about a week ago. Perhaps the Mrs MacKinnon meant was her, not Mary? But why on earth would Mrs Southam be concerned with *her* marriage prospects? Only if—

No! That's ridiculous. She rubbed her face with her hand, feeling a blush rising in her cheeks. She'd had a difficult couple of days, starting with her father's visit, and now her mind was playing tricks.

"I suppose it's possible it was me they meant," Charlotte said. "But I don't have any idea why someone would ask after me, either." She hoped her expression did not give her away.

Mary opened her mouth, her eyes on Charlotte's face, then pursed her lips and said nothing.

"No matter," Charlotte added quickly, wanting to change the subject before Mary made any uncomfortable speculations. Sometimes her friend was *too* perceptive. "What are you going to get for a new dress?"

Charlotte and Davie set out for Birchanger after breakfast the next morning. As soon as they turned off the lane, Davie ran on ahead. Charlotte caught the odd glimpse of him through the trees, but he was soon well in front of her. Pausing to admire a bank of early primroses, she caught a flash of movement on the path behind her and turned to look properly. Nothing moved, and she put it down to the wind, or perhaps a deer.

As she walked up the drive to Birchanger Hall, she saw Davie following the major into the kitchen garden. Curious, she paused when she reached the door into the garden, and looked inside. The large sheet of paper Davie had been looking at last time he was here must be a plan, for the two of them were holding one end each, with the major pointing to parts of the plan, then to different sections of the garden.

Charlotte left before they spotted her. She greeted Mrs Jackson in the kitchen and left her cloak, then took her cup of coffee to the housekeeper's room to confer with Mrs Malplass. When they had decided which rugs and pieces of furniture needed to be moved to allow the painters to complete the remaining rooms, Charlotte went to help Webb with the ledgers.

She wasn't hiding from the major, not at all.

$\sim$

Matthew finished explaining the new layout of the kitchen garden to Davie, then sent him to ask Jackson to sort out pegs and string to start marking where the paths would be. When Davie arrived, he had said his mother was on her way, so she must be here by now.

Mrs Jackson confirmed that Mrs MacKinnon had indeed arrived, and was talking to the housekeeper. Matthew nodded, and requested a tray for two in the parlour when it was time for luncheon. Then he headed for the library. There was no point interrupting her work, but he was pleased that whatever had upset her two days ago hadn't prevented her returning.

"Will you join me for luncheon, Mrs MacKinnon?" Matthew asked, waiting by the door to the kitchen as she came out of the steward's office.

Mrs MacKinnon glanced at his face, then away again, a small crease between her brows.

Something is still wrong? He waved a hand at the kitchen table, which was rapidly filling up with the gardeners and the Jacksons. "I seem to have been evicted from the kitchen."

That last comment raised a small smile. *Good.*

"I... er, thank you, Major." She nodded, and they crossed the hall together. He'd left the newspapers he'd obtained from the squire at one end of the table in the parlour. Mrs MacKinnon looked at them, then at him, one eyebrow raised.

"I thought it was time I took an interest in the world beyond Birchanger," Matthew explained, holding a chair out for her. "I borrowed some recent copies from the squire. He said he misses your conversations."

"I... yes, it... I mean, it was useful for me to keep abreast of things, too, without the expense..." She looked down at the table, a faint flush reddening her cheeks. What had he said to make her blush like that?

"Perhaps you would like to take some of them away with you?"

Matthew offered. "Thompson said you used to do that when you visited him."

"Er, yes, thank you. As long as you have finished with them." She glanced at him briefly, but returned her gaze to the table. Odd—as far as he knew, he wasn't suggesting anything different from her previous routine with the squire.

Mrs Jackson brought a tray in, and set dishes out on the table. While they ate, Matthew described Davie's latest hidden mathematics lesson in the marking out of the kitchen garden. She smiled at that, then asked what he was planning to plant. He mentioned the agricultural advice Staines had given him, happy to find the conversation flowing more easily on such impersonal subjects. Although she did seem to spend a lot of time looking at her plate rather than at him.

"I wanted to ask if I may borrow some of the agricultural journals you sent back from Farleton," Mrs MacKinnon said when he'd finished talking about draining some of the upper fields.

"By all means. Take whichever ones you wish."

"Thank you. I... I thought they might give me ideas for... for some of the articles I write." She seemed ill at ease again, meeting his eyes only briefly.

"Borrow anything you wish from the library," Matthew said. He couldn't imagine most women being interested in any of the books he had here, but Mrs MacKinnon was not 'most women'.

"Thank you, Major. That is very kind." She stood as she spoke. "Thank you for luncheon."

Matthew stood too, and watched as she left the room. There was definitely something wrong—this was not the same woman who had seen off his stepmother. Something must have happened since then, but he had no idea what. Her problems with her father wouldn't make her ill at ease around *him*, would they?

He rubbed his hand through his hair. It could be worse—she could have declined to eat with him at all. He turned to the pile of newspapers. If she didn't come for them, he'd send a couple with Davie when the lad returned home.

CHAPTER 41

Matthew made his first appearance in St Peter's church in Edgecombe on the morning that Mary MacKinnon married John Deacon. The church was full—he guessed that the new Mrs Deacon was both well known and well liked in the village. Mrs MacKinnon acted as the bride's attendant, dressed in a dark green gown rather than her usual blacks. Unfortunately, he could only see her back view from the Birchanger pew, with most of her hair hidden by her bonnet.

He stood, sat, and kneeled at all the appropriate times, although his mind wasn't on the service. In the three weeks since he'd returned from Farleton, he'd seen Mrs MacKinnon on only a handful of occasions. He'd asked her to show him around the house to explain her plans for the remaining rooms, and persuaded her to eat luncheon with him a few times. The conversation then had been lively enough, once they had started discussing the newspaper reports on the progress of the war and the intentions of the new government in France. She took some papers away with her on the days she came to Birchanger, and Matthew sent them down with Davie or Tilly on the days when she did not. He'd have liked to take them down himself, to enjoy her company for a while in the warmth of the cottage kitchen, but he wasn't sure he'd be welcome.

When the newly-weds went into the vestry to sign the register, most of the congregation headed for the Hare and Hounds to celebrate. Toby Minching somehow managed to cram what seemed like the whole village into his pub. Matthew had paid for a couple of barrels of ale to help the wedding breakfast along, mostly as thanks for the excellent work Deacon had organised on his roof.

Matthew stayed at the inn for a while, talking desultorily with a few of the workmen he recognised from Birchanger. Mrs MacKinnon and Davie were present, too, but she sat with a group of village women and he didn't feel he could join her. He was a stranger to most of the people here, and soon felt they would be able to celebrate more enthusiastically without his presence.

As he left the inn to see about getting his horse saddled again, a groom rode up the road. Seeing Matthew, he asked if he was Lord Tillson.

"Letter for you, my lord," the man said, when Matthew nodded.

It was from Sir Vincent Kinney, in his role as magistrate, asking Lord Tillson to pay him a visit as a matter of urgency, although it gave no further details. Puzzled, Matthew considered ignoring it, but as the skies were now clear after the morning's rain he had little excuse not to go. Besides, the ride to Leverton Park would be a pleasant one, and Sir Vincent, although a bit of a slow-top, would at least be someone different to talk to. He asked the groom to tell Sir Vincent he would be along later that afternoon and rode back to the Hall to change.

Charlotte enjoyed talking with the village women for a while, trying not to let her eyes dwell on the major at the far side of the room. He looked uncomfortable, and she wasn't surprised to see him leave after less than an hour.

She did not stay much longer herself. She felt self-conscious talking in this setting with the village women, despite knowing all of

JAYNE DAVIS

them. Although they were used to asking her for advice, it was quite clear that the class distinction would never allow them to treat her as a friend. Besides, she did not want Davie exposed to the kind of drunken behaviour she was sure would follow the draining of the barrels of ale.

The new Mr and Mrs Deacon hadn't yet managed to find a suitable house to rent, so Charlotte and Davie were going to stay with Letty at Northridge Hall for a couple of nights to give them some privacy. They walked back to Upper Edgecombe to collect a small bag each to take what they would need, and for Charlotte to change back into her blacks.

There were still a couple of hours of daylight left when they set out again for Northridge. Charlotte turned to look back at the cottage for a moment as they walked down the lane. It had been her home for nearly ten years, and would continue to be so, but it would feel very different when Mary no longer lived there. She was very happy for Mary, but she would miss her company when the couple moved out.

She should really find another woman to live with her, she thought, turning into the path leading up through the woods. As a widow, it was acceptable for her to live alone, but she didn't want any gossip at all about her for the sake of Davie's future. Lost in thought, she didn't notice that Davie had been quiet for some time.

"Davie?" She stopped, and called again. There was a rustling off to one side, and Davie appeared from the trees with mud on his knees, and bits of twig and dead leaves sticking to his coat.

"I was tracking you, Mama," he explained, having the grace to look a little guilty at the state of his clothing. "Like the red Indians do…"

Charlotte frowned at the state of him, but it was too late now—he was already a mess. At least he had spare clothing with him so he wouldn't be a disgrace at the squire's.

She sighed. "You'd better give me your satchel to carry," she said, resigned, then put the strap over her shoulder. "Mantraps?" she asked, in sudden anxiety.

"They've checked this bit," he replied before he vanished again.

416

Rustling noises came from the undergrowth; there was an occasional sharp crack when Davie must have stepped on a dead stick, with some of the noises coming from one side and some from behind. She shook her head, wondering if she'd ever had so much energy when she was younger.

Charlotte crossed the Birchanger drive and carried on along the path leading to Northridge Hall, but she hadn't gone far when a horse whickered. She stopped to listen, tilting her head. She heard the noise again, not from the drive but from somewhere just ahead. She walked a bit further and listened again, finding the animal tied to a tree a few yards off the path. It was far enough into the trees to be hidden from anyone on the drive.

She frowned. It looked like the major's horse, and she thought she recognised the saddle bags as his, as well. If the major had tied it up on his way back to Birchanger, it must have been here for several hours. But surely he wouldn't have taken saddle bags down to Edgecombe for the wedding? Perhaps he had been back to the Hall and had been on his way somewhere else when he stopped.

The horse tossed its head and whinnied again. Charlotte realised it had been tied in a way that prevented it from reaching the ground to crop the grass. Why would the major leave his horse tied up so uncomfortably, so far from the drive?

Matthew's head pounded, pain radiating from the back of his skull. *Where am I?* He opened his eyes to darkness, and the feel of damp, still air. He was sitting, his back against a hard surface, his wrists above his head.

Trapped! His breath came fast, his pulse accelerating and turning the throbbing in his head to shooting pains.

No, I'm in England.

Think! He took a deep breath, then another. *England, not India!*

Dark? It could be night? *No, there's light, up there.* A thin line, above and in front of him. But too dark to see anything.

Why were his hands above his head? *A dream?* His fingers felt cold, colder than the rest of him. *I've never dreamt cold fingers before.*

He tried to bring his hands down towards his face. He could move them a little way, but then something pulled against his wrists and they would move no further. He tugged again. Although they must be fastened together he couldn't feel anything against his arms other than the tightness when whatever was holding him pulled taut.

Where am I?

Twisting his body round, he tried to move his hands far enough to feel behind him, but he couldn't reach anything. He shifted his weight, and something rustled beneath him. *Straw?*

Standing was difficult without being able to use his hands to push himself up, but he finally managed to grasp the rope holding his hands in the air, using it to pull himself to his feet. The movement made his head throb again, and pain shot up his left leg as he stood on it.

Gasping, he transferred his weight to his right leg. He gingerly tested his left leg again, adding weight then flexing his knee and ankle. The pain gradually eased. He couldn't be sure without being able to touch it, but it was probably bruised—nothing broken or sprained. He wriggled his fingers, feeling them gradually warm as his circulation returned.

When the pain in his head had eased to a dull ache, he realised there was now enough slack in the rope for him to feel the wall behind him. He turned around, running his hands over as much of it as he could reach. Hard, rough, with regular grooves.

Brick?

He tugged on the rope, hearing a creaking noise from somewhere above his head, but a series of sudden, hard pulls did nothing more than make his shoulders hurt. A smell of damp vegetation rose as his feet moved whatever was spread over the floor.

Straw? A stable?

Why did he think he was inside? No light around him, no breeze, no moving air. The rope must be fastened to a roof beam above him.

"Hello?" There was no distinct echo, but his shout reverberated as if inside a small building.

He shut his eyes, sinking back onto the straw. Somehow, the dark seemed less menacing if he tried to convince himself that it was dark because his eyes were closed, not because he was shut away. In a small space...

He was not back in that cell. He wasn't! He was fully dressed. His back didn't hurt. He could remember events *since* that hell-hole.

He *could* remember Birchanger, Richard arriving, mapping, Mrs MacKinnon. Those were *not* just dreams of what would happen when he escaped.

Not dreams. Dreams of escape wouldn't include failing to put a bullet through his brain on Christmas Day.

Who had put him here? And why?

Charlotte regarded the horse thoughtfully, then took pity on the beast and untied it, refastening the reins so it could crop the sparse vegetation. She heard footsteps behind her and turned, ready to ask Davie what he thought, but her words died in her throat as she saw two men coming through the trees. Her heart began to race as she took in the blond hair of the one in front. The deserter, Smith. Behind him was a burly man she did not recognise.

She waited, with tension knotting her stomach, hoping they would pass her by. That hope died when they stopped a few feet in front of her.

Smith gave a triumphant leer. "We'd like you to come along with us, Mrs MacKinnon," he said, with a politeness so overdone it was insulting.

"I think not," Charlotte said, tilting her chin up and forcing herself to sound both calm and firm. She turned to walk further along the path, moving at a normal pace in spite of the sick feeling in her stomach. Running would be useless; they could easily outpace her.

"I think *so*," Smith said, catching up and gripping one arm tightly enough to hurt. "You're coming with us."

"There were a nipper with 'er," the other man said.

"Well, he's not here now," Smith said. "Southam said nothin' about a brat."

"But if the brat saw..." The other man put an unshaven, ruddy face into Charlotte's, his foetid breath almost making her gag. "You got a brat with you?"

"It must have been one of the village children," Charlotte said, frightened for Davie now. She had no idea what the men wanted, but they must not get hold of her son as well. She hoped he didn't try to rescue her on his own.

Smith started moving, pulling on her arm.

"Let me go!"

"Can't do that. You're coming with us," Smith said again, continuing to force her onwards.

"Where are you taking me? Let me go!" She allowed her voice to rise to a shriek, hoping Davie was close enough to hear. "Someone will fetch help from the village. You won't get away with kidnapping me!"

"Shut up," Smith snarled. "I owe you for gettin' beaten by that one-armed fancy man of yours. Just keep your pretty little mouth shut, or I'll do it for you!"

"Can't do that," the other man said. "We're supposed to—"

"I know!" Smith snarled at him. "You keep your mouth shut too, Braddon. There's too much noise. We don't want anyone else to find them. Not yet."

Them?

"Where are you taking me?" Charlotte asked, pulling despite the painful grip on her arm and hoping they would give some information that Davie might hear. Davie fetching help was likely to be her only hope of escaping unharmed.

"You shut your mouth," Braddon said. He put a big, meaty hand close to Charlotte's face, as if he was about to cover her mouth. She pressed her lips together, trying to make it clear that she had stopped talking. Smith pulled on her arm again and she stumbled forwards.

"You really want this bitch if the plan don't work?" Braddon asked.

Cold spread though her body, making her hands clammy, as she recalled Smith's attack on Sally. It was just as well she wasn't prone to swooning. *Swooning?* If she did...

She let her body go limp and closed her eyes.

"Bugger!" Smith produced a string of profanity as Charlotte collapsed onto the path. She managed not to cry out as her elbow and hip hit stones on the ground and leaves and twigs pressed into her face. She lay as still as she could.

"What d'you do to her?"

"I didn't do nothin'!"

Something poked her hip. Perhaps one of them had prodded her.

"She still alive?" Braddon's voice.

"Yes."

"You'll have to carry 'er if she don't wake up."

"Me? Why me?" That was Smith.

"Why not?"

"You bring them bags, then. Don't want to leave nothin' lyin' around."

There was further muttering, then one of them grasped her arm and legs and slung her uncomfortably over his shoulder. One arm steadied her, his hand uncomfortably far up her thighs. She was glad she was wearing a thick skirt.

It took a real effort to stay limp, but she hoped one of them would reveal some information if they thought she could not hear.

She was bumped about painfully as the man walked; breathing was difficult as his shoulder dug into her stomach. Hoping she was not going to swoon in reality, she concentrated on breathing steadily, and the feeling of her bonnet gradually slipping off her head as the strings came loose.

CHAPTER 42

atthew didn't know how much time had passed, but his hands were beginning to grow cold and numb, so he struggled to his feet again. The throbbing in his head had eased. His leg, although still stiff and sore, held his weight. Rolling his shoulders eased the ache there; he flexed his arms to help the blood flow into his hands.

He moved his wrists to his face, touching his cheek. He felt a thin rope binding his wrists, but also a soft cloth wrapped around his arms beneath the rope. *Why would someone do that?*

Using his teeth, he worried blindly at the knots, but they had been pulled tight and he soon gave up.

His gaze shifted around his prison, trying to make out something, anything, in the darkness. The thin line of light he had seen earlier was no longer there. His pulse accelerated, blood pounding in his ears.

It's dark because it's night outside. This is not *Seringapatam.*

Breathing deeply, he reminded himself that it was too cold for India. There were no iron manacles around his wrists.

But he *was* helpless, and trapped, undoubtedly by someone who meant him harm. That part was no different. He rested his aching head on his bound arms and shut his eyes.

Deep breaths. Just breathe deeply.

He made another attempt to loosen the knots. He thought he detected a little movement in one strand, but his bonds didn't slacken, and further efforts made no difference. It would be easier if he could bloody well *see* what he was doing...

This is England. Not India.

He sat to rest his leg, stretching it out before him.

He would be missed—if not tonight, then by tomorrow. He wasn't hungry, or even thirsty, so it wasn't likely he'd been here for long. That meant they, whoever they were, couldn't have taken him very far. He *would* be found.

He flexed his left leg. If it was just bruised, moving it now and then might prevent it stiffening up too much.

Don't think about the hours ahead.

He would be in the dark for hours. It was cold, and getting colder. There would be no Webb or Reena to wake him.

Hours, not days. Remember that. He took more deep breaths.

He pushed away his memories of the stinking straw in that cell, the rats running over him...

Don't let the bastards win. Work out the hours. Count, then try the knots again.

Charlotte clenched her jaw to keep from crying out as Smith stumbled and lurched forwards. One of the men swore as Smith released his grip and she crashed to the ground, her shoulders hitting something hard enough to knock the breath out of her. Smith landed on her legs, crushing them painfully. She gasped, but managed not to cry out, then forced her body to go limp again.

"What the bloody 'ell are you doin'?"

"I tripped," Smith said defensively. "'Sides, we're nearly there."

"Right. Put 'er down by the door when we get there."

Door? In the middle of the woods?

Smith grabbed her and slung her over his shoulder again, staggering on at a slower pace. Without warning, she was dumped back on the ground, and reflexively put out a hand to break her fall. She glanced at the men, eyes only half-open. They weren't looking at her.

"Filled the bucket, did yer?" Braddon asked.

Smith grunted. "Yeah. Bloody long way down to the stream it were, too."

Why did they have a bucket of water in the middle of the woods? If they were going to use it to wake her up…

"Where am I?" she moaned.

"Damn, could 'a done with 'er stayin' out for a bit longer!" Braddon stuck his face in front of Charlotte. "Keep quiet," he hissed menacingly, the reek of his breath bringing bile to her throat. "Stay sittin' there."

Charlotte closed her eyes, fighting down rising panic and desperately hoping that Davie had run to get help. Braddon stood up. Charlotte sucked in a deep breath of clean air, then opened her eyes again. She felt she should try to run, but they would soon catch her again.

"Get the bloody door open," Smith said. "And we'll need the lantern. I'm not goin' to fill that damned bucket again if we miss."

Braddon grunted. She heard a flint striking, then saw Braddon placing a lit lantern beside a door in the hillside. He turned the key in a padlock and the hinges creaked as he pushed the door open.

The space beyond the door was dark.

Smith came over, putting his face close to hers with another leer. "Don't struggle, darlin', or I'll have you now—"

"Chuck 'er in," Braddon interrupted.

"I thought we wasn't supposed to—"

"Don't matter now. It'll look like he done it. And if he don't, we'll sort 'er out when we come back later. We got to get back to the inn and show ourselves now. Come on."

Charlotte stood as Smith approached. This time he grabbed one hand and twisted her arm behind her back. She gasped as pain shot through her shoulder. She tried to bend forwards to relieve the pressure, but his other hand grasped the collar of her coat.

"Quiet, darlin'," he hissed, jerking her trapped arm up to make his point and pushing so she had to move forwards. She heard him mutter under his breath as she stumbled over roots scarcely visible in the gloom beneath the trees. Then they were at the door.

The lamp Braddon held lit the stone floor of a passage. Her arms were freed, and a push in the small of her back sent her staggering forwards. She took one step, then felt nothing beneath her feet. She screamed as she fell, then pain shot down her left side as she landed. She gasped, winded and struggling to breathe.

Sucking in air, she heard words from the two men, a splash, then a shout of rage from further inside the building.

"Quick, lock the door." That was Smith's voice.

"Hang on—chuck them bags in, don't want them lyin' around."

A couple of thuds, then the light vanished. Blinking in the darkness, Charlotte pushed herself up, wincing at the pain in her bruised shoulder and hip. She moved her limbs tentatively, but could feel no further damage.

Then she became still. The unsteady breathing she could hear was not her own.

That shout—that hadn't been the two kidnappers. Even as the thought occurred, she heard a rustle of straw, the sound of movement, then a curse.

The horse—the major's horse. They had talked about a 'he'…

Matthew heard a metallic creak, then voices, too quiet or muffled to make out the words.

Rescue?

He suppressed a sudden flare of hope. It was more likely to be his captors returning. He struggled to stand, pulling on the rope above him. His ears registered footsteps, and a shriek cut short. Then a light flashed in his eyes and cold water drenched his face.

He gasped. Screwing his eyes shut, his weight was momentarily taken by the rope as he swung to one side, his wordless shout of rage ringing in the confined space. The rope he was pulling on suddenly came loose, sending him sprawling into the straw again.

Breathe, I can breathe...

For a moment he lay on the floor, unmoving, breathing hard. His initial panic faded as nothing further happened. The water was doing nothing more than soaking into his neckcloth and running uncomfortably down his chest.

There had been light...

Pushing himself to a sitting position, he rolled onto his knees and scrambled up on his feet. He moved in the direction he thought the light had come from, only to be brought up short as he tripped over the rope. Pain shot through his knees and bound wrists as he landed on something hard and rough, with sharp corners and edges.

He swore, sitting where he had fallen while the pains gradually lessened to aches. He held his breath for a moment as he heard a rustle to his right—someone else moving in the darkness.

"Major?"

A woman's voice, quavering with uncertainty.

"Major, is that you?"

A woman he knew. "Mrs MacKinnon?" *What is she doing here?*

"Yes." Her voice strengthened. "What's happening? Where are we?"

Matthew felt the obstacle he had run into, his bound hands making his movements clumsy. Steps, starting at thigh level.

"I don't know," he said. "I woke up here with a sore head. Are *you* all right?"

"I think so. What is this place?"

"An outbuilding?" he suggested.

"In the middle of the woods?"

"Ah." The steps and the straw began to make some kind of sense. "We're in the ice house."

The rope would have been fed through the pulley in the middle of the ceiling, normally used for hauling up ice blocks. Their captors must have released the other end of it before they left. He shook his head—he could puzzle that out later.

The room was silent for a moment before she spoke again.

"Are you hurt, Major? Your head?"

"Nothing to speak of. But my hands are tied. Until you were pushed in here, the rope was also attached to something in the roof."

"They untied you?"

"Not exactly. My wrists are still tied together, but no longer tied to anything else." Matthew heard her moving.

"Perhaps I could try?"

That sounded more like the efficient Mrs MacKinnon he knew. "A light would help. I don't suppose you have anything with you?"

"No, I'm afraid not."

He held out his bound hands in the direction of her voice. He was still standing at the bottom of the steps from where she had fallen, so she must be quite close. "It's quite safe to stand up," he said. "The roof is high."

"Oh, yes, of course."

After a moment he felt a touch on his arm. More touches followed as her hands explored until they came to the rope, then all he felt was an occasional pressure and pull on his wrists as she worked on the knots.

"Major, why are we here?" He could hear the return of doubt in her voice.

"I have no idea," Matthew said. "I set off to see Sir Vincent, then I woke up in here. I didn't see who attacked me."

"One of the men who brought me here was Smith," Mrs MacKinnon said, still trying to undo the rope. "He said... he wanted to..."

Her voice broke off, and he heard her take a deep breath as her hands stilled. He mentally cursed the rope that still prevented his hands from moving, and tried to put as much reassurance into his voice as he could.

"I won't let him hurt you, don't worry." How he was going to stop Smith, he didn't know, but he would. Somehow, he would.

He felt her hands moving again, until the tightness around his wrists slackened.

"There," she said at last, satisfaction in her voice

Matthew pulled his wrists apart and the rope unravelled. "Thank you." He stretched his arms out sideways, then backwards, trying to ease the stiffness. He couldn't help letting out a small groan as his cramped muscles protested.

"You *are* hurt!"

"Just stiff, that's all. Are you sure they did not hurt you? Did they push you in? Did you fall?"

"A few aches and pains, but nothing is broken."

"That's good. I doubt they left the door unlocked, but it would be as well to check."

He heard a faint murmur of agreement as he felt for the steps. Running his hands along the edge of the bricks, he worked out that he was to one side of the steps. The lowest point was to his left. Moving that way, he muttered a curse as he stumbled over something on the floor.

"Major?"

He crouched down and explored with his hands. Leather, a buckle, a strap.

"You had bags with you?" he asked.

"We were going to stay with Letty for a couple of days," she told him.

"We?"

"Davie was with me. I was carrying his bag—"

"They didn't get him as well?"

"I don't think so. Not while they were bringing me here."

"Davie's bag is the smaller one?"

"Yes."

Fumbling in the dark, he unfastened the straps on the smaller bag, felt inside, then tipped the contents out onto the straw, running his hands over them. A book, clothing, a couple of toy soldiers…

"Ah!"

"Major?"

"Candle ends," he said, with satisfaction, standing and placing them carefully on the bottom step. He pulled his tinder box out of his coat pocket and lit one. The small glow of light was immediately comforting.

"How did you know?" Mrs MacKinnon asked.

Her voice was close; he turned to see her surveying the small pile of her son's possessions. She had no bonnet, and her hair had partially come loose from its pins, strands of it tumbling down her back.

He dragged his attention back to her question, taking a deep breath before speaking. "He's a boy. And when we came here before, he had a candle end in his pocket." As he spoke, Matthew looked through the other items. He extracted a small knife before stuffing the rest back into the satchel and turning back to Mrs MacKinnon. She had sat down against the wall and was watching him, her arms wrapped around her chest.

"You're cold," he said, concerned. He shrugged out of his coat and draped it over her shoulders.

"You'll get cold," she protested.

"I'm all right," he stated. For the moment, at least. His wet neck-cloth was uncomfortable, so he unwound it and put it in his pocket.

He moved the candle to one corner of the bottom step, then lit a couple more. He scrambled up the steps and carefully made his way along the short passage to the door. He pushed at it but, as he expected, it didn't move. He tried to force it with his shoulder, but only once. His shoulder would give out long before the door.

Returning to the floor, he could see Mrs MacKinnon's face turned towards him, eyes wide in the candlelight.

"I'm afraid we can only wait," he said.

"Until they come back?"

"Until help arrives," he said firmly. He sat down on the straw beside her, back against the cold bricks. "Will you tell me exactly what happened? What they said?"

The light from the candles was enough to show movement beneath his coat. Rubbing her arms? Still cold? He hesitated for only a moment, before reaching over to feel in the pockets of his coat, finding his flask. He took a cautious sniff and then a taste to make sure it hadn't been tampered with.

"Have a drink, Mrs MacKinnon," he said, putting the flask into her hand. She obediently took a mouthful of the brandy, and then another, and he took the flask from her again.

"Better?"

"A little."

"There are some advantages to knowing drunken wastrels, after all," he said, smiling in the dim light.

Charlotte frowned. "You're *not* a drunken wastrel," she said. He'd never been a wastrel, and the 'drunken' was no longer accurate. "I know you better than that now."

"In that case, do you think you could drop the 'Major'?" he asked.

She glanced sideways; she could see that he was looking at her, but in the flickering shadows she could not make out the expression on his face. It wasn't proper to call him by his given name, but it would be much... friendlier. Now was not the time to worry about such things.

She rubbed her arms again. She *was* chilled, but that wasn't the reason for her shivers. With nothing she could actively do, her thoughts were returning to what might happen if those men found Davie in the woods. Or if Davie couldn't find help before the men returned.

"You *are* cold," the major—Matthew—said. He lifted one side of his coat and shuffled closer, stopping when their shoulders touched, and rearranged the coat so they were both beneath it.

She stiffened, catching her breath.

"I'm sorry to force the proximity, Mrs MacKinnon. We *will* be warmer together."

She couldn't deny the truth of that. Nor that the solid feel of his shoulder against hers, his thigh against her leg, were comforting as well as warming.

"Can you tell me what happened?" he asked again.

She leant her head back against the wall, describing briefly how she had been captured and carried here.

"You didn't see, or hear, Davie?" Matthew asked, when she had finished.

"No, not after they captured me."

"Good. He'll be bringing help."

Charlotte hoped he was right, but she was still worried for Davie's safety, alone in the woods in the dusk with those two men.

"Tell me again what they said. Word for word, if you can remember."

"Does it matter?"

"I'm trying to work out why we are here."

Charlotte thought, and repeated what Smith and Braddon had said, as well as she could from memory. The reminder of Smith's threat to 'sort her out' later made her shiver. "One of them said 'Southam,'" she finished.

She felt Matthew shifting, then his arm was around her, gently encouraging her to rest her head on his shoulder. He pulled his coat up and tucked it snugly around her neck. He must have thought she was shivering from cold.

She shouldn't allow it. Not only was it highly improper, but she was a grown woman, a mother. She should not *need* another person like this. But it was so good to be held, to have someone else who could take charge and do the worrying.

She wriggled slightly to get into a more comfortable position. His arm slackened, as if he were about to let go, then tightened reassuringly again when she made no further movement.

"I'm very much afraid you have been caught up in an attack on me," Matthew said, after a few moments of quiet between them. "You said they mentioned my brother's name. My coat still had money in it, and nothing else is missing as far as I can tell, so the motive is not robbery. Then there was the water they threw at me..."

A memory stirred in Charlotte's mind from the time of his illness. "Webb said you didn't like your face getting wet?"

"Something like that," he said. "I nearly killed my brother's valet when he put wet towels on my face. Webb had to knock me out to get me off the man."

"Richard's?"

"No. My other brother's valet—Charles—the one who's been stealing from the estate. It's possible he worked out I don't like being shut in the dark either, I did always sleep with the curtains open in London."

"It doesn't seem to be bothering you much at the moment," Charlotte commented, surprised at how calmly he was admitting such things. "How would your brother know Smith?" She felt his shoulders move as if he was shrugging.

"Smith's bearing a grudge," he said. "If Charles has been making enquiries locally they may have encountered each other. I can't think of anyone else who would have a motive for attacking me. Or you."

She recalled again some of the things Smith and Braddon had said, the implications of their words working their way through her head. "It sounded as if they wanted you to attack me. Why would they want that?"

"Charlotte—I would *never* do such a thing, I hope—"

"I know," she stated. "But what could your brother hope to achieve by it?"

She heard a sigh and felt the movement of his chest as he breathed out.

"All I can think of is that Charles is trying to get me to commit some crime, such as killing or harming you, for which I would be imprisoned or hanged." Matthew's voice held a tired note of resignation. "Or perhaps to get me certified as insane and so be able to take control of the family finances."

CHAPTER 43

"*B*ut that's... evil!"

Matthew could clearly hear the horror in her voice as she stiffened in his arms.

"Yes," he said. He didn't want to believe it—Charles was family, after all—but what other explanation could there be?

"And when those men find you haven't harmed me, they'll make things look as if you had when they come back for us?"

"It's possible," he admitted. It was almost certain, in fact. He hoped she had not worked out the next implication. A living Charlotte would be a witness, so she was in as much danger from Charles as he was.

"Matthew, why aren't you bothered by the dark now?"

He closed his eyes for a moment. *Good! Keep her talking about other things.*

"We have the candle," he pointed out. "In any case, it's never so bad when someone else is with me."

Someone alive, to be more accurate.

He suspected it might also have something to do with having this woman nestled against him, his body and most of his brain focussed on more pleasant, if extremely improper, thoughts.

He made an effort to concentrate on their current predicament. "They will be expecting me to be maddened, or panic-stricken, and you to possibly be injured. We are not. And Davie—"

"They won't have caught him, will they?"

He could only hope not. That, however, wasn't what she needed to hear. "If he's the lad I think he is, he will have followed to see where they were taking you. You—or the men—didn't hear or see him?"

"No."

"I think if they had seen him, or captured him, you would have known. He will have gone to find help."

"Everyone's at Mary and John's celebration," Charlotte said. "The men said they were going back there. They might have caught up with him in the woods."

"No, no. He'll be perfectly safe." He remembered the two remaining mantraps, but said nothing. Davie was a smart lad, with enough sense to watch and wait rather than spring into impulsive action. The last thing Charlotte needed was further doubt. "They probably set off as soon as they'd pushed you in here—Davie would still be watching. *He'll* be following *them*. He knows these woods like the back of his hand."

He wondered how long that would take. As he felt in his waistcoat pocket for his watch, his hand accidentally brushed against the front of her dress. He heard a short indrawn breath as he jerked his hand away.

"I'm sorry. My watch is in my pocket." His face flushed with embarrassment even as his heart beat faster. He hadn't intended to touch her, not there. She hadn't pulled away, so hopefully she was not too offended.

He retrieved the watch, tilting it to catch the faint candle-light.

"It's nearly six o'clock," he said. "Most of the Birchanger staff will probably still be at the celebrations." He thought for a moment, estimating times. "It can't be much more than half an hour since you arrived—possibly less. Davie could take around an hour to get back to Edgecombe, longer if he tries to find help at Birchanger first." Perhaps best not to remind her that Davie would soon be making his way in the dark.

"Then half an hour more for help to get back here; plus time for him to tell his story and for Webb to decide what to do." And to try to sober up a little, no doubt. "I'm afraid we are likely to be here for another two or three hours."

"What if those men come back first?"

"You said they had to show themselves at the inn? They'll be establishing an alibi. They'll want to stay until late to do that, so help should arrive first." It was a reasonable deduction, and he hoped it would hold true. "We'll hear them opening the lock. Neither of us is in the state they'll expect."

She took a deep breath.

"What can we do?" Her voice was determined, and he smiled. This was the practical Charlotte he'd come to know.

"I took a knife from Davie's bag, and there's the rope. There may also be some bits of brick we could use. I should look..." He was reluctant to move.

"Oh, yes." She straightened, drawing away from him. "Should I try to undo the rest of the knots in the rope?"

"If you can see well enough." Matthew pushed himself to his feet. He handed Charlotte the rope, then used his hands to sweep away some of the straw near the steps. The floor beneath the covering was stone-flagged, and clear of any bits of brick or stone he might be able to use as a weapon.

He muttered a curse. Jackson had been too damned efficient at getting the place cleaned out before laying the fresh straw. To be certain, he moved around the edges of the space, shuffling the straw to the side with his boots, but found nothing.

"What will we do with this?" Charlotte asked, holding the rope out.

"Hold the rope across the steps, and pull it tight when they come in. It should trip at least one of them." They would be easier to deal with on the ground. "Can you do that?"

"I think so, yes. Did you find anything?"

"I'm afraid not."

"What about the bags?" she suggested. "You could swing Davie's satchel at them?"

Matthew picked up the satchel, hefting it. It wasn't really weighty enough to make a decent weapon.

"My bag has some books in it," she said, opening it and rummaging around. "Will they help?"

"Indeed they will." Their fingers touched as he took the books from her, his pulse accelerating at the feel of her skin.

Concentrate!

Putting the books in the satchel, he fastened it and swung it experimentally. It might do—it could at least put one of the men off-balance long enough for him to use the knife or his boots. Perhaps Charlotte could take the satchel, leaving him with both hands free.

He turned to make the suggestion, and his words went unspoken. Charlotte was twisting her shoulders back and forth, one hand rubbing her neck, then she stretched her hands above her head. Matthew couldn't tear his eyes away from her face and the smooth line of her neck, pale in the flickering light. She lifted her hands to her hair, picking out bits of straw, then gathered the loose strands and wound them back into a knot, her breasts lifting enticingly under her gown.

She gave a final pat to her hair and Matthew looked away hurriedly, his heart racing uncomfortably. He sat against the wall, in their original position facing the steps, keeping his gaze firmly on the straw in front of him. She sat next to him, resuming her position with her head on his shoulder. He pulled the coat across them both again, wanting to thread his fingers through her hair, to pull her towards him. With great restraint he restricted himself to brushing bits of straw off her shoulders.

"More straw?" she asked, her voice sounding slightly sleepy. "I must look like an old witch indeed!"

Her body shook against his. *Laughing? I hope so...*

"I only saw your boots and dress," Matthew protested. He couldn't recall now what had prompted those unjustified and ungentlemanly thoughts. He was just thankful she now found it amusing.

"That was my oldest dress. The one I use for gardening."

"The first time I saw you properly, I knew you were not what I had thought."

You were... you are, beautiful. The words almost came out, and he closed his mouth firmly. In this situation, such words could be misconstrued. They reflected his wishes, not his intentions.

She said nothing more, and he heard her breathing deepen, grateful for the trust she was showing by letting him hold her like this. He leaned his head on the wall behind, wishing this moment would last in spite of the cold, the damp straw, and Charles' evil plan. She was beautiful, but that wasn't the half of it.

Birchanger Hall had looked like a home when he returned from Farleton. It felt like a home, too, on the days when she was there. She made it a place he wanted to be, where he could be happy. Birchanger was filling up with servants, but it would be empty without Charlotte's presence.

He looked down at her head, tucked against his shoulder, wanting to stroke her hair, but afraid to wake her. He hoped Webb would be needing help for some time to come.

Then her head slipped downward as her body relaxed further. The movement woke her.

"I can't believe I went to sleep," Charlotte said, her voice low. "That doesn't seem right."

"Shock, or a sudden fright, often has that effect." He shifted a little in the straw, and she drew back.

"I'm sorry," she said, her gaze resting on his face for a moment, then away. "I'm warmer now. I... I'll just move—"

"It's not going to get any warmer in here," he said. "Stay under the coat. You should sleep if you can." Sleep was the last thing he was thinking about.

"I never can sleep well sitting up," she said, her voice hesitant.

"You could lie down," he said, doubtfully. "The straw is rather damp, though." He paused, knowing what he wanted, but not sure he should suggest it. The suggestion came out anyway. "Sit on my lap, I'll stop you slipping down if you fall asleep again. We'll be warmer together under the coat."

For several moments she was still, then she moved closer. He released a breath he hadn't realised he'd been holding. Putting his hand out to guide her, he helped her settle across his lap. His left arm curved around her body, supporting her as she rested her head on his shoulder.

"Thank you, Matthew," she whispered.

"My pleasure," he said. She couldn't know how true that was. It was a pleasure to hear his name on her lips; a pleasure holding her. He hoped the layers of clothing between them were thick enough to conceal the effect she was having on his body.

"Are you sure you're comfortable?" she asked, her breath warm on his neck.

No.

"Yes." he said. "Try to rest. I'll wake you as soon as I hear anything."

He loved the feel of her weight on his legs and the feel of her in his arms, the soft pressure of the side of her breast against his chest, and the faint scent of something floral from the hair tickling his face.

Jumbled memories wandered through his mind as he looked down at her face. He pictured coming across her in a dusty dress looking over the pile of furniture in the main hall, making one of her lists. He was entranced by the way she tilted her head slightly when she was thinking, and the warmth in her eyes when she was not-laughing at him conjured a matching warmth within him.

He shifted slightly when his legs began to numb. She wriggled, steadying herself by slipping an arm under his coat and curling it around his waist. The pressure of her hand against his body felt good —so good he worried that she *must* be able to feel what she was doing to him, even through her skirts.

He put his hand up to her hair again, wanting to feel it under his fingers. He tucked an errant curl behind one ear. He couldn't resist stroking her face with his fingertips, then again with the backs of his fingers. Heat washed through him at the feel of her skin.

In the faint, flickering light, he saw her face turn up to his, her eyes open and wide. He pulled his hand away, guilt overriding his ardour. Instead of protesting, she lifted her own hand, laying her palm against his cheek. He closed his eyes and swallowed hard, involuntarily drawing her closer to him.

Her hand lifted, leaving him bereft until it touched the back of his head, gently pulling him down towards her. Praying he had not misinterpreted her intent, he bent his head until his lips were close to hers.

Charlotte woke slowly, breathing in the scents of the man holding her: soap, a faint aroma of wool from his clothing, and a trace of the brandy they'd shared earlier. The strong arm at her back was comforting, safe.

Matthew.

A wonderful warmth flooded through her. She shifted slightly, moving her hand against his shirt, warm from the flesh beneath. She turned her head, wanting to see his face, and the unbearably gentle touch of his fingers stroking her cheek sent a wave of pleasure through her body.

No one had touched her in that way for far too long. Whatever notions of propriety and decorum she might still have clung to vanished without a trace; there was only now, and only this. She laid her palm against his cheek, feeling the prickle of stubble rough against her skin.

She wasn't thinking. Her hand seemed to move to the back of his head its own accord, curving around the back of his skull to draw him down. A request, a demand? His breath came faster as their lips met, her heart hammering in her chest. The feel of his free hand tangling in her hair added to the heat inside.

Too long...

The kiss could have lasted seconds, or hours. He drew back, slowly. She reluctantly released her hold on the back of his head, resisting the impulse to demand more. She thought he might speak, but he just rested his forehead on hers.

She wanted him to kiss her again, but the sensible—annoying—

part of her brain started to work. *A decent woman doesn't demand a gentleman's kiss.*

The admonition had surprisingly little effect on her body or emotions. Perhaps she'd been too willing to hide away in the cottage with Davie and Mary, assuming that most marriages would be like her parents', or her aunt's.

Not all men were like that. *This* man was not like that.

A rattle interrupted her thoughts. At first, she wondered if her ears were conjuring sounds after the long silence below ground. The next rattle was louder, and Matthew lifted his head.

"Charlotte," he whispered urgently. "The rope..."

She took a deep breath, pulling her arm from his coat and taking his arm as he helped her to her feet. The door rattled again.

"Major! Major, sir, are you in there?" It was Webb. She almost collapsed in relief.

"We're here, Webb," Matthew shouted. "Break the lock if you have to!"

"Goin' to shoot it off, sir."

The shot didn't sound very loud from inside the ice house, and it was followed by a few blows that must have been from a rock or the butt of Webb's pistol. The door burst open and lantern light shone in.

"You all right, sir?" Webb asked. "Mrs MacKinnon, are you there?"

"Here, Sergeant," she said, then Davie pushed Webb aside, almost toppling him off the steps, and rushed down onto the straw.

"Mama!" Davie found her in the dim light and wound his arms around her waist, clinging on tightly.

"I'm fine, Davie. Well done for fetching help!" She crouched down to his level, pulling him into a hug again. She could feel his shoulders shaking a little and guessed he was crying, so she found a handkerchief in a pocket and gave it to him.

"Mrs MacKinnon?" Matthew attracted her attention. "Ma'am, Webb says we need to be gone from here quickly. Are you ready to go?"

"Yes, of course."

"Davie, you did well," Matthew said. "Can you go up and wait outside? Just for a minute or two."

Davie gave a final sniff, then nodded. Matthew lifted him up to the bottom of the steps and he climbed out. Matthew picked up the two bags and put them partway up the steps. He collected the rope and the cloth that had been around his arms and threw those up too, even prying the candle-ends from the bottom step.

"Why—" Charlotte started to ask, but stopped mid-sentence. This wasn't the time for questions.

"I don't want it to look as if we've been here," Matthew said. "I'll explain later."

Charlotte spotted a few hairpins glinting in the lantern light. She picked them up, then let Matthew help her up the steps. Deacon had another lantern, and was holding Matthew's horse.

"You all right, ma'am?" Deacon asked anxiously.

"No real harm done," she said, trying to convince herself as much as him. She moved out of the way to allow Matthew and Webb to come out behind her. They closed the door and rested a rock against it to keep it shut.

"Mrs MacKinnon, can you walk as far as Birchanger, do you think?" Matthew asked.

"Yes." The effects of the kiss were still fizzing in her blood.

"Good." He looked around. "Webb, you take Davie on the horse— we'll have to follow the main path and hope we're clear of it before anyone else comes up."

CHAPTER 44

*C*harlotte sank onto one of the kitchen chairs, thankful to take the weight off her feet. Davie came over to her and she pulled him onto her lap.

"Coffee, ma'am," Mrs Malplass said, putting a cup down in front of her, then glancing at Davie. "Shall I get him some hot milk?"

"Thank you, yes. But where are Sally and Mrs Jackson?"

"They're all down in Edgecombe. Jackson came back up just now."

She looked around. Matthew, Deacon and Webb were sitting at the table with hot drinks in front of them, while Mrs Malplass was busy putting more water on the range.

Charlotte thought she should be relieved now she was safe, but she could feel herself on the verge of tears. She swallowed hard. She would *not* cry now. She hugged Davie a little tighter.

"If you can hang on a little longer, Mrs MacKinnon?" Matthew put a hand on her shoulder. It felt reassuring and comforting, and she struggled to resist the urge to rest her head against his arm.

"I think you need to hear this." His voice was encouraging, but his face was grim. "Webb?"

"Sir. There was a couple o' men in the private parlour upstairs at the pub, while we was all drinkin' downstairs. One of 'em came out to call for Minchin'. It were your brother, like I told you." Webb took another mouthful of coffee.

"Mrs MacKinnon needs to hear it too, Webb. My brother Charles, not Richard?"

"Yessir. But Minchin' didn't know who 'e was, 'e never give his name. Seems a Captain Beauchamps 'ired the room—not long after you left, it must'a bin. They was 'avin' a meal and wine and the like. Another nob... er... gentleman come while we was there."

Charlotte wondered who Captain Beauchamps was. She noticed one of Matthew's eyebrows rise when he heard the name.

Webb continued his story. "I asked Mrs Minchin' to take in their next drinks, 'stead o' the girl, but she couldn't 'ear what they was sayin'. But she said the new bloke were Sir Vincent Kinney. She reckons the other two was tryin' to persuade 'im to do somethin'."

"Major, didn't you say you were going to see Sir Vincent?" Charlotte asked, frowning.

"Yes. He sent me a note." He felt through his pockets, then got up to search the pockets of his greatcoat. "It's not there."

"You said nothin' were missin', sir?"

"That's right, Webb. Just the note."

"So, mebbe it weren't Sir Vincent what sent it?"

"That is beginning to seem very likely. Go on, Webb."

"Well, not long after that Smith come into the taproom, and another I didn't recognise. You know him, Deacon?"

Deacon shook his head.

"Anyways, just after they come, young Davie found me. 'E must 'ave seen Smith in there, cos 'e crept in real quiet and told me what 'appened. And 'e brung your 'orse so I could ride, but that meant you was likely caught as well. I reckoned it must be somethin' to do with your brother, sir, so I thought it wouldn't do to make a big fuss—and anyhow, young Davie said 'e knew where Mrs MacKinnon was so we didn't need a search party."

Charlotte looked down at her son, still sleeping on her lap, and was overwhelmed with thankfulness that he was not only unharmed, but had been so brave and sensible. The need to hug him tightly was strong, but she didn't want to wake him.

Webb was still talking. Although she was tired, she forced herself to focus on his words. She *did* want to know why she had been kidnapped.

"...groom from Wickwar, said 'e were sent up to Edgecombe by the blokes in the parlour with a message for you, sir. They must 'a come up to Edgecombe themselves not long after 'im." Webb took another mouthful of his coffee. "You said somethin' about Sir Vincent when 'e give you the note, but Sir Vincent weren't one of the men what give it 'im. So I reckoned your brother was up to no good, what with not showin' 'is face and not givin' 'is name."

Charlotte followed Webb's recital with difficulty, but the main point seemed to be that Charles Southam *was* responsible. She glanced at Matthew's face; he was frowning, and rubbing the back of his head.

Angry? She didn't know how she would feel if one of her sisters had done such a thing. Sad perhaps, as well as angry.

"Mrs Malplass?"

Matthew was looking beyond Charlotte, towards the housekeeper still standing by the range.

"My lord?"

"Before you left London, was there any servants' talk about me?"

"Talk, my lord?"

"I want to know what was being said, Mrs Malplass. Don't worry about passing on gossip—that is exactly what I want to hear."

"Well..."

Matthew nodded encouragingly.

"Gregson, Mr Southam's valet, said you attacked him. For no reason, he said. And Mr Southam—Mr Charles, that is—some of the maids heard him saying things about you to Mrs Southam. Nothing specific, like, just complaining and saying things were all your fault, that kind of thing."

Matthew nodded, as if he already suspected what Mrs Malplass told him.

"Thank you, Mrs Malplass. Now I know it isn't one of your normal duties, but could you please go to my room and lay out a clean set of clothing—as you can see, I am slightly the worse for wear and I am expecting visitors soon. Some water for washing, please, and see that the fire in the parlour is still going."

Charlotte heard the woman's footsteps cross the kitchen, then the door closed behind her. Mrs Malplass had confirmed that Matthew's brother knew about the valet incident. That did explain the bucket of water.

She shivered at the evil intent behind Charles Southam's plan. Who was the other man? "Major, who is the other man Webb mentioned?"

"Beauchamps?" He looked at her, then Webb. "If it's the same man... You didn't see him, Webb?"

Webb shook his head.

"Captain Beauchamps was on the ship back from India," Matthew explained. "He took rather too much interest in a young lady on board. Webb and I helped the ship's officers prevent him from seducing her."

He shrugged, running one hand through his hair. "I suspect he holds a grudge. He may even have sought me out in London, and found my brother instead."

Charlotte nodded, checking on Davie again as Matthew related their conclusions about the plot to Deacon and Webb.

"...imagine Sir Vincent has been summoned to be a witness, as the local magistrate." He ran a hand through his hair again.

"We could get Smith and that other one at the ice 'ouse," Webb suggested. "There's three of us, if we leave Jackson to guard 'ere."

"No, I think it is better to pretend that nothing happened at all. If we capture them, there will be talk."

There would indeed, Charlotte thought. Nothing as exciting as a kidnapping had happened in Edgecombe in all the years she'd lived there. Exciting if you weren't part of it, that is. She rubbed her free hand across her eyes. There had been gossip enough when she'd first moved to the village, a woman with a child and no husband. Some would recall that, and would delight in resurrecting the old whispers about illegitimacy...

"Mrs MacKinnon—are you all right?" Matthew's brow was creased in concern.

She swallowed hard, looking up at his face. "Yes." That came out too faintly, so she tried again. "Yes, thank you. I'm just tired. Avoiding gossip is the best plan, if it can be done."

Gossip could harm him, too, she supposed, although the unfairness of life meant that women usually got the blame for... improper behaviour. Heat rose in her cheeks as she recalled their kiss, and she forced her gaze away from his mouth, thankful he was listening to Webb and not looking at her.

"You just lettin' 'im get away with it, sir?" Webb asked.

"Not if I can help it—but we can think about that later." He paused for moment, staring into space. "Here's the plan," he went on. "So far, the only people who know we were locked up in the ice house are the people here, and Smith and Braddon. No-one will take their word against mine, so it's Sir Vincent we need to concentrate on."

It made sense to Charlotte. Webb and Deacon, too, nodded in agreement.

"I think they will call here with the expectation that I am absent. They would then find my horse—accidentally, as far as Sir Vincent is concerned—and pretend to search the woods. Smith would have arranged to remove all traces of foul play on their part." He glanced at Charlotte, rubbing his wrists reflectively. "They even thought to pad the rope so there were no marks on me to show I'd been tied up. But if I am here, then it can go no further."

Charlotte shivered again, making Davie stir this time. Matthew hadn't explained what Sir Vincent would have seen, had the plan worked, but Smith's leer and his threats came back into her mind.

Matthew's hand was on her shoulder again, comforting. He hadn't slept, he'd spent part of the afternoon tied up, yet he seemed now not to be affected by it.

I'm safe now. It isn't going to happen.

"Mrs MacKinnon—are you up to going back to your home?"

Charlotte looked up, then back at Davie.

"It is possible that after the story my brother may have spun, Sir Vincent will want to check that you are safe," Matthew explained. "It is best if he finds you at home. Deacon will go with you."

Charlotte just wanted to crawl into bed and hide from the world for a while, but he was right.

"I can carry the lad, ma'am," Deacon said.

"All right. Letty—Mrs Thompson—might send to see if I am safe. I am already far later than she was expecting me." She shook Davie's shoulder to wake him. "I could say Davie was taken ill?"

Davie yawned, then stretched, and she set him on his feet. "I take it we should not be starting off down the drive?"

"You might meet them on their way here."

Charlotte nodded. "If we go down to the cottages, there's a path from there. We'll find it."

Matthew looked worried. "You can stay here if you wish, naturally, but—"

"No. As you said, it is best if I go home." She got to her feet, slightly revived by the coffee and the rest.

"Best be off, then, ma'am," Deacon said.

"John—I'm so sorry about breaking up your wedding night—"

"Don't worry about that ma'am. I wouldn't be in a position to be wed if it wasn't for you and the work his lordship gave me."

"Leave the bags," Matthew said as she moved to pick them up. "I can have them brought down in the morning."

Charlotte thought for a moment, then agreed.

"Mrs MacKinnon, I can't tell you how sorry I am you have been caught up in this mess—"

"It's not your fault, Major. None of it is your fault." She shook her head slightly and turned to follow Deacon.

Matthew watched Charlotte leave, wishing she did not have to walk further in the dark after her ordeal, or that he could go with her and make sure she was safe.

He shook his head. Deacon would look after her. Smith and Braddon, if they were wandering the woods, would be in the opposite direction, near the ice house.

Concentrate, man!

He turned, seeing Webb and Jackson waiting for orders.

"Jackson, get the horse unsaddled, please. Webb—powder? *Dry* powder? Just in case we need it."

Webb didn't argue this time, but disappeared in the direction of the cellar.

In his room, he found that Mrs Malplass had laid out a change of clothing and set a bowl of water by the fire to warm. He stripped off his dirty clothes, kicking them under the bed for now. He couldn't imagine why Charles might come to his bedroom, but it was best to have them out of the way just in case.

He dipped a cloth in the water and wiped himself down, concentrating on the visible parts, his face and hands. Checking there was no mud left, he dragged a comb through his hair.

His hand stilled for a moment, remembering the feel of Charlotte's hair on his skin. He breathed the faint scent from the bowl of pot pourri on the chest, another reminder.

Guilt washed over him, and he closed his eyes. *Did I take advantage?* She hadn't struggled; she had even returned his kiss.

At least, he thought she had.

Get on with it, Southam. Charles will be here any minute.

Did he need to shave? Rubbing his chin brought back the feel of her hand on his face. *Had she wanted that kiss?* God, he hoped so.

Dragging himself back to the present, he decided there was no time for a shave, and probably no more stubble than usual for this time of day in any case. He towelled himself dry, then dressed.

CHAPTER 45

The knock on the front door came as Matthew was putting the finishing touches to his neckcloth. He grabbed his coat and the book from his bedside table, took the stairs at a run with Reena trotting behind him, and reached the hall just as Webb emerged from the kitchen.

Webb looked at him in enquiry.

Matthew shrugged himself into his coat, pulling his shirt sleeves down, and gave Webb a nod.

Good man! Webb had already set out a decanter and glass on a side table. He put the book on the table open and face down, as if he had been interrupted while reading it, then poured himself a glass of brandy. Reena settled herself by the fire.

Listening carefully, he could make out the sound of voices, then footsteps and a knock on the parlour door, still ajar.

"Some gentlemen to see you, my lord," Webb said. "Are you at 'ome?"

Matthew surprised himself by smiling—he remembered trying to explain the concept of being 'at home' to Webb some time ago.

"Who is it, Webb?"

"Man says 'e's your brother, sir. And Sir Vincent Kinney and a

Captain Beauchamps. Jackson's taken their three 'orses round to the stables."

That meant the three men waiting for admittance were the only ones. Smith and the other man had presumably gone to make sure that things in the ice house would look bad for him. He gripped the glass hard, fury rising again at what they'd planned to do.

Webb was still looking at him. Matthew took a deep breath; he must act as if nothing out of the ordinary had happened.

"Show them in, Webb." He rose as his visitors entered, brandy glass still in hand.

"Gentlemen—how may I help you?"

Matthew was gratified to see Charles frowning. He couldn't tell if his brother was angry, but he *did* seem confused. And yes, this Captain Beauchamps *was* the same man he had kept from molesting Miss MacLeod on the *Amathea*. He, too, looked annoyed. Sir Vincent looked from Matthew to Charles and back again, his brows starting to crease into a frown.

Webb took up a position by the door, trying to look butler-like and doing very well, apart from his muddy boots.

"How may I help you?" Matthew asked again, when no-one answered his first query. "Charles, you pay me a visit at last!" The bonhomie in his voice sounded false to his own ears, and Charles would not believe it, but Sir Vincent was the one to be convinced here. "Do take a seat, gentlemen."

"Tillson." Sir Vincent tipped his head in acknowledgement and sat down.

"Brandy, Sir Vincent?" Matthew offered politely.

"Don't mind if I do." Sir Vincent said, taking the proffered glass. "Thanks, Tillson."

Charles sat, his gaze flicking from one piece of furniture to the next, then to the carpet.

"Admiring the furniture, Charles?" Matthew asked, unable to resist needling his brother. "There were some lovely pieces that came with the Hall, just needed a little polishing up." The look on his brother's face confirmed their earlier supposition that Charles had been here before, when the best furniture had been in storage.

Silence fell. Matthew waited for Charles to speak, but it was Sir Vincent who broke the uncomfortable silence.

"Tillson, you are well?"

"Why, yes, Kinney. Thank you for asking." Matthew's gesture took in the room. "Enjoying my new property, now I've got my staff organised."

Sir Vincent just nodded, turning to face Charles. "Seems you've brought me on a fool's errand, Southam," he said angrily. "All the way from Leverton to Wickwar, then up to Edgecombe and now to here. What the hell do you mean by it? I've better things to do than traipse all over the countryside at night for nothing!"

"Whatever is the matter, Kinney?" Matthew said, remembering that he was supposed to have been here all afternoon and evening. "Is something wrong?"

"Got a note from Southam there," Sir Vincent nodded towards Charles. "Says he's your brother?"

"My *half*-brother, yes."

"The note said he was worried about you. And..." He ground to a halt.

Matthew wondered exactly what Charles had said. "Do go on."

"He said he was worried about Mrs MacKinnon."

Matthew raised his eyebrows. "Really? Why come to me, then?" He was fascinated to see Sir Vincent's face gradually turning red.

"Dammit, Southam!" Sir Vincent said, turning to Charles. "*You* can repeat the farrago of nonsense you told me!"

"Really, brother, you are not being very welcoming," Charles started, ignoring Sir Vincent.

"So sorry, Charles." Matthew got up and poured two glasses of brandy, handing one to his brother and one to Beauchamps. "I assumed you'd help yourself, as usual."

He heard a faint snort from the direction of the door. The others appeared to have heard nothing. When he looked round Webb was still in his butler pose, gaze fixed expressionlessly on the far wall.

"Now then, Charles. To what do I owe this... brotherly concern?"

Charles took a mouthful of brandy before answering. "Mama visited you last month, but you were not here. There was a most encroaching—" He suddenly stopped.

Remembering the letter he'd had from Charlotte, Matthew suppressed a smile. "Do go on, Charles," Matthew said encouragingly

"Yes, well. Mama met a Mrs MacKinnon here—"

"Here?" Sir Vincent asked sharply.

"Why, yes, Sir Vincent, Matthew said. "Mrs MacKinnon acts as a secretary for me a couple of days a week."

Sir Vincent frowned.

"She comes for a few hours each week, that is all. While I was away she was supervising the renovations. She is very efficient, and has helped to make sure the staff I take on are all respectable." Matthew made sure he sounded suitably respectful.

He turned to his brother. "Charles, you were about to tell us why you are concerned about Mrs MacKinnon?"

"I... er..." Charles recrossed his legs, his hands fidgeting with the brandy glass. "Well, Beauchamps here said he sailed back from India with you."

"On the same ship, certainly."

"Said you'd made improper advances to a girl on the ship. When I heard, I was worried you might... and you attacked my valet. I was worried in case you might attack—"

Matthew put his brandy glass down with a snap. "Is that what he told you, Kinney?"

"More or less," Sir Vincent admitted, looking puzzled.

"Very well. Allow me to set you both straight on the matter. If you doubt my word, Kinney, Charles, you may apply to the ship's first officer for corroboration. I can supply you with his name and the name of the ship, the details will be in the log. There *were* improper advances made to a young lady on the ship, by Captain Beauchamps. I assisted the officers in thwarting his attempts. I suggest that Captain Beauchamps bears me a grudge for this, and I will take legal action if he repeats his slanders."

Beauchamps shuffled in his seat, wiping his palms down his breeches, but did not speak.

"However, if I am such a danger to the female population, why has it taken you this long to come here? And why be concerned only about Mrs MacKinnon, as opposed to all the other females in the area? Including your own sisters, Kinney."

Sir Vincent was still frowning. Matthew could almost see the wheels turning in his head—Charles must have been very pleased to find the local magistrate so slow-witted.

"Southam, why did you say your men would help to look for Tillson?" Sir Vincent asked eventually.

"I'd asked him to meet us in the inn," Charles said. "When he didn't arrive, I was worried he might... that something might have happened to him. I'm very glad to find *he* is safe and well."

"Your note must have gone astray, brother. All's well, then." It was time to bring this to an end. "Charles—I assume you and Beauchamps have taken rooms in the village? It shouldn't take you long to make your way back. Kinney—you have some way to ride home—I'm sure my housekeeper can find you a room for the night, if you wish to stay here."

"Thank you Tillson, but I should get home."

"Should we not make sure Mrs MacKinnon is unharmed?" Charles put in, before Matthew could escort him to the door.

"What makes you think anything has happened to her?" Matthew asked.

"I heard she left the celebration at the same time as you did," Charles said.

"She was still at the wedding celebration when I left," Matthew said. "That was in the early afternoon, with several hours of daylight left. Have you any reason to think she might have come to some harm today, as opposed to all the other days on which she must have walked to her home?"

"It's at least a mile along a lonely lane..." Charles muttered.

"Really, Charles, you know where she lives? You seem remarkably interested in a lady you've never met."

"Indeed, Southam," Sir Vincent said, getting to his feet. "What exactly is *your* interest in Mrs MacKinnon? *Do* you have any reason to think she may have come to harm?"

Of course he did, Matthew thought angrily, but he could not say so. He fought to keep his expression bland while Charles muttered something indistinct about overhearing talk in the pub.

"Perhaps I'll just call to make sure," Sir Vincent said, not sounding convinced. "It's not far out of my way."

There was a cough from the doorway. "Excuse me, my lord," Webb said. "I did overhear durin' the celebrations that Mrs MacKinnon was goin' to stay at Northridge 'All for a couple o' nights."

"Ah, thank you, Webb. So she probably will not be at home in any case."

"We'll just call there then," Charles said. "You know the way, Sir Vincent? We could call on our way back to Edgecombe."

"It's not *on the way*," said Sir Vincent, sounding irritated.

"Sir Vincent, you and I could ride over just to put your mind at ease, then you could come back here for the night?" Matthew didn't wait for a reply. "Webb! Get Jackson to saddle my horse."

"We'll accompany you, brother," Charles said.

"Very well," Matthew said, then turned to Sir Vincent. He was pleased to see that Sir Vincent was now looking thoroughly annoyed —he needed the man on his side.

"This way, gentlemen." He led the way out of the Hall and round to the stables, managing to place himself next to Sir Vincent. There was one more piece of misdirection he could try.

"Do you find it easy to get outdoor staff in this area?" he asked. Sir Vincent frowned at this apparently random change of subject, but Matthew didn't give him much time to think. "I only recently had to turn off someone for molesting my cook. It turned out he was a thief and likely a deserter from the navy as well. Smith, he called himself."

He was pleased to see, out of the corner of his eye, that his brother suddenly paid attention to what he was saying.

"Small loss, though," he added. "The man was bone idle—always lied about the amount of work he'd done, when most of the time he'd

454

done very little at all." He thought that was enough. No magistrate would take Smith's word against the word of a peer, but Matthew hoped that Charles would now also have doubts about what his men had *really* managed to do this day.

In the stables, his three visitors went to their horses, and Matthew managed a quiet word with Webb. "Why did you mention Northridge?"

"Make sure Mrs Captain 'as enough time to get 'ome, sir," he said.

Matthew mentally cursed himself—why hadn't he thought of that? "Good thinking, Webb. What about Smith and the other one —Braddon?"

"Probably still wonderin' why there's no-one in the ice 'ouse." Webb held out the pistol that usually resided on the mantelpiece in Matthew's bedroom. "Loaded, sir. I've got one too, sir, in case they try anythin' on the way, or Smith and that other bloke find us. Jackson's got a shotgun and 'e'll stay 'ere to make sure Mrs Malplass is safe while we're gone."

"I wish you'd been one of my sergeants, Webb," Matthew said, taking the pistol.

CHAPTER 46

The route home was along unfamiliar and slippery paths with only the lantern light to show the way. It took nearly two hours. Mary was anxiously waiting for them in the kitchen, a hot bath ready by the range. She took Davie from her new husband and helped him to strip off his muddy clothes and get into the bath, almost before Charlotte had taken off her cloak.

Charlotte sank into a chair, grateful to take the weight off her feet for a while. The hot water seemed to revive Davie a little, and when he had finished washing, Charlotte dried him down and gave him a huge slab of cake and a cup of hot milk. She sat beside him, drinking the mug of tea Mary gave her.

"Mama, what did those men want?" Davie asked, through a mouthful of cake.

"Davie, you were so brave," Charlotte said, immensely proud of her son. She gave him a big hug. "We can talk about it in the morning, but we both need some sleep first." She dropped a quick kiss on his head, then took him upstairs and tucked him in, something she hadn't done for years.

"Goodnight, Davie."

He gave her a sleepy smile as she shut the door.

. . .

Deacon had been assembling plates of bread and ham, and spooning out bowls of soup that Mary had been keeping warm on the range. Charlotte tried again to apologise for spoiling his wedding night.

"Don't worry about that," he said. "In fact, if Davie hadn't fetched me from the pub, I'd probably have drunk too much ale to appreciate it myself. And there's nowt stopping us..." He trailed off, concentrating on his soup.

Charlotte could see that the back of his neck had gone rather red, and pursed her lips against a smile. That was *not* the kind of thing people normally discussed with their employer. Although he wasn't really an employee, not any longer. He was a partner in her writing, and likely to be running a building and carpentry business of his own before much longer.

What a strange thing to be thinking about after all that's happened this evening! She knew why, really. It was to stop herself from remembering the way she'd kissed Matthew—the major. *What must he think of me?* Warmth rose in her cheeks. *My face must be as red as Deacon's...*

"You all right?" Mary asked. "You look ever so hot. Not caught cold, have you?"

"No, no," Charlotte said hastily. "Just warming up." She could see that Mary wasn't quite satisfied with this explanation. "It's possible we might have callers," she added, hoping to fend off further enquires.

"Who'd come—"

"I'll explain later," Deacon said.

"I'll answer the door if someone comes," Charlotte said. "You two go off now." The look Mary and Deacon shared as he followed her up the stairs brought heat to Charlotte's face again. Envy washed over her, mixed with the remembered arousal of that shattering kiss in the ice house, and a feeling of mortification that she had initiated it.

She put her hands to her cheeks, reliving the moment, in spite of that irritating voice telling her that a decent woman did not think about such things. Intimate relations with Angus had been enjoyable, but that single kiss from Matthew... she could remember nothing to compare with the way it had felt. And it was just a kiss. What would—

Standing abruptly, she went into the scullery to splash some cold water on her face. *Don't dwell on it. Men kiss women all the time—it doesn't mean anything.*

She managed to bring her thoughts back to the present. If Matthew...

The major. He's your employer.

If the major was right about his half-brother's plans, she may be having visitors soon. She must not be found in the kitchen with muddy clothing and footwear this late in the evening.

Charlotte quickly checked that the doors were locked and took a bowl of hot water upstairs to have a wash. As she donned her night-rail, she hesitated, debating whether or not she should go to bed—it might be better to stay awake until any visitors arrived. Cold feet and goosebumps on her arms swayed her to crawl into bed. Lying down felt wonderful, and her limbs began to relax as the bed warmed. She'd need to be alert if visitors did come. Perhaps she would close her eyes, just for a few minutes...

Loud knocking woke her. She lay in bed, confused at first, before memory returned and she realised someone was knocking at the door. Pulling her dressing gown on as she got out of bed, she was about to go downstairs to answer the door when she thought better of it. If the person responsible for the kidnapping was outside, she shouldn't be letting him into the house.

"Charlotte?" Mary stood in the doorway holding a lamp in one hand, the other hand holding her dressing gown closed. Her hair was loose and tousled. "Should John go?"

"No. I'm going to talk to them out of the window. Can you make sure Davie stays in bed?"

Mary went off to Davie's room. Charlotte pulled the curtains back and opened the casement.

"Who's there?" she called. There was still a bit of moonlight, allowing her to make out the shapes of four men on horseback, and one horse without a rider. "Who's there?" she called again, hearing her voice shake despite her efforts. Who were they all?

A figure stepped away from the house, peering upwards. She still couldn't make out who it was.

"Mrs MacKinnon, it is Sir Vincent. I came to see if you were well. We have been to Northridge. Mrs Thompson said you were expected but had not arrived."

"Oh, Sir Vincent!" Charlotte said. Matthew's supposition had been correct, which meant he was probably one of the other men. She couldn't make out which one he was in the pattern of moonlight and shadows.

"You frightened me so, knocking like that in the middle of the night!" she went on. "Davie was not feeling well, so we didn't go, and I had no-one to send with a note. We are all perfectly safe, thank you." She looked around again. "But who are all those other men? Why have you brought so many?"

"I'm very sorry to have woken you, Mrs MacKinnon," Sir Vincent said. "If I may, I will call in the morning to explain."

One of the other men spoke. Charlotte did not recognise the voice. "We should go in to—"

"That is enough, Southam!" Sir Vincent turned to face the speaker. "You have dragged me all over the countryside on a fool's errand, and worried Mrs MacKinnon into the bargain. Be off with you! If I see your face again I'll have you arrested."

"I'm so sorry, Charles…"

That was Matthew's voice, and Charlotte's fears finally subsided.

"…I really only have the staff at Birchanger to look after Sir Vincent. The inn at Edgecombe is along that road—only a mile or so."

Sir Vincent waited by the door while two of the riders moved off down the lane. He did not move, even when they were out of sight.

"Sir Vincent?" Charlotte called, wondering if he was now expecting to be let in. "Thank you so much for your concern. I must get back to see to Davie." She shut the window and drew the curtains. It felt wrong not to have said anything to Matthew, but it would have looked quite odd to Sir Vincent if she had.

Mary stuck her head around the door again. "Gone?"

"Soon will be. Davie's asleep?"

"Like a log."

Charlotte smiled her thanks and climbed back into bed. Exhaustion sent her to sleep for a time, but flashes of the day came back to her in dreams: the sudden fall into the ice house, the recollection of Braddon's foul breath in her face, the futile struggles she'd made against Smith. Each time she awoke, shaking and frightened, she forced herself to remember that she was now safe, that Matthew would deal with his brother and the two men. She had no further need to worry. Unfortunately, logical thought had little effect on her sleeping brain, and when she awoke for the third time she got out of bed and put her dressing gown on.

She spent the rest of the night downstairs, sitting by the kitchen range with a cup of tea and desperately trying to keep her mind on her *Woodland Tales*.

Her stories didn't work as a distraction, but the delicious memories of being held in Matthew's arms did. Snuggled in a chair under a blanket, she indulged in them for a while. She had felt safe, even though they were locked up. Then the comfort of his arms had turned to much more. She put one hand to her cheek, recalling the feel of Matthew stroking the skin there, his hand tangling in her hair, the sensation when their lips had met and the kiss had deepened.

A sudden flash of the way she had pulled his head towards hers intruded. She put her hands to her cheeks in embarrassment. *What must he think of me?* Many men, she knew, would accept an offered kiss. He had returned the kiss, and looked as if he had enjoyed it, too. *I'm sure he did, but that isn't what I need to know.*

Davie found her sitting there in the morning, well before the usual time for breakfast. His eyes looked puffy, reddened. Had he been crying?

Charlotte held her arms out and he came to sit on her lap, as he used to do when he was younger. He didn't say anything, just snuggled against her. Charlotte felt tears pricking her eyes as she stroked his hair. He was the reason she was here in this little house—her son, who depended on her, who had helped to save the pair of them last night.

"Mama?" He was looking up at her, so she brushed a finger across her eyes to wipe away the moisture before he could see it.

"I'm so proud of you, Davie," she said. "You were so brave, and you did exactly the right thing." She kissed his forehead, then moved him so she could stoke up the range and make some breakfast. He climbed onto her lap again while the tea was brewing, then she poured and they drank their tea in silence for a while.

"Did you sleep well?" she asked. He shook his head wordlessly. "Would you like to sleep with me tonight?" she said.

"Yes, please," he said, smiling then snuggling his head into her shoulder.

"Good. It will help me sleep better too. Do you want to tell me what happened? You don't need to, if it will make you feel bad again."

Davie looked worried. "I should have tried to rescue you," he said. "But I was afraid of those men."

"You were very sensible not to try that, Davie," Charlotte said, thankful once again that he had kept his wits about him. "They were much bigger than you, and you might have been hurt." He *would* have been hurt. *Or even killed?* She put that thought firmly out of her mind.

"There's nothing wrong with being afraid," she went on. "It kept you from doing something that would not have worked nearly as well as going to find Mr Webb. I was frightened, too, but I knew you were out there and you would bring help."

Davie didn't look convinced.

"What did you do?" she asked.

"I followed them when they carried you. I thought you were dead," he said, with a gulp.

"I was pretending to be unconscious to see if I could find out what they wanted," she said. He digested this for a moment, nodding as he approved.

"I felt better when I saw you talking to them, then they put you in there. I tried to open the door after those men went away, but I couldn't. I had to be quiet in case they heard and came back. I followed them back to the village. They made a lot of noise walking," he added in disgust, making Charlotte smile. "Then I found Mr Webb."

Charlotte hugged him tightly again. "Mr Webb told me what happened after that," she said. "You were very brave, Davie. You did just the right thing." He still frowned, biting his lip; she feared her words had not provided reassurance.

As she got up to serve their porridge, she wondered what Davie would do if anything *had* happened to her. Nothing had, but life was uncertain; she could have an accident or fall ill at any time. She did need to spend some time making contingency plans.

They were just finishing breakfast when they heard a knock at the door. With a start, Charlotte realised she was still in her night-rail and dressing gown. Davie ran into the parlour to peer out of the window, and came back frowning.

"It's Sir Vincent, Mama."

Damn! She'd forgotten he'd promised to call.

"You go and let him in, Davie, then light the fire in the parlour. Tell him I'll be down in ten minutes."

Davie looked worried, still, but did as he was bid while she hurried upstairs to get dressed. She pulled the night-rail off over her head, fleetingly wondering what it would feel like if someone else was doing that for her. She stilled for a moment, closing her eyes.

There were many reasons she had not accepted Sir Vincent's previous offers. Now, after sharing that kiss with Matthew, intimacy with any other man would never be anything more than a duty.

Sir Vincent stood by the window, staring at the rain. He turned as Charlotte entered the parlour, making a small bow in greeting. His hair looked immaculate, as usual, so he must have spent some time peering into the mirror while waiting for her; even his neckcloth looked neat. Only his boots had lost their gloss with the rain. Impressive, she thought irrelevantly, if he had stayed at Birchanger overnight without a valet.

"I came to apologise for waking you in the night, Mrs MacKinnon," he said. "I take it David has recovered?"

Charlotte's mind went blank for a moment, before she recalled the excuse she'd given for not going to Northridge Hall last night.

"Yes, thank you Sir Vincent. It was only an upset stomach. He probably ate too much at the wedding breakfast." Sir Vincent looked puzzled. "My companion got married yesterday," she explained. "Won't you sit down?"

He waited until she sat, then took the chair on the other side of the fireplace. She noticed him glancing at the landscape picture above the mantelpiece. She almost wished she'd told Davie to change the picture before letting him in.

She sighed. It was time for a bit more honesty.

Sir Vincent didn't start in the usual way. "Do you know a Charles Southam, Mrs MacKinnon?"

"I know *of* him, Sir Vincent," she replied. "He is one of Lord Tillson's half-brothers, but I have never met him."

Sir Vincent nodded.

"Why do you ask?"

"Oh, nothing you need worry yourself over, my dear. Nothing at all." He glanced up at the mantelpiece again. "He had some cock and bull story about you being in danger from Lord Tillson—utter nonsense, I'm sure."

Charlotte suppressed her irritation at his patronising manner. "Indeed. Lord Tillson has never been anything but the perfect gentleman. But I do thank you for your concern, Sir Vincent."

He smiled. "Nice picture you have over the fire, Mrs MacKinnon," he went on uncertainly, fiddling with one of the buttons on his coat.

Charlotte glanced at the sunny landscape in the painting. "Indeed, I find it cheering in this gloomy weather." She knew what he was implying, and waited for the inevitable.

"Mrs MacKinnon, that fool Southam would not have been able to cause such a bother if you had the protection of a husband."

"But Lord Tillson was no danger to me, was he Sir Vincent?" Charlotte asked calmly. She felt ashamed to be lying to him, but if the truth came out it wouldn't do her reputation any good, nor would it help Matthew—the major.

"No, no, my dear. You were perfectly safe. I apologise for rousing you so late at night. Southam should not have been spreading such stories."

"I am most appreciative of your concern, Sir Vincent." In that, at least, she could be sincere.

He looked at her again, running a finger nervously around his neck beneath his neckcloth. "Er, Lord Tillson said you have been working for him."

Charlotte nodded. "That is correct, yes." She raised an enquiring brow. It really was none of his business.

"Mrs MacKinnon—Charlotte—I do not like the idea of you having to work at all! Your writing, well, that is genteel at least, but acting as a secretary? Man's work, my dear. Not suitable, not suitable at all."

"Many ladies have secretaries," Charlotte said, her voice becoming a little sharp. "And many ladies are in charge of large households."

"My dear, they instruct the housekeeper. They do not renovate houses. Ladies have *social* secretaries."

And must lead very boring lives.

"I'm sorry if my actions offend you, Sir Vincent." Charlotte was surprised to realise she *did* mind what he thought, to a degree. She didn't *dislike* Sir Vincent, she just found him uninteresting and didn't agree with his ideas of how women should behave. At least he was well-meaning.

"I am not offended, Mrs MacKinnon," he said, but his frown made her think he was, a little. "I am just concerned that you *need* to work. You know I would—"

Charlotte still felt drained from her largely sleepless night, and didn't want to have this conversation now. Last night's events had clarified things, however. It was time to end it. Kindly, if she could.

"Sir Vincent," she said firmly, then waited until she had his attention. "Sir Vincent, you have been a constant admirer, but I wonder if the idea of courting me has possibly become a habit. I fear it may be just a way of stopping your mama introducing too many young ladies to you as prospective brides."

His race reddened. "Mrs MacKinnon, I do assure you that you are the most suitable lady of my—"

Suitable? How flattering!

"Sir Vincent, I do not think you know me very well."

"That can be remedied. Would you do me the honour of spending the day at Leverton soon? My mother and sisters will be there, naturally. I can send a carriage."

Charlotte shook her head. "Thank you for the invitation, Sir Vincent, but I must decline."

"Mrs MacKinnon, it would—"

"Sir Vincent, you should know that I am a very capable woman."

"You have *had* to be, my dear. You should not need to be."

"But I enjoy managing things. Your mother is very capable as well, you know," she added, hoping she wasn't causing offence.

"She's run the house for thirty years. You do like the house, don't you?"

"It is a fine house, yes." In truth it was comfortable enough, although some of the decorations were rather ostentatious for her taste. "There is no dower house, though, is there?"

He shook his head, another frown drawing his brows together.

"Do you think Lady Kinney will be happy to give up the management of the house while still living in it, too? Whoever becomes your wife, *she* would expect to run your home. How do you think your mother will like being superseded?"

"I'm sure you will be guided by her experience, my dear."

"Sir Vincent," Charlotte said firmly, trying not to sound impatient. "I am twenty-nine years old, nearly thirty, in fact. I'm not a young miss straight out of the school-room, and I have been making decisions for myself and my son for ten years. I will *still* be making decisions for my son if I do marry again."

"My dear, you don't need to worry about making decisions. That's why ladies need husbands."

Charlotte pursed her lips and took a deep, slow breath. She couldn't work out if he really didn't understand what she was saying, or was *choosing* not to understand. *How different from...*

She shook her head, concentrating on the man in front of her, not the one her imagination kept conjuring up. "Sir Vincent, it *is* a woman's place to make decisions about household matters. I am perfectly capable of that, and I would not be happy being told what to do by someone else."

She took another deep breath. "I do thank you for your offer—for the many offers and kind attentions you have paid me over the years —but I must decline."

He stared at her, his mouth open slightly.

"Do think about what I have said, dear sir. I am sure you will be happier with a younger lady, one who would be happy to learn from your mother." *And live under her thumb.*

Sir Vincent rubbed his hand across his forehead, looking at the floor. Charlotte heard footsteps on the stairs, then Davie's voice greeting Mary.

Sir Vincent stood. "You have indeed given me much to think about, Mrs MacKinnon."

Charlotte rose as well, holding out her hand. He bowed over it, picked up his hat and walked over to the door.

"Mrs MacKinnon, I hope we may still remain on friendly terms?"

Charlotte smiled. "Indeed, sir, I hope we may." She followed him out and down the passage, then stood watching as he mounted and rode down the lane. She felt lighter, a weight removed from her shoulders. She should have made that decision long ago, without needing—

"Mama?" Davie stood behind her in the passage. "Mama, you didn't say 'yes' did you?"

"No, Davie, I did not. I told him 'no'. Not ever. Now, I'm still tired so I'm going back to bed for a nap. Why don't you come with me?"

CHAPTER 47

*M*atthew didn't sleep well, in spite of the brandy and port he'd drunk. Sir Vincent had a surprisingly high tolerance for alcohol. Even with his own recent overindulgence, Matthew felt he'd consumed more than enough by the time Sir Vincent finally retired to his room. Much more.

In his dreams, the familiar image of the prison cell transformed to the ice-house, the dim candle-light showing Benson dying on the floor near him but out of reach, as always. Waking to Reena's whine, he took deep breaths until his heart rate slowed to normal.

Will the past never leave me?

In the dark, staring up at the invisible bed canopy above, he revisited his sleeping thoughts. He remembered the ice house as it had really been: the weight of Charlotte on his legs, the scent of her hair, and the feel of it beneath his hands.

That kiss... nothing he'd experienced before came close to the taste of her mouth beneath his. What would it be like if they had—

No!

He wasn't sure how much advantage he'd taken of her in the situation. He recalled persuading her to sit closer, and remembered the way she fitted against him when she sat on his lap. He also recalled—

too well—the feel of her lips beneath his, but not how that had come about. She *had* kissed him back.

Hadn't she?

Turning over, he buried his face in the pillows. He tried to keep his thoughts on mundane things: the progress on the kitchen garden, how many fields to plant, how well Charlotte had organised—

He sat up abruptly, contemplating having another drink, but dismissed the thought. Climbing back into a bottle was not the answer. If he could not stop his brain working, at least he should think of something useful, like what to do about Charles.

Eventually, he drifted off into restless sleep again, until Webb woke him to say Sir Vincent was up and wanted breakfast.

Thankfully Sir Vincent was in a hurry to be gone, so breakfast was quick. Matthew stood by the front door, watching him ride away down the drive. The sun had risen an hour before, but thick clouds covered the sky. Matthew rubbed his eyes, tempted to go back to bed until his headache eased.

Closing the door against the damp air, he headed to the kitchen for more coffee, and to order hot water to be sent up for a bath. Back in his room, he held his hand out—good, steady enough to shave. He rolled his shoulders and stretched, wincing at the stiffness in his muscles. Once Webb and Mrs Jackson had filled his bath, he sent Mrs Jackson off to brush his coat and make sure he had a starched neck-cloth, and directed Webb to check that his boots were polished.

When they had gone, he stripped and got into the bath, relaxing as the hot water helped to ease the aches in his limbs and clear his head a little. He needed to decide what to do about his brother.

Anger flushed through him again. He hadn't thought Charles would go so far as attempting to kill him, for that could easily have been the result of last night's actions. Involving Charlotte in his plans was evil indeed.

Charles, he hoped, had no idea that his plan had almost succeeded. Even if Smith told him what the two men had done, Charles would probably not believe him. In that case Charles would think he had nothing to hide, and would probably just return to London and make further plans to get his hands on more money. Matthew could decide how to deal with Charles later.

Smith was a different matter, a more immediate danger. He was already resentful about being driven away from Birchanger. If Charles had promised Smith money for the kidnapping, it was more than likely he had not paid it. In which case, Smith would want to take his frustration out on someone else. Charlotte, who regularly walked from her house to Birchanger, or to Northridge, was the easiest target.

Damn Charles for involving her in his plot!

Matthew hurriedly washed, then towelled himself off and donned a shirt and clean breeches. Charlotte had been on her way to Northridge Hall when she'd been kidnapped. He had to make sure she did not set out again today, at least not without an escort.

He set up a mirror and shaved, thinking through the possibilities. Another aspect occurred to him. Sir Vincent had said he was going to check that Charlotte really was all right. Matthew hadn't mentioned that he was going down there himself later, trying to maintain the impression that Charlotte was purely a business acquaintance in order to uphold her good reputation.

A widow with a child—people often wondered about the legitimacy of such children. Hell, he'd thought the worst himself at one point. Although Sir Vincent had no idea what had really happened, Charles could easily start a rumour, or get Smith to do so, and men like Halliton would revel in spreading it. Her position in the village could become untenable.

He wiped his face with a towel, then ran his hands down his cheeks. The action reminded him again of the sensation of Charlotte's hand against his face, and how *her* skin felt beneath his touch. Her softness, the trust she'd shown by allowing him to hold her…

Dammit man—concentrate!

He grimaced, wondering what would have happened if Webb had not arrived when he did. He'd taken advantage of Charlotte—Mrs

MacKinnon—when she was in a vulnerable position. He should have had more self-control.

There was one obvious solution, of course. A woman with a husband would not be subject to that kind of gossip. And he'd have Charlotte here permanently, sharing his life, sharing his bed...

If she'll have me.

The thought acted like a bucket of cold water on his head. He couldn't help thinking that he'd get the most out of any such arrangement. It wasn't fair on Charlotte to have to accept him for such reasons.

He put that thought out of his mind, drank the rest of his coffee and finished dressing. Breakfast wouldn't take long, then he would go.

The grey skies had turned to rain by the time he was finally ready. Matthew debated riding instead of walking, but he'd get wet either way. His greatcoat would keep most of the rain out and Charlotte wouldn't mind muddy boots.

Turning his collar up, he set off at a brisk pace down the drive, then took the path through the woods. The cool, damp air and the exercise helped to clear his head.

His thoughts kept returning to the idea of marriage. Specifically, his marriage to Charlotte. The idea felt so right, he wondered why he hadn't thought of it before. Would she want it though? What did *she* think about that kiss? What would it be like to be married to Charlotte if she didn't feel the same way he did?

Of course, from her point of view, marriage to any respectable man would remove the risk of rumours. He frowned. Sir Vincent had already been there this morning.

Remember the portrait!

If Charlotte had wanted to marry Sir Vincent, she could have done so any time in the last few years.

Hold onto that thought.

How could he persuade her that he was a better prospect than Sir Vincent? He suspected that his title meant as little to her as it did to him. Trudging up the muddy lane to Upper Edgecombe, he turned over a variety of arguments. Being married would mean that busy-bodies, like Sir Vincent or that fool Bretherton, would stop trying to tell her how to run her life. However, using that as an argument, he realised with dismay, would make him sound just like them.

Money? In spite of Charles' thefts and the costs of renovating Birchanger, he was still comfortably off. He didn't think money would sway her, though, and such an approach could easily be misinterpreted.

He opened the front gate to the cottage, his stomach churning with nerves as he realised he still hadn't worked out exactly what he should say to her.

He knocked, feeling disappointed when Mary opened the door. She showed him into the parlour, saying that Mrs MacKinnon had gone for a lie down.

"She's unwell?" Matthew asked, concerned.

"Just tired, sir," Mary said.

Perhaps this isn't the best time to talk to her?

"I'll get her," Mary added, before he could protest. "She'll want to see you. I'll bring tea while you're waiting."

She added some wood to the fire before she went out. Matthew took off his greatcoat and hung it over the back of a chair. Mary returned with the tea tray, followed by Davie, his clothing rumpled and his hair sticking out in all directions.

"Hello, sir," he said, rubbing his eyes.

"Good morning. How are you feeling today?" Matthew asked. "Have you only just got up?" It was almost noon.

"No, I got up ages ago, but then Mama wanted me to go for a nap with her."

"You must have been very tired last night, Davie. I wanted to thank you again for fetching help—that was very well done."

Davie flushed, but didn't meet his eyes. There was no smile indicating pleasure at the praise.

"What's wrong, Davie? Those men have gone, and I'm going to

make sure they don't come back." He didn't know how he would manage it, but manage it he would.

"I was afraid," Davie said, his gaze remaining on the floor. "I should have tried to stop them taking Mama."

"I've been afraid lots of times," Matthew said, careful to keep his tone light and conversational. "There's nothing wrong in being afraid. In fact, only very stupid people are *never* afraid."

Davie's head lifted, his eyes widening in surprise. Matthew hid a smile, recalling his own reaction when this idea had first been put to him.

"The important thing," Matthew went on, "is to not let being afraid get in the way of thinking what to do. And sometimes being afraid *helps* you to decide what to do."

Davie frowned.

"What do you think would have happened if you had tried to stop those men? They probably had pistols, you know." Matthew let that sink in for a moment. "So being afraid of the men kept you from attacking them. That was the right thing to do. Then you thought about what to do, and you followed them without being caught—yes?"

Davie nodded.

"You found out where they had your mother locked up, followed them to the village, and then you found Mr Webb—all without them knowing you were there at all—yes?"

"Yes."

"That sounds like a very successful reconnaissance mission to me. Deserving of a mention in dispatches, even!"

Charlotte stood in the doorway, her cheeks warm, swallowing against a sudden jumble of emotions: pleasure at seeing Matthew again, gratitude that he seemed to have reassured Davie when she could not, and embarrassment at the memory of their kiss and what he might be thinking about that.

"What's that mean, a dispatch?" Davie asked.

Her heart was racing, so she took a deep breath as stepped into the room. "Good morning, Major."

Matthew stood, a smile curving his lips for a moment, then he rubbed the back of his neck and dropped his gaze.

Charlotte wiped damp palms down her skirt. *Davie first...*

"It's a *good* thing to be mentioned in dispatches, Davie" she said. "I'll explain later," she added, seeing his frown. She sat down, and Matthew resumed his seat.

"Sir, why did those men lock you and Mama in the ice house?"

Charlotte glanced at Matthew, hoping he could give her son a better explanation than she could.

"I'm afraid it was because of me, not your mama," he said to Davie, his gaze flicking to Charlotte then away again. "My brother sent them. The brother you haven't met," he clarified, "not Lieutenant Southam."

"But why—"

"He wants to be Lord Tillson," Matthew said. "If I were dead, he would be the next Lord Tillson."

"Why do people want to be lords?"

"They think it makes them more important."

Charlotte caught his dismissive shrug; he'd never seemed to value his title.

"Is that why you—"

"Davie, why don't you go to the kitchen," Charlotte interrupted, to divert the stream of questions she knew would follow. "I'm sure Mary can find you more cake or biscuits."

Davie gave what passed for a small bow to Matthew and took himself off.

Getting up to make sure the door was firmly closed, Charlotte returned to her chair without looking at the man sitting on the other side of the fire. Her doubts about her behaviour, easy to ignore while Davie was present, flooded back. Her cheeks flushed again.

"Charlotte," Matthew started, his voice hesitant. "I hope you have recovered from yesterday's events."

"Yes, thank you, Major." She met his eyes, then quickly looked away. Was he going to mention their kiss? The silence stretched out uncomfortably. "I'm a little tired," she added. "I did not sleep well."

"No, I mean, I'm sorry to hear that. I... er... Davie, is he all right?"

"I think so. You seem to have put his mind at rest regarding his actions."

He nodded, clearing his throat. "Mrs MacKinnon, I came to apologise for—"

"It wasn't your fault, Major," Charlotte broke in, hoping he wasn't going to say it had been a mistake, or had meant nothing. "Not at all."

"It might not have been my fault, but it was due to me." He looked her in the face for a moment, then his gaze slid sideways and he rubbed the back of his neck again. "I could have spoken to my brother," he said, "instead of just curtailing his spending."

Charlotte rubbed her palms on her skirts. He was talking about the kidnap, not their kiss. Perhaps it *hadn't* meant anything to him. Trying to ignore the sinking feeling in her stomach, she gave herself a mental shake; he was still talking.

"...go to London to... I mean, to make sure he does not do such a thing again." Matthew paused for a moment, fiddling with a button on his coat. "I think... I mean, it is possible that my brother will still try to cause trouble, even though it will gain him nothing. If there are rumours, gossip—"

"I'm sure there will be no problems, Major, but thank you for your concern."

He nodded, his gaze meeting hers for a brief moment before he looked away again, a faint crease between his brows. He took a deep breath. "There is also... we... that is, I, did not..." His voice trailed off, his brows drawing together. "That is, I...well, I realised... there were some moments that weren't..."

Is he talking about the kiss? Apologising for something *she* had initiated? Perhaps he was just being a gentleman, taking the blame to spare her embarrassment?

"I don't want to see your name besmirched." Matthew continued, his hands pressed against his knees and his knuckles white. "I'd be very honoured if you'd consider... I'm not suggesting you *need* to..."

Charlotte frowned. Did he consider her actions to be forward? Had she seemed too desperate, needing him?

He took another deep breath. "In short, Mrs MacKinnon, will you do me the honour of accepting my hand in marriage?" The words came out in a rush, and once more his gaze slid away as he looked down at his boots.

Charlotte turned her head away, tears pricking her eyes, unable to speak through the tightness in her throat. She hadn't expected a proposal, nor the sudden yearning—a wish that he had offered marriage because of the kiss and how it had made him feel, that he *wanted* to share his life with her.

"That is," Matthew went on, his expression uncertain, "I am offering you the protection of my name, if you will take it, in case there is..."

He stopped speaking.

Charlotte examined his face, her heart heavy when she took in his expression of discomfort. She couldn't work out if he was offering marriage to protect her against possible damage to her reputation, or because of their inappropriate kiss in the ice house. It was immaterial, though; a marriage undertaken for either reason would be painful. Insupportable.

Hands bunching her skirts, she swallowed hard before speaking, making an effort to keep her voice level.

"I thank you for your offer, Major, but there is no need. No need at all."

He glanced at her again, briefly, his expression blank. "I see," he said, returning his gaze to the floor.

The silence lengthened, until he finally stood. "I will take my leave, then. I hope you will continue to... that is, I think Webb would still benefit from your help and advice." He cleared his throat. "I will be going to London, and expect to be away for around a week. If there is anything you need while I am away, do ask Webb. He will have my direction."

Charlotte stared down at her clenched hands, lifting her gaze only as he left the room. She had caught a movement out of the corner of her eye—had he held his hand out?

She stood and walked over to the window in time to see him close the gate and set off down the lane, her knees feeling weak and wobbly. He walked slowly, turning just before he was out of sight to look back at the cottage, but he was too far away for her to make out his expression.

She sat again, hands on her cheeks, frowning. His bearing hadn't been one of a man relieved of an onerous duty. Had she misunderstood?

"Charlotte? Are you unwell?"

Charlotte started at the interruption to her thoughts. Mary stood in the doorway, concern on her face.

"I... I'm still rather tired," Charlotte said, managing a normal voice. It was true, she *was* still tired. She could not just retire to bed again, leaving Mary to supervise Davie; she had to do something to keep her mind busy.

CHAPTER 48

*I*diot!

Matthew kicked at a stone in the path, sending it skittering off into the trees.

Charlotte had been wearing one of her old black dresses, with faint shadows under her eyes, but never had she appeared more beautiful to him. He'd managed to keep his mind on what he was saying while he was talking to Davie, but as soon as she shut the door behind her son his wits had gone wandering.

You made your proposal sound like some kind of business arrangement.

Shoving his hands into his pockets, he kicked morosely at more stones as he walked up through the woods. It was hardly surprising she'd turned down someone who couldn't even string a coherent sentence together, let alone his catastrophic failure to tell her he admired her and *wanted* to marry her.

He went over the interview in his mind, turning up the drive and taking his usual route round to the back of the Hall. It was only then that another thought occurred to him.

Not only did you completely botch that proposal, you also forgot about making sure she stays safe.

At the moment, that was more important. He *could* do something about that.

"Webb!"

~

Davie sighed as he added up the column of numbers for the third time. Charlotte felt slightly guilty. Perhaps it had been unfair to give Davie a mathematics lesson as a means of keeping her own thoughts in order.

"Mama, are we still going to go to Northridge? Bertie has some new soldiers."

Charlotte frowned. The original reason for the visit—to give Mary and John some privacy—still applied, but how would they get there? She wasn't going to walk through the woods without an escort, not with the possibility of Smith still being around.

"Mama?"

"I'll think about it, Davie." Perhaps Letty could send the carriage? She should, at the very least, write to make a proper excuse to Letty. Although both of those options would mean asking Deacon to take a note over, and he had better things to do at the moment.

A knock on the front door interrupted her thoughts. Davie jumped up to answer it, leaving the door open. Charlotte heard Webb ask if he could come in to talk to Deacon, and went to the parlour door. She suspected that the newly-weds had retired to Mary's room, but she couldn't tell Webb that. Although if she made enough noise offering refreshments, perhaps they would hear and come down.

"Do come in, Sergeant," Charlotte said, leading the way into the kitchen. Webb put his bag down inside the kitchen door and took a seat at the table, while Charlotte put the kettle on, 'accidentally' knocking a pan to the floor as she did so. By the time the tea was brewed and cake had been offered and accepted, Deacon and Mary had come downstairs, both tidily dressed and showing no signs of marital activity. Nevertheless, Charlotte was amused to see Webb's face redden, guessing he had just worked out what he might have interrupted.

"The major sent me, Mrs MacKinnon," Webb started, looking worried. "'E's gone to London to sort out 'is brother. But 'e's worried about that Smith. It won't be safe for you, ma'am, walkin' through the woods, not until Smith 'as been caught, but 'e can't put word out in case Smith—"

"Yes, I understand that," Charlotte said, not wanting to go into the implications of possible gossip and rumour while Davie was present.

"Right, ma'am. 'E reckons you ain't safe, neither, Deacon."

"Nor Mary," Deacon said. "He'll resent her giving me a job here instead of him. If I get my—" He stopped as Mary's elbow met his ribs. To Charlotte, his muttered threat had carried more menace than shouting or outright anger would have done.

Webb coughed, and pulled his bag towards him. Taking out a pistol and a small box, he pushed them across the table to Deacon. "You're to borrow this. There'll be another pistol coming from Bath, if you want it."

Deacon took the pistol and examined it. Charlotte wondered if he could load it with one hand, but was sure he'd manage somehow. It was good of... of the major to think about Deacon's safety. She closed her eyes for a moment, wondering yet again if she had misinterpreted him this morning, or if this was just the action of a decent man trying to put right something his family had caused.

"...so Tilly or one of the other Jacksons'll come down in the mornin', to see if you need to go anywhere, ma'am."

Charlotte realised she had missed part of what Webb had said. Had he offered her transport in the wagon? It would be inconvenient having to arrange such a thing in advance, but that was a small price to pay when the alternative was being trapped in the cottage.

"Sergeant, could you take a note to Northridge Hall for me? Mrs Thompson might be able to send the carriage for us, so Davie and I can stay there for a few days. John, you will be able to protect Mary better if you don't have the two of us to worry about as well."

"I'll do that, ma'am," Webb said, his face lightening. "Smith likely won't think to look for you there, if 'e is still around."

Charlotte got up to fetch paper and pen.

"Best stay indoors for a few days, then," Charlotte heard Mary say cheerfully, and felt a pang of envy.

Matthew looked around with interest while he waited for the butler to return. The Earl of Marstone's townhouse occupied a position along one side of Grosvenor Square, an address with the sort of prestige Serena had always coveted. The marble floors and pillars in the hall demonstrated wealth, but the walls were decorated plainly, setting off the family portraits hanging in the spaces between the doorways. The whole was tasteful, even restful, particularly compared to what Serena had done to his own house.

"His lordship will see you now," the butler said, and ushered him into a library. Leather-bound books on polished wooden shelves lined most of the room, with the walls above painted dark red to match the velvet curtains. Two men stood by a desk near one of the windows.

"Major Lord Tillson, my lord," the butler intoned, closing the doors as he backed out.

Phineas Kellet approached, his hand held out. "Good to see you again, Major."

"Kellet," Matthew said, shaking his hand.

Kellet turned to the earl. "My lord, may I introduce Major Lord Tillson? My lord, the Earl of Marstone."

"Tillson, welcome." The earl gestured towards a chair. His hair was beginning to turn grey, but was still thick above piercing blue eyes. He was expensively dressed, but not ostentatiously so; the quality being evident in the cut and the cloth, not in gold buttons and embroidery. Matthew couldn't help but glance down at his own clothing, and decided to find a tailor after his next call.

"Thank you for seeing me, my lord," Matthew said, taking the indicated seat. Kellet sat further away, in a chair by the window.

"How are you, Tillson? You seem to be better than initial... ah... reports described."

"Very well, thank you. Thanks in no small part to Mr Kellet's recommendation of his brother as my legal man."

"Are you planning on going back to India?"

Matthew didn't really want to discuss his plans, but it would be rude to refuse. "No, I'm settled in this country." Settled where, he wasn't sure. If Charlotte couldn't forget or forgive, he didn't think he could continue to stay at Birchanger. But there was always Farleton.

"You are resigning your commission?"

"I am planning to, yes."

"Before you do that, have you considered transferring to the regular army?"

What use would he be to an army? It shamed him to admit it, but the possibility of being captured again could easily prey on his mind enough to affect his judgement—at least it would at the moment.

"I don't think I'm fit for war any longer, my lord."

The earl regarded him thoughtfully for a moment. "Go to Horse Guards while you're in town. Kellet will make you an appointment. We could use someone with experience and sense in an advisory capacity."

"Very well, my lord." He could listen to them, at least.

"Now, how may I help you?"

"A relatively small matter, but if you could spare about an hour of your time in a day or so, I would like an unimpeachable witness, preferably one of rank."

The earl leaned back in his chair. "I sense a story. Brandy?"

Matthew didn't really want a drink this early in the morning, but thought it would be impolite to refuse. Kellet poured the amber liquid from a crystal decanter, then Matthew outlined his plan.

～

Charlotte strolled between the tall yew hedges, keeping pace with Letty and almost gritting her teeth in frustration. The weather was glorious for early spring, with puffy white clouds drifting slowly across a pastel blue sky, and a chilly bite to the air. She was well wrapped up, and warm enough, but on such a day she should be striding through the woods, with the sun shining through the still-bare trees. The ground would be brightened by yellow celandines and white wood anemones, and there would be clumps of daffodils flowering by the stream. The exercise might even help her to think more clearly.

Letty took the air every day, strolling around the formal gardens, but it wasn't what Charlotte regarded as exercise.

"Are you all right, Charlotte?" Letty regarded her with concern.

Charlotte realised she had been frowning, and forced a smile. "Sorry, Letty. Just trying to work out a story." She hated having to lie, but she could not tell Letty what was on her mind, nor complain about the way she'd been spending her time over the last few days. It was good of Letty to let them stay, busy as she was with the new baby.

"I don't know how you do it," Letty said, admiringly. "You must give me a list of all the stories, so I can read them to little Arthur when he's old enough."

"Certainly," Charlotte said, guessing what Letty would say next.

"I think I'll just go to the nursery to see how he's getting on."

Naturally; it was nearly an hour since she'd last seen her new baby. Charlotte felt a twinge of envy. Her own first weeks with Davie had been filled with arguments with her father, fighting to be allowed to spend even an hour a day with him.

They turned and made their way back along the yew walk towards the house. Letty went straight up to the nursery, while Charlotte went to stand by the window in the parlour, looking out over the lawn. She really *should* be thinking of another story, or the next *Cotswold Diary* article, but she wasn't in the mood. Perhaps she should rescue Davie and take him for a turn around the garden? A smile curved her lips as she recalled Davie's disgust at learning that, in addition to his new soldiers, Bertie had a new tutor whose lessons Davie could share while he was staying at Northridge Hall. However, once Charlotte had quietly reminded him that it was not safe to play in the woods at the moment, he hadn't made too much fuss about it.

She followed Letty upstairs, the schoolroom being on the same upper corridor as the nursery. The nursery door stood open, and she looked in. Squire Thompson was there as well as Letty, dandling baby Arthur on his knee and tickling his ribs gently to make him squeal. The squire was showing a side Charlotte had never expected. She had always thought he'd married Letty to get a new mother for Bertie. Perhaps he had, originally, but judging by the way he was now doting on both Letty and the baby, she was sure this was no longer the case.

Davie had never known a father. She swallowed a lump in her throat as she moved on. Davie was better off fatherless than he would have been with a father like her own, or even the kind of indifferent step-father Sir Vincent might have made. She paused outside the schoolroom door, closing her eyes and putting a hand to her forehead. Matthew, on the other hand, would be an excellent father for Davie, and if they had a child—

Stop it!

She took a deep breath, turning her mind away from Matthew. Time enough to think on that later, when she was alone.

Davie looked up eagerly when she opened the schoolroom door. She had a word with the tutor, who agreed that Davie could finish his translation later. They went out into the sunshine to look for insects and birds.

CHAPTER 49

*J*oshua Kellet welcomed Matthew into his offices. Charles Southam was already seated in the outer room, a foot tapping. Matthew tensed at the sight of him, but controlled his anger. Success depended on Charles not knowing for sure whether any part of his plot had worked.

"Matthew," Charles said in greeting, a bland smile on his face. "I'm glad you finally saw reason about increasing my allowance—as I said, living in India, you would have no idea of the expenses of a gentleman in society."

"Charles," Matthew acknowledged, carefully expressionless.

"If you would be seated over here, gentlemen?" Kellet gestured to a large desk in one corner of the room. "I'm afraid there has been a leak in the roof, and my private office is temporarily out of commission. We will have to discuss our business here."

Matthew looked at the two clerks in the far corner of the room, scratching away busily at their high desks, and his lips twitched. Charles ignored them and took his chair.

"I'm afraid all is not as rosy as you seem to think, Charles," Matthew said. "I am willing to pay your allowance only for another ten years. It is a generous allowance, and you should be able to make investments or buy an estate to keep you in sufficient comfort. I *have* back-dated the increase for a few years."

Charles' expression slipped a little at the first part of Matthew's statement, but brightened slightly at the end. Then his bland smile returned.

No doubt thinking ten years is plenty of time to get rid of me.

"If you could just examine these figures, Mr Southam," Kellet said, turning the document on his desk around so Charles could read it. Charles flicked through the pages, until he came to the total at the end.

"The other thing is, Charles," Matthew continued, while his brother was looking at Kellet's document, "I'm giving you the lot now, rather than paying you quarterly. If you're happy with that, you just need to sign the document."

"Sign?" Charles looked offended. "You cannot take my word?"

"I wish to avoid any future misunderstandings," Matthew explained. "It isn't usual to give you ten years' allowance in one lump sum, so I just need a signature as your acceptance of the arrangement."

"Oh, very well." Charles took the proffered pen and scribbled his signature at the indicated place.

"And the copy, if you please."

Charles muttered under his breath, but signed the second copy.

"If you gentlemen would witness this?" Matthew said, raising his voice slightly so it carried to the clerks' corner. The two clerks shuffled over and added their names to the bottom of both documents, then returned to their desks. Matthew handed one copy to Charles.

"Before Kellet pays you the sum, Charles, I'd like you to read this." Matthew handed over a folded document.

Charles opened it, his brow creasing as he saw the heading. "This is your will?"

"As you see."

Charles skimmed his eyes across the document and then read it in more detail, his frown changing from puzzlement to red-faced anger.

"Is there a problem, brother?" Matthew asked.

"You show so little regard for your family?" Charles' voice grew louder. "This is preposterous! I— we are entitled to more consideration than this!"

"Your mother has the settlement made on her marriage, and I have settled a sum on Julia that should be sufficient to give her another season or two, and a marriage portion. As you see, if she remains unwed, I have increased the allowance to your mother to enable her to meet the additional expense."

"But Birchanger—I won't be able to keep it running without other income—"

"Oh?" Matthew pretended surprise. "You assume I will predecease you, *and* you have gone into Birchanger's finances in detail?"

"Well, I... er... at one time it was thought you would not be returning. You were reported missing. Birchanger would have become my responsibility."

"Ah, I see. Well, brother, as I am only a few years older than you, it is unlikely to be a burden for you for many years yet—I shouldn't worry about it if I were you. I should point out that if I am fortunate enough to marry, I will, of course, make provision for my wife, and any children we are blessed with. However, the bequests to you, your mother, Julia, and Richard would remain the same."

Charles' eyes narrowed before he regained control of himself. "Just considering the possibilities, brother. After all, you never know when an accident may befall you."

"Indeed—or when someone may attempt a kidnapping, for example." Matthew raised an eyebrow and enjoyed watching Charles' eyes widen momentarily before he resumed his normal, bland expression.

"An unlikely event, surely," Charles said, after a brief moment.

"One would hope so," Matthew agreed. "Now, Kellet, would you be so good as to give my brother the balance of what he is owed for the next ten years."

Kellet opened a drawer in his desk, pulled out a leather purse, and handed it to Charles.

Charles looked puzzled, then opened it and extracted the roll of bank notes inside. He quickly flipped through them, his face darkening in fury.

Matthew compressed his lips, trying not to laugh.

"What the hell is this?" Charles said, his voice loud in the small room.

"The balance of the amount owed you for the next ten years," Kellet stated patiently.

"But this is barely one year's worth!"

"Yes, but you've already had the rest," Matthew said. It wasn't Kellet's argument—no need for him to draw Charles' ire.

"What do you mean, I've had the rest? Kellet's only given this to me now."

Matthew leaned back in his chair. "Charles, you've been drawing far more than your allowance for the last five years, haven't you? And you took Richard's allowance and stripped Birchanger Hall of anything you thought you could sell." *And probably a lot you couldn't, for spite.* "Show him the accounts, please, Kellet."

Kellet brought out another set of papers. Even from a distance, it was clearly a set of very detailed accounts. Kellet started to go through the list, reading out each entry, but after only a few items, Charles got up and slammed his hand down on the list. Kellet sat back.

"The steward at Farleton was responsible for that."

"Under coercion from you," Matthew said.

"You can't prove it!"

"I know I'd have a hard time proving it in court, even if I was prepared to air family problems in public, which is why we are doing it this way." He moved Charles' hand away from the list. "Well, now is your chance to question the accounting. Is there anything there you disagree with?"

Charles looked at the list blankly. It was many pages long, and would take some time to go through. "I was the head of the family when Father died," he said eventually.

Matthew tilted his head. "How so? I am the oldest."

"You weren't here—my position required me to spend more." He stood and pulled the document he had signed out of his pocket. "Besides, this document is rubbish—witnessed by a couple of clerks?" He tore the papers in two and flung the pieces on the floor.

Matthew smiled, savouring the moment. "Kellet, would you care to introduce your clerks?"

"By all means, my lord. My brother Phineas Kellet—a respected man of business. And my brother's employer, the Earl of Marstone."

The two 'clerks' stood up and looked straight at Charles for the first time. Charles' face gradually drained of colour.

"You recognise me then, Southam?" the earl asked, a humourless smile on his face. "I'm afraid there's no going back—you agreed to the arrangement Lord Tillson has offered you. If I hear any rumours about this arrangement, or about Tillson, you will not be welcome in society again. I will see to that."

"But I cannot live on this!" Charles complained, still hoping for some kind of favour.

Matthew's smile became wider. "Oh, don't worry, Charles—I've arranged employment for you. A choice, even."

Charles took a step back from the desk, shaking his head. "What? Employment? Me?"

"Well, why not? I've been employed for ten years in a perfectly respectable career in the army. And you *are* a younger son."

"I can't... I'm not suited for soldiering."

"Don't worry Charles, I wouldn't inflict you on any army. No, but I'm sure there are nabobs in India who would love to have a social secretary with links to the aristocracy."

"India? A secretary?"

"Or you could go to Australia," the earl put in. "I could see if the governor there needs an assistant?"

"A *penal* colony! Matthew, why are you doing this to me? What have I done to you apart from spending a bit of your money?"

Matthew stood and faced his brother, his face now grim. "You kidnapped me in what was no doubt an attempt to kill me or have me declared incompetent. In the process you risked the life and honour of a perfectly innocent woman."

"You can't prove..." Charles' voice trailed off as he realised he had just incriminated himself.

Matthew gave a humourless smile. "And you cheated Richard by having his allowance stopped. I know I cannot prove it, but I have no doubts, which is why you will be leaving the country. Kellet will give you your ticket. You will be departing—"

"You *bastard!*" Charles shouted, pulling a fist back as if he was going to strike Matthew. A couple of coughs from the doorway caused Charles to pause. Two footmen stood there. Although not particularly large, they looked solid and tough.

Charles stilled for a moment, then dropped his hand, his shoulders slumping.

"As I was saying, *brother,*" Matthew went on, "you will be departing this evening. And you will be escorted home to pack—arrangements can be made to send your other belongings on. I should also let you know I have signed a power of attorney, so even if there are any future... accidents... Lord Marstone will administer the estate, not you."

Charles stared at him for a moment, nostrils flaring, but made no further move to attack. He turned and stormed out of the door, the footmen following closely behind.

Without saying anything, Kellet took a bottle of brandy from a cupboard and poured four glasses.

"I think this is commiseration, rather than celebration," Marstone said seriously. "Family divisions are never pleasant."

"My lord, thank you for your help," Matthew said. "For *all* your help."

"The War Office has found a use for you? I should point out that the rifle testing wasn't 'make-work'—your input was very useful, I'm told."

"A few uses, yes. Part time, probably, but that suits me well." At least he appeared to be good for something.

The men shook hands, and Marstone took his leave. Matthew thanked Kellet again, and arranged to meet him the next day to finalise various remaining matters, then went back to his hotel. He supposed he would have to confront Serena too, to explain, but that joy could wait for a day or two. He'd give her some time to calm down a little after hearing Charles' version of events. He still had to call at

Doctor's Commons as well.

~

Matthew was tired and cold as he turned the horse up the drive to Birchanger. He'd obtained an outside seat on the overnight mail to Bath, and had spent most of the journey trying to decide when he should visit Charlotte again. He needed to reassure her that Charles was out of the country and no longer a danger to her. Unfortunately, that did not make it any less likely that Smith or Braddon would be a threat. He should also try to make a better proposal of marriage, but he was reluctant to take that step in case she turned him down again. Two refusals would be final, he felt.

His spirits lifted a little as the Hall came into sight, smoke from the chimneys rising straight up into the still blue sky. His stomach growled—it had been a long time since the hurried breakfast he'd eaten in Bath. One of his saddle bags held the various documents he'd obtained, safely wrapped in oiled silk. At the moment, he just wanted to be back in the now-familiar surroundings of his home, enjoying a hot bath in front of the fire.

Jackson must have seen or heard him arrive, and came out to the stables to take care of the horse. Matthew slung his bags over his shoulder and headed for the back door.

He didn't know whether to hope that Charlotte would be at the Hall or not. He'd thought about his botched proposal to her many times over the last few days. Having the chance to talk to her again would be good, but he did need to think about exactly what to say first. He had to get it right this time.

Webb's voice roused him from his thoughts. "Welcome back, sir. Did you get all you went for?"

"A little more than I bargained for, Webb. I'll tell you later—for now, I'm in urgent need of a bath."

"Mrs Malplass is sortin' it out, sir. It'll be a few minutes, but there's coffee on the range. Mrs Jackson's gone to light a fire in your room.

My office is warm, though, if you want to sit there for a bit." He picked up Matthew's bags.

Matthew took up Webb's suggestion and went into the steward's office, taking the chair nearest to the fireplace. He rubbed his forehead, wondering if this was the chair Charlotte used when she was helping Webb.

Webb returned and set a cup of coffee in front of him, taking the seat behind the desk. "No sign of Smith since you left, sir," he reported. "I asked Toby Minchin', down at the pub, to put word out that Smith's been stealin' from Birchanger, and to let 'im or me know if anyone sees 'im."

"Good idea, Webb, thank you."

Webb grinned. "There's no gossip in the village, neither."

Matthew raised an eyebrow. "How can you be sure?"

"Listened in the pub, sir. 'Ad to go down there every night, just to be sure."

Matthew shook his head, smiling. "Such dedication to duty, Webb."

"Yessir, thank you, sir."

"Cut it out, Webb. Anything else happen?"

"Ordered a lot o' stuff for the kitchen garden, sir. Took the lists over to Mrs MacKinnon to check first."

"She hasn't been here?" That was not a good sign, he thought, much of his pleasure at being home evaporating.

"She went to Northridge 'All, sir, the day you left for London. I took a note over for 'er, and the squire sent 'is carriage to take 'er over."

Matthew frowned. Was she staying away deliberately? Perhaps it was not wise—

"Everythin' all right, sir?"

"Yes, of course," Matthew snapped. "Why shouldn't it be?" He took a deep breath. None of this was Webb's fault, and the man was regarding him curiously.

"No reason, sir. Sort your brother out, did you?"

"Oh, yes—he should be a couple of days into a voyage to India at this moment."

Webb grinned again. "Excellent, sir. Mrs MacKinnon will be glad to hear that, too. Reckon it might be safe for 'er to go 'ome now you're back?"

Matthew rubbed the back of his neck. "I'm not back for long. I've been given another job, I need to—"

"Bath's ready, sir." Mrs Malplass knocked at the door as she called out, but she did not wait for an acknowledgement.

"I'll talk to you later," Matthew said, before picking up his coffee and going for his bath.

Soaking in the welcome hot water, he considered what Webb had told him. Northridge was probably the safest place for Charlotte to be at the moment, so it was good that she had gone to stay. That probably explained her absence from Birchanger, too. If she needed to come up, she would have to ask the squire for someone to escort her, or to drive her. She would have to explain that it was too dangerous to walk over, in case Smith was still around, and that would lead to the further explanations and possible gossip they had both been hoping to avoid.

He rubbed his face. He supposed Webb could have called for her and escorted her here, but that could also have necessitated explanations to the squire or his wife. So her absence from Birchanger was because of the threat of Smith, not necessarily because she had been avoiding the place.

He washed, then got out of the tub and dried himself. The fact remained that she was still at Northridge. How was he supposed to call on her there? He could hardly ask for a private interview. He'd be obliged to make polite conversation with the squire and his wife beforehand or, even worse, afterwards.

He'd have to write a letter.

CHAPTER 50

*C*harlotte looked at the paper in front of her. She had to write the *Cotswold Diary* article for May in the next couple of days, and all she had achieved since sitting down here after luncheon was a few scribbled words and a lot of random patterns on the page. Being in Letty's parlour didn't help her concentration. Letty didn't talk, but Charlotte could tell it was an effort for her to keep quiet while she had company. It would be impolite for Charlotte to retire to her room.

The weather did not help her mood, either. The spell of fine, cold weather was still with them, and she wanted to be out walking the woods, not cooped up indoors.

She clenched her fists. *Damn Smith, and Matthew's brother.*

Although without Charles Southam's plotting she would never have shared that kiss with Matthew. She felt her cheeks heat, and hoped Letty didn't notice.

That thought led to Mary and John. They'd had nearly a week to themselves now, so perhaps it was time she returned home. She wasn't sure how long Letty was expecting her to stay, but she could find some excuse, such as a need to refer to some papers at home.

She stood and went over to the window, stretching her arms and fingers to provide an excuse to stop working. She idly watched a rider approaching the Hall, taking more interest as he drew closer and she recognised Webb. He *could* be bringing a message to the squire, but—

"Letty, I can see someone coming with a message for me," she said. "I'll just step out to meet him."

"More gardening advice?" Letty asked, looking up from the baby's cap she was embroidering.

Charlotte made a sound that could be agreement, and made her way out to the stable yard.

"Letter for you, ma'am," Webb said when he saw her. "The major got back today."

Charlotte felt a blush rising again. *Really—just like a silly girl!*

Webb fumbled in a saddlebag and handed over a folded set of pages, sealed. "Said his brother's gone out o' the country."

"Thank you, Sergeant." That was good—Charles Southam would no longer be a threat to Matthew. She turned the letter over, not wanting to open it while Webb was watching. While *anyone* was watching, come to that. Why had he written instead of calling?

Why should he call? I turned him down.

Of course, the letter could just be details about Birchanger...

"Another letter come for you, Mrs MacKinnon," Webb said. "Think it's about the rest of the furniture you ordered. I was wonderin' if you was likely to be comin' up to Birchanger soon?"

Charlotte took the second letter and opened it. "They'll deliver it in a couple of days," she said. She thought for a moment. "I'll probably be returning home tomorrow. I may call on my way. If the squire's man can drop me at Birchanger, could you or... could you escort me back home afterwards?"

"Yes, ma'am. That'd be no trouble. I'll be off back, then." Webb nodded and remounted, kicking the horse into movement.

Charlotte turned the letter over again. She'd tell Letty she was needed at Birchanger tomorrow, and would go on to Upper Edgecombe from there.

The bedroom Letty had given Charlotte was comfortable, and three times the size of her room at home. Charlotte had pleaded tiredness, retiring early with a cup of hot chocolate, which was now ignored and cooling on the little side table.

She tucked her feet up into the chair by the fire and read Matthew's letter again. She skimmed over the part where he explained what he had done about his brother, and how Webb had asked the landlord at the Hare and Hounds to put word out to watch for Smith.

It was the final section she concentrated on, even though she'd already read that part several times.

Arriving back here this morning brought home to me what a huge difference you have made. Birchanger feels like a proper home now, one that is a delight to be in. I do hope you feel able to continue with the remaining rooms.

Unfortunately Smith is still a potential danger, but Webb or Jackson—or both if you feel it necessary—will be happy to escort you whenever and wherever you wish to go, you need only ask.

I have to go away on business again. However, I am happy to leave all decisions about the Hall in your capable hands. I know Webb will value your continuing advice, as well.

I will miss our conversations while I am away, but I look forward to seeing what further improvements you will have made to the Hall when I return.

It only remains to assure you that my offer remains open, should you change your mind.

Your sincere friend,

Matthew Southam

Charlotte rested her head on the back of her chair. That comment about her turning Birchanger into a home—it sounded as if he were taking no credit himself for the improvements. So much had changed: the tenants had decent homes again; the Jackson children were well-fed and happy; there were more jobs for local people.

Granted, most of the day-to-day decisions had been taken by herself and Webb, but he'd agreed to them. He'd also given Webb the steward's job, even though Webb was demonstrably not yet capable of doing it on his own. And he had treated her as if she had a mind of her own and opinions to be respected, giving her far more responsibility than was normally given to a woman.

She read the letter again. It *was* good to know that he appreciated her efforts, and wanted her to continue. Their last meeting had been so awkward that she hadn't really been sure he'd meant his request for her to continue.

That last sentence—it could just mean he would still be willing to give her the protection of his name if any gossip did start. Or it might mean he *wanted* to marry her. She couldn't shake off her impression that she'd missed something when he had made his proposal.

Folding the letter, she placed it on the bedside table and got into bed. She *would* go to Birchanger on the way home tomorrow, and find way to talk to him in private.

Charlotte left Davie in the kitchen stroking Reena, and went through to Webb's office, asking if the major was available.

"Sorry, Mrs MacKinnon, 'e's not 'ere." Webb stood up from his desk as she spoke, looking surprised, as if she should have known that Matthew was not at Birchanger.

Charlotte paused in the process of removing her bonnet and cloak. "Oh. His letter did say something about going away on business." She hadn't realised he meant so soon. "When will he be back, do you know?"

"A month or so, 'e weren't sure, ma'am."

"A month!" The nervous knot in her stomach got worse. A month was a long time to wait to resolve things.

Webb looked surprised again. "'E said it depends on who they give 'im, could be longer, but not likely to be shorter. Are you working 'ere today, ma'am? There's some coffee made, then the furniture what's comin'."

"I... no. No, I've got some writing to get done. I came up for a word with the major. I can tell Mrs Malplass what to do with the furniture."

"Are you feeling quite well, ma'am?"

"Yes... yes, of course. Well, then. I'll be back up in a day or so, to see if you need any help, Sergeant." She picked up her bonnet.

"Mrs MacKinnon, do have some coffee before you go back. It's cold out. The lad could do with warmin' up as well, I reckon."

She agreed, and took a seat while Webb went to fetch coffee. No doubt Davie would persuade Sally or Mrs Jackson to give him some cake while he was in the kitchen.

"Has the major gone back to London?" she asked, when Webb returned. It was none of her business, really, but she wanted to know.

"No, ma'am. 'E was startin' in Exeter, 'e said. Workin' 'is way west from there." Webb handed her a steaming mug.

"Exeter?" She sounded like a parrot, for heaven's sake. She took the coffee, and sipped it to cover her embarrassment.

"Surveyin', ma'am. Somethin' to do with places for buildin' defences, if they decides they want them. Attached to the Royal Engineers, 'e said."

"That's good, is it?"

"Yes, ma'am," Webb said, with surprising enthusiasm, but then pressed his lips together, looking as if he'd said too much.

"You're glad he's staying in the army?" The idea of him being sent away—further away than Exeter—filled her with dismay. She'd consider that later.

"It's not that, ma'am. It'll do 'im good to be needed for somethin'. 'E was thinkin' 'e wasn't no good for—" He pressed his lips together again, looking embarrassed, as if he would take the words back if he could. "Excuse me, Mrs MacKinnon. I need to get on."

She finished her coffee and left him to his letters. As she had thought, Davie was just gathering up the crumbs from a piece of cake in the kitchen.

"Ready to go, Davie? Mr Jackson's going to take us down in the wagon."

"Can I just get a new book first, Mama?"

"New book?"

Davie rummaged in his bag and pulled out a book. "The major lent me this," he explained. "He said I could choose another one when I finished it."

Charlotte held her hand out, and he gave her the book. It was an adventure story of ships at sea, but clearly one written for boys and not an adult novel.

"Can I go and choose one?" he asked again.

She nodded absently, and Davie dashed off. She'd been so busy with her own thoughts over the last week she hadn't even looked at what Davie had been reading. In fact, she was surprised Matthew had any books suitable for a ten-year-old boy.

She'd been in the library since the boxes of books had arrived from Farleton, but she hadn't taken a close look at the shelves since Matthew had sorted them. Curiosity overcame her now, and she followed Davie into the library and wandered along the shelves. She had long thought the books a person owned—or the absence of books, if that were the case—could say a lot about what that person was like. The books here were the ones Matthew had *chosen* to bring from his other estate.

There were still a lot of empty shelves, but the books on the occupied ones were organised by subject. The first shelves she inspected held various classics translated from the original Latin or Greek. The next case contained a variety of technical and mathematical books— the kind one might expect to see on the shelves of someone whose business was surveying and fortifications. Then there were histories and travel descriptions, many of parts of Asia and the Americas as well as various places in Europe. She even found some less expected books about gardens and farming. There were one or two novels whose titles Charlotte recognised, but the final shelf she examined made her pause, gazing at them blankly.

"I've got one, Mama," Davie said. "Are we going now?"

"What? Oh, in a while, Davie. I've just... I've just thought of something I need to do first. Why don't you take your book back to the kitchen and ask Sally for some more—"

He'd gone before she finished the sentence, and she turned her attention back to the bookshelf. A pile of periodicals was stacked at one end, back copies of the titles published by Mr Berry—the ones with her articles in.

Next to those was a selection of books with titles that looked to be stories for boys—flicking through them, she saw they were indeed tales of derring do and adventure. The front pages of some had name plates with Matthew Southam or Richard Southam written in. Her heart began to race as she worked out the implications. It wasn't surprising that the Southams still had books from their childhood— what *was* surprising was their presence here at Birchanger. Had Matthew brought them here specifically to lend to Davie?

Charlotte sat down heavily in one of the chairs, suddenly feeling weak at the knees. She *had* completely misunderstood the situation, misunderstood him. She had quite possibly rejected the one person she needed, the one man who would not try to order *her* life solely for his own advantage, and the one man Davie might not resent too much as a stepfather.

And if she were to be honest with herself, Matthew was the one man she *wanted*.

Why had he looked so ill at ease when he called on her? He'd been so tongue-tied. He'd apologised for what his brother had done... *hadn't he?*

She distinctly remembered that she had wanted that kiss, but perhaps he hadn't seen it that way. Had he been apologising for imposing himself on her? Why would he think so?

Well, she *had* been avoiding him for a couple of weeks before the ice house, ever since she'd seen him exercising in the stables. She'd been doing it because she was afraid to admit to her own feelings and needs, not because he had offended her—but there was no way he could have known that. If he really lacked confidence in himself as Webb had implied, perhaps he had misread her actions and could be blaming himself.

"You all right, ma'am?" Charlotte jumped when Webb spoke from the doorway. She realised she was still holding one of the adventure stories, and she quickly put it down, trying to gather her wits. *What to do now?*

"Ma'am?"

"Sorry, Sergeant. I was wool gathering." She stood up. "Tell me, how are the men getting on with clearing the kitchen garden?"

⁓

Matthew's room at the Ship Inn in Dawlish was comfortable, if a trifle shabby. It was too small to dine in, so he was sharing his meal in a parlour downstairs with Lieutenant Meadows. Meadows was friendly enough, but didn't seem to have any interests outside his current job.

Well, he did have one other interest. Meadows had just got engaged to the daughter of a vicar near his home town, and after only three days in his company, Matthew knew almost everything there was to know about dear Susannah. Far more than he wanted to know.

He felt a little envious of someone who seemed to be settled and happy in his choice, even if the young woman did sound dull, but he was too tired to feel anything much. He'd come on horseback, and so hadn't brought Reena with him. As a result he was having nightmares again—thankfully not as bad as they used to be, but he still wasn't getting a full night's sleep.

Matthew and Meadows had spent the first couple of days being shown around the coastal defences near Exeter. They needed to meet the colonel of militia based in Exeter, but the man was difficult to pin down, so they were working their way down the coast until a meeting could be arranged. It was enjoyable work, checking for possible landing sites away from the already-fortified ports—not too taxing, and it helped to keep his mind off his failure to win Charlotte's hand.

Almost as if thinking about her had worked some kind of magic, the girl who came to clear their dishes handed him a letter from her apron pocket.

"This come today, Major."

Matthew recognised Charlotte's handwriting. He felt a mixture of hope and dread—but whatever it said, he was not going to open it and read it in public.

"Letter from home, sir?" Meadows asked.

"Just a business letter," he said, managing nonchalance. "I think I'll take a bottle to my room. We need an early start in the morning?"

"Yes, sir. Goodnight, sir."

He went to the taproom for a bottle of port, then to his bedroom. Once alone, he propped the letter on the small table and poured himself a glass. It would either be good news—she had changed her mind—or the end of all his hopes if she was writing to say, once and for all, that she did not wish to accept his offer.

Stupid! It could just as easily be some business matter, perhaps even written on Webb's behalf. Even that would be good, in a way. It would mean she hadn't taken against him so much that she didn't want to work for him any more. He finished the glass of port he'd poured out, then picked up the letter and broke the seal.

It wasn't what he had expected. It wasn't any of the things he had thought it might be.

He scanned it again, just to be sure.

...Webb fell off Daisy... dignity hurt more than his person...

...dining table looks very well in the room... looking forward to showing you the improvements...

...organise a celebratory dinner when you return, even if just the squire and his wife...

...Davie enjoying the adventure books you sent up...

...kitchen garden coming along nicely... men can start ditching in the fields...

...Jackson found two more mantraps, Webb says that's all of them now...

There were no decisions for him to make, or spending to authorise. It was just a letter from a friend, telling him what she'd been doing and... and looking forward to his return? He read it again. Yes, it read that way.

A feeling of lightness spread through his body, as if a burden had been removed. It wasn't *just* a letter from a friend. It was a letter from a friend he thought he'd lost.

On that thought, he firmly corked the remains of the port and undressed. Lying in bed, he allowed himself to think of her grey eyes, the way the sun brought warm lights to her brown hair, and her smile. Those, at least, he would still have. He tried to keep his thoughts away from the other things about her he wanted but might never have.

He fell asleep remembering how good she had felt in his arms.

CHAPTER 51

$\mathcal{M}$ary walked up the lane from the village, turning the letter over in her hand. As far as she could tell, it had come from London, so it must be from Charlotte's aunt or her father. If it was from Charlotte's father, it wasn't likely to be good news.

She hung up her coat and removed her muddy boots, debating whether to give the letter to Charlotte right away, or to let her concentrate on her work for a bit longer. Charlotte had not been doing well lately—Mary had entered the parlour several times in the last few days to find her staring at nothing. Mary's eyebrows rose. Come to think of it, she'd been like that ever since she'd been imprisoned with Lord Tillson in the ice house. *Interesting...*

Best get it over with. She went into the parlour and gave Charlotte the letter.

"Your father?" Mary asked, seeing her friend's frown. "Bad news?"

"It will be," Charlotte said, breaking the seal. She scanned the letter, then closed her eyes for a moment. Her hand trembled slightly.

"Charlotte?"

Charlotte shook her head, passing the letter over.

Mary read it, struggling to decipher the scrawled handwriting. She did not understand a few of the long words, but she got the gist. "He's going to get a magistrate to take Davie away? Can he do that?"

"I don't know," Charlotte said dully. "He probably can. If I won't return to London—which also means marrying whoever he decides I should—he's going to claim I am not educating *his* grandson properly, nor keeping him in accommodation suitable for the grandson of a gentleman. He'll say that I am not a fit mother, and so should not be left in charge of Davie."

"The boy's healthy, happy, and even learnin' Latin!" Mary said indignantly.

"Yes. But we're only women, Mary," Charlotte went on bitterly. "Who are *we* to judge the right way of doing things?"

"But I thought he wanted to sell you off to someone? Who'd want a wife who was a bad mother?"

Charlotte shrugged. "Who knows the way some men think? If he's found some ancient lecher who wants a legitimate heir, the child can just be handed over to nurses and tutors." She took the letter back from Mary, glancing over it again before putting it on the table. "He may just want to impose his will on me. I defied him twice, after all— running away with Angus, and then when I bought this place with you."

"What will you do?"

"I don't know." Charlotte stood with her fingers pressing her temples for a minute. "I don't know," she said again, looking at Mary with a frown. Then she glanced down at the pile of papers she'd been working on, suddenly sweeping them all onto the floor.

"Charlotte!" Mary made a movement to pick them up, but stopped herself. The papers weren't important at the moment.

"What's the use?" Charlotte started pacing up and down the small space in front of the fire. "We've struggled for years to make ends meet, just so I can keep Davie out of my father's clutches. And just when things were beginning to go really well, this happens!"

"There's always Sir Vincent," Mary started to say. "He could—"

"Bloody *men!*" Charlotte almost shouted, her temper flaring. "*I* can't do anything? Only a *man* can? I'm not worth anything except as some man's *wife?*" She took a deep breath.

Mary realised she was staring with her mouth open, and closed it quickly. She watched as Charlotte gradually calmed down. She'd never seen her in such a state before.

"I'm sorry, Mary—"

"I weren't suggesting you had to marry Sir Vincent," Mary said. "Only, he's a magistrate, in't he? That's all I meant. Maybe he'd know if your father can really do this."

"Oh." Charlotte took a deep breath, and rubbed her forehead. "Yes, I suppose he might. I'd better write... or should I go and see him? Do you think—"

"I think you should go for a walk," Mary said firmly. "Oh, maybe not. There's that Smith." She frowned, glancing at the letter still lying on the table, then out of the window. The weather looked pleasant. "I reckon you should dig the garden for a bit."

Charlotte frowned.

"Really, a bit of exercise'll do you good. You've bin sitting in here too long, it's no wonder that letter has overset you so. And imagine stabbing the spade into your father every time." Mary smiled, humourlessly.

Charlotte stared at her for a moment, then out of the window. "Very well, I'll go and change my dress. Digging might help me think what to do." She put her hand out for the letter.

"No, don't take that," Mary said. "Try not to think about it, then you'll have a clearer head when you come in again."

Charlotte nodded, and went to change.

Mary waited until she saw Charlotte safely wielding a spade in the garden, then found a clean sheet of paper and a pen. She sat down at the table, pulling the letter towards her. When she finished copying it, she'd get John's spare pistol and take it with her up to Birchanger; that Smith would regret it if he came near her.

～

Charlotte felt a little better after an hour's digging, using the time to think about her situation. No matter how unfair it was, bemoaning the way men ran the world for their own benefit wasn't helpful. For the moment, she had to accept things the way they were, and that she needed the assistance of a man.

Her father had said he would call on her in a week for her decision—accept his choice of husband and have Davie sent to school at his expense, or have her son taken away from her and be allowed no further contact with him. From the date on the letter, she should have five days left. But she wouldn't put it past him to arrive earlier than he'd said.

Mary wasn't around when Charlotte went back indoors. She put the kettle on and called Davie in for a cup of tea, then sat down in her parlour to write to Sir Vincent. She'd have to ask John to go down to the village again with it when he came in.

She took a deep breath.

She would also write to the major... Matthew. She would accept his offer of marriage, and try to explain that she was not doing so only because of her father's threat.

She hoped he had not offered only out of duty. She would have to hope he *wanted* this.

∿

Webb scratched his head as he tried to decipher the writing in front of him. Mary resisted the temptation to tap her foot, but eventually held her hand out for the copy of the letter she'd made. "Should I read it to you?"

"It'd be quicker," he admitted.

Mary took it back and read it out loud, halting slightly over some of the longer words.

Webb frowned as she read. "It's a bad business, right enough," he said when she finished. "But I dunno what I can do about it."

"If she was married," Mary said, "her husband would have charge of Davie and her father couldn't do anythin' about it."

"Makes sense," Webb said.

"Only to a man!" Mary muttered. "So I was thinking…" She broke off as she saw Webb's expression change to one of shock. "No, not *you*, you daft fool!"

Webb gave a weak smile. "No, 'course not. Who, then?"

"Who d'you think?" *Men—can't see what's in front of them!*

He frowned, then eventually his face cleared and he grinned. "Oh, of course. Just the ticket for the major, too, I reckon. Do you think 'e's interested?"

"What?" Mary sighed. "He come down to see Mrs Captain the day before he went off to London, didn't he?"

Webb nodded.

"Just got out of bed and come down, did he?" *Like getting blood out of a stone.*

"No, 'e spent ages 'avin' a bath an' shavin'. Got Mrs Jackson to press 'is…" Webb trailed off. "Oh. I see what you mean. But 'e's in Exeter, or even further."

"Well get him back then!"

"They'd need the banns…" Webb looked thoughtful. "'E brung an awful lot of papers with 'im from London. 'E give some to me and Mrs Captain—accounts and such. But 'e kept quite a lot. D'you reckon there might be a special licence?"

"Where's the papers?"

"In 'is room. But I can't—"

Mary stood up decisively. "*I* can. You can send for the constable if you want, or you can help me look. If I've guessed right, he'll *want* you to send for him."

The Mermaid, one street back from the sea front in Teignmouth, had a comfortable parlour, warmed by a crackling fire. Matthew sat at a small table, a glass of ale to hand, reading over his notes from the last couple of days. Lieutenant Meadows had, thankfully, decided to spend the rest of the afternoon sampling the local brews in a more lively establishment, so Matthew had the place to himself.

Voices in the corridor warned him he was about to have company, then the door burst open. Looking round to protest this noisy intrusion, the words died on his lips as Richard entered the room. His coat and hat dripped water onto the floor, and his face was lined with tiredness.

Matthew stood, his chair scraping along the floor.

"Rich, what are you doing here? Is something wrong?"

"Bloody hell, Matt," Richard said, pulling off his hat and putting it on a table. "I've asked for you in nearly every inn in this damned town. Webb said you'd be in The George."

Matt shrugged. "They were full. What—"

"Ale," Richard said to the landlord. "And food. Whatever you have that's quick." He glanced at Matthew. "For two."

The landlord hesitated a moment then, at Richard's glare, left the room, pulling the door closed behind him.

"Rich, what's happened?" Matthew asked again, his voice more urgent this time.

"No-one's died, don't worry." Richard took off his wet coat and sat by the fire, stretching his legs out towards the blazing logs. He fumbled in a pocket and took out a folded paper. "Here, read that."

Matthew took it, puzzled. He didn't recognise the handwriting. "Who's this from?"

"Mary..." Richard snapped his fingers. "The other Mrs MacKinnon. Copy of a letter your Mrs MacKinnon received. From her father, according to Webb. Webb rode to Farleton with it."

"What has—"

"Just read it, Matt. Then I'll explain."

Matthew puzzled out the scrawled writing, his lips thinning and brows drawing together as he realised what the letter was saying. "You know what's in this?" he said to Richard, his hand almost shaking as he tried to control his anger.

"Yes, Webb explained. Nasty bit of work, your Mrs MacKinnon's father. Makes Mama look almost pleasant."

"Webb sent you? Why?"

"The other Mrs MacKinnon told him to bring me the letter, so, like a good chap, he did as he was told." Richard smiled.

Matthew took a deep breath. "I'll help if I can, of course, but I'm not sure what I can do. Pay for a lawyer, I suppose, if she'll accept that."

"If she were married, her husband would be the lad's guardian. Her father couldn't threaten her again like this."

Matthew felt heat rise in his face, his gaze sliding away from his brother.

"Looks like she was right," Richard said, grinning.

A maid entered with a laden tray.

"Ah, ale. And the food. Eat up, Matt, we need to be on the road again sharpish. Landlord's sorting out a change of horses."

"Who was right?" Matthew asked, desperately trying to make sense of what his brother was saying.

"Mary... the other one." Richard waved a hand.

"Mary Deacon. She got married a couple of weeks ago."

"Lot of it about," Richard said, grinning again. "Eat. I'm in the curricle, I'll take you to Exeter. You can try for a seat on the overnight mail—it'll be quicker. If not, we'll have to drive. You can hire a horse in Bath to take you the rest of the way."

Richard tucked into the plate of stew and, after a moment, Matthew did the same, trying to read the letter through again as he ate. This time he noticed the statement that Metcalf would call on his daughter within a week. Checking the date, he finally realised why Richard was in such a rush.

Damn. That meeting with the colonel of militia in Exeter was in two days.

Charlotte is more important.

He'd have to leave the meeting in Meadows' hands, and hope he would ask all the right questions. He bolted down the rest of the stew, scribbling a quick note for the lieutenant before going to his room for his coat and hat.

~

The booking office in Exeter could only offer him an inside seat on the mail, but Matthew bought the ticket without hesitation. Richard looked dead on his feet now and he didn't feel much better; they were too tired to drive themselves, and would take a lot longer than the mail in any case. Richard found a room for the night; he would drive himself back to Farleton the following morning.

Once the coach was moving, Matthew leaned back in his seat, resting his head on the panel behind and closing his eyes. Thankfully the other passengers did not seem to want to talk, but he doubted he'd get any sleep anyway with the thoughts spinning through his head. Perhaps that was just as well—no sleep meant no nightmares.

There hadn't been much time for thought in the curricle—he'd either been driving, or ensuring Richard did not lose the way in the gathering dusk. Now he went over the contents of Metcalf's letter again. *Despicable!*

Marriage. There was no doubt that marriage would allow Charlotte's new husband to take guardianship of her son and so prevent Metcalf's coercion, although that would still mean she would lose control herself. Would she trust *him* not to dictate her actions?

Matthew frowned. The idea of marriage appeared to have come from Webb, or Mary Deacon, not Charlotte herself. Would she want that solution? The friendly letter he'd received a couple of days ago, now worn from re-reading, made him hope she might not be too averse to the idea. He should forget her reaction to his disastrous proposal—any sane woman would have turned him down after that.

He did his best to stop thinking—about anything—as the coach jolted on. He still had a long ride from Bath to Edgecombe before him, and he'd be no use to anyone if he was too tired to get there. He managed to sleep for part of the night, getting out for a few minutes at some of the stops to stretch his legs and take some air. Now and then the walls of the coach began to close in on him, but he resolutely turned his mind to grey eyes and chestnut hair, and although the feeling didn't pass, it moderated enough to allow him to doze off again.

~

"My lord!"

Matthew didn't hear the voice amid the bustle in the busy inn yard. He stretched, stiff after sitting in the coach for so many hours, and rubbed his face.

A horse. He needed to hire a horse.

"Sir, Lord Tillson!" This time there was a touch on his shoulder, and he looked around.

"Deacon?"

"Yes, my lord. Webb sent me. I've got your horse, and Webb says you've to go to Leverton Park, not Birchanger."

"What? Why?"

"He didn't say." Deacon gave a wry smile. "Mary's been sorting things out, I reckon. Glad I caught you here. Reckoned the mail was the quickest option."

Matthew nodded, too tired to really take in what Deacon was saying. Only the bit about going to Leverton registered.

Hell. Richard had suggested that marriage was the way out, if she'd have him; he'd assumed *he* was the intended husband. If Webb had summoned him back just to be a witness while Charlotte married that slowtop Kinney, he'd have the man's guts for garters.

"Sir?"

"What?" He realised Deacon must have been trying to say something.

"Best have a quick bite before you set off, my lord. They're still serving breakfast. I'll get the horse saddled."

Matthew rubbed his face again. He'd get some coffee, at least.

CHAPTER 52

*M*atthew rode straight round the side of the house to the stables when he arrived at Leverton Park, feeling in no fit state to present himself at the front door. Webb must have been watching for him, as he appeared before Matthew had finished giving one of Sir Vincent's grooms instructions about the horse.

"Sir! You all right, sir?" Webb's initial greeting turned to concern when he took in Matthew's appearance.

"As well as can be expected after travelling for most of a day, Webb. Is Mrs MacKinnon safe? Well?"

"Yessir."

Matthew released a breath.

"So far, sir," Webb continued. "'Er father ain't come yet. 'E could come any time, though."

"If Sir Vincent is taking care of things, why did you summon me here in such a rush?"

"With all due respect, don't be daft, sir." Webb's tone seemed to indicate that not much respect was actually due. He held out a packet. "I brung these for you."

Matthew took the packet and pulled the string undone. He recognised the special licence he'd obtained in London and the other legal documents Kellet had helped him draw up. He'd been hopeful when he made those preparations. Hopeful, and determined to make a better job of his next proposal, but not confident. Even those feelings were better than the sense of loss and finality now forming a cold knot in his guts. Webb must have rifled through his private papers, but he couldn't bring himself to be annoyed about it. Not now the woman he loved was to marry someone else.

"What do I need these for?" he asked bitterly. "Webb, what the hell am I doing here?"

"What do you think, sir? She ain't married that bag of wind, if that's what—"

He broke off as Charlotte's voice interrupted them. "Sergeant, that's not a very kind way to talk about Sir Vincent!"

Matthew turned, and his breath caught as he saw her. She met his glance with a smile, her cheeks turning pink.

Webb's last words had sown a little seed of hope, and he returned her smile, a lump lodging in his throat.

"Sir, just do as you're told, sir," Webb muttered so only Matthew heard, and sidled out of the stable.

Charlotte had seen Webb rush out of the house and followed out of curiosity, not expecting Matthew to arrive for another day or two. The sight of him standing in the stables set her heart racing, filling her with happy anticipation instead of the worry of the previous few days.

Her blush deepened as Matthew smiled, then she took in the state of his clothes and the lines of tiredness on his face. Concern dampened the happiness and relief she felt at seeing him here so soon.

"You haven't married Sir Vincent?" Matthew asked, his smile fading.

"No." She bit her lip, her happiness receding further. He wouldn't have asked that question if he *had* received the letter accepting his proposal. "You didn't get my letter?" Better to be sure.

"I got your letter about the gardens a few days ago." He ran one hand through his hair, now beginning to look confused.

Why is he here? Surely any business with Sir Vincent would not require him to have travelled in such haste?

The knot of nerves in her stomach intensified. It had been difficult enough to write that letter accepting his proposal—now she had to *say* it.

And hope that he is still willing to marry me.

"I sent another letter two days ago. If you didn't get it, why are you here now?"

"Webb sent a message via Farleton—Richard brought it to me, and got me on the mail from Exeter. He sent a copy of your father's letter. You know nothing about this?"

My father's letter? How...?

Mary! It must have been Mary. No-one else knew about the letter until she'd told Sir Vincent about it. Meddling woman, although she was very glad Mary *had* meddled, under the circumstances.

Matthew's expression lightened, then he ran his hand through his hair again. "Why are you here? Has Sir Vincent—"

"I came to ask his opinion, as a magistrate. He confirmed that my father could do nothing if I were married."

"I see," Matthew said flatly, looking away, his lips pressed together.

"And I thought it was better to be here in case my father came before you arrived," Charlotte ploughed on. "Sir Vincent might have been able to stop him taking Davie away. I'm not sure how, but he said he would try."

She broke off and took a deep breath, blushing again. *Why is it so hard to say?* At least he'd turned back to face her.

"I... well, I was hoping you meant what you said in the letter you sent to Northridge with Webb. That *your* offer still stands. That was what I wrote to you, but you have not had that letter."

Matthew gazed at her, stunned, and a flush of hope sent his heart racing. This was what he wanted, and he worried for a moment that he was only hearing what he wished to hear.

She needs my protection, that's all. He shook his head, pushing the thought away.

"Major?" She sounded concerned.

"My apologies, Mrs MacKinnon." He blinked, then took a deep breath, standing straighter. "I would be honoured if you would accept my hand. Will you?" *Damn—that proposal was little better than the first!*

"Yes, sir. With pleasure. And thank you."

He smiled, feeling rather dazed.

"You look exhausted, Major. You should—"

"Matthew," he said. "Or Matt, if you prefer. If we really are to be married?"

"Matthew," she said, smiling up at him. The smile lit her face, and his breath caught again. He wanted to reach out and touch her cheek, to pull her close.

"I hope it wasn't too inconvenient, dragging you away from your job," she said, her smile fading a little.

The thought of that meeting with the colonel crossed his mind, and he dismissed it. He wasn't sure Meadows could handle it, but he'd deal with that later. It was not important compared to this. Nothing was as important as this.

"No, not at all."

"I have, haven't I?" Charlotte said, biting her lip.

He could see a frown forming. He'd paused too long before replying. "Really, Mrs... Charlotte. You haven't interrupted anything of importance, I assure you."

She still looked worried. "I think Mr Bretherton should be able to issue an ordinary licence instead of waiting for the banns to be read, but he's away at the moment." She glanced at him, then away again, hands gripping each other hard. "It might take a few days—"

"Don't worry, Charlotte." *She must be concerned about her father turning up.* He glanced down at the packet of papers Webb had given him, happy this problem could be resolved so easily. "I... er, at one point it was possible we would *need* to marry, if my brother or Smith started to spread gossip, and if that were the case I thought it best done quickly. So I got a special licence. We can get married as soon as you wish."

He hoped she wasn't offended by his presumption, but her face showed only relief. He held out the packet of papers to her. "Charlotte, if you are sure you want to do this, read these while I get cleaned up." He looked doubtfully at his clothing. "I'm not sure how clean—"

"I think Webb will have brought some of your things," Charlotte interrupted him. "A most efficient sergeant."

"Indeed." He held out the papers again, and this time she took them. "They can be changed if you wish," he said.

She looked at the packet, then back at him. "What—"

A discreet cough stopped her, and they both looked towards the doorway. Webb stood in the middle of the courtyard, far enough away not to have overheard anything.

"If you would come this way, Major?" he called.

"I suspect your bath is ready," Charlotte said, smiling again as she turned to follow Webb.

Matthew picked up his bag and went after them, a warm glow spreading through him as he began to believe this really *was* happening.

Charlotte made her way to the bedroom Lady Kinney had reluctantly assigned to her; it was the only place she could read the papers without interruption. She had hardly set foot on the stairs when Sir Vincent opened his library door and called her name.

"Mrs MacKinnon?" She looked around and he made an inviting gesture. She sighed, but he *had* been very kind to her, so she turned and followed him into the library.

"I saw Lord Tillson arrive," he said. "Have you spoken to him?"

"Yes, sir. We are to be married."

"Good, good. I'm glad that is settled." He smiled, showing genuine pleasure. Charlotte was amused by the irony of the fact that she liked him better than she ever had before. Now that he no longer regarded her as his future wife, he seemed to have stopped thinking of her as a little woman who needed guidance, and considered her to be simply a person.

"I am very grateful for your help, sir."

Glancing down at the documents in her hands, she thought she should read them before going any further. *No—there can't be anything in them that would make me change my mind.* The knot that had lodged in her stomach since receiving her father's letter was gone, a small bubble of joy growing in its place. *This is the right thing to do, for many reasons.*

"Lord Tillson brought a special licence," she went on. "Do you think your vicar would be able to marry us tomorrow? I don't wish to take him away from his duties any longer than necessary."

"I'll send a man down with a note immediately," Sir Vincent promised. She thanked him as he turned and left the room.

Charlotte put the packet of papers on a table, then took two letters from her pocket. The first was her father's letter, read many times since it arrived. The other was from her aunt, Lady Henbury. She opened it for one last time, words jumping out at her.

...Meerbrook says Metcalf... Earl of Billesdon...needs an heir... second wife... fifty if he's a day... dissolute...

She screwed it up, along with her father's letter, and threw them into the fire, then stabbed at the curling fragments with the poker until they turned completely to ash.

Dusting her hands, she sat at the table and picked up Matthew's packet of papers.

Charlotte first looked at the special licence, then put it to one side. There were two documents headed Last Will and Testament—she did not read these but, curious to see why there were two, glanced at the signatures at the end. One of them was unsigned, while the other had been signed and witnessed. She mentally calculated the dates; it had been drawn up when Matthew had been in London, just days after his proposal to her.

She put those to one side, too. No doubt she would find out at some point why there were two copies.

The final document was a marriage settlement. She paused for a moment. The special licence—he had given a reason for buying that, which made some sense. Paying his solicitor to draw up a marriage settlement seemed strange, though, before a marriage had even been agreed. Had he been so confident she would change her mind?

No, not confident. Hopeful, perhaps?

Charlotte unfolded the settlement and read through it carefully, since some of the legal phrasing was not immediately clear. Then she read it again, still not sure she had understood it correctly.

A marriage settlement was supposed to provide for a widow after her husband died; she knew that, even though she had not had one for her marriage with Angus. But the sum of five hundred pounds per annum was generous. He had also included two hundred pounds a year for her sole use during his lifetime as well as a provision for school fees for Davie. That was generous indeed. She would have expected to be given some pin money, but not so much.

She put the paper down with a shaking hand. He must have arranged all this in London, when the reason for marrying her would only have been to avoid scandal. No, when she *thought* that was the reason. These documents made it clear that his offer had not been intended only to protect her good name.

Tears prickled her eyes, and she resolutely blinked them away. She would make this marriage work—for both of them—and she could start by *not* crying at her wedding!

CHAPTER 53

*C*harlotte heard a knock on the door, and a maid came in with a message that Sir Vincent requested her presence in the parlour. When she entered, she saw that Matthew was there too—bathed, shaved and in clean clothes. His expression, she thought, was somewhere between anxious and worried.

"Ah, Mrs MacKinnon," Sir Vincent said as she came in. "I've had word from the vicar. He has to go to London tomorrow, but he can perform the ceremony this afternoon if you wish." He glanced at the clock. "In an hour."

"Very well," she said, without hesitation, feeling suddenly breathless. She glanced at Matthew, relieved to see him smile.

"Tillson?"

"If Mrs MacKinnon does not feel rushed, then this afternoon suits me very well."

"Sir Vincent, do you know where Davie is?" Charlotte asked.

"Want the little chap to be present, do you?" Sir Vincent said. "Samuel took him fishing, I think." He glanced at the dusk outside the window. "They should be back soon. I'll ask the housekeeper to make arrangements, then send someone to find him." He nodded in their general direction and left the room.

"I'm afraid I didn't buy a ring," Matthew said apologetically. "I do have this…" He held out a signet ring. "Or perhaps Lady Kinney would—"

Charlotte shook her head, taking the ring and holding it against her finger. It would be a loose fit, but she could find some way to fasten it so she did not lose it. "I would rather use this," she said, handing it back with a smile.

"Did you read the documents, Charlotte? Are the terms acceptable?"

"The settlement terms are exceedingly generous, thank you. I was not expecting so much."

"Well, most of it won't be relevant for some time." He looked uncomfortable. "I'm afraid I need to get back to my duties fairly soon."

Her heart sank—not just from the prospect of having to face her father alone. They needed some time, some privacy, to talk. But, according to Webb, this job was important to him.

"I understand," she said, trying to sound reassuring. "Really I do. When do you need to be back in Devon?"

"In a day or two, if possible." He cleared his throat. "I was going to ask," he went on, "if you, and Davie of course, would care to join me. We could travel down tomorrow, and arrive some time the next day. I would usually be busy during the day, I'm afraid, and April is a bit cold for staying by the sea, but there should be plenty to see or do. And if your father comes…"

She smiled at the idea that she might need persuasion to agree to such a trip. "Matthew, it's an excellent idea. Davie has never been further than Bath, so I think a stay near the sea… with you… would be wonderful. For *both* of us."

"Excellent. It won't be as comfortable as Birchanger, but—"

Someone knocked at the door, then opened it without waiting for an acknowledgement. They both turned towards the door.

"Ah, sorry to interrupt," Sir Vincent said. "Mrs MacKinnon, one of the grooms is fetching young David back. I thought I'd let you know."

"Thank you, Sir Vincent," Charlotte said, suppressing her irritation at the interruption.

Sir Vincent nodded at them as he left, pulling the door closed behind him.

Charlotte looked at Matthew, a small smile curving her lips as she raised an eyebrow. "Even a room at an inn will feel more... private... than here."

He returned her smile, looking more relaxed.

She gestured at the dress she was wearing. "Now, I think I ought to get changed in honour of the occasion."

"You look beautiful whatever you are wearing," he said, his voice deepening with unmistakable sincerity, the expression in his eyes making her catch her breath.

He lifted her hand and kissed it, sending a flush of heat to her face.

"In an hour, then," he said.

Mary was waiting in Charlotte's room when she got there, looking pretty in her best blue gown. She was supervising a couple of maids filling a bath. "All workin' out then?" Mary asked.

"I think so. That is, yes, very well." Charlotte looked Mary in the eye. "Thank you for getting Webb to fetch Matthew... the major."

Mary shrugged. "Someone had to show some sense!"

"We're going to Devon with Matthew tomorrow." She felt her face reddening—again—at the thought. His given name was coming more naturally to her now.

Mary frowned, then a knowing grin spread across her face. "I'll be off back home this evening then, an' I'll send a trunk down with the things you need. Unless you want to go back for it?"

Charlotte shook her head. Her father might arrive in Edgecombe, and she didn't want to have to face him alone. She undressed and enjoyed a good soak in the hot water, before drying herself and putting on clean undergarments.

Mary laid out Charlotte's favourite dark green gown. "You'll not be wearing blacks for your wedding," Mary stated.

Charlotte smiled. "Thank you for bringing that one."

A knock on the door heralded a maid with a small bunch of

hothouse flowers 'with the compliments of Sir Vincent'. Charlotte suspected that the housekeeper was responsible, but she was touched anyway.

Mary helped her to put up her hair in a loose knot at the back with a couple of the flowers in it, and a few curls teased out to frame her face. She pinned two more of the flowers to her dress, and Mary used a length of green ribbon to make the rest into a nosegay.

There was another knock on the door. This time, Sir Vincent stood in the doorway, holding a slightly grubby Davie by one arm. Charlotte frowned, but her son's sulky expression suggested why he had arrived in such a fashion.

Mary took one look at him and pulled him into the room. "Into the bath now, young man," she said firmly, hands on hips.

"You go on down," Mary said to Charlotte, and stood over Davie as he reluctantly started to remove his clothes.

Sir Vincent offered his arm, and Charlotte followed him out onto the landing, pulling the door closed behind her. She stopped a few paces from the bedroom door.

"I'm sorry if my son was misbehaving, Sir Vincent," Charlotte apologised.

"Needs a man's guidance, my dear. I've always said so."

He had, and for the first time Charlotte wondered if he might be right.

"Tillson's welcome to the little..." He stopped, pressing his lips firmly together.

"Sir Vincent, I cannot thank you enough for the help you've given me over the last few days," she said, trying to ignore her irritation at his last words.

He patted her hand comfortingly. "My pleasure, my dear."

"I do need to talk to my son, Sir Vincent. I will follow you down in a few minutes."

"Very well, my dear."

He went off down the stairs, and Charlotte returned to her room. Davie was just finishing washing, so she handed him a towel, ignoring the scowl on his face. Davie perched on a chair by the fire while Mary picked out a clean set of clothes for him.

"Davie?" Charlotte said, pulling up a chair to sit next to him. "I'm marrying the major. I thought you liked him?"

"Don't want you to get married," Davie muttered.

Charlotte sighed. "Davie, I'm sorry I didn't tell you what was happening, but I didn't want you to worry."

Davie's scowl lightened a little, but that was all.

"Davie, I *want* to marry the major." She knelt on the floor in front of him, her hands on his shoulders. "Remember I told you we came here to keep my father from taking you away?"

He nodded silently, eyes wide. Charlotte thought he'd managed to forget that threat over the last couple of days, and was sorry she'd had to remind him. She rubbed his shoulders through the towel. "If I marry the major, that won't happen. My father will not bother us again. Ever."

Davie frowned.

Thinking this time, not sulking? She wasn't sure.

She rubbed his shoulders again. "Davie, it will turn out well. Trust me?"

Someone knocked at the door before Davie could answer. She heard Mary move over to open it, and a low-voiced question and answer.

"You're wanted downstairs," Mary said, crossing the room to where Charlotte still knelt. "You go," she said. "I'll bring him down when he's dressed."

Charlotte paused just inside the door to the front parlour, noting that the furniture had been rearranged. A small table stood in front of one of the windows, with a bowl of flowers on it matching the ones she was carrying. The vicar had set out his prayer book and other paraphernalia. Beyond the window the lowering sun lit the lawn and the trees beside the drive.

Matthew stood by the table, his eyes widening and his body going still as his gaze fell on her. Charlotte felt a shiver of pleasure as she noted his reaction. She met his gaze for a moment, then dragged her attention away to take in the rest of the people present.

Sir Vincent stood next to Matthew. Lady Kinney and her daughters were sitting on chairs to one side, their expressions neutral. Charlotte supposed that Lady Kinney's relief at not having her for a daughter-in-law was warring with annoyance that the highest ranking man in the near neighbourhood was no longer a possible suitor for one of her daughters.

Charlotte waited by the door for Mary and Davie to arrive. Mary must have done a quick job tidying up Davie, for they didn't have to wait long. Davie still did not look happy. Charlotte, dismayed, met Mary's eye, but Mary just shrugged.

"Davie, won't you come up to the front with me?" Charlotte asked.

He gazed at her, but shook his head.

She held out a hand. "Davie?"

He shook his head again, his lower lip trembling a little.

Charlotte sighed. Perhaps she should have talked it through in more detail with him but, until a couple of hours ago, she hadn't known herself what was going to happen. It was too late now.

"Sit there then," she said, pointing to a chair by the door.

"Ignore him," Mary said. "He likes Lord Tillson usually, doesn't he? He'll get over it."

Charlotte gazed at her son for a moment, as he reluctantly went to sit on the chair, but then decided that Mary was right. She turned and walked towards the waiting men, Mary beside her.

Matthew was looking concerned. "Do you want to talk to Davie? I'm sure we can wait…"

The vicar interrupted, clearing his throat and frowning.

Charlotte shook her head. "No. This is *our* wedding. It's in his best interests too, even if he doesn't realise it yet."

Matthew touched her shoulder. "You're sure?"

Charlotte nodded, taking comfort in the warm feeling radiating from his hand.

The vicar opened his prayer book.

"Dearly beloved, we are gathered together here in the sight of God…"

～

Once the ceremony was over, Sir Vincent, showing unexpected tact, shepherded everyone else out of the room. Matthew stood facing Charlotte as she twisted the signet ring around on her finger.

"I…" She cleared her throat and tried again. "I wanted to thank you for coming so quickly."

"It was nothing." What else could he have done? She'd needed him. "I will always—"

They were interrupted by a knock on the door, and Sir Vincent's butler stepped in without waiting for an acknowledgement.

"What is it?" Matthew asked, impatient at the interruption.

"Excuse me, my lord. Sir Vincent sent me to inform you that a Mr Metcalf has arrived. He is in the library, and wishes to see Mrs… er… Lady Tillson. He has been waiting for some time, I understand."

Her father had caught up with them, then. His lips thinned. Metcalf would *not* be allowed to bully Charlotte any further.

"Very well. You may inform him that we will see him shortly."

CHAPTER 54

harlotte's brow was creased with worry, her face white and drawn. Matthew clenched a fist, trying not to let his anger show.

"I can get rid of Metcalf for you, if you wish," he said, putting a hand on her shoulder and giving what he hoped was a reassuring squeeze. "He has no legal hold over you."

Charlotte shook her head resolutely. "I think I should see him. But... will you come with me?"

"Of course."

"Davie?"

"We'll find out where he's got to first, and make sure he stays out of your father's way."

Charlotte nodded, biting her lips and taking a deep breath. She crossed to the mirror over the fireplace and pulled the flowers out of her hair.

"What are you doing?"

"I'm dressed for my wedding, not for a... a confrontation."

Matthew walked over and stood behind her, stilling her hands before she could pull any pins out. "Leave the rest, you look wonderful."

"I don't need to be dressed up to see my father," she protested, brows drawing together at the idea.

"You are dressed up for *you*, not for him. Remember, you are Lady Tillson, and he's just a mister."

"I don't care about—"

"No, but *he* does. Remember that. Now you're married, he can't do anything to you, apart from upset you and worry you—*if* you let him. You've stood up to him before."

"The stakes were not as high before," she stated, her lips turning down at the corners. "He was trying to threaten Davie as well this time."

"Not any more," Matthew said.

Charlotte thought it was better if Davie didn't know her father had arrived until after she had dealt with him. She went upstairs with Matthew and found Davie in his room. Mary was with him, and Charlotte quietly asked her to keep him there.

The butler awaited them at the bottom of the stairs. "Mr Metcalf is in the library, my lord, my lady. Sir Vincent is with him."

"Thank you," Matthew said. "If you would announce us formally, please?"

The butler gave a stately nod, then led the way across the hall. "Lord and Lady Tillson," he announced as he opened the door.

Charlotte took a deep breath.

Her father turned as they entered, his lips pursed and a frown on his brow. "You took your time! I've been kept here for over an hour. I have never been treated with such—"

Matthew coughed. "We were only informed of your arrival ten minutes ago."

"Some... some *lackey* held a pistol on me. On *me!* Prevented me from seeing my own daughter."

Webb? He must have prevented her father interrupting the wedding. Charlotte closed her eyes, thankful that this confrontation had not happened earlier. Matthew's hand closed gently around hers, and Charlotte's nervousness eased a little. Her father could do nothing to her now.

"Father," she said. She walked over to a chair near the window and sat down. "How nice of you to call. What brings you to this part of the country?"

"You know damn—"

Matthew cleared his throat. Metcalf glanced at him, drawing in a breath before he continued. "You know very well," he said, in a more moderate tone.

Indeed, you wish to bully me and my son for your own gain and spite.

"You were concerned that my son did not have a proper tutor, a large enough home, or adequate male guidance," Charlotte said, starting with the statements in his last letter. "I have remedied the last two. The matter of his education will be taken care of as soon as we identify a suitable school." She pressed her lips together, resisting the impulse to carry on talking.

"You've 'remedied' the matter by running off again, like you did when you married that Scottish wastrel! MacKinnon wasn't faithful to you, was he? I made enquiries. What did you expect from someone you coerced into marrying you?"

"Coerced? No. At the time, I *was* about to be coerced by you into a marriage with someone nearly three times my age." She was surprised —and pleased—to find that her voice was steady.

"You would have been a viscountess! And he was wealthy. Did you tell your new husband about the footman—or was it a groom—you gave yourself to in an attempt to try to get out of the match I'd arranged for you? Then you seduced MacKinnon so he'd run off with you."

"I seduced no-one," Charlotte said, managing to keep her voice calm. Before, her father's insinuations would have upset her; now they merely made her angry at his spiteful attempt to harm her new relationship. An attempt that would not succeed.

She glanced at Matthew, managing to relax her features enough to give him a smile. His lips curved slightly, and he nodded. The knot inside her faded a little more, and she turned back to face her father.

"As far as my current position goes, I had a letter from Aunt Henbury. She told me about the match you were trying to arrange for me with the Earl of Billesdon."

"So you married this—"

"Baron," Matthew said, sounding deceptively calm. Charlotte shivered at the controlled anger in his voice, but her father seemed oblivious to it.

"I've heard about you, Southam," her father spat, glancing at Matthew. "A lunatic, a seducer of innocent young girls—"

Matthew strode across the room and twisted his fists into Metcalf's lapels, slamming him into the wall. Metcalf's rant was cut off abruptly and his face lost its colour, his throat working as he swallowed.

"That is slander," Matthew said, his voice calm but his face only inches from Metcalf's. "You will *not* repeat that. I have ways of finding out what is said in London and, believe me, you *will* regret any repetition."

"How... you..."

"You know of the Earl of Marstone?" Matthew paused, but Metcalf said nothing. Matthew raised an eyebrow. "No? Above your class, is he? Well, he's a good friend of mine, and he will take a dim view of any slurs upon me or upon *my wife*. He could easily ruin you—financially and socially."

He let go of Metcalf's coat, and the man almost fell to the floor. "Do you understand me, Metcalf?" Matthew asked.

"I... er... yes." Metcalf pushed himself away from the wall and straightened his coat. He turned to his daughter, his face red with anger and shining with perspiration.

"What did you do, daughter? Offered yourself to this man to make him marry you? How else could you find someone to marry you so quickly?"

Charlotte took a deep breath, suppressing her anger. "You are mistaken," she said, keeping her voice level with an effort. "Your actions only hastened the wedding. I had already received an offer from Lord Tillson, and had already decided to accept. You should not judge everyone by your own low standards, Father."

She drew in another breath, carrying on before her father could speak. "You married my mother for money, and made her life a misery. You married off Augusta and Beatrice for your own gain, not their happiness or—"

"They have titles, wealth—"

"You clearly value those things above happiness. I do not." She gazed at him, seeing the angry flush on his cheeks and realising how ridiculous it was that he was still trying to force her to his will. She suppressed a small smile as the realisation finally dawned on her that she was free of him, for good. Until she met Matthew—or even Deacon and Webb—she hadn't really understood how venal and selfish he was.

"...no idea how the world works, *daughter*." Metcalf had regained his temper a little. "You should take advice from those who know—"

"I have sufficient advice, from better sources than you."

She stood. She owed him no respect, no duty as a daughter. It felt good to finally tell her father what she thought of him, but she needed to end this, and at a time of her choosing, not his.

"You have no hold over me or ... or *our* son." She glanced at Matthew, and received an encouraging smile. Squaring her shoulders, she spoke more firmly. "I don't know what you hoped to achieve by coming here, and I have no wish to see you ever again. Good day."

Charlotte turned her back on him and walked to the door.

"Come back here, girl," he shouted. "You cannot—"

She closed the door behind her as she left the room, cutting off his words.

"Impertinent hussy, I'll see—"

"You will do nothing." Matthew glared at Metcalf. "If you upset my wife again, in *any* way, I will call you out."

"*You* will... ha! From what I heard, you'd be too drunk—" He stopped talking abruptly as Matthew took a couple of steps towards him.

"Too drunk to hold a pistol straight?" Matthew asked, his anger under control now that Metcalf's spite was only directed at him. "Do you wish to test that theory?"

Metcalf swallowed and shook his head. Then his eyes narrowed. "I'll get the marriage annulled. There must be some irregularity. You haven't had time to call the banns."

"You will find all is in order," Matthew stated. He was tempted—so tempted—to physically throw the man out, but that would not prevent him trying to cause further trouble. "Why don't you consult a magistrate?"

The bell pull was near Metcalf. The man's face whitened as Matthew walked towards him, and he backed away a few steps and sat down. Matthew pulled the bell. When the butler appeared, Matthew asked if Sir Vincent could be summoned.

Sir Vincent must have been waiting close by, for he appeared almost immediately. "What can I do for you, Tillson?"

"Not me, Sir Vincent. Metcalf thinks the marriage documentation was not in order. He wishes to consult a magistrate."

Sir Vincent met Matthew's eyes, then looked away again. Matthew smiled to himself. Perhaps Sir Vincent was not quite the slowtop he sometimes appeared to be.

"I saw the licence myself," Sir Vincent said, addressing Metcalf. "There was nothing wrong with it. Why do you think there was?"

"Give me the direction of the local magistrate," Metcalf said. "I'm sure he can be persuaded to find an irregularity in the proceedings. And while you're here, what do you mean by allowing one of your staff to point a pistol at me?"

Sir Vincent clasped his hands behind his back, rocking on his feet slightly. "Firstly, Metcalf, the person who prevented you barging in on a private ceremony to which you had not been invited is not one of my employees. However, although it was given after the fact, he has my *full* approval for what he did in *my* home."

"Hmph."

"Secondly, are you suggesting that a magistrate can be... persuaded to find an irregularity where none exists?"

"Most men can be persuaded, given sufficient inducement," Metcalf said. "I could make it worth your while, as well. The magistrate?"

Sir Vincent smiled. "*I* am the magistrate. You should also know that I, too, proposed marriage to your daughter. You will not convince me that she has done anything wrong. If I hear of any attempts to interfere in the future, I will make it plain that you attempted bribery. Now, take yourself off, or I'll have Tillson's man with a pistol escort you from the premises." He crossed to the door and held it open, instructing the butler to have Metcalf escorted to his carriage.

"My thanks, Sir Vincent," Matthew said, once Metcalf had gone.

"A pleasure."

"If you'll excuse me..."

Sir Vincent nodded.

Matthew made his way to the room where they'd left Davie. He found Charlotte sitting with her son, a cup of untouched tea on a small table beside her. She looked up hopefully when the door opened, her worried expression changing to a small smile as his eyes met hers.

"He's gone," Matthew said, with no preamble. Davie looked up hopefully. "He's gone for good," Matthew went on. "You don't need to worry about him any more."

He glanced around. Davie's room was small, and felt cramped with the three of them in it. "The sun is still shining," he said. "Shall we all take a turn in the gardens?" He'd prefer to have Charlotte to himself, the woman he had finally admitted that he loved, but Davie was part of her. Davie needed to be happy with this marriage.

"That's a good idea," Charlotte said, standing.

Five minutes later, after fetching coats, they strolled along a path in the garden behind the main building, the borders still largely bare but with patches of daffodils and primroses brightening the beds in the gathering dusk.

"Your grandfather won't be coming back," Matthew said again, wondering if Davie's slight frown was still due to worry about being taken away from his mother.

"Thank you, sir," Davie said, his voice far more subdued than usual.

"Your mama saw him off," Matthew said.

Davie looked up, surprise clear on his face, then he grinned.

Charlotte shook her head slightly, but did not contradict him. She cleared her throat. "Davie, I think you have something to say to... to the major."

Davie, head hanging, muttered that he was very sorry for having made a fuss at the wedding. Charlotte opened her mouth, but closed it again when Matthew put a hand on her arm.

"May I talk to him?" he asked quietly. "If I am to be his stepfather."

Charlotte stared into his face for a moment, then nodded with a small smile. "I'll go back into the house," she said. "Davie, you may stay out here with the major for a little while." She didn't give Davie a chance to reply, but met Matthew's eyes once more with a fleeting smile, and walked away.

Matthew watched for a moment, then dragged his mind off the sway of her hips and turned to Davie.

Charlotte walked to the house, then stopped and looked back. If she'd left Sir Vincent or someone like the squire with her son in similar circumstances, she would have expected to see him shouting at Davie, and waving an arm or pointing for emphasis. Instead, Matthew stood with his hands in his pockets, looking almost casual. He was obviously talking *with* Davie. After observing them for a moment, it was clear that Davie was answering. A few minutes later they turned and walked together further into the garden. She saw them shake hands and then, from the way Matthew was moving his hands, he must be describing something, perhaps the things they would see in Devon.

She felt... she wasn't quite sure *what* she felt. She'd been respon-sible for Davie all his life, with the assistance of Mary, of course, but there had never been any doubt he was *hers*. By law, Matthew would now be Davie's guardian, but even without that it would be nonsensical to try to maintain Davie as her sole responsibility. It felt as if she were giving him up, partly, and it was only now that this reality struck her with a pang.

There was no-one better to share the responsibility—Davie and Matthew were already friends, as far as a ten-year-old could be with someone twenty years his senior. And after Matthew's upbringing with a stepmother who did not want him, Charlotte had few worries that Davie would not be treated as well as any children they might have together. That thought brought a blush to her face.

She wondered if they were wrapped up well enough for the chill evening air, realising with a flash of amusement that she was thinking of them both in the same way—checking they were well fed and warm enough.

Silly to think like that about Matthew, he's a grown man!

Then her heart filled, and she swallowed hard as she recognised her feelings for what they were. Love. In different ways, but still love. She closed her eyes for a moment, thankful that her initial refusal of Matthew's offer had not put him off. Life in the cottage with Mary had been good, yet the prospect of life with Matthew held so much more.

Seeing the pair of them walking back towards her, she turned and hurried into the house, not wanting to be caught watching.

Sir Vincent's household kept country hours. Although Davie was younger than the youngest Kinney children, he joined them at table, seated between Charlotte and Matthew. Davie, as usual, concentrated exclusively on his food to start with. Charlotte ate a little, but the combined feelings of unreality and anticipation took away her appetite. And her ability to make conversation, too, she thought, when the only thing she said to Matthew was a request to pass the salt. Talking with her new husband felt awkward in front of the whole

Kinney family, and she was glad when the meal ended and she took Davie back to his room.

"Bed for you, Davie," Charlotte said. He made a token protest, but got undressed and put his nightshirt on. Charlotte tucked him in, then sat on the edge of the bed.

"Sleep well, Davie. And don't get up in the morning until I come to get you. You've got a book to read."

"Mama?"

"Yes?"

"I'm sorry I was rude and upset you."

"I'm sorry I didn't tell you properly what was happening," she replied seriously. "Do you mind so very much?"

"Oh no! I *like* the major." He thought for a moment. "He said he is my guardian now."

"That's right. But I am still your mother, and I still love you. That hasn't changed."

Davie nodded. "That's what he said."

"Did he tell you to say sorry to me?"

"No. But he said he was sad that I had been rude because it upset *you*. I *am* sorry."

Charlotte gave him a big hug, then tucked the covers back around him.

"No more sulking then?" He nodded, sleepy. She sat there for a few more minutes until he was sound asleep, then let herself quietly out of the room.

CHAPTER 55

$\mathcal{W}$hen Charlotte came back downstairs, Matthew was waiting for her in the hall.

"Sir Vincent has offered us the use of his library," he said. He held up a key. "No interruptions."

She smiled, suddenly feeling uncertain again, but followed him into the room. She sat in an armchair near the fire.

"Davie is settled?"

"Yes. Thank you for talking to him—whatever you said to him outside seems to have reassured him."

Matthew sat down facing her. "This Earl of Marstone I mentioned, he's an acquaintance rather than a friend, but I think he would do what I said. Your father certainly has no legal hold over you or Davie. You are both safe from him now."

Charlotte nodded. "I know, but it's difficult to believe—"

"You don't have to stand up to him alone any more." Matthew put a comforting hand on her knee. "I will be there for you."

Charlotte took a deep breath, and managed a more confident smile.

"Did you read the second will I had made?" Matthew asked.

Charlotte shook her head.

"The second one was written to be valid if we married; Sir Vincent witnessed it. It makes you and Richard joint guardians of Davie should anything happen to me. I can change that if you wish. It would have been perfectly possible for you to be sole guardian, but I included Richard to keep your father from claiming—"

"Thank you," Charlotte said. "Richard is a good man. And so are you." She felt drained now, but calmer.

"Wine?" Matthew gestured to a decanter on a table in one corner of the room.

"Please."

She straightened her skirts while he poured the wine. She took the glass he offered, and he sat down opposite, looking as awkward as she felt. Now they were finally alone together, with time to talk, she was nervous again, her stomach fluttering.

What if I'm wrong? A true gentleman, which he undoubtedly was, could not really have said 'no' when she asked him if his offer of marriage was still open. He hadn't shown any signs of regretting it, but he *did* seem a little ill at ease.

She didn't know how to start, so she asked him if he was allowed to tell her about the task he was doing in Devon.

He smiled. "It's not a secret. Every harbour master and militia commander along the south coast wants to make sure their own area is well defended if the French come, so they ask for another fort, another wall, more or bigger guns. The War Office wants an impartial view as to which ports or sections of coast need better defences." He shrugged. "I suspect they really want the answer that nothing more is needed so they don't need to spend more money on it."

"So you'll be moving on down the coast?"

"I'm afraid so. I'll need to move on from Teignmouth two or three days after we get there."

She frowned. She'd thought they would have more time. "That isn't long. If we came with you, would we be a distraction, or get in your—"

"Not at all," he interrupted. "At the moment we're just gathering information. The more difficult part will be making the final recommendations, but I cannot do that for some time yet."

"So we could come with you?"

Another smile spread across his face. "You won't mind moving on every few days?"

"Matthew, I've been stuck in Edgecombe for nearly ten years. I like it there, but it's…" She waved a hand. "Small. Confined. The same people all the time."

Lonely, too, now she had the possibility of more.

"Then yes, I would… like to have your company. Very much." The smile was back.

His lips do have a lovely curve to them, and—

She brought her thoughts back under control. "Thank you." There were still things to be said between them. She eyed the glass of wine he'd poured for her. If she was wrong, she was about to make an enormous, and embarrassing, fool of herself. "I was wondering if it was too early to retire to bed?"

"You must be tired after the day you've had," he said, leaning forward with concern.

"No. Not at all." She looked at the wine in her glass again.

Dutch courage, but why not? She drank half of it, and took a deep breath.

"Matthew, when you came to see me the day after… the day after the ice house, I…"

Another deep breath. *Just say it.*

"I was embarrassed about kissing you and didn't know what to think, and you could hardly look me in the face and only talked about getting married to stop any gossip and I didn't know—" *Stop babbling!*

"I was ashamed of my behaviour." His gaze slid away from hers for a moment.

"You had nothing to be ashamed about," she said. *Heavens, it's difficult to have such a frank discussion.*

"I took advantage…" he said stiffly, his face reddening slightly

"No." She could feel the heat rising in her own face, but ploughed on. "You did nothing I did not want to happen. You were holding me, but I kissed you." She reached for her glass again, swallowing a mouthful of wine, keeping her eyes on the red liquid.

"When you wouldn't look at me," she went on, not able to meet his eyes, "I thought you must be disappointed by my behaviour. I thought you were offering for me because it was the honourable thing to do—"

Good God, is that what she thought?

He stood, taking her glass and setting it on a table. He knelt in front of the chair so he could look directly into her face.

"Charlotte..."

She glanced at him briefly, and he put a hand out, cradling one cheek. He heard her breathing deepen, and stroked his thumb gently along her cheek. She finally fixed her gaze on his.

"Charlotte," he said softly, "one of the best feelings comes from finding out that someone you... someone you want, wants you too. You could never disappoint me. Never."

He stood, taking her hands and gently pulling her to her feet. She rose with no resistance, and his own breath caught at her closeness, the faint scent from her hair, her lips so near...

"Come to bed?" he whispered, hoping he wouldn't mess *this* up as he had messed up so much else in the last year.

He curled one hand around the back of her head, feeling the silky texture of her hair. His pulse accelerated as she mirrored his action, her hand pulling his head down gently as it had once before.

He controlled himself, making the kiss nothing more than a gentle brush of lips, part of his mind aware they were in a public room, even though the door was locked. When he pulled back a little she was smiling.

"Bed," she whispered.

Matthew glanced around the room assigned to Charlotte. It was much larger than the one he'd used to bathe and change in earlier, with a larger bed. A fire had warmed the bedroom nicely, and the lamps gave a golden glow to Charlotte's skin as she stood uncertainly near the bed. He deposited the decanter and glasses on a chest, and returned to the door to turn the key. He took off his coat, suddenly feeling *too* warm.

Charlotte raised her hands to her hair, starting to pull hairpins out. Matthew crossed the intervening space in a couple of steps, putting his own hands over hers. "May I?"

Her hands stilled as she looked into his face, eyes wide, then moved her hands away.

"It's a long time since I—"

"I know," he said softly, and turned her gently around so she was facing away. His fingers delved gently into the coils, breathing the lavender scent, finding pins one after the other and pulling them out. His heart rate quickened as he ran his fingers through her hair, as long and thick as he'd imagined.

Take it slowly.

Charlotte turned to face him, pulling at her fichu, then dropping it on the floor. She looked up, her lips parting. That was invitation enough. He pulled her close, lowering his mouth to meet hers. The sensations spreading from the kiss, and from her hands pressing against his back, almost undid him, but he finally managed to pull away, breathing hard. Her face was flushed, her eyes half closed.

"Charlotte, I—"

She silenced him with a finger on his lips, then moved her hands to his waistcoat buttons, working them loose one by one. The gentle pressure of her hands against his chest sent shocks of awareness through him. He fumbled at the laces on the front of her gown, managing to push it off her shoulders, sucking in a breath as he took in the swell of her bosom showing above her stays.

More damned laces!

By now, Charlotte's need seemed as urgent as his own, and he undid his neckcloth with shaking hands before unlacing her stays. Exerting more self-control than he'd ever needed before, he let her set the pace as more of their clothing came off. For the first time, he got as much—more—joy from seeing her pleasure as he did from his own feelings as they explored each other with hands, eyes and lips, finally moving to the bed.

They lay in each other's arms for some time afterwards. Matthew stroked the waves of her hair, needing the feel of it beneath his hands, and the warmth of her body close against his own, to convince himself that this was real, this was happening. Eventually he moved, needing to stoke up the fire, letting her go with reluctance.

Charlotte watched as Matthew put more wood onto the fire, her limbs feeling relaxed and heavy. Her previous doubts about his feelings, and why he had offered to marry her, seemed silly now. She closed her eyes for a moment. She'd poisoned her own thoughts about men and marriage for too long. Her mother and her aunt had undoubtedly experienced miserable marriages; her mind shied away from the idea of intimate relations in those circumstances. Angus— Angus had been fun to be with, and she hadn't minded his indiscretions too much. But nothing compared with the experience of making love with Matthew; love and trust made so much difference. A lump blocked her throat, and she was grateful once more that Matthew had not been put off by her initial refusal.

She turned slightly, admiring the way the muscles moved beneath his skin as he moved around, picking up the clothing strewn across the floor, then searching for hair pins he'd dropped in his enthusiasm. Even though he was still a little thinner than he should be, he had a lean beauty to him, marred only by those lines across his back. No, not marred—they were just there, part of his history.

Matthew turned and saw her looking, and braced himself for the questions. Sympathy, whether real or false, would not be welcome. But all she said was, "That must have stung a bit."

He surprised himself by giving a crack of laughter. "It *was* a bit sore at the time." He got in beside her and put an arm around her. She turned on her side so her head rested comfortably in the hollow of his right shoulder.

"They don't do that to officers, I thought."

It was a question, and it wasn't. He knew that if he chose to ignore it, she would not ask him about it again. He glanced down. She had draped her right arm across his chest and closed her eyes—she wasn't gazing at him waiting for an answer.

"A case of mistaken identity," he said.

"That's not what gives you nightmares, is it?"

"It's part of what happened," he said after a moment of silence. "But you are right, it's not the part that haunts me." He paused. Did he really want to tell this story and risk it triggering more nightmares? This marriage had got off to a strange start, although at the moment it was going far better than his wildest hopes. There should be no secrets between them.

"The mistaken identity was deliberate," he began, picking through his memories to mention only the relevant facts. She didn't say anything, but the slight change in the way her body lay against him told him she was listening. "The war with Tipu Sultan was likely to end in another siege at Seringapatam. I was sent with a few men to survey the fortifications, to see if anything had changed since the last siege in '92. We were in uniform, but I was wearing a private's uniform."

Stevens had been on sentry duty for the first part of that night. Their attackers must have been very quiet, or Stevens had fallen asleep at his post.

"They captured two of us," he went on. He'd seen Stevens dead; Havers must have been killed when the Tipu's soldiers caught him with the dispatch.

"Benson?"

"Yes. The Sultan has... interesting... ways of dispatching his prisoners. Benson was afraid..."

He'd been afraid, but also resigned.

"I tried to comfort him a little by pointing out that at least it would be quick, unlike the several hundred lashes the British army often handed down to miscreants. I was overheard."

"Ah."

Good, he didn't need to explain every little detail. "But part way through, Benson apologised for getting us into that situation. He called me Major. Unfortunately they heard that too, and decided I was worth preserving in case I could be exchanged, or had useful information. They gave Benson the full two hundred. Then they threw us into a cell, chained to opposite walls. They put water and some food in with us, but Benson couldn't get up to get it, and I couldn't move far enough to give it to him."

"He died?"

"Yes."

A flash of Benson crying for his mother went through his mind. Charlotte's arms tightened around him. Her presence was comforting, and he marvelled again that she was here with him. She didn't speak, but he sensed that she knew there was more to be said.

"I didn't have any useful information," he continued, when the silence was on the point of being too long. His chest tightened, panic threatening to pull him under as he recalled the consequences.

"Troop numbers and so on, they already knew. It didn't stop them trying to get more. Breathe in enough water through a cloth on your face and you know you're about to drown."

And the next time you know what will happen. Even though you know you will probably come out the other end alive, it doesn't make much difference while you are trying not to breathe water.

Charlotte held a hand up to his face, and he tilted his head, pressing his cheek into her palm. She didn't say anything more, but her touch, the warm body pressed against his, helped to calm him. He'd trusted her with his guilty secrets, his shame, and she had not judged him. She would never try to use his past against him.

He stroked her hair as his racing pulse gradually eased, a feeling of deep contentment spreading through him as he pulled her close again with his other arm. Then she turned her face to his and their eyes met.

His heart started to beat faster again as her lips parted slightly in silent invitation.

They took longer this time, Matthew learning from her reactions to his touch, little gasps or moans of pleasure. Learning, too, what he enjoyed from her fingers and lips on his skin. Although less urgent, he found their lovemaking even more satisfying this time, the mutual trust between them deepening the satisfaction he got from her enjoyment as well as his own.

Matthew heard Charlotte's breathing become deep and regular, and felt more physically relaxed himself than he could ever remember being. He hadn't slept well for some time, but despite that he wasn't feeling drowsy. He looked at the long hair spread over the pillow next to his head, his pulse accelerating as he recognised the lack of confidence that had so nearly lost him this woman. His nightmares had done more to him than rob him of sleep.

For the first time, he let himself remember details of the past events that had caused those nightmares. It was time to face them, not hide from them.

The mine—he hadn't told Charlotte about that, but he was surprised to realise that he no longer felt shame, or guilt, over failing to get word back to headquarters about it. Regret, perhaps, as he had not completed his mission, but Webb's assurances had convinced him that it had caused no casualties.

So just Benson, then.

You're an engineer—be objective.

Visions from his nightmares ran through his head: Benson weakly asking for water, crying for his mother, cursing him. Which of those were memories? Had he conjured them up as a result of his feelings of guilt?

He hadn't been to blame for Benson not being able to reach food and water. Although he'd been able to reach some of it himself, the chains had prevented him giving any to Benson.

He recalled flashes of campfire talk: Benson talking with Havers, describing his life before the army in the slums of Bristol. The life Benson escaped by joining the army had been just as likely to end up with him dead from disease, or a knife in the back. As with many such men, the army became his family, and he had been proud to volunteer for the surveillance mission. That didn't detract from the horror of his death, which Matthew would probably never forget. He doubted that his nightmares would ever go completely, but perhaps he could prevent them affecting his waking hours too much.

Matthew turned and settled himself against Charlotte's back, curling himself around her sleeping form, and was comforted by the scent of her hair and the soft sounds of her breathing. He didn't quite manage to put all thoughts out of his mind, but the ones that lingered were of grey eyes and the taste of her skin. Eventually, he fell asleep.

CHAPTER 56

$\mathscr{M}$atthew woke early the next morning, only the first grey streaks of dawn visible through a slight gap in the curtains. Charlotte still slept beside him, her hair tickling his face. The peace he'd felt after their lovemaking last night returned to him— Charlotte would look after him in the ways he needed, just by being there. As he would look after her in any way he could.

The memory of the previous night brought other feelings, too. Nothing he'd experienced in the past compared with last night. It wasn't *what* they'd done, so much as *who* he'd done it with. She stirred against him, and he stroked her hair, remembering what she had told her father the previous day.

"Charlotte," he whispered, quietly enough not to wake her if she was still asleep. "When you were talking to your father, was that true?"

She stiffened in his arms, turning suddenly to face him, eyes wide in shock.

"Oh!" She put her face in her hands, her voice coming muffled through her fingers. "If..." She gasped a breath. "If you believe the things he says, then he's still won. He's still managing to destroy—"

"Charlotte, no!" Horrified, Matthew realised she had completely misunderstood what he was asking. "Charlotte?" He stroked her hair gently, feeling her shoulders begin to shake.

Is she crying? "Charlotte?" He wrapped his arms around her as well as he could with her arms in the way, holding her close until her body stilled.

"Charlotte?" This time she looked at him. There were traces of tears, but she was no longer crying, thank goodness.

"Charlotte—I'm going to tell you a story. Are you listening?"

That got her attention. She gave a little gulp and an almost imperceptible nod of her head. He lay back, putting an arm around her and pulling her towards him. He settled her against him so her head rested on his shoulder.

"Once upon a time, not so very many years ago, there was a beautiful young girl. Her father wanted her to marry an older man. A much older man, and not a nice man, I think?"

Charlotte lay still for a moment, then he felt movement on his shoulder and hair tickling his chin as she nodded her head.

"But the girl was not going to be forced into this marriage. She may have threatened to give herself to someone else, hoping the marriage to this older man would not happen, or would be annulled afterwards if she wasn't untouched. But that threat did not work."

Hair tickled his chin again.

"She found someone else to marry. Someone she liked?"

A small nod.

"Someone you loved?"

This time the movement was different—was she shaking her head?

"No—I didn't love him, but we were friends in a way." She paused for a moment and took a few deep breaths, her body relaxing into his.

"Angus was in London on leave. His colonel thought he should settle down, so he didn't mind getting married. He never promised to be faithful, and he wasn't. But he was good fun, and he was fairly discreet about his liaisons. That was far better than being in the power of the man my father had chosen."

"Then he died, and you came home."

"Yes, and I found out on the ship that I was going to have Davie.

Then my father tried to start all over again. I had some money from Angus. He had a winning streak just before he went upcountry and fell ill with cholera. Mary had just buried her third husband—Sergeant MacKinnon. He left her a little money, too. She'd had enough of India so she came home with me. When my father became overbearing I contacted her and we bought the cottage between us."

He held her close for a few minutes before he spoke again. "When I asked if it was true, I was asking if what *you* said was true."

"What did I say?"

He hesitated. *Does it matter?* Even if it was not true, she was here in his arms, and she needed him.

"Matthew?"

Hell. He'd have to carry on and ask her now. "You said your father only hastened the marriage, that you'd already decided."

"Oh, that." She wriggled free of him and moved away a little, making him roll onto his side so they faced each other.

"Now it's my turn to tell you a story," she said, a smile lighting her face. "Are you listening?"

"Yes, ma'am." He wasn't sure he was going to like it though.

"Once upon a time, a wagon arrived in our village. A tall, thin man got out and fell at my feet. A drunken wastrel, I thought, and he thought I was an old witch."

Matthew opened his mouth to protest against this, but she laid a finger across his lips.

"No, don't interrupt—this is *my* story!" She smiled again, sliding one hand around his waist. "He was good to my son, and helped him understand things I couldn't. This man didn't assume I needed a man's guidance to run my life. Instead, he trusted me to sort out his home."

She paused again, gazing into his eyes. His breath caught at her expression. Love? He swallowed hard.

"This man thinks he isn't needed."

"I—"

Charlotte put a hand over his mouth and he subsided. "But he *is* needed. He has a brother who thinks the world of him. He has people who admire him; Webb told me you said you wished he'd been one of your sergeants—you should have seen how proud he was."

Her hand moved to cup his cheek. "You protected me after the ice house," she continued. "All this while you were fighting demons from your past. I realised I'd made a big mistake when I thought you were only offering out of duty. I wanted to talk to you, to make sure you *wanted* to marry me, so I wrote to you—"

"—about the garden!"

"Yes. It seems silly, doesn't it? I didn't want to make even more of a fool of myself if I was wrong, so I thought I should start by making sure we were still friends."

"Just friends?"

"No. Not just friends. I wanted to talk when you got back. I hoped I hadn't spoiled things by refusing you. Then my father's letter came. I wrote to explain that I'd already changed my mind, but you never got that letter. You came back so quickly when Webb sent for you, and you still said you would marry me. I took the chance that you *wanted* to, and weren't just offering again out of kindness. Despite my father, yesterday was one of the best days of my life..."

Her eyes closed, and Matthew saw a tear forming in the corner of her eye. He wanted to brush it away, but she was still talking.

"One of the best days," she went on, her voice slightly unsteady. "With someone I love..."

"Charlotte." Matthew's voice wasn't steady either. "With someone who loves *you*." Now he did brush the tear gently with his thumb.

"You remember I said one of the best feelings is finding out that someone you want, wants you too?" he said. "Even better is when you find out that someone you love, loves you too."

He rested his forehead on hers. "And when someone you need, needs you too."

EPILOGUE

Three months later

Charlotte sat at a small table set on a gravelled area in the kitchen garden. Behind her, the workmen sweated in the July sunshine as they put the finishing touches to the succession house, but she was cool beneath a large sunshade. She looked around the garden with satisfaction. The ground before her was now neatly laid out, with vegetables growing in neat lines and beds of flowers to be cut for the house adding glowing colour around the edges. Fruit trees espaliered against the walls would not produce much fruit for a couple of years, but it wouldn't be long before Birchanger was self-sufficient in other fruit and vegetables.

Paper and pencils were scattered on the table in front of her, along with the remains of her afternoon tea. She was supposed to be writing another story, but her concentration was lacking.

She took her aunt's last letter from the back of her notebook to read again. Lady Henbury gleefully reported that Metcalf—Charlotte had stopping thinking of him as her father—had finally decided not to contest the trust fund, and Charlotte's money would be sent to Joshua Kellet to be invested for Davie's future. That was one of the pieces of good news for Matthew, when he returned. Another was a report that Smith had been arrested for desertion in Bristol and was now awaiting trial, and Braddon had been sentenced to transportation for stealing.

She picked up her watch, lying on the table next to the plate of uneaten cake. Matthew had been in London on business for a week, and she missed him badly. He had arranged to collect Davie from his lodgings with Doctor Lorton in Bristol, and should be back soon. She smiled at the main piece of news she had for him, resting her hand on her midriff in satisfaction. She'd been fairly sure before he set off, but the recent bouts of nausea and tiredness had confirmed her suspicions. It would probably be a January baby.

Webb entered the garden and scrunched along the gravel path to check on the workmen's progress, giving her a nod as he passed. Turning her chair a little, Charlotte eyed the timber and glass structure Matthew had designed, with Davie's help. It stretched half the length of the south-facing inner wall of the garden, and its interior would probably feel like an oven in this weather. He'd arranged heating from a new stove behind the wall, which was also used to heat the stable. As well as growing fruit, it would be a lovely place to sit in the winter months, giving the feel of the outdoors without being cold. Davie's enthusiasm for the design work had convinced her to send him to a school in Bristol that could provide a more technical education than the usual topics studied by gentlemen's sons. He came home every other weekend. From the stream of chatter about his lessons, his friends, and the sports they played, he was not just resigned to school, but actively enjoying it.

More footsteps crunched on the gravel. Mrs Malplass came into the garden carrying a tray laden with glasses and a large jug of ale. She had changed greatly from the anxious woman who had arrived at Birchanger in February. The clean air of the Cotswolds suited her, giving a healthy glow to her skin. Webb hurried over to take the tray from her, and helped her to pour out the drinks for the workmen.

Charlotte narrowed her eyes, her suspicions deepening. Webb did seem to be taking more care of his appearance recently, and that coat he wore was new only a few weeks ago. She looked more carefully at the housekeeper. Was that a new ribbon in her hair? She smiled. Webb deserved to find someone for himself.

Looking at her watch again, she decided to take a stroll down the drive. The sound of the workmen chatting over their ale faded away as she left the kitchen garden, and was replaced with the humming of bees on the flowers planted along the front wall of the Hall. She stopped to watch some of them, wondering if stories about insects would be too unbelievable, then turned as she heard voices in the distance. Shading her eyes, she made out the shape of horses and a curricle emerging from the trees, and her heart lifted. They were back at last. She smoothed the sprigged muslin of her summer gown, and tucked a stray curl behind her ear.

Matthew saw Charlotte waiting near the front door as soon as the Hall came into sight, her pale gown bright against the mellow stonework. He'd thought she was beautiful when she wore mourning gowns, but the paler colours she wore now suited her even better. He felt a little breathless as the curricle drew close enough for him to see her smile. He'd only been away a week, but it felt like an age.

Davie was still chattering away about his last fortnight at school, but Matthew wasn't listening any more. He pulled the horses to a halt. Davie leapt out of the curricle almost before it stopped moving and dashed over to his mother for a hug. Straight away, he started telling her everything that had happened since Matthew had dropped him off two weeks earlier. Charlotte met Matthew's eyes over her son's head, and she smiled.

A smile with a promise.

Matthew gave her a sympathetic grin and set the horses into motion again, calling for Jackson to see to them as he entered the stable yard. In the shelter of the building, the air was still and hot. He took off his coat and left it in the curricle, walking back around the Hall.

Charlotte stood looking through the doorway into the kitchen garden, but turned as he approached.

That smile again.

She stepped away from the door and moved towards him. "I've sent Davie to see how the succession house is coming along," she said, taking his arm.

Matthew glanced towards the stables. Jackson was inside, seeing to the horses, and they were out of sight of the workmen in the garden. He took her in his arms, holding her close and breathing in her scent.

"I've missed you," he whispered into her hair. "I love you."

Charlotte wound her arms around his waist and hugged him tight for a moment, then he felt her pull back.

"I hope you've got some to spare," she said, pursing her lips in her trying-not-to-smile face.

He frowned, puzzled. Charlotte patted her stomach, then a happy smile spread across her face.

It took him a moment to work out what she meant. "You're sure?"

She nodded. He pulled her close again, resting his forehead against hers.

"Charlotte, that is..." He closed his eyes and shook his head slightly. So much had changed in the last seven months, since he'd arrived here. Since he'd met her.

"Are you well?" he asked, stories of difficult births springing into his mind.

"Yes," she said, a mischievous smile spreading across her face. "I do feel the need to lie down, though."

He frowned in concern. She put a hand to his cheek, stroking it lightly.

"I think you should come and lie down with me." She took his hand and pulled him towards the door while he was still working out what she meant.

Inside, he picked her up and carried her upstairs in his arms.

THE END

AFTERWORD

Thank you for reading The Mrs MacKinnons; I hope you enjoyed it. If you can spare a few minutes, I'd be very grateful if you could review this book on Amazon or Goodreads.

You can find out about new releases or special offers on my website:

www.jaynedavisromance.co.uk

You can sign up there for my mailing list—I promise not to bombard you with emails. My website also has links to my Facebook and Pinterest pages, and a contact form if you'd like to email me about anything.

ABOUT THE AUTHOR

I wanted to be a writer when I was in my teens, hooked on Jane Austen and Georgette Heyer (and lots of other authors). Real life intervened, and I had several careers, including as a non-fiction author under another name.
That wasn't *quite* the writing career I had in mind!

The Mrs MacKinnons is my first novel, but won't be the last - there are several more being worked on.

ACKNOWLEDGEMENTS

Thanks to my critique partners on Scribophile for comments and suggestions, particularly Alex, Daphne, Erin, Georgie, Jean, Lynden, Toni, and Violetta.